The man had composer. She sho two tables from the counter where the peanut butter and jelly were stored. TJ's back was to her, so she couldn't see his reaction.

"Abe, he likes his little store, and we need to respect that," Celia said.

Abe. The name rang a bell, and she tried to remember why it sounded familiar. It took a few seconds, but it finally came to her. It was the name of Celia's ex-husband. Abe…Abe…Abe Bannister. That was it.

Holy cow! Seriously? Bannister? No, it couldn't be. TJ would have said something. He'd told her about being James True, and she'd kept his secret. Well, actually she'd discovered his secret, and he'd admitted to it. But still, he trusted her, right? Maybe it was only a coincidence.

Standing up, TJ leaned on the table. His tones were low, but she heard him clearly.

"Cut the doting parent act. I'm not buying it. You didn't know how to be parents when I was a kid so don't try and make up for it now. Take your vacation on Martha's Vineyard and leave me alone. But thanks for the offer. Mom. Dad."

He turned and stopped cold when he saw her standing there. Color leeched from his face, and she realized he hadn't wanted anyone to overhear. But there was no denying it now. It wasn't just coincidence, having his songs sung by Python, his Python tattoo, his music ability.

TJ Bannister was the son of Celia Muñez and Abe Bannister, king and queen of the rock world.

True Dreams

by

Kari Lemor

Storms of New England, Book 2

This is a work of fiction. Names, characters, places, and incidents are either the product of the author's imagination or are used fictitiously, and any resemblance to actual persons living or dead, business establishments, events, or locales, is entirely coincidental.

True Dreams

Contact Information: info@thewildrosepress.com

Cover Art by *The Wild Rose Press, Inc.*

The Wild Rose Press, Inc.
PO Box 708
Adams Basin, NY 14410-0708
Visit us at www.thewildrosepress.com

Publishing History
First Champagne Rose Edition, 2020
Print ISBN 978-1-5092-3000-6
Digital ISBN 978-1-5092-3001-3

Storms of New England, Book 2
Published in the United States of America

Dedication

To my very own Sagey.
Thank you for being such an amazing supporter
and motivating me to continue writing.
Those purple pom-poms have kept me going
so many times when I wanted to quit.

Acknowledgements

I want to thank everyone who has supported me and my writing. Without you, this book wouldn't be here.

To Judi, who makes sure my words shine. To Pamela for helping me navigate the waters of the publishing industry.

To Delia DeVry for her help with the lyrics to some of the songs.

To Peggy for talking me off the ledge more times than I can count.

To my family and friends, who humor and support me and give me encouragement when I need it. I appreciate you more than you know.

To my amazing TEAM! My beta readers, Kris and Emily, who make sure my characters have enough angst and my conflicts are strong. I couldn't do this without you both! You make my books sing.

To MA Grant, my beloved Critique Partner, who helps me brainstorm and create the world for my stories. Who asks the tough questions, so I don't skimp on putting quality in every part of my books. You are a gift!

And to the beautiful region of Cape Cod and The Knob for all the fun we've had there.

Chapter One

Ten Years Ago

The bottle was empty. Damn!

True Bannister stretched his arm out and relaxed his fingers. The heavy container dropped onto the plush carpet with a dull thud. He shifted in bed, trying to remember last night. Obviously, it involved the bottle of Chivas Regal he'd emptied.

Swinging his legs out from the sheet, he planted them on the floor, his head spinning. He sat for a minute taking inventory. Naked, and at least a half dozen used condoms littered the bed and floor. The smell of sex wafted through the air.

He chuckled dryly, remembering the girls he'd been with last night. Sisters? Yeah. They'd offered him the bottle of scotch, then their gorgeous bodies. Refusing either would have been stupid.

After crossing the room, he picked through his dresser for a clean pair of shorts, then glanced around the chaos. Everything on his dresser had been swept off so he could screw the blonde up there. Twice. The redhead he'd done on his desk and up against the wall. Oh, and bent over the chair by the sliding door. Couldn't forget that time.

The bed was in disarray, highlighting where the girls had rocked his world, both of them at the same time. They'd been skilled. A small patch of the sheets still clung to the bed where he'd pulled them to cover himself once he'd kicked the girls out. His father taught him to take what he could but not to let them stay. They'd think they were something special and want more. He wouldn't mind more right now. What were their names? Something rhyming? Sandy? Candy? Mandy? Didn't matter. There were always more where they came from.

Being the son of Abe Bannister, lead singer for the rock group Python, certainly had its benefits, and True took full advantage of them. He'd shared his father's groupies for years, since he'd become a teen, and last night was no exception. He'd been celebrating the life of a musician since he was in diapers. Python had done a small venue for charity, and the after party had moved to their Malibu mansion. As it always did.

Sitting on the edge of the bed, he admired the snake tattoo on his right thigh. It was Python's trademark, and he'd gotten it on his sixteenth birthday. His eighteenth was only a few days away. He'd been hinting to his parents he wanted a Maserati. They better not disappoint him.

Shaking hands slid the shorts over his hips. A quick fix would get him through the morning. He glanced at the clock. Yup, still morning, for another thirty-two minutes. Maybe some of last night's party goods were still available.

He left his room and wandered down the hall, overlooking the large atrium and living room below. The stillness and silence strange compared to the music and laughter from last night. The house was trashed. Bottles and remnants of joints littered the floor. White powder dusted the table tops. The scent of alcohol and smoke still permeated the air. A few people lingered, asleep, or passed out.

Where had his parents spent the night? They each had their own room, but it wasn't uncommon for them to share it with someone else. Theirs was an open marriage. Celia Muñez, as popular in the rock world as Abe, didn't like to be alone. At home or on the road.

Maybe once he'd gotten another hit, he could find someone to help him finish off the box of condoms in his room. There was a half-naked brunette draped over the love seat. He'd be happy to wake her up.

Better wake his sister first. It was Sunday, church day. Sonni had gotten in the habit when their grandparents, Celia's mom and dad, had lived with them. But Mamita and Papito hadn't liked the wild life here and moved back East where they had family. Sonni used to drag him along to church, and he'd let her for lots of years. Not recently.

He walked around the corner to Sonni's room. She liked the quiet nook, especially when she wanted time with her music. Her voice was like their mom's, pure and sweet. But then Dulce, *sweet,* was her middle name. Sonata Dulce. Nothing boring for their eclectic parents.

Sonni hated having a unique name. She preferred her nickname and even called him TJ to make his name sound normal. He reveled in its uniqueness. True Jam Bannister. No one else had anything like it. He loved the attention he got being the son of superstars. Abe had let him go on stage with them a few times, so he'd gotten even more notoriety. It hadn't hurt he'd written Python's last two hit songs. He wasn't sure which he liked better, writing music or performing it.

He tapped lightly on his sister's door but didn't expect an answer. She was a deep sleeper. Turning the handle, he entered. A tiny bit of light slipped through the opening in the curtains, and he saw the shadow of Sonni in her bed.

As he passed her book shelf, he picked up one of the novels lying on top, a romance. One of the cheap ones promising a happily ever after with the white picket fence. She adored these books. Did she really think love was so sublime? Giving yourself to one person forever and ever? After growing up with the parade of people passing through Abe and Celia's bedrooms? Love didn't exist. Not in Los Angeles. Probably not anywhere.

Sonni had spent hours reading to him when they were younger, especially when they got dragged along on tour. She'd made him love reading, too. Shown him all the places you could escape to inside a book. What would he have done without his sister? She'd been his only friend for the longest time. Kept him from being lonely when they'd been too young to be allowed downstairs. Lately, they hadn't been hanging out as often. Sonni wasn't into the party scene, and she definitely wasn't into sleeping around. He was glad. He'd hate for guys to use her to get their kicks. Yeah, pretty hypocritical of him, but he only screwed girls who were looking for a quick fuck with a superstar, or at least the son of one. They certainly weren't being taken advantage of. Soon, he'd be known for being True Jam Bannister, not for who his parents were.

True walked across the room and picked up Sonni's guitar. Waking her with a song might be nicer than jumping on her face like he'd done as a kid. Strumming a few chords, he sat on the edge of her bed. Did she have a book nearby? Many times, she'd fall asleep while reading.

There was only a bag of pills. Ecstasy? He could use one right now to get him through after a busy night. She'd been using them more lately, finally loosening up and enjoying some of the benefits of being Abe and Celia's kid.

Strumming his fingers along the strings, he played an old melody Sonni liked. He reached toward the pills, craving one. No, he should wake his sister first. Maybe they could have breakfast together. It had been a while since they sat and talked. It'd be nice. He could find the brunette later.

He strummed louder and poked Sonni with his elbow. She didn't respond.

"Come on, Sonata, wake up." Using her full name always got a rise out of her. That should do it.

Still no response. He placed the guitar carefully on the floor and shook her shoulders. "Sonni? Come on, wake up."

Her body felt stiff, and the tremors in his hands intensified. Heat, then coldness rushed through him. His stomach tightened. He pushed the rigid body once more, refusing to accept the possibility.

"Sonni! Wake up, damn it! This isn't funny!"

He touched her face. Her skin was frigid. As cold as the chunk of ice forming in his chest. He pulled his hand back, ignoring how much it shook, which had nothing to do with needing a fix.

Terror pounded into him like a freight train. Screams tore from his mouth. Tears streamed down his face. He couldn't breathe. "Don't you dare leave me alone, Sonni. You promised me you'd always be here for me. Wake up!"

He lowered his head to her chest, sobs wracking his body. His voice wobbled, barely audible. "Don't leave me. I love you. And you're the only one who loves me."

****

Present Day

Help Wanted

Sara Storm grinned at the sign in the window of the bookstore/coffee shop, *Tea and Tales,* on the quaint Main Street in Hyannis on Cape Cod. She took a deep breath and pushed open the door. Confidence. She'd been lacking it all her life, but she'd never get anywhere unless she showed she knew what she was doing.

Her eyes adjusted to the dimmer light inside, then she looked around. The owner had combined two store fronts to make one massive business. A bookstore on the left while the right side tables, chairs, and sofas clustered in groups. This wasn't a place where they rushed through your order and pushed you away for the next paying customer. The interior invited you to sit and enjoy your beverage and pastry at your leisure.

Sara wanted to sit with a cup of tea and take in the ambiance of the place. She'd love to select a book and skim through it while sipping her drink. Not her goal right now. She needed a job.

A woman in her late fifties wiped down the counter on the far right. Sara strode over, as confident as she could be.

"Hi, what can I get for you?"

"I'm interested in the job you have advertised."

The woman looked confused, and Sara pointed. "You have a sign in the door."

"Oh, right. We forgot to take that down."

Her heart sank down to her toes. Damn. Why hadn't she come down earlier to apply for jobs? Or realized her part-time job at the Melody Tent didn't pay enough to live here? Every other place she'd looked, especially the ones with live music, already had full staff.

Sighing, she smiled politely. "Thank you anyway. It must be great working here. I'd never want to leave."

As she turned away, the woman stopped her.

"Fill out an application. Some of the summer staff might not work out, and it's good to have someone waiting in the wings."

The woman was only being polite, but Sara waited for her to get the application. She could be polite, too. Maybe someone would leave. And maybe it would snow in July.

"I'm Mary."

She took the application. "I'm Sara. I have a résumé, too."

Mary signaled for her to sit at a table, and Sara dug in her bag for a pen.

"Do you live around here?"

Her hand stilled, and she looked up. "No, I'm from New Hampshire. I'm here for the summer. I've got a job working a few hours at the Melody Tent but hoped to find another job for the rest of the time." What she really wanted was to connect with a music promoter who'd listen to her sing. She'd love to travel the world and be known for her great voice, not for being the youngest Storm sibling.

Mary pointed to her resume, and Sara handed it over, then began filling out the application. When done, she gave it to Mary, flashing another big smile. Supposedly, it was one of her better attributes. After five years of orthodontic work, it should be.

"You worked in a library for a year?" Mary tucked a piece of wavy silver hair behind her ear. "Can you stick around? The boss'll be here soon, and I'd like him to talk to you."

Hope flared inside, but Sara didn't dare get excited. "I have time. May I look around while I wait?"

Mary waved her hand. "Enjoy."

Sara did. The coffee side was great, but the book side seriously called to her. Tall, built-in bookshelves lined the walls, and hand-crafted bookcases and tables were scattered here and there near comfortable chairs. Sprinkled among them were racks of novelties, jewelry, and smaller craft items. Singing a little tune under her breath, she took a closer look, noting they were all locally made on Cape Cod.

A staircase took up the back, left wall, rising to a second-story loft area. She longed to explore but didn't want to miss the owner, so she stayed where she was. Good first impressions were everything.

Child-sized furniture formed a small nook near the large front windows. It was surrounded by lower bookshelves and a box of toys and puppets. Children sat on a brightly colored area rug, flipping through picture books. Moving closer, she picked up a familiar one.

"Are you gonna read to us?" A red-haired girl looked up hopefully. "I like that book."

"I like it, too," Sara answered. "It's one of my

favorites." She looked around, seeing some adults nearby, checking in their direction. The other children gathered close and sat at her feet, so Sara dropped next to them, smoothed the long skirt of her sundress over her legs, and opened the book.

As she read, the children scooted nearer and gazed intently at her. She'd always had the knack for attracting children. Her brothers had called her The Pied Piper when she babysat the neighborhood kids. The children's section of the library she'd worked at was where she'd been most popular.

When she finished the book, a boy, no more than three, shoved another book in her hands. "Wead dis one, please."

The other children bobbed their heads enthusiastically. She happily complied.

More books followed, and somewhere along the line a black and white spaniel wandered over and curled up next to her with its head in her lap.

"That's Freckles," a girl with brown ringlets informed her. "She belongs to Mr. B. She likes stories, too."

"I see. Does Freckles come here often?"

"Yup, if Mr. B. is here, Freckles is here." The littlest boy patted the dog's head. "He don't like to be by himself."

"Well, this is a place I'd want to be, also." She wanted this job. To work for someone relaxed enough to bring their dog to work would be wonderful. The atmosphere spoke of comfort and serenity.

Another book was placed in her hand, and Sara scratched the dog under its chin before starting. Their family dog growing up had been a spaniel. When she leaned down to talk softly to the dog, she was rewarded with the animal licking her face, then squirming further into her lap. She laughed and continued reading.

****

TJ Bannister shouldered the back door of *Tea and Tales* open, depositing the large box of sugar packets onto the counter. He hadn't meant to leave Mary so long, but the holiday weekend traffic had started and it was only Thursday. Memorial Day always signaled the beginning of the summer crowd pouring onto Cape Cod.

As he peeked into the shop, customers milled around, but it was past the morning rush and still early for vacationers. Most would show up in full force tomorrow or Saturday.

After pouring hot water into a mug, he threw in his favorite cinnamon tea bag. When he looked around the shop, it appeared ready for the big weekend. Thank God, Mary had stayed on after he'd bought the business.

He should tell her he was back. She wouldn't do Story Hour with him gone. He tossed his tea bag, glanced toward the children's section, and froze, cup halfway to his lips. An angel sat on the floor reading to the kids.

Okay, maybe not an angel, but with the sun streaming through the window, highlighting her blonde hair, and her innocent face filled with laughter, she sure looked like one. Even her voice was soft and ethereal as she sang along with the words of the book. Who was she? And why was she doing Story Hour? Where was Mary?

TJ tried to look away from the vision by the

window to find his wayward manager, but there was something about the girl that glued him in place. She was breathtaking. He continued to stare, taking in her features. By themselves, they weren't anything special. Her long, blonde hair was straight and tucked behind her ears. Her oval face, small nose, and full lips were nothing out of the ordinary. And her figure, what he could see of it, wasn't movie star quality. But the whole picture she made…it was straight out of his dreams, the few he allowed himself to have.

She wore a sundress in some soft color and had a sweater-like thing around her shoulders. Her legs were covered by the dress.

"She's doing a nice job, isn't she?" Mary appeared at his shoulder.

"Who is she?"

Holding up some papers, Mary said, "Her name is Sara Storm, and she's looking for a job."

A job! He couldn't hire her. Not a lick of work would get done because he'd spend the whole day staring, imagining what he could do to the soft curves filling out the conservative top of her dress. Picturing the long legs he imagined were under her loose skirt, wrapped around his waist. God, he had to stop this, get her out of here.

"We don't need help, Mary. We're all set with those two I hired last week."

Mary narrowed her eyes. "Darcy called out today. First day of sunshine in a week, and she's suddenly sick. What's going to happen when the real summer weather hits? We could use someone reliable."

"What makes you think *she's* reliable? She looks about fifteen." She didn't, but he needed an excuse.

Mary handed TJ the papers. "College degree in English Literature and worked in a library for a year. My guess is she's around twenty-three."

Not jail bait. Even worse. He'd have no reason to keep his filthy thoughts under control. Mary's smirk screamed *matchmaking* again. Couldn't she get it in her head he wasn't interested in a relationship with anyone right now? This porcelain-skinned angel would run in a different direction at top speed if she ever knew who he was and what he'd done. Nope, she had to go.

"We'll be fine for the summer. Keep her application on file if we need it later." He wouldn't need it. Might even burn it.

Mary crossed her arms over her chest. "Stop running away, TJ."

"And you stop trying to hook me up."

Mary rolled her eyes. "I'm not trying to hook you up. Look at her. She must have a million boyfriends. The fact remains, those two you hired last week won't stay the whole summer. This girl could fill in for me at Story Hour. She's a natural with children. And she doesn't mind your dog sitting in her lap, shedding all over her nice dress. At least talk to her."

TJ had noticed the dog. Traitor. Freckles was curled with paws on Sara's lap and face between her breasts. Sara rubbed the dog's ears and neck, pulling the animal closer to her chest. He wanted to be the dog right about now.

"Fine, I'll talk to her, but I'm not guaranteeing anything. I need to call her references and check she's legit."

Mary chuckled. "Yeah, 'cause she looks like someone who'd falsify documents."

"Ted Bundy was charismatic and charming." He flinched at Mary's playful slap. "I could fire you for hitting the boss."

"You'd never do it." Mary grinned. "You can't manage this place without me."

"And that's the only reason I put up with your crap. Otherwise, you'd be toast."

Mary waved to Sara. Untangling the dog from her arms, she gave Freckles another scratch, then gracefully rose. Damn, the legs were even longer than he'd imagined. *Talk to her, then show her the door.*

"Sara, this is TJ Bannister, the owner. TJ, Sara Storm. I'll let you two talk. I have work to do."

"Hi, Mr. Bannister." Her eyes sparkled, while her smile lit up the room. "Thank you for speaking with me. I appreciate it."

TJ clutched the application to his chest and turned to sit at one of the tables. Anything to avoid shaking her hand. He'd most likely get third degree burns.

"Tell me about yourself? Something not in the resume which I can read myself." Maybe she'd be vapid and self-centered. Or immature and giddy. Anything that would give him an excuse not to hire her. And make his groin stop aching.

"I'm from New Hampshire. I have three older brothers. I came to the Cape this summer for some independence. I have a part-time job at The Melody Tent and—"

"You have another job?" This was perfect. How could he hire her if she had another job? It would interfere with working here. "I need someone who's available for more than a few hours a week."

Her eyes opened wide, and TJ swallowed hard at

the bright blue irises hypnotizing him. Her face fell, and she scrambled in her purse, pulling out a folder. She set a piece of paper between them, her lips curling up again. Did she ever stop smiling?

"I have plenty of time to work. The Melody Tent is only open certain dates for concerts. Mostly weekend nights. Here's my schedule, and you'll see I noted all the times I'm available for a second job."

TJ glanced at the paper and conceded she had lots of time free. She wasn't even starting for another three weeks. Her innocent face turned toward him, and his heart unfroze a tiny bit. Could he have her underfoot all summer? Her sunny disposition would send him to the nut house in no time. Like he didn't already belong there.

"I need someone during our busy nights and weekends."

A sigh escaped her perfect lips, and she swallowed hard. She took a deep breath, squaring her shoulders. "Please, Mr. Bannister, I need this second job to pay for my apartment. I promise, I'll never call in sick, I can work as many hours as you want, and even come in early or stay late to help clean. You're open at seven. I can be here earlier and make coffee or come in after hours and pick up or stock books."

No doubt she was determined. And she actually had Freckles climbing in her lap. His dog was friendly but had been abused as a puppy and shied away from strangers. Freckles seemed to trust Sara for some reason.

He glanced at her application again, stalling for time. Mary's voice in the back explained to a customer how busy it was during the summer. Yeah, he got the hint.

"The shelves and racks need dusting at least once a week."

Her smile blasted his way again. Couldn't she turn the strength down?

"I don't mind at all. Whatever you need me to do."

His lap had a few suggestions, but he clenched his fists under the table to control the urge. "There's a whole second floor of books, too." She couldn't say he hadn't warned her.

Instead of resignation, her eyes opened wider, and she looked ecstatic. "Really? I didn't get up there. The kids asked me to read."

"Yeah, Mary usually does Story Hour, but during the summer it's busier. I'd need you available every Tuesday, Thursday, and Saturday morning at ten."

TJ waited, hoping she'd want Saturday morning off if she had to work late the night before at the Melody Tent. Her damn smile just got larger and was about to swallow her whole face.

"I love reading to the kids. It was my favorite thing when I worked at the Portsmouth Library. Does Freckles always join in, too? She's adorable."

"If I'm here, she's usually here."

Her overabundance of cheerfulness was too much. It had to go away. He stood. "I'll go through your application. If I'm interested, I'll be in touch. Thank you."

The sunshine toned down but only a notch. She reached out, grabbing his hand. TJ nearly fell over. Yup, third degree burns.

"Thank you for speaking with me today. Even if you don't need help, I'll probably come in often. What you've done here is amazing."

Pulling his hand away, he said, "I like it."

He walked away, indicating their meeting was over. After taking a look around, she left. TJ sighed. How could any one person be so filled with joy?

"She's sweet, isn't she?" Mary asked at his shoulder. She needed a bell around her neck.

"Who? Sara Sunshine? That's a little too much happiness for me."

"Only because you're a miserable old grouch. She'd be good for you. Make you start living again."

He frowned, proving her point. His first eighteen years he'd done more living than anyone should. Look at where it'd gotten him.

"Enough with the Cupid's arrow. She'd never be interested if she knew who I was…what I really am."

Mary pointed her finger at his face. "Stop. You aren't the same wild teen you were ten years ago. Or even the young man who asked me for a job six years ago. You need to let it go."

Damn, he wanted to. But deep inside, he was still the same twisted person. He might be a revised edition with a shiny new cover and up to date formatting, but the story was still trash. If Sara stuck around long enough, she'd see it. That would wipe the smile off even her face.

Chapter Two

"Your phone was ringing, Sara."

Sara whipped her head around, clutching the shower curtain to her. What was the creeper doing?

"Leave it there, Dan," she growled. "I'll check it when I'm done."

"Okay." Her temporary roommate stood in the half-open doorway, staring at the not-quite opaque plastic curtain.

Her cheeks grew hot, and her body tensed. "Leave it and go."

Dan took his time placing the phone on the counter and backing out. Sara clenched her teeth. "Get out of the bathroom and shut the door!"

The door finally closed, and Sara waited to see if he'd open it again. When it remained in place, she quickly rinsed the shampoo from her hair. Chills pricked the back of her neck as she stepped from the tub and wrapped a threadbare towel around her. She rushed to the door and shoved it to stay closed. Silly, Dan, who rivaled the incredible Hulk, could rip it from its hinges in one yank.

She hated living here but didn't have much choice. She'd come to the Cape later than most, and all the decent rentals had been taken. The ones she could afford anyway, which wasn't much. Even living at home last year, her college loans had sucked up any extra money.

Kayla, her cousin Sofia's college roommate, had a small rental in Hyannis, minutes from the Melody Tent. Unfortunately, it meant Sara had to sleep on the couch and put up with Kayla's slimy boyfriend, Dan, who also lived here. But she'd already accepted the job at the Melody Tent and quit the one at the library. Not the smartest move in the world, but she was determined to reach her music goal, not the one her family had planned for her.

She hastily dried off and dressed. Since she didn't actually have a bedroom, she had to do everything in the bathroom, but the lock on the door was broken. She'd have to buy a lock even though they weren't supposed to alter anything in the apartment. She couldn't live all summer with the threat of Dan walking in on her.

After pulling a comb through her wet hair, she looked at her phone. Most likely one of her family. It had only been five days and they were already suffocating her. She loved them more than anything, but sometimes she couldn't breathe.

The number on the screen was unfamiliar, so she pressed the keys to listen to the message. She froze and hope soared when she heard the voice of the bookstore manager.

"Hi, Sara, it's Mary Prentice from *Tea and Tales*. We'd like to offer you the job here if you're still interested. Please stop by the shop sometime today to fill out paperwork. If you've decided to go elsewhere, call and let us know. I look forward to seeing you again."

She actually flapped her arms. Good thing no one

was around to see. No word for days, so she figured they hadn't wanted her. Oh, this job would be a little slice of heaven. Cozier than the library and much more relaxed.

How relaxed she'd be with the owner hanging around, she wasn't sure. She'd expected someone more Mary's age, not hovering near thirty. And certainly not drop-dead gorgeous with piercing eyes practically dissecting her. His dark coloring, angled features, and days' worth of scruff were intense, and his demeanor serious. Unfortunately, he hadn't seemed to like her. Hopefully, she'd simply read him wrong.

Once ready, she walked the few streets over, bolstering her courage the whole time. Why she needed courage, she didn't know. It was only a summer job. But the way TJ Bannister had looked at her a few days ago made her nervous. College-aged boys or fatherly types were the kind of guys she was used to. This man made her heart race like nothing she'd ever experienced before.

The shop was moderately crowded, and Mary stood behind the coffee counter waiting on a customer. There were a few more in line. Standing back, she looked around again. Yup, this would be a great place to work.

Mary handed change back to the customer, then called out the name 'Darcy,' in the direction of the back room. A girl about Sara's age came out and began to help the next person in line. The girl's black hair was cropped short, spiked, and at least five pair of earrings decorated from the top of her ears to the bottom. More piercings decorated her eyebrow and nose. Heavy, dark make-up accentuated her features, making her look mature and world wise.

Sara touched her own simple hoops, feeling plain in comparison. Maybe she should start wearing more make-up. Or *some* make-up, as she hadn't bothered with any today. Would it help her appear older and more mature? More confident with her appearance? Too many years of being the skinny, gangly girl with braces and glasses had dictated how she saw herself. It was hard to replace the image in her mind.

"Sara, nice to see you again," Mary greeted. "I hope you're here to tell us you'll take the job."

"Yes, thank you. Mr. Bannister didn't seem keen on hiring me."

"Don't worry about TJ." Mary picked up some papers, then steered Sara to a table by the window. "He's harmless enough. Simply doesn't like to be told what to do by me. Can you start Story Hour this Thursday?"

Sara nodded, then noticed the little girl with brown ringlets and the smaller boy wandering their way. Mary turned to them. "I'll be right with you, Jasmine and Eddie. I have to do a few things first."

"Can't she read to us like she did the other day?" Jasmine asked. Sara saw a resemblance and figured the boy must be her brother.

"You wouldn't have time now, would you, honey? I wouldn't ask, but a new shipment came in, and TJ wants it out before tonight."

"Happy to. Can I finish these forms later?"

Mary nodded, then waved Sara off with the kids. Three more children sat on the area rug as she settled on the floor.

"Mrs. P. always sits on the chair when she reads," a

blond boy, maybe seven or eight announced, like Sara had done something wrong. He hadn't been here last week.

Before she could reply, Eddie snuggled next to her, grinning. "She wead here before. She sit on a floor to be near us, wight?"

Sara ruffled his hair. "Right. Maybe Freckles will come and sit with us, too. Is she here today?"

The children all nodded, making Sara's stomach flip. TJ Bannister was here. She gazed around the room but didn't see him. Or the dog.

"Does Mrs. P. usually pick out the books, or does she let you decide?"

Eddie's eyes lit up with mischief. "We pick the books."

The starchy, blond boy sat up straighter. "Not all the books. She picks a few, and if there's time, she'll let some of us choose."

Sara tried not to grin at his imperious tone. She took a book and opened it.

"What's your name?" Jasmine asked as Sara turned the page.

"Sara Storm. Maybe I should learn your names, too."

"I'm Elliot," the starchy boy announced. "And Sara Storm is the Invisible Woman. You aren't invisible."

He had no idea how close to the mark he'd been. With her popular brothers, she often felt invisible.

"Actually, *Sue* Storm is The Invisible Woman. My name is Sara. And before you ask, no, we aren't related."

"I want to be invisible." A set of twin boys who had wandered over and settled on the edge of the rug said in unison. "Then mom wouldn't know when I took a cookie," one of them finished.

"That's Harrison and Benson." Elliot leaned in closer. "Sometimes I wish *they* were invisible."

"Believe me, being invisible isn't all it's cracked up to be."

Once she'd learned the names of all the children, she began to read. After several books, the hair on the back of her neck stood on end. Freckles walked over from the corner stairs, but it couldn't have been the dog making her senses go on high alert. As she looked to the top of the stairs, her breath whooshed out of her body. TJ Bannister stood there, staring, a frown on his face.

****

TJ unloaded the box of romances and checked he'd put them correctly on the shelves. The tranquil beach scene on the cover of one caught his attention, and he read through the back blurb. Glancing around to make sure no one saw, he put it in the drawer of the table holding the Science Fiction best sellers. He'd get it later.

As he grabbed another box, Freckles wandered out of his office and to the stairs. It was time for Story Hour, and the dog loved reading with the kids. Unfortunately, it meant Mary wouldn't be able to get any work done.

It didn't matter. More important was for those kids to develop a love of reading. The shelves could be filled any time. Sonni had always made time to read to him, no matter how much she wanted to be doing something else. He'd never forget. Those times had made him feel special, and he learned how much books could take you away from all the negative in the world. Like your parents never having time for you.

TJ followed Freckles' journey. Little Miss Sunshine had returned. Her soft voice floated up to the loft, and he moved closer to the railing to hear better.

Elliot said something about the Invisible Woman. With her looks? Hardly.

"Believe me, being invisible isn't all it's cracked up to be." Regret flashed in her eyes.

Seriously? How had anyone passed her by without a second and third glance? He was supposed to be unloading stock, and he couldn't tear his eyes away.

Freckles walked toward her, and she looked up, her eyes meeting his. Damn. He nodded, then realized he was frowning, so lifted one side of his mouth. Her face lit up. Man, he was a goner.

Get it over with and welcome her to the shop. He took his time down the stairs. No sense in Sara Sunshine thinking he was in any hurry to see her.

"Thanks for coming in, Miss Storm."

Her sea-blue eyes held him in place as she returned the greeting. At least he thought she did. His head was elsewhere. She rose and held out her hand.

He eyed it, trying not to look like it was a snake, but he couldn't have been successful because her eyes dimmed. Or maybe it was because he still hadn't shaken it. Manners.

After grasping her hand firmly, he quickly dropped it. Kept the tingling to a minimum.

"Thank you for the job, Mr. Bannister. I'll work hard, I promise."

TJ forced a nod. "Are the forms filled out?"

"No, Mary asked me to read to the kids first. I'll

finish them now."

Filling a rack with postcards, Mary glanced up, then quickly lowered her eyes, the smirk on her face clear. She had to stop with the matchmaking.

Sara sat, writing furiously. Her brow furrowed, and the tip of her tongue poked out between her lips. It seemed to be a subconscious gesture, but it stirred something inside him. It was going to be a long summer.

Walking to the children's area, he took a look at what might need replacing. The books Sara had read were still stacked next to the big wicker chair Mary usually sat in to read. Obviously, Sara liked getting on the floor with the kids. It's where he always sat when he read to them.

Freckles wandered near, and TJ leaned over to scratch her ears. The dog lifted her head for more.

"You spoiled little girl," he crooned to the animal as he knelt on the floor next to her and rubbed her tummy. "That's right, spoiled." The dog's tail thumped a beat on the carpet.

"You wead to us, Mr. B?" Eddie asked, as he plopped next to TJ. The boy's sister had taken to a corner with a picture book.

"Why don't you read to me? Pick a book you know."

Eddie's eyes lit up. Like his had done whenever Sonni let him read to her. He hadn't known how, but with the book memorized, he felt like he could.

The boy scrambled to the shelves, grabbed one, then scooted back to lean against TJ. He opened the book and proudly began, "One fish, two fish…"

TJ scratched the dog as Eddie 'read'. When Sara

got up from the table, she caught his attention, and his heart flipped as she walked over. Her hips swayed gently but not overtly, and he was mesmerized yet again by the overall softness of her appearance.

He turned his gaze to Eddie but couldn't keep it there as she lifted her skirt to lower herself to the floor. Again, those legs sent his mind into a spiral. The looseness of her top belied her curves but also fell open as she sat. She had plenty to satisfy a man.

But it wouldn't be him. It couldn't be him. He wasn't the type of guy she'd ever take a second look at. Not if she knew him. He certainly didn't deserve an angel, even if Heaven had sent her down just for him. As she leaned over and patted Freckles, he pulled his hand away, pretending to help Eddie turn the page.

She didn't notice and whispered endearments to the dog. Closing his eyes for only a second, he envisioned her whispering the words to him. They'd be sitting around an open fire, close enough to touch. Freckles would be sitting at their feet, and they'd be peaceful and happy. It had been a dream of his for so long. Finding the one woman who would love him for who he was and forgive him for what he used to be. Who would help him be a better person.

He stared openly at Sara, and her eyes radiated warmth. Yes, he'd had that dream often, but the woman in it never had a face. Now she did. And she looked like Sara Storm.

Chapter Three

"Sorry it took so long, Mary," TJ apologized as he entered the shop, carrying a box of coffee stirrers. "The traffic is heavy already."

Walking behind the counter, he placed the thin, plastic straws in the correct location.

Mary leaned on the counter. "Traffic isn't that heavy. Don't think I didn't notice exactly what time you slipped out to run your errands."

He tried for innocence, like he'd ever mastered that and certainly not with Mary. "Don't know what you're talking about. Mid-morning is always a good time for errands. There's no line out the door?"

"I meant right before Story Hour. Avoiding our new employee? What do you have against the poor girl?"

"Nothing," he fibbed. Unless he counted being too upbeat and a danger to his libido. His gaze slanted toward the front of the store, then down at his watch. "Is she gone? I'm not paying her for more than reading to the kids today."

"You stingy miser," Mary accused. "She took your dog for a walk. Freckles was whining to go out. You were too busy trying to escape."

"I wasn't trying to escape." More like avoid. "We needed supplies. I would have taken Freckles out when I got back."

"Then wet-vacced the carpet where she peed."

Sticking his head back under the counter, he pretended the napkins needed organizing. *Should have taken the dog out. Can't believe I forgot.* Damn Sunshine was making him do all sorts of stupid things. Like wear his button-down shirt and pressed khakis. It made no sense why he hadn't worn his typical jeans and T-shirt since he was going out of his way to avoid her. Not that he'd ever admit it to Mary.

He peeked over the counter, seeing Mary with a customer. Good, he could go to his office and do paperwork without her accusing him of hiding. Which is what he planned to do until his happy-go-lucky employee left for the day.

"Hey, boss," Darcy called out as he grabbed a cup of cinnamon tea and an apple muffin to take with him. She was coming in from her cigarette break, probably her third for the day. "What's with the outfit? And you shaved. You look like you got shit on by a preppy bird."

"Darcy, language. And I'm not wearing a suit and tie, for Pete's sake. I have to meet someone this afternoon and didn't want to look like a reject from the slums."

Good excuse, huh? He *was* meeting with someone. Granted it was only Jim Reese, his AA sponsor. It wouldn't hurt to look like a professional and not some recovering addict. Which unfortunately, he was.

"Sure, boss, but remember I offered to take you shopping. I could make you look totally badass. All the chicks would be hot for your bod. Any time you want."

He glared, and Darcy held up her hands to ward him off. Sauntering behind the counter, she began wiping it down. She was a good worker, when she wasn't taking one of her many breaks.

The back door opened, and Sara walked in with Freckles on a leash, humming along to a song in her head. Damn, he'd wanted to be upstairs when she got back, and Darcy had distracted him. But not the way Sara distracted him.

When she bent to unhook Freckles' leash, TJ had to bite his lip to keep the groan from escaping. No sundress today. This was even worse. White slim-fitting Capri pants accentuated her legs and showed him her firm, rounded ass was equally as gorgeous. A simple T-shirt hugged her curves, and boy, did she have some nice ones. Understated but definitely there.

The invoices were on the table, so he couldn't slip out without at least acknowledging her. Not without appearing like a total jerk.

"Thanks for taking Freckles outside. I meant to do it earlier but got held up in traffic." Shit, he'd rot in hell for the number of lies he'd told today. It's what Mamita would have said. She'd know. He'd told her enough lies to go to confession for a few decades. He touched the cross around his neck, the one that had been Sonni's, hoping it would absolve him.

"No problem, Mr. Bannister. Happy to do it. It's beautiful outside, and I love walking."

"It's TJ. We aren't very formal around here." Why had he said that? Calling him Mr. Bannister would keep the formality of boss and employee strong. It might remind him how much he needed to stay away from her and her sunshiny personality.

He picked up the forms. "I'll have next week's schedule finished when you come in Saturday."

Sara scratched Freckles, then smiled again. Why couldn't she stop?

"Do you mind if I stick around? I wanted to check out how the books are organized and see upstairs."

Did he mind? Yes, but he could hardly kick her out. "Fine, but you're off the clock. You'll get a tour next week with your training." Maybe she'd take the hint and leave.

No such luck. She actually chirped. "I could stay in a bookstore all day." Then she wandered into the shop.

Bookstores had been his favorite places, too. But now she was here, infiltrating his mind and stirring up parts of him he didn't want stirred up, he wasn't so sure. After gathering more invoices, he walked to the stairs. He pretended he wasn't looking to see where she'd gone or listening for her voice as she cooed to the dog.

When he got to his office, he left the door ajar. Maybe if he told himself enough times it was to hear if Mary needed help, he might eventually believe it.

****

Sara replaced the books she'd read in the basket. It was almost noon and Jasmine and Eddie were still here.

"Jasmine? Did your mom think Story Hour lasted longer today??"

She didn't want to leave the kids without a parent, but TJ seemed like he wanted her gone.

"Mama's working," Eddie piped in as he played with blocks. "She come back later."

"It's okay," Jasmine added. "Mr. B. watches us while Mama works. He doesn't want her paying a babysitter. As long as we behave, he says we can stay here."

"Is this only for today or all the time?" Had their mother been here the last few times? She didn't think so.

"Yep, all the time." Jasmine never looked up from her book.

Wandering around the store, she kept her gaze on the kids. She'd gotten a feel for where things were. Children's section, cookbooks, travel guides, and other non-fiction downstairs. Plus a few tables filled with the newest best sellers and lots of tourist stuff.

Climbing the stairs, she looked down where the two children sat quietly playing and reading. Did her new boss actually allow them to stay here three times a week so their mom could save money? He'd been nothing but surly and short with her. Her mind had trouble balancing that person with someone essentially providing free day care.

Her heart pounded when she explored the upstairs. It extended to the area above the coffee shop, too. Unique pieces of upholstered furniture littered the nooks and alcoves of the floor. Sara could live here she loved it so much.

Of course, if she did, her lifelong goal wouldn't happen. She couldn't become a singer if she shut yourself in a bookstore all day? She loved singing even more than she loved books.

Passing another alcove, she saw an open door where TJ sat at a desk inside. He stared at some papers, marking them. The glasses he wore made her inside lighter. She'd worn glasses since the fourth grade and had been incredibly self-conscious. Kids had been cruel, especially once she got braces, too. The quintessential dork. Her long monkey arms and stilt-like legs hadn't made it any better.

TJ looked good with glasses. They weren't the thick-rimmed ones most of the in-style guys wore. They were roundish, seeming to have no rim at all and blended in with his face so she hardly noticed them. Lucky guy. She'd made sure to get contacts as early as possible to tone down her geekiness.

When TJ straightened, Sara took a step back. *Not too embarrassing, getting caught mooning over the boss.* Even if he was gorgeous and made her pulse hop around like a frog in a jumping contest.

TJ checked his watch, then removed his glasses, setting them on the desk. Scrubbing his face with his hand, he stood up. Sara scooted behind a high shelf as he left the room and jogged down the stairs.

Curiosity got the better of her so she peeked downstairs. Unfortunately, he disappeared into the coffee shop part. But before she could go back to the book section, he came out calling to the kids.

"Lunch. Mary made your favorite, peanut butter and jelly. Yum!"

Jasmine closed her book while Eddie put his Lego creation in the basket and laughed. "But you don't like peanut butter and jelly."

Sara watched as TJ sat comfortably at the table with the kids. How long had he been babysitting them?

He asked the children questions about what they were reading and building. Freckles threw sad eyes at the children, so Eddie held part of his sandwich out.

"No, you need to eat your crust, Eddie. Freckles has her own food out back. She'll get spoiled if you give her scraps."

Jasmine chuckled. "Mama says you feed Freckles

scraps all the time. *You're* spoiling her."

TJ's eyes lit up with mischief, and he held his finger to his lips. "Shh. It's a secret. You can't tell anybody. They'll think I'm a softy."

"You are an old softy, TJ."

Sara adjusted her position to see who'd spoken. It was an attractive young woman with dark hair tied back in a ponytail. She had a cute figure in jeans and a T-shirt.

"Mama!" The woman scooped Eddie into her arms and kissed his cheek. "Time to go home?"

"Time for your nap."

The boy frowned but settled his head onto the woman's shoulder.

"You don't have to feed them lunch every day, TJ. You already watch them all morning."

He shrugged. "It's only PB and J, Gabby. No big deal."

The woman looked at TJ with adoring eyes. "It is a big deal to me, and you know it. I plan on paying you back someday."

"Oh, I know. And it'll be something really big." TJ spread his hands wide to indicate a huge amount.

Gabby playfully patted his arm. "You goof. Come on, Jasmine, let's get home and allow TJ to get back to work. He can't spend all day watching you."

Gabby shifted Eddie in her arms. "Say thank you to TJ."

The children obeyed, and Gabby kissed TJ on the cheek. Something twisted in Sara's stomach. What it was, she didn't know, or even why it happened, but it was unsettling.

They left, and TJ walked off, so Sara couldn't see

him anymore. She grabbed a book and settled into one of the farthest alcoves. Seeing TJ all sweet and tender with the children made her curious. He'd been the same with Gabby. They must be close. No surprise. A guy like him wouldn't be hurting for female companionship. Like her brothers. They never had trouble finding a date.

Not her. She couldn't find the right kind of guy if she tripped over him. Nothing she did even got her boss being nice to her. He apparently had the ability. Clearly, she wasn't worth the effort.

****

"Perfect timing," Jim Reese called out as TJ walked inside the restaurant. "I already ordered. It should be ready soon."

The plastic lobster in Jim's hand vibrated, and he chuckled. "See, I told you, perfect timing."

After walking to the counter, they claimed the loaded tray. Jim grabbed the cups. "Iced tea or soda today?"

TJ threw him an exasperated look. "You didn't ask what I wanted to eat. Now you're concerned about my drink choice?"

Jim grinned. "Okay, iced tea it is. Find us a table. I'll be there in a sec."

Balancing the tray, TJ headed to the picnic tables outside. Jim had ordered the Clam Plate for him, with onion rings instead of fries. It's what he would have ordered. What he always ordered when they came to Seafood Sam's. Was he too predictable?

He chose a table away from the building and settled in. Jim showed up a minute later and sat across from TJ, pulling the Haddock Plate toward him.

Tossing a few fries in his mouth, he chewed, then asked what he always asked each time they met.

"How long has it been?"

TJ sighed, yet knew exactly how many years, months, days, and minutes since his last drink. Would he ever get to the point where he didn't know right off the top of his head?

"Seven years and five months next Tuesday."

Jim nodded. "Twenty-five years, eight months, and twelve days."

TJ swallowed hard. Jim still counted. How long would he? "Do you ever get tired of focusing on the time since your last mistake?"

Jim took a bite of his coleslaw, sipped his drink, then stared at TJ straight on. "I think of it as focusing on the amount of time I've been successful. You need to think that way, too, my friend. You've been very successful."

He didn't answer, just squeezed ketchup onto his plate and dipped one of his clams into it. They ate in silence for a while, then TJ asked, "How's business at the lumberyard? Picked up since tourist season started?"

Jim managed Hyannis Home Center but lived in Falmouth, a twenty-five minute drive, so they usually met here. TJ liked being away from the town he lived and worked in when they met. Customers nearby might overhear their conversations and judge him. Not that he cared what people thought, but he was a member of the community who owned a business and had started becoming involved with the Chamber of Commerce. Baby steps. Little by little, he hoped to be the contributing member of society he'd never been as a spoiled kid.

"Yup, summer residents are getting supplies to fix up the place since they left last year. Can we push off our basketball game until later on Sunday because I have to train some of the new staff. Does five work?"

"Sure." They had a standing game every Sunday at two. "I have some new staff myself starting this week."

At his sigh, Jim looked up curiously. "You don't think they'll work out?"

Thinking of Sara and her sunny disposition, his mind immediately flashed to the way her hips swayed when she walked, and how her nose crinkled when she smiled. His body reacted in ways it hadn't in far too long. Man, he needed to get control. Or get laid.

"We'll see," he answered vaguely. "You know seasonal staff. They think it's great living down here, but when you make them work during the best beach hours, they aren't happy about it." Except Sara. She'd probably say she was happy she wasn't where the sun could burn her alabaster skin.

Jim pulled a brochure out of his pocket, setting it on the table. "This was by the counter. Seen it yet?"

TJ didn't need to open it. It was the brochure for The Cape Cod Melody Tent. He knew what was in it.

"Second weekend in August has some great bands. You plan on going?"

TJ shrugged and pulled apart an onion ring. He liked the crunchy coating more than the actual onion. Maybe he should just order some fried batter.

"Did you know he'd be here this summer?" Jim was digging, and TJ would eventually talk, but it might take some time. Jim knew this. And he'd wait. He always did.

"Yeah, he emailed me. Not sure how I feel about it. I haven't seen my dad in almost two years."

When he opened the brochure, his gaze immediately zeroed in to the picture of his father's band. They were all old. It was ridiculous they performed like they did thirty years ago. But people still bought tickets and followed them everywhere.

The group's trademark, a black, stenciled Python, decorated the corner of their picture. He rubbed his thigh, the connection one he couldn't deny, no matter how much he wanted to.

"When was the last time you saw your mom?" Jim's voice was casual as he finished off his fish.

"She shows up every year to visit my grandparents. I'm sure she'll stop in this summer, too. If she's got time, she may make an attempt to see me. Usually, she wants me to drive there when she comes. Heaven forbid, she goes out of her way to see her child."

Jim didn't respond, so TJ concentrated on his meal. He'd abandoned the thought of ever having a loving family the day Sonni died. It was another unrealistic dream.

"What's up with the summer staff? You seemed a bit edgy when you mentioned them."

Sara's smiling face appeared in his mind, and he found himself grinning. Why, he didn't know. She was a menace to his libido. His severely underused libido.

Jim noticed right away. "Someone interesting?"

Maybe he needed to talk it out. He trusted Jim more than anyone else. Except maybe Mary, but he'd never have this conversation with Mary. She'd have him and Sunshine married by the end of the month.

"I'm not sure interesting is the word I'd use.

Dangerous, maybe."

Jim's eyebrows rose. "Dangerous, as in emptying the cash register dangerous? Or dangerous to the nice, neat little world you've been carving out for yourself?"

"You don't beat around the bush, do you?"

"Twenty-five years, eight months, and twelve days."

TJ chuckled. "Dangerous to my peace of mind."

"Female?"

His chuckle turned into a snort. "Yeah, very."

"Tell me about her, and how she's gotten your knickers in a twist."

"Her name's Sara. She came in looking for a job, and Mary fell in love with her. I will admit she's perfect for Story Hour. Even has Freckles crawling in her lap."

"Seriously? I've known you for six years, and your dog won't come anywhere near me. This girl must be something special. She look like a fashion model?"

TJ frowned. "She looks like a goddamn angel."

"I don't think God damns any of his angels."

"She's this porcelain doll with blonde hair and innocent eyes. She dresses like she's going to church and never stops smiling."

"Smiling." Jim cringed comically. "Yeah, you have to watch out for those ladies who smile."

"She's got a degree in English Literature and attracts kids like the freakin' Pied Piper."

"Sounds like the heroine of those romance novels you read."

"Don't make me regret telling you," TJ scolded. "That's the problem. Whenever I allow myself to have dreams of a normal life, one like they have at the end of those books, I picture someone like her right beside me.

It's a dream, not reality."

"Why can't it be reality for you?" Jim leaned closer. "You deserve a happy life as much as the next guy. Stop blaming yourself for what happened in the past. Let it go and move on. Maybe this Sara is exactly what you need."

"I don't know." TJ shook his head. "She's a *nice* girl. I've never dated a nice girl before. Come to think of it, I don't think I've ever really *dated* anyone before. Usually I hookup with a chick someplace, we do it, then say goodbye. Sara's not the hookup type."

"When we first met, you were seeing someone."

TJ thought of Kerri, and his insides revolted. "Don't mention that bitch. Our relationship was mostly about sex. You don't jump into bed with someone like Sara."

"Then ask her out on a date and don't sleep with her."

Sleep. TJ had never slept with a woman before. Had sex, screwed, banged, yeah, he could get cruder in terminology. But sleeping with someone meant commitment. Something he'd never had or knew how to do. His role models were limited.

"Did I mention she's a nice girl? I have no clue how to treat one of those. Not one I'm interested in romantically anyway."

Jim started to talk, and TJ interrupted him. "And don't tell me to ask Mary. She's already got us practically engaged."

"Why don't you let time takes its course. Get to know her. Talk about what she likes and wants to do with her life. Treat her like a friend first and see what grows from there."

TJ didn't think this would work. Jim always gave him good advice. But how was he supposed to act like friends with someone whose lips called out to be kissed? Whose slender arms asked for his fingers to caress them? Whose mile-long legs begged to be wrapped around his waist. He knew he should only listen to the sweet voice coming from her mouth, but the rest of her body was far noisier than her words and much clearer in his mind. Staying away from her, so he couldn't hear, seemed like the better solution.

Chapter Four

Sara walked into *Tea and Tales* a half hour early Saturday. She didn't see Mary or TJ. Her insides fluttered. *Come on, confidence!* Darcy stood behind the bookstore register, and two unfamiliar girls each helped a small line of customers at the coffee counter. A cup of tea and pastry would be calming before she started.

Some of the kids playing in the children's section caught her eye as she waited in line. There was Jasmine, Eddie, bold as brass Elliott, shy little Hope, and the redheaded girl who had been here the day Sara applied for the job. She turned back as the line moved and faced a redheaded woman behind the counter. She looked familiar, and Sara turned to view the redheaded girl, then back to the woman.

"Yup, Fiona's mine. Can't even try to deny her. What can I get you?"

"Cinnamon tea and a piece of coffee cake, please."

The woman left and was back in seconds with a cup and pastry quoting a price. Sara pulled bills out of her purse and held them out.

A hand reached from behind her, grabbed the money, and pushed it back at Sara. "Nope, she works here, Becca. Boss hired her last week to do Story Hour and other stuff."

Darcy had come up behind her.

"We haven't officially met, but I'm Darcy Marx,

and this is Becca Miller. She's the assistant manager in charge when Mary or Jason isn't here. Your name's Sara, right?"

"Yes, Sara Storm. It's nice to meet you both. Are you sure about the cake and tea? I planned to pay for it."

"When you're working, it's on the house," Darcy explained.

"Unless you eat and drink all during work." The other girl walked over from her position behind the counter. She had wavy dark hair with bright pink on the tips. Her figure was voluptuous and not at all hidden in the low-cut top and tight shorts. Sara felt plain and frumpy beside her.

"I'm not working until ten," Sara said. "Maybe I should pay."

"You're fine." Becca pointed to the pink-haired girl. "This is Hunter Crump. She started last week."

Darcy waved in Hunter's direction. "And she better learn to keep her boobs inside her shirt if she doesn't want to end this job. TJ's in his office and wants a clean, family friendly store. That ain't it."

Hunter pouted but tugged on the top slightly. Sara looked down at her own flowing skirt and loose sleeveless top, feeling a bit overdressed.

Taking her tea and pastry, she thanked Becca and sat at an empty table. The crowds moved in and out, but it was still slow paced. Kind of like the small New Hampshire town she grew up in. She couldn't say she missed it since she'd only been gone a week, but it was strange not to have her parents around to talk to or her brothers to tease her. Of course, her oldest brother, Erik, was stationed overseas, and she hadn't seen him in almost ten months. She missed him and worried about him being in a war zone.

As ten o'clock approached, more kids shuffled in, claiming rug space in the children's section. Sara finished her snack and tossed her trash.

Getting this job had been perfect. The only small worry was how TJ treated her. He hadn't exactly been mean, but the warmth he gave to the children wasn't there when he spoke to her. Children had a way of spreading it to everyone. He obviously wasn't immune.

"Mary isn't working today?" Sara asked Becca, hoping the older woman's friendly face would be around to make her more comfortable. It usually took a while to warm up to people, yet she was always outwardly friendly. Inside, she was a bundle of nerves.

"Mary has Fridays, Saturdays, and Sundays off."

"Is it time to read, yet, Sara?"

A tug on her skirt had her looking down into Jasmine's bright face. She took the child's hand and led her to the colorful carpet. There were more children than usual.

"Hi, everyone, I'm Sara. Are we ready to begin?"

Some loud whoops and a few softer, "yups" came her way, and she sifted through the books, pulling out her favorite. As she began to read, her anxiety drifted away, leaving her calm and in her element.

The hour flew by, and soon the parents herded their children out, disposable coffee cups in their hands. Only Jasmine, Eddie, and Fiona were left. She hated leaving the children by themselves, but TJ would consider this time *off the clock*.

Becca walked over, scooping Fiona into her arms. "Okay, munchkin, Grammy's here. Be good, and I'll see you later." She planted a few sloppy kisses on the girl's face, making the child squeal in delight.

"Hey, Sara?" Darcy called out from behind the coffee counter. "There's a lull right now. I'll show you how the equipment works."

TJ said she'd get trained next week. Would he be okay with this? He hadn't shown his face since she'd been here, though Freckles had joined Story Hour as usual. If he stayed put, she could learn a few things now, then look like a great student when she officially trained later.

"Did TJ ask you to show me this?" *Cover your bases. No sense getting the new boss upset before you even start.*

"He'll be fine. You're here now, and it's not busy. On Monday, we've got stock coming in, and it's mostly new people, with only Mary for the morning. Better to learn now."

Sara walked behind the counter noting Becca was at the book register. Hunter stood near the end, talking with a few guys who'd gotten coffee. Following Sara's gaze, Darcy rolled her eyes.

"Don't do that, huh? Especially when TJ's around. Being friendly to the customers is one thing. Ignoring your work to flirt, not too cool."

"I'm not really the flirtatious type."

Darcy chuckled. "Didn't think you were but figured I'd say it anyway. If you're wearing nice clothes," she pointed to Sara's skirt, "you might want to use an apron. There's some in the back room. It's not required, but even when you're careful, you end up with coffee drips all over you."

She listened carefully as Darcy explained the large

variety of coffee makers and warmers, and which blend was used for each flavor of coffee. “We always have at least two pots of hot water for tea. Those stay on the end burners.”

So many details. What if she screwed up? It wasn’t hard, but she wanted to prove to TJ she wasn’t some brainless idiot. Maybe he’d be nicer to her. Like he was to Jasmine and Eddie and their mom. Okay, maybe not like their mom, as she had a feeling it might be more than friendship there.

“Hunter, can you show Sara how to empty the grounds filter and refill it? I have to take care of these customers.”

Why couldn’t Hunter take care of the customers? Sara turned. It was another group of good-looking guys. Either Darcy wanted them to herself, or she didn’t trust Hunter not to flirt hopelessly with them. Hunter left the group she was talking to and reluctantly came over.

“These are the filters for the coffee. It’s pretty simple if you’ve ever made coffee at home.”

She was more of a tea drinker but didn’t want to start that conversation. Hunter pulled out the handle of the filter holder on the right and emptied the used grounds into the trash.

“These are the different types of coffee. Did Darcy tell you what each color means?”

“Yes, orange is decaf, brown is hazelnut, white is vanilla, and green is regular. The pots are marked the same way. The other specialty coffees are made in single cups and not in pots.”

“See, easy.” Hunter ripped open a packet, then dumped it into the filter before shoving it back into the coffee maker. “You do this one. It’s Hazelnut.”

When she pulled on the filter handle, it wouldn't come out. Hunter was back flirting with the guys at the end of the counter and no help. Suddenly the girl grabbed a dishrag and started wiping things down. Turning to see what had motivated Hunter to actually work, she saw TJ crossing the room toward them.

As she tugged harder on the handle, the filter flew out, spilling hot coffee grounds and water all over her hand. She jumped back with a yell, then cursed herself. Couldn't she do anything right? And with the boss watching. But damn, her hand hurt.

She bent down to clean up the mess, but TJ pushed past Darcy and grabbed her burned hand.

"Under cold water, now."

Pulling her to the sink near the back wall, he turned on the water. "Darcy, clean that up. Hunter, get upstairs and finish straightening the shelves."

"Let me see," TJ said right near her ear, still holding her hand under the water. A shiver ran up her spine at his nearness and the gravelly tone of his voice. He was upset. Would he even let her stay now after this stupid mistake?

"I'm fine, really." Why was her voice so small and timid? When she dealt with her brothers, she was plenty loud. She tried to pull her hand away and make light of the injury. But damn, it stung. Heat and pain throbbed across the nerve endings on the top of her hand.

"You're not fine. You can get severe burns from hot water. Darcy should have warned you about that filter. It sticks and needs to be pulled out in a certain way. I'm sorry you got hurt."

His last words came out much softer than anything she'd heard him say yet. He actually meant it and didn't sound angry. Maybe she could keep her job after all.

"Keep it under cool water for at least ten minutes to get as much of the heat out as possible. It should help. Then we'll wrap it."

"No, I'm sure I don't need—"

"It's basic first aid for burns. I made sure to learn this when I first started working here. I had a few accidents like this, too."

He stood right behind her with one hand holding hers. His firm chest pressed against her back, and she liked it. She didn't know why, but there was something comforting in his presence. He grasped some paper towels from the roll and put his arms around her. God, what was he doing? She stood inside his embrace.

****

TJ pulled Sara's hand from the water, carefully dabbing the paper towel over it. The skin had turned red. He glanced down, and her face was as red as her hand.

Both his arms were around her, and she was pressed against him. What had he been thinking? Only to check the burns weren't more than first degree. But the feeling starting to infiltrate his body headed for second degree or higher.

Yet, he couldn't let go. This was nice. More than nice. When was the last time he'd simply held a woman in his arms without being in the middle of screwing her? Maybe never. Or probably only the few seconds it took to get her to agree to go off and have a good time with him. God, what a sleaze. But had he changed?

He wouldn't say no to sex with Sara, but he couldn't see it happening. Not right now. She was too sweet, and no way he could have a quick screw with her, then let her go. She wasn't the type. Still, he'd met women who'd appeared innocent but ended up as experienced as him.

"Feel any better? Is the sting going away?"

She nodded, yet her eyes held moisture. Moving her hand out of the water stream, she winced. "The water makes it hurt less."

"Good, leave it here for a bit longer." His left hand rested on the sink edge but shifted closer to her waist. Leaning down on the pretense of checking her hand, he nestled his nose next to her hair. Some light, fruity scent floated his way. Strawberries? Maybe her shampoo. Definitely not heavy enough for perfume. It smelled soft and feminine, like Sara.

After a few minutes, her body relaxed, and she leaned back against him. *Oh, damn,* he enjoyed this too much. Parts of him hardened when her bottom pressed against his front. Time to let her stand on her own.

Easing away, he grabbed more paper towels. "Keep it there a few more minutes. I have some gauze in the First Aid kit. I'll get it ready."

As he walked toward the back room, her soft "thank you" floated his way, her voice truly melodious. Like she belonged in an angels' choir. He sifted through the kit, putting out the materials he'd need. Doing it where the customers could see wouldn't be good for business.

When he poked his head out, she was patting her hand dry with a softer towel Darcy had given her.

"Thanks, Darcy, and for cleaning up the mess. I'll do this in the back. Can the three of you handle everything for a few minutes?"

Darcy gave him her typical 'are you kidding me?'

look. "You've been in your office all morning even through the rush times. Yeah, I think we can handle it." She looked at Sara, "Hey, maybe you can get Workman's Comp."

TJ glared. "And maybe you can get Unemployment."

Darcy made a face, laughed, then went back to working behind the counter. He took Sara through the back, into the bathroom, closed the lid on the toilet, and said, "Sit here. I'll bandage it up."

"It'll be fine. I don't want to be any problem."

Her anxiety was clear. Why? She'd been great with the kids. He'd peeked again today while she'd read, and the kids loved her. Her expressive tone and distinctive voices made the children laugh. That's what he wanted for this place. Children were supposed to have fun. They shouldn't be molded into their parents. They should simply be kids.

Picking up the gauze, he crouched down in front of her. Her eyes were dry now. Good. Yes, he'd bitched about her exorbitant amount of happiness, but he hated to see it gone.

He took her hand gently and wrapped the gauze loosely around it. "No problem at all, Sara. We need to make sure you're okay. If it gets worse or discolored at all, let me know. You might need to have a doctor look at it."

"I'm sorry. This was my fault. I pulled too hard."

When finished with the gauze, he placed some tape on the edges. Keeping her hand resting on his, he tapped lightly against the tape a little more. To make sure it didn't come up. *Sure.* It couldn't be due to the tingle he got with his fingertips touching hers. A tiny smile played about her lips as she stared at their hands.

"It wasn't your fault. That filter's been sticking for a while now. I keep meaning to get it fixed or replace it, but I haven't gotten around to it yet. Everybody here knows to be cautious. Darcy should have warned you."

"It's not Darcy's fault. She was helping a customer because Hunter—"

Her eyes flew up, realizing what she was about to say. Loyal of her.

"I know. Hunter was preoccupied with other…customers." Mary had warned him some of the new help might not work out. He'd hoped that wouldn't be the case. If only Hunter would keep her mind on business and her body inside her clothes. No way Sara would ever wear anything so revealing. He'd love to see it, but he'd never want anyone else to. Now where did that proprietary thought come from?

Needing some distance from this angel who was casting some sort of weird spell over him, he stood, cleared his throat, then walked out of the tiny washroom. "I made next week's schedule. Get a copy from my office before you leave."

TJ walked out through the shop, and Darcy eyed him cautiously. "She gonna live, boss?"

Sara rolled her eyes, and he was glad to see some of her spirit return. "I'm fine. Sorry I caused such a scene. Thank you for cleaning up after me, Darcy. I owe you one."

Darcy rubbed her hands together, wiggling her eyebrows. "Ooh, someone owes me a favor. Loving this."

As he trotted up the stairs, Sara close behind, he shook his head. Hunter chatted with a customer again.

Flirted actually. The girl could teach a class on it. Reprimanding her would be a waste of time. He wanted to get Sara home so she could rest.

Picking up a copy of the schedule, he passed it to her. "I usually hand out copies to everyone. If you aren't around, make sure to get one here." He pointed to the table they were on. "I also have one posted in the back room downstairs."

Sara skimmed the paper. "You gave me lots of hours."

"Monday you're training. You've got Story Hour the three days, so I gave you hours then. Then Wednesday night, I'll teach you how to clean. Cleaning is Wednesday and Sunday night. I don't work Sundays, and I don't want Jason staying late either, so I'll give you a key to lock up when you leave."

He started back downstairs with her beside him. When they got to the back door, he looked around. "Where's your car? If your hand still hurts, I can drive you home and walk back here. Your address wasn't too far."

"I don't have a car. It's only two blocks over. I took this job and the one at The Melody Tent because I can walk to them."

TJ glanced out the window. Dark clouds hovered in the sky. "I'll give you a ride. I don't want it to start raining while you're walking home."

"I'm not afraid of a little rain. I certainly won't melt."

She was sweet enough to. "But you shouldn't get the bandages wet, so I'll give you a ride. Freckles can come with us, if you need a chaperone."

He whistled for the dog, and they went outside to

his dark blue 4X4. After TJ opened the door for Sara, Freckles followed him around to the driver's side and jumped in first.

Putting the truck in gear, he pulled out of the parking space, taking a right, then doubling back on the one-way street. When they came to the intersection, Sara pointed to the right.

"It's the second building."

An insurance agency. A kind of sketchy one.

"You live here?"

"Upstairs. I share it with a few people."

Pulling over, he eyed the building warily. He wasn't sure he wanted to let her out. "I'll walk you up."

"No," she answered quickly. "I'm fine. Thanks for the ride. I'll see you Monday." She leaned in, and TJ stopped breathing, but she scratched the dog and crooned a good bye to her. He should have left the dog back at the shop. When he leaned across to open the door, she stiffened.

"Wave from the window, so I'll know you got inside." His face was inches from hers, and her pupils got larger. Maybe she was as affected as he was.

"You don't—"

"Humor me," he cut in, then leaned back. He'd rather stay right where he was.

After pulling keys from her purse, she hopped out. Her hips swayed in the ultra-feminine way she had of walking. Barely a minute later, her face appeared at the window upstairs. She waved shyly, and he could practically see her blush from here.

As he pulled out into traffic, he thought about his plans for tomorrow, Sunday, his day off. Usually he loved having a full day to himself where he didn't have to worry about going in and checking on the business. But for some reason, all he could think about was Monday morning when he was back at work.

Chapter Five

"Thanks for showing me the science fiction books…what was your name again?"

The customer she'd brought upstairs leaned in closer, causing Sara to step back.

"It's Sara. You're welcome. Um, I'll let you shop." She turned to go.

"Pretty name, just like you." He put his hand on the shelf, blocking her exit. "I'm Gavin. Maybe you could help me. Have you read any of these?"

"I'm not much for science fiction. I can get someone else to help you. I'll go ask." She tried to walk past him in the other direction, but he positioned himself in her way.

Her heart stopped for a second. If this was one of her brothers, she'd simply push him. With a customer, she might get fired. She needed this job.

Gavin leaned closer. "What kind of books do *you* like to read, Sara? Maybe we could get together and discuss one sometime."

Okay, get yourself out of this one. She'd always used her ex-boyfriend, Robby, as an excuse. Should she lie and say she was seeing someone?

"Sara, do you have a minute?"

TJ stood behind Gavin, his face impassive. Great. Did he think she was flirting? "Of course."

Her boss glanced at Gavin and raised an eyebrow.

"Is there anything else you need? I have to go over some scheduling if you're all set."

Gavin's smug expression fell away, and he dropped his arm. "No, fine. Thanks."

Gavin turned to the shelves but didn't appear to actually be looking. Sara skirted around him, walking over to TJ's office door. He had disappeared back inside.

Stepping through the door, she breathed a sigh of relief. Although maybe she shouldn't. Was she about to get a lecture on fraternizing with customers?

"Did you need me for something?"

TJ leaned against his desk. "Yes, relax. You don't have to put up with rude behavior from customers."

"But we're supposed to—"

"Be polite to them, I know. But if one of them makes you uncomfortable, you have permission to walk away, or get someone else to help you. Do you understand?"

Sara nodded. She wasn't getting fired.

Walking closer, he picked up her bandaged hand. "I don't ever want you to feel uneasy working here."

She stared at their hands. What she felt right now wasn't exactly uncomfortable, but it was something she had no experience with. When Robby had held her hand, her heart and nerves had stayed calm. Not the case with TJ.

"Is the hand feeling better?"

"Yes, thanks. It's been four days now, so the sting is gone. It's a little sensitive where the blisters popped."

He continued looking at her hand, like he was studying an ancient artifact. "I'm glad to see you're taking care of it."

He let go of her hand and leaned on his desk again. "How are you doing here? Getting the hang of things? Mary said you did great on the register yesterday."

She smiled at his acknowledgment. "I've worked a register before. It's easy enough. The hardest part is trying to remember coffee orders if they want cream, sugar, and extra flavors to go in it. I'm more of a tea drinker myself."

TJ chuckled. "Me, too. When I bought the coffee shop, I thought of changing it to only tea, but here in New England, people are pretty serious about their coffee. I couldn't do it and stay in business. I compromised."

Her comfort level around TJ had improved the last few days. Ever since her accident, he'd been much nicer to her. Made small talk and asked how she was. She liked it, was beginning to realize she liked him.

"It was a good decision. Seems like you sell as much tea as coffee." She peeked out the door. "I guess I should let you get back to work. Thanks for…um…"

His eyes held humor. "You're welcome. Let me check if your suitor has made his choice and left." He glanced out the door. "All set. Wonder if he actually bought a book."

As they walked out, TJ looked at his watch. "It's only two. You aren't scheduled until four because you're cleaning tonight."

Cleaning. Yeah, she was thrilled he'd given her the job with so many hours. But Wednesdays were the nights they did open mic at the brewery across town. It was the only place on the Cape she'd found she could get a chance to sing. Of course, it was a few miles away and not walkable, which meant trying to find a taxi and paying more money. She shouldn't complain.

Sara shrugged. "I'm not actually on the clock now. I came in to look around, and Cam asked if I'd bring this guy upstairs."

"What was Cam doing?"

"Busy with another customer? I didn't ask. It was only going to take a minute."

TJ looked thoughtful. "Take an extra break tonight to make up for the time you spent with Romeo." He looked over the railing into the bookstore. "Looks safe."

Her cheeks heated, and she lowered her eyes. What was it about this man that made her go all stupid and blushing? Right there. He was a man. She was used to dealing with boys her age. TJ wasn't old. Mary had said he wasn't thirty yet. But the way he acted and held himself with such confidence and maturity said it all.

Sara skipped down the stairs.

"Did you give Gavin your number?" Camden Gregoski, another summer hire, sidled up behind her.

Sara's head whipped around. "What? You knew he'd hit on me?"

Cam shrugged, a stupid smirk on his face. "Yeah, he thought you were hot, so I arranged for the two of you to have a little *alone* time."

"Well, maybe I didn't want any alone time with him. Don't do that again, Cam. It made me uncomfortable."

"What's your problem?" Cam made a face. "Summer is for hooking up and having fun."

Cam looked like the type to have fun. He had the whole sun-bleached hair, tanned beach bum thing going on. Even smelled like the beach.

"Know who I'd like to hook up with." Hunter strolled over. The tips of her hair were a bright aqua-blue today, matching the top barely holding up her Double D's. Sara gazed down at her barely B's, wondering if she stuck them out there whether she'd get noticed more. Although the kind of guys who would probably notice would be like Gavin or Cam. No, thank you.

"Who? Maybe I can arrange it." Cam apparently considered himself a dating service.

Hunter tipped her chin in the direction of TJ, who knelt near the shelves in the children's section, rearranging books. "He is yummy. I bet he could show a girl a good time."

Cam's eyebrows rose. "He's too serious to have a good time."

"He's only serious when he's here because it's his business. I heard he has a big house down on the beach. He must be rich."

"So, you're only interested in his money." Cam's mouth twisted.

Hunter's eyes lit up. "And his body. Don't you think he has a gorgeous body, Sara? Love those snug T-shirts."

She couldn't disagree but would never gossip about their boss. Cam wandered off, so she turned to straighten some postcards. Hunter stepped closer.

"Sara, you aren't working Saturday night. Could you switch with me? I have a beach party I want to go to. You're not busy then, are you?"

"I, uh, no, I'm not, but—"

"Awesome, I'll go ask TJ. Thanks. You're a doll."

Sara kept her eye on Hunter as she walked away.

The girl smoothed out her short skirt and tugged on her top, causing her curves to pop out more than ever. TJ looked up only briefly when Hunter approached, and his gaze went straight to her face. He didn't fall for the free cleavage.

He listened, shook his head, and said a few words. Hunter bent over, her lip out in a pout, her figure very much on display. TJ gave a tiny smile, said a few more things, then continued his work. Hunter came back, her shoulders slumped.

"He wouldn't let me. Said you had to do Story Hour in the morning, and it wouldn't be fair to make you come back again at night. I already told this hot guy I'd go. Guess I'll call in sick."

Sara shook her head as Hunter walked away. If you wanted to make it anywhere in this world, you needed to show up and do your best. Sara was determined to make it.

****

"What made you decide to run away to the Cape for the summer?"

TJ showed Sara the cleaning routine but was curious about this angel who'd popped into his life. Over the past few days, she'd been an exemplary worker. Like resisting the advances of the customer this afternoon. The guy had been good-looking and certainly someone Hunter would have been all over. That girl needed to be restrained at times. Like when she tried to flaunt her over-sized chest in his face and get him to change her hours. He'd seen Sara's wide eyes and tight lips when Hunter had talked to her. She hadn't wanted to switch but had been railroaded.

"I needed a change of scenery." Sara continued

dusting the shelves. Even when she was chatting with the boss, she still did her work. "I live in a small town and wanted to see new faces."

"So a few months down here was the answer."

"Yeah, I love music, and I saw The Melody Tent was looking for seasonal workers. I didn't realize how few hours it actually was, or how much rent would be, even sharing a place. Plus, my brothers hated the idea of me coming down. I needed to shake them up a bit."

He paused in his cleaning. "You don't get along with your brothers?"

Sara's eyes twinkled. "Oh, no, I'd do anything for them. And they'd do anything for me. But they're very overprotective, and sometimes it's tough being their little sister. All three of them were super popular in high school, played lots of sports, and were liked by everyone. I was simply their baby sister, invisible whenever they were around."

Her gaze roamed the room as her shoulders rose and fell. "I just wanted to be known for me, Sara Storm, not as Erik, Alex, or Luke's little sister."

Or Abe and Celia's son. He completely understood. Maybe they were more alike than he thought.

"Good for you. I hope this is what you need, and you can start standing on your own and being yourself. I know what it's like to be under someone else's shadow."

"Really?" Her face lit up, and he felt a connection. He moved to the next row of books not wanting to get too deep into that discussion. She wasn't ready to know his past, and he wasn't ready to tell her.

For the next hour, they worked alongside each

other, TJ showing her what needed to be done and how to do it. She was strong and capable. Smart and well-read, too. Not surprising since she'd been an English Literature major.

"I think my favorite part," Sara commented a while later, as they were cleaning the coffee makers, "is when Mr. Brownlow looks at the portrait of his niece and sees the resemblance to Oliver Twist. It always gives me chills."

"I love seeing old Fagin and the boys. Although, I think the old man met his match when Bill Sykes grew up and began upping the ante in his crimes."

Sara shivered. "Bill Sykes was an awful man, but Fagin, I don't know, he always struck me as somewhat noble in a small way."

"What are you talking about? The man trained little boys to pickpocket and steal people's wallets and jewelry. What's noble about that?"

"Okay, maybe not exactly *noble,*" Sara back-pedaled. "But truthfully, what he did for those boys was better than their other options. He gave them a place to sleep and food to eat. If they hadn't had him around, they would have been on the streets and possibly dead in a short period of time. Yes, he used them for his own gain, but I think he cared for them a little, and they got something out of it, too."

"Yeah, the tricks to petty larceny."

"Oh, stop." Sara swatted him with the dishtowel she used to dry the coffee pots. "You have to admit Fagin was a better choice than the streets, living on their own."

Debating with her was fun. She had many opinions on the classics. Some he shared and some not, but he took the opposite side from her on most of the ones they'd discussed, simply to get a rise out of her.

"Okay, I'll agree on that."

She looked smug at his admission, and he wanted to kiss her. Wipe the smile off her face and replace it with one filled with desire. But could she ever desire him?

"But Nancy sure didn't make good choices," he continued. "Certainly not being with Bill Sykes."

Pausing in wiping the pot, she seemed pensive. "No, it probably wasn't the best decision on her part, but she was in love, and love makes you blind to many things."

"Love is blind, huh? A bit cliché, isn't it?"

Her nose wrinkled as she chuckled. Man, he couldn't get enough of the innocent action.

"Maybe, but Bill probably wasn't always as bad as he was in the book, and he took care of Nancy to a certain degree. She probably would have needed to do worse things if she hadn't been with him."

Crossing his arms over his chest, he narrowed his eyes, wanting to taunt her. "You're saying Bill was as noble as Fagin?"

"Oh, God, no," she yelped. "He was a horrible man. What I'm saying is Nancy's decision to be with him wasn't as stupid as we might think. She was in love with him, and people overlook quite a lot when they're in love."

Had Abe and Celia ever really been in love? They certainly overlooked an awful lot with each other. But then they weren't married anymore. Sonni's death had turned into a blame game, and it had only gotten worse from there.

Sara saw the good in everybody, like Nancy had done with Bill Sykes. But she wasn't stupid. She'd seen exactly what the customer had wanted from her this afternoon and tried to back away. If she fell in love with someone, would she be able to overlook any terrible things they'd done in the past? Could she possibly forgive him for the way he'd lived his life for far too long?

Wiping the last pot, she placed it under the counter, then turned to face him, her head tilted as if to say, *what next*?

"There's still a little hot water left. Do you want a cup of tea before you head home?"

It was silly to ask, but he wanted to extend his time with her.

"I'd love some." The brilliant smile appeared again, the one he'd balked at the first few times he'd met her. He'd never malign it again.

"Okay, Sunshine, pick your poison." He held out the basket with the tea bags for her to choose one.

Picking up the cinnamon tea, she gazed at him strangely. "Sunshine?"

"You're always smiling, no matter what. It lights up the room, like the sun."

Her cheeks turned pinks, like they'd done a few times before. Another aspect of her he liked. No one blushed any more. No one was innocent enough to. At least none of the women he'd met. But Sara was in a category all her own.

"Go and sit by the window, and I'll bring it to you."

He poured the water, dipped the tea bags inside, then carried the cups over to the table. The lights were dimmed in the shop, but the street lights from Main Street shone bright and illuminated where they sat. Like something from a romance novel. But that would mean the heroine, Sara, was attracted to the hero. Him? Or was he the antagonist who stood in the way of the heroine getting what she wanted?

What did he want? To get to know her better. Their discussions while cleaning had been invigorating. It wasn't often he met a woman who had a mind and actually used it. Of course, he'd never really been looking for one before. Now he'd found Sara, he couldn't imagine why not.

"So, *Jane Eyre* or *Wuthering Heights*?" TJ knew she'd have an opinion. Sure enough those expressive eyes lit up.

A half hour later, he wondered if they should continue the great debate they were having but decided it was late, and they both needed to work in the morning. As Sara finished describing a scene in her favorite book, he allowed his gaze to wander. His focus was only on her beautiful voice.

She must have thought he wasn't listening, because she turned to see what he stared at. Her head cocked when she saw the poster advertising their Friday and Saturday entertainment. Jason had put up a new one.

"You have live music here on weekends? Are they singers I've heard of?"

"No, mostly locals. It's pretty low key. I don't serve alcohol, but we do have sandwiches and desserts for sale, and we get to keep the place open a little later. It's a nice option for the tourists who want some entertainment but don't want the club scene."

"I love the idea. I wish I had more weekend nights

off."

"What kind of music do you like?" He loved all kinds. Even though Abe and Celia had been straight rock and roll, they'd made sure he and Sonni had learned the classics and knew a variety of styles.

"Everything. I learned to play classical early but later was allowed to do more contemporary."

"You play an instrument?" Could she be more perfect?

"I started piano lessons when I was six. I taught myself the guitar until I saved enough babysitting money for lessons."

"I'd love to hear you play sometime, Sara."

He was certain she'd be amazing. Or maybe he just wanted to spend more time with her and share another thing that mattered to him. First books and now music. The dream he kept at bay in the back of his mind began to drift closer and have more clarity than ever before. For the first time, he actually had it in sight hoping it would come closer and eventually be within his grasp.

"I brought my guitar with me. Do you book the performers ahead for the summer?"

"Jason does, but I think he only books them a few weeks in advance and adds to them as we go along. Sometimes, we get a tourist who wants a go, and we let them."

"Really?" Excitement glowed in her eyes. "Do you think if I have a day off, I could perform?"

"Play your guitar, you mean?"

"Yes, and I also sing. It's one of the reasons I came down here this summer and got the job at The Melody Tent."

A deep blanket of foreboding settled like a shroud

over him as Sara's enthusiasm grew. She kept talking, but this time he wasn't mesmerized by her voice.

"I know there are music promoters and managers who come with the groups. I was hoping to catch the attention of one of them. If they heard me sing, maybe they'd sign me on or at least help me know the best way to get noticed."

The knots in his stomach doubled, then tripled. Memories flew through his mind of weeks on the road with only Sonni to keep him company, while their parents, the band, and all the groupies lived by the musician's creed: sex, drugs, and rock and roll. Sara couldn't possibly want that. Not his innocent Sunshine.

A wistful expression appeared on her face. Her words were ones he dreaded to hear.

"It's been my dream for a long time to become a singer and tour all over the world. I'll do anything to get there."

His vision fogged as he gazed out the window past Sara's angelic face. The dream that had been moving closer, and had almost been within his grasp, suddenly made a sharp U-turn, flittering away faster than the wind in a Nor'easter. Another feeling crept toward him, a familiar one, but it had kept its distance of late. One he wanted to avoid. But Sara's revelation had awakened the power it had over him.

He needed a drink.

Chapter Six

Music blared from the windows of her apartment. Kayla and Dan were having *another* party. A dozen in three weeks. Sara always had to wait until everyone left to sleep.

Tonight she wasn't in the mood to be patient. Going for a walk or sitting on the back stoop until everyone staggered off home, wasn't her idea of a good time.

She'd put in her first night at The Melody Tent, and it was well past midnight. Tomorrow morning bright and early, she had to deal with a dozen children. TJ might get mad if she wasn't on her game.

The night a little over a week ago, when he'd taught her the cleaning routine, confused her. After her accident, he'd acted nicer, and that night they'd definitely connected, discussing many of her favorite books. His eyes gleamed with mischief whenever he gave an opposing view, like he was waiting for her to get riled up. It had been fun, and she thought they'd started on the road to friendship. But right after she'd told him she wanted to be a singer, he'd clammed up again. Why?

Ever since, the camaraderie they'd shared was missing. He didn't go out of his way to talk to her and only interacted with her when he needed something. Maybe he was busy or in a bad mood, but he'd still been wonderful with the children and sarcastic with Mary and Darcy. With her, it was almost back to the way he'd been the first week they'd met.

She slogged up the back stairs, wanting to simply crawl into bed without battling her roommates. But as the apartment was Kayla's, she had no right to be demanding. Kayla had allowed her to stay here as a favor to Sofia. The money Sara paid in her portion of the rent probably didn't hurt either.

When she pushed the door open, her heart fell all the way to her toes. A dozen people sat drinking or smoking, and a couple in the corner were going hot and heavy, unaware there were others in the room. Or maybe they didn't care.

No one in the room noticed her. They were all laughing and getting high. Sara found Kayla near the front window sucking down a beer. Dan sat at her feet, puffing on a joint. The smell in the room made Sara's stomach turn. How would she sleep here after they'd all gone? The stench was worse than ever.

"Kayla?" She had to repeat the girl's name before she looked up. "When is everyone leaving?" She hated to be pushy, but this was also her place. Would Kayla get the hint and shoo everyone out?

Kayla stared back, her eyes unfocused. Damn.

"Hi, Sara. Want a drink? We've got plenty in the fridge."

Her shoulders slumped. "No, thanks, Kayla. I'm really tired and need some sleep. I have to work in the morning. Will this last much longer?"

Her roommate's eyes cleared for a second, then unfortunately glazed over again.

"Kayla," Sara strengthened her tone, like she did

with her brothers. “I can’t sleep on the couch if there are people there.”

Kayla’s gaze swung to the couch. “Okay, we can sit on the floor.”

She clenched her teeth to keep from screaming. “I can’t sleep with people in the room, Kayla. I need to go to bed. I have to work in the morning.”

“Well, use my room. No one’s in there.”

Sucky option since it was Dan’s room, too, but these people looked like they weren’t ready to leave. Dan popped some pastel pill in his mouth, and she groaned. Seriously? These people were a mess.

“Fine,” she snapped, knowing sleep may not come with the noise. It was still better than sitting outside on the stoop until they all left. She grabbed a tank top and shorts and shuffled into Kayla’s room.

The sheets were questionable, so she pulled the comforter up and slept on top. A cool breeze from the ocean, only a mile away, filtered in. That and her exhaustion lulled her to sleep quickly.

****

Sara woke with a start as the mattress dipped next to her. Blinking to focus in the dim light, she knew immediately who it was. Dan. The scent of weed assaulted her as he crawled closer.

“Hey, baby,” he slurred, the smell of alcohol strong. “Come here and give me some.”

She swatted him and scooted in the opposite direction, but the bed was against a wall. Damn. She attempted to slide toward the end, but Dan grabbed her arms and pressed her down.

“Dan! Get off me!” It did no good when she pushed. He had to be over two hundred pounds. His mouth lowered to hers, and the putrid stink of his breath made her want to puke. When he forced his tongue into her mouth, her stomach heaved in protest. Slapping at his face, she turned her head, but his lips only moved to her neck. God, what the hell was he thinking? Her skin crawled at his touch.

"Get off me! I'm not Kayla, you idiot! You're hurting me."

He paused for a second, then a nasty smirk appeared. "This'll hurt real good, baby. You'll see."

Her breath froze in her lungs. *Need to get out of here.* She continued pushing, but his hands clamped her tightly in place, squeezing her arms. Twisting, turning, he wouldn't budge. *Get. Him. Off.* She screamed as loud as she could, her voice echoing in the silence. Nothing. The party sounds and music had stopped. Where the hell was Kayla? Passed out again?

Dan moved one hand from her arm and lowered it to grope her breast. She'd definitely throw up soon if he didn't stop. Alcohol-tinged perspiration assaulted her nose. Panic rose inside as his mouth attacked hers again. His other hand slid inside her shorts. His weight held her in place no matter how hard she bucked and pushed. She couldn't get leverage. Her heart pounded in her chest as she struggled against the invasion.

"No!" She got her arms in front of her and shifted her leg to try to get him away. Dan didn't move. His hand slid deeper into her shorts. *Stop! Oh, please, stop!* Pounding on his chest was fruitless. He knocked her hands away. She clawed at his face. He growled, leaning more of his weight on her. *Can't breathe. Can't move.*

Dan smirked and grabbed her thrashing hands,

holding them above her head. He pressed his hips into hers, fully aroused. Shit. This wasn't happening.

"Let's have some fun, baby."

Sitting back, he gripped her waistband, pulling at her flimsy shorts. Not if she could help it. She lifted her knee, shoving it in his groin.

He reared back, howling. *Take advantage, crawl around him*. She got to the edge when he grabbed her hair, yanking her back. His other hand wrapped around her waist, his fingers digging into her hip.

"You bitch!"

Twisting, she swung her fisted hands in his direction, colliding with his head. It was enough to loosen his hold for a second and allow her to get her footing. But he lurched off the bed and landed on top of her on the floor, a knee on either side of her hips. His face tightened as he pawed at her clothes, finally lifting her top and yanking at her bottoms.

Sara screamed as loud as she could. How could no one hear her? Tears filled her eyes, but she blinked them back. *Don't give up. Fight*. When she opened her mouth to scream again, he slapped his pudgy fingers over her lips. Bile rose in her throat at the salty tang, and she swallowed it, along with the last remaining thoughts of rescue. She opened her mouth, chomping down hard. He reared back, his eyes red and crazed, like he was about to hit her.

Grabbing the floor lamp, she sent it crashing into him. He rolled to the side, pushing it away, and Sara scrambled to her knees, trying to crawl away. Dan caught hold of her shirt and pulled, but the thin fabric ripped and slipped through his fingers.

Get out. Don't look back. Racing across the floor,

she tugged her bottoms back up and flung open the bedroom door. Her mind focused enough to grab her bag as she raced down the stairs and into the night air. Dan's growls echoed behind, and she sprinted faster, intent on escape.

The concrete sidewalk reminded her she was barefoot, but she didn't stop. *Never going back there. Ever.* But where would she go? Everything was closed, and she didn't even have shoes on.

She reached for her phone but stopped before she could dial. Her family was hours away—and they'd make her come home. No.

As she ran a little farther, no footsteps followed. Her shoulders sagged, and her steps slowed. The hands clutching her bag shook. Her whole body shook. Shit, she'd almost been raped. Her stomach clenched, and she twisted to puke the contents onto the grass next to the sidewalk. She coughed and spit, then stepped away to lean against a tree.

Think. A safe place to sleep? She had to work in the morning. Work. The store. Could she go there? TJ had given her the key to lock up after she cleaned.

She sped up again, almost jogging once she had a destination, stumbling a few times on rocks. Once there, she silently let herself in the back door. First stop, the sink to rinse out her mouth, the rancid taste of Dan's lips still lingering. She wanted to crawl into the basin and scrub off the filth covering her. Not now. One of the upholstered benches on the second floor should be good enough to rest on.

As she stumbled through the darkened store, the events of the night began to sink in. Memories of Dan, heavy and unmovable, touching her intimately, paralyzed her. The trembling in her body grew until she was afraid she'd break into little pieces. Sinking into the nearest chair, she pulled her legs to her chest and burst into tears.

****

The tone of TJ's phone roused him from his slumber. Sitting up, he squinted at the clock. Almost three in the morning. Who the hell…?

After unlocking the phone, he tapped the flashing app. The store's security system. He scrolled through until he came to the cameras inside *Tea and Tales*. The motion detectors indicated the intruder's location. He enlarged the screen to see someone walking from the back room, stopping at the sink before moving toward the stairs.

The room was dim, but he could tell the person was small. A kid? They wouldn't find money. Anything not deposited was locked in the safe in his office. They stood there as if lost.

Zooming in, his breath caught when he realized it was a girl. As he studied the screen, she turned. Sara. Suddenly, she crumpled into a high-backed chair and curled into a ball. What the hell?

He sprang out of bed and jammed his legs into the jeans he'd thrown on the floor earlier. Thrusting his feet in a pair of Docksiders, he grabbed a T-shirt and his keys. Freckles roused from her spot on the floor and padded over.

"Down, girl. I'll be back soon."

He hoped he'd be back soon, but he couldn't fathom why Sara was at the store at this hour. Looking terrified. Horrifying scenarios ran through his head as he remembered her sketchy apartment. Jumping in his truck, he tore off down the road. Good thing he was only ten minutes away.

The back door was locked, and he growled as he fished for the right key. When he darted to where he'd seen her, the chair was empty. His heart raced as fear, deep and intense, shot through him. Had someone followed her? Where was she?

He crept through the store, and when he didn't see her there, headed to the stairs. The second floor was equally as silent. Passing the science fiction shelves, he moved deeper and finally saw her curled up on the Victorian love seat in the corner under the window. He approached cautiously, not wanting to scare her.

"Sara?" His voice was low as he nudged her shoulder.

Her anxious cry startled him as she sprang up and pressed back against the upholstery. The fear in her eyes clearly showed her state of mind.

"It's okay. It's TJ. Why are you here? What happened?"

The glow from the emergency lighting kept her in shadow, but he could see her face. Nothing close to a smile.

She only managed a small squeak before her face crumpled, and she sank back into the fetal position he'd found her in. Sitting next to her, he drew her trembling form into his arms.

"Sara, what happened? Come on, Sunshine, look at me and tell me what's wrong."

The tremors continued, and sobs racked her body. *Don't think the worst. Maybe she and her boyfriend broke up, and she's feeling uncharacteristically dramatic*. God, he hoped it was something so minor.

"You're making me nervous, Sunshine. Tell me why you're here in the middle of the night, and maybe I can help."

Sara snuggled closer and his arms tightened automatically. When had he become protective, and of some girl he'd only known a few weeks? But he'd hold her if she needed it. Was beginning to think he'd do anything for her.

Pushing her hair out of her eyes, he flicked it over her shoulder. Her strap, broken and hanging, sent waves of fear splashing over him. He placed his finger under her chin and lifted.

"Sara, tell me what happened. How did this break? Did someone do this to you?"

She straightened slightly but stayed leaning against him. Glancing at her shoulder, she nodded. More tears coursed down her cheeks.

Rage boiled up inside. He wanted to hit something. Who could do something like this to his angel? But if he went crazy and started ranting, he'd probably scare her more. Banking his fury, he took a deep breath.

He stroked one hand down her back, then touched her cheek with his other. "I want to help you."

A few ragged breaths came out. "Roommates…having a party when I got back from work tonight." Her voice shook.

"You weren't working tonight." He knew where she was every second at the shop.

Sara shook her head. "At The Melody Tent. They like to party. My roommates. And they had a bunch of people over."

"Someone from the party did this? Ripped your shirt?"

Sara tossed her head, looking all around, her breathing uneven. Another sob escaped, and she closed her eyes briefly.

"I told Kayla I wanted to sleep. I had to work in the morning. I sleep on the couch."

Her disjointed words were scattered, but he didn't interrupt.

"She said to use her room. I was tired. It was late, so I did."

What the hell had happened? Gritting his teeth, he waited. She trembled, then let out a sob, biting her lip to stop it.

"Later…" Sara shuddered. "I woke up and Dan was…was crawling into the bed."

"Dan?" Whoever this Dan was, he'd made the number one spot on TJ's shit list.

"Kayla's boyfriend. He lives there, too."

"Dan ripped your shirt? What else did he do?" Heat rose inside, and he struggled to keep it at bay. Sara needed his support and comfort right now, not his anger.

"He started kissing me…touching me. He held me down, and he's so big, and I couldn't get up."

She sobbed harder now, her head pressed against his chest.

"I tried to push him off, but I couldn't…he kept touching me…he tried to—" She pulled her legs even closer to her body. "But I stuck my knee in his…and he moved back, and I tried to leave. But he grabbed me again…got me on the floor…"

Her sobs rang out, the desperation in them slicing through his gut like a jagged knife.

"I didn't know what to do. I pushed the lamp on

him, but when I tried to leave, he ripped my shirt. I just ran. I don't even have my shoes or anything."

Her shoulders heaved up and down as she cried. He tightened his grip, stroking her back and hair.

"I didn't know where to go, and I had to work in the morning…"

She was babbling, but he let her get it out. Finding this Dan and ripping him to pieces, was utmost in his mind, but Sara needed him right now. There was one thing he needed to know. Was almost afraid of the answer.

Lowering his forehead to touch hers, he whispered her name. "Sara. Listen. I need to know. Did he rape you?" If the bastard had, she'd need to go to the hospital immediately and call the police. He couldn't spend time holding her.

Her head shook vehemently as she burrowed into his chest. Her hands gripped the front of his shirt which had grown damp from her tears. His relief was palpable. This may have been horrifying, but it could have been much worse.

They sat on the love seat for a while, and he held Sara until her breathing slowed and sobs lessened. He didn't ask any more questions, and she fell silent.

His arms remained around her until she was nearly asleep. They'd been here an hour. Every now and then she'd shiver and snuggle closer. Not sure why. Snuggling had never been his thing. If it helped her cope, he didn't mind.

"You need sleep. You can use one of my guest rooms for tonight."

Sara roused slowly and sat back, pushing the hair from her face. For the first time, she actually seemed aware of her surroundings, and an expression of embarrassment covered her face.

"I'm sorry. Sorry you had to come here in the middle of the night. I didn't want to bother anyone. I didn't know where else to go, and I had a key. I'm sorry." She put her fist to her trembling mouth.

TJ reached for her arms, and she winced. They were red and beginning to bruise. He loosened his grip. "No need to apologize. I'm glad you had enough thought to take the keys with you. I hate to think of you wandering around Hyannis in the middle of the night."

For the first time, he noticed her clothes. How had he missed the skimpy shorts and snug tank with no bra? The broken strap had been apparent, but he hadn't seen past, too worried about Sara. It blew his mind he could do that. And felt good.

He stood. "Come on. Sleep."

As she stood, her shoulder strap flopped, exposing the top of her creamy breast. He kept his thoughts clean. "I'll get you a sweatshirt."

Grabbing one from his office, he was out in seconds, draping it over her shoulders. She pushed her arms in, and he zipped it up to her chin. The sleeves hung low over her hands, and the bottom brushed her knees. Still so beautiful.

Freckles welcomed them when TJ unlocked his front door, the animal's tail wagging fiercely. Sara knelt down and scratched the dog, cooing to her in that amazing voice.

"Guest rooms are upstairs."

She followed him up the stairs and down the hall.

"I don't use this room much, so the sheets are clean." Rarely, did he use any of his guest rooms. He'd bought the house because it was on the beach. It hadn't mattered it had five bedrooms.

"I'm sorry to be so much trouble."

She stood there, unhappy as he'd ever seen anyone. It seemed out of place on her.

"Get some sleep, and in the morning we can file charges against this bastard, Dan."

Her eyes grew wide and filled with fear. "No, I don't want—"

"We'll talk about it in the morning. You need some rest." He glanced at the sweatshirt hanging on her slight frame. "I'll get you a T-shirt to sleep in."

"Thanks."

"Back in a sec. Bathroom's through there. There might be a new toothbrush in the drawer."

When the dog started to follow him, he pointed. "Freckles, stay." The dog obeyed and sat at Sara's feet.

He bolted down the stairs, got an old T-shirt, then rushed back up. The bathroom door was closed, and the sound of running water came through. While he waited, he turned down the sheets and plumped the pillows. It wasn't long.

Handing her the T-shirt, he said, "If this isn't good enough, I can find something better."

"It's fine. Thank you. For the shirt and everything you did tonight."

"I didn't do anything, Sara. I was simply there."

"I know. Thank you for being there."

She stepped into his arms. This was getting familiar, and he liked it. After giving her a quick squeeze, he reluctantly let her go.

"Freckles can stay up here tonight, if you want."

"She can?" A tiny smile found its way to Sara's

face as she sat on the edge of the bed. "Can she sleep up here?"

He'd make an exception for tonight. "Sure."

Patting the bed, she called the dog's name. Freckles got excited but gazed at TJ first. He snapped his fingers near the bed, and said, "Up."

The dog didn't wait for another signal. She jumped up and settled next to Sara's hip. Sara scratched her ears.

"If you need anything, let me know. My room's to the right of the front door."

"Thank you again, TJ."

She nestled her nose into Freckles' fur, and he walked out. After one last look, he whispered, "Good night, Sunshine."

Chapter Seven

Sara woke to a sticky feeling on her fingers. Opening her eyes, she saw Freckles sitting next to the bed, her nose nuzzling Sara's hand.

Memories of last night swamped her mind, and she shot up, lungs burning as if she were drowning. Dan grabbing her. Holding her down. It played through her mind like a video clip stuck on a loop. Her gaze darted around the room. She was safe. TJ had brought her here.

She started to lie back down, but the dog whined and paced the floor. Probably needed to go out. Flinging back the covers, she followed the dog into the hallway and down the stairs to the kitchen door.

The yard was fenced in, so Sara let Freckles out and stepped onto the back porch. The grassy backyard surrounded a kidney shaped pool, and she tipped her face to the warm sunshine. It was higher in the sky than she expected. What time was it? Was TJ still sleeping? She'd woken him in the middle of the night after all.

Freckles came back quickly, they went inside, and Sara checked out the kitchen. It was spacious with the newest equipment, granite counters, and cherry cabinets. Her mom would be envious. For years, she'd bugged Sara's dad to update the old Victorian they had.

When her gaze skimmed the clock, she panicked. It was ten-thirty. She was supposed to be at the store reading to the kids. She almost missed the note as she flew past, but it floated off the counter and fluttered in front of her. On it was TJ's bold writing.

Sara,

Saturday is my day to open the shop. Don't worry about Story Hour. I'll take care of it. Help yourself to anything in the fridge or cabinets. Remote control is on top of the TV. Freckles will need to be let out. She can go in the backyard by herself. I'll be back before lunch, and we can talk.

TJ

Relief swept through her knowing she didn't have to face anyone right now. Her emotions were a confusing mess. It had been sweet of TJ to let her sleep here last night, but she couldn't stay. She had to find another place to live.

First, she needed food. The fridge was packed, and she wondered if TJ had other people living with him. A wife or girlfriend stashed away? How much did she know about him other than he owned *Tea and Tales,* and he'd read classic literature enough to discuss it?

Her hunger needed satisfying more than her curiosity, so she pulled some things from the fridge and made scrambled eggs, then cleaned up after she'd eaten.

"Can I do some exploring, Freckles? You won't tell, will you?"

The spaniel stopped eating from her dish on the floor and wagged her tail as if to say, "Go ahead."

She'd seen the large, open living room in the center of the house on her way to the kitchen. There was a hallway off to the right, and she followed it past a bathroom to a dining room. The room was fancy yet looked unused. From there, she went to the next room in the front corner and stopped. Holy Cow. A dream come true. Two walls had large floor to ceiling windows. She could see the ocean and even out to Martha's Vineyard from here. But the thing taking her breath away was the concert grand piano sitting dead center in the room. There wasn't much else in it.

Her eyes never left the instrument as she automatically walked closer. She'd dreamed of playing a piano like this someday but wasn't sure it would ever happen. Stopping a few feet away, she itched to touch it but didn't dare. These things cost a fortune, more than she'd made last year working at the library.

But, unlike the dining room table, this was obviously used. Sheet music littered the holder and was scattered on the upholstered bench. Where had TJ gotten the money for it? It was a Steinway Concert Grand for Pete's sake. *Tea and Tales* might get busy in the summer, but she doubted it was that lucrative. Although, some people paid this much for a car, and TJ only drove a used Ford. Maybe music was more important than anything else, and he invested his money here.

Of course, his oceanfront house on Cape Cod had to be worth close to a million. Unless it was his family's house. What did she know about him? She hadn't even known he could play an instrument.

The night they'd cleaned, he'd shown interest in her ability to play the piano and guitar. It was only when she'd mentioned becoming a singer, he'd shut down. Strange.

Moving closer, her gaze focused on what type of music he liked. As she flipped through the sheets, she made sure she didn't touch the piano, no matter how much she was dying to sit and play. Some of the music was classical, but much of it was by James True. Her contemporary music class in college had studied him. James True had been around for about ten years and written songs for many of the famous rock or pop groups. His music had won numerous awards and become hits in the Top Forty. Not much else was known about him. He'd never shown up at the Grammys when his songs were nominated, and he didn't give interviews. All communication was exclusively through his manager.

She approved of TJ's choice as she enjoyed True's music, too. But now wasn't the time to dwell. Getting dressed would be good, except she didn't have any clothes with her. No way was she putting the ripped stuff from last night back on. The thought made her feel dirty. TJ wouldn't mind if she had a shower, right?

There wasn't any shampoo in the upstairs bathrooms, so she jogged downstairs and cautiously entered TJ's room. It was the same size as the music room, not surprising since it took up the other front corner of the house, with large windows on two walls overlooking the ocean.

Stepping in further, she saw a line of doors on one wall. Closets? The last wall held a king-sized bed and a door. The bathroom? She scooted around the bed, thinking her mother would be appalled she was wandering in a man's bedroom alone. Although it was more appropriate than being here with him, she supposed.

TJ's intense eyes and crooked smile came to mind. The gentleness of his arms, as they'd held her last night, had been unexpected but nice. You'd think after what had happened with Dan, she'd be freaked at the thought of any guy getting within ten feet of her. But TJ's embrace had felt safe. Like nothing could hurt her.

Aside from a few dressers and some artwork on the walls, the bedroom was fairly sparse. As she walked toward the bathroom, two framed photos on his bedside table, next to a paperback novel, caught her attention. One was a young woman, maybe her age or a little younger, with long dark hair and almost black eyes. She was beautiful and had a Hispanic look she sometimes caught in TJ's features. Who was she? His girlfriend? Then who was Gabby? A tiny flicker of jealousy wove its way through her, surprising her.

She picked up the other picture. It was a boy and girl, maybe ten or twelve, laughing with each other. The girl was younger, but Sara realized it was the same person in both pictures. The crooked smile of the little boy let her know it was TJ. It must be his sister, if the resemblance was anything to go by. Where was she now? Were they still close? Replacing the pictures exactly as she'd found them, she accidentally knocked over the book.

She expected some mystery or crime novel, but her heart lightened when she saw it was a romance. The cover showed a couple holding hands on the beach, walking into the sunset. The scene was idyllic, and she longed to have this with the right man. First, she'd have to find him. Setting the book back down, she moved to the bathroom.

Holy cow. It was the size of her bedroom at home. A whirlpool tub filled one corner, and a separate shower enclosure, larger than any she'd seen outside of magazines, took up the other. Two sinks molded into the long granite counter completed another wall along with the toilet.

She grabbed shampoo and body wash from the shower and a face cloth from the counter. Back upstairs, she vigorously scrubbed her skin as the water sluiced down her back, wanting every trace of Dan's hands off her. But was the terry cloth capable of removing it from her memory?

She finger-combed her hair, after rubbing it with a towel, then wrapped the towel around her body. It looked like it hadn't ever been used, it was so soft and fluffy. She took the items back downstairs and replaced them in their exact spots. Sara adjusted the towel around her and walked out of the bathroom. TJ stood in the middle of his room, staring.

****

The house was quiet when TJ entered. Was Sara still sleeping? It was noon, but they'd been up late last night with her ordeal. It had taken all his control not to drive over to her apartment and smash Dan's face in. But he'd wait and see what Sara wanted to do. The scum couldn't get away with attacking her.

He walked into his bedroom to find something Sara could wear. Last night's outfit wouldn't be a good choice. He leaned over to dig through his dresser, but noise from the bathroom had him straightening up. Out walked Sara, a towel wrapped around her delicious body.

"Oh, you're back." Her wide eyes looked wary. Had she showered in his bathroom? Not a picture he needed rolling around his mind.

"I borrowed some shampoo and body wash. There wasn't any in the upstairs bathroom."

“It’s fine.” He searched her face, wanting to avoid looking lower, but he couldn’t help notice the bruises on her arms were darker today. “How are you feeling this morning?”

Her mouth tightened as she tucked a strand of hair behind her ear and blushed. “I just needed to clean up and get it all off, you know.”

“I know. Let me find something that might fit without falling off you.”

“Do you have a brush I could use? If I don’t comb out the tangles soon, I’ll never get them out.”

He pointed to the brush sitting on his dresser, and she picked it up. The towel loosened as she struggled, and he thought it might drop. He wouldn’t mind seeing Sara, and all her glory, but if anything came to pass between them, he wanted to do it properly. Like he even knew what proper was.

The black silk robe Celia had brought him from one of her overseas tours would look gorgeous on her. He’d never worn it.

“Here, this should be more comfortable while brushing your hair.”

Sara shrugged into it with a “thanks.” When she turned her back, he dug through the drawer but could see her in the mirror. She did a little twist with her hips and pulled the towel out from under the robe. He shivered. Belting the robe, she sat on his bed, pulling the brush through her long locks. The sight of her sitting there, doing something so casual, had longing crawling through him.

He found a pair of cotton shorts with a drawstring and another T-shirt. This one thick enough to hopefully hide the fact she didn’t have a bra. Of course, he would still know. Dropping them on the bed, he moved to the door.

"Are you hungry?"

"I had some eggs an hour ago, but I could eat again. Thanks."

When she strolled into the kitchen a few minutes later, the sandwiches were ready, and he had two glasses of iced tea on the counter.

As she scooted onto the high stool, he tossed a bag of Cape Cod potato chips in between their plates. He sat down, and they ate in silence.

"Any thought to what you want to do?"

Sara concentrated on her sandwich. After a few chews, she said, "I need my stuff from the apartment and to find a new place to stay."

"Not an easy time of year. We should go to the police first and press charges against the bastard who did this."

Fear returned to her eyes, and TJ hated he'd brought it back. He wanted to make everything perfect for her. But how?

"I know he's a creep, and what he did was horrible, but if I press charges, I'll have to go to court and actually tell people what he did, and…I'm not sure I can talk about it in front of others."

He took her hand. "Sara, he can't be allowed to get away with almost raping you. What if he tries it with someone else, and they aren't as lucky as you and don't get away?"

She pulled at her arm and rubbed her hands together. "They'll just call me a slut and say I brought it on myself."

"Why do you say that?"

Her gaze stayed on her food. “It happened to my friend, Shelbie. Since she wasn’t actually raped, they chalked it up to him being drunk and her flirting.”

He wanted to argue but knew sometimes it happened. It shouldn’t, but it did.

This Dan bastard was going to pay for what he’d done, regardless of what Sara did. Maybe not in court, but TJ would make sure the man knew what fear was. As Sara had last night.

“Finish your lunch, and we’ll get your stuff. You can use my guest room until you find another place.”

“I’m ready. I don’t look ridiculous, do I?” The baggy shorts hung to her knees, and she’d knotted the T-shirt on the side. Probably to keep it from hanging past the shorts. The look was adorable.

TJ tilted his head and grinned. “You ever get your brothers’ hand-me-downs?”

Her shoulders slumped. “Yes, sometimes, but only for play clothes. Is that what I look like?”

Gently grasping her chin, he made her look at him. “You look as beautiful as ever. And it’s only until we get your stuff.”

They got in the truck, letting Freckles sit between. It didn’t take long to get there, but she grew tenser the closer they got. By the time he parked, she was gripping the door handle like it was a life line.

When he opened his door, Sara looked at him with panic in her eyes. “I don’t think I can go in. I’m sorry.”

Reaching over, he tucked a stray strand of hair behind her ear. “It’s okay. I’ll get your stuff. Where is it?”

“In my suitcase, which is under the table by the front window. I didn’t have a dresser, so I left it all in there. Can you get my guitar, too, please? It should be right on top."

"Sure. Roll up the windows and lock the doors if you want." He scratched the dog's head. "Freckles, stay."

His fists clenched as he took the back stairs up to the apartment. What would he do if Dan was there? What he wanted to do wasn't exactly legal. Pounding on the door, louder than he needed to, he waited a few seconds. It opened, and a tall, gaunt brunette stood there, looking at him curiously.

"I'm TJ Bannister. Sara works for me and—"

"She's not here," the brunette jumped in. "I don't know where she is. Haven't seen her all morning."

TJ's jaw tightened. This girl had no clue what happened last night. "I know she's not here. She won't be coming back either. I came to get her stuff."

The girl, Kayla, he assumed, made a face but stepped back allowing him to enter. "Really? She doesn't seem the type to shack up with her boss, but I guess it's better than sleeping on the couch."

"She's not shacking up with me," he ground out, trying to remain calm, especially when he saw the large slug sitting on a recliner. The guy was huge, and his stomach turned thinking of this bastard touching Sara, holding her down, and how terrified she must have been. "Your boyfriend didn't tell you what happened?"

Dan paled. He remembered. Kayla turned to him with a curious look, but Dan remained silent. TJ had no compulsion to keep the truth from her.

"He tried to rape Sara last night. She managed to get away, though she's got a few bruises to show for it."

Kayla's expression grew thunderous. "What the hell?"

Dan jumped off the chair, moving quickly for someone his size. He shook his head, his eyes wild. "No, baby, I didn't. I mean…I thought it was you. You know how much dope I did last night…I thought it was you."

"The fact she was fighting back and screaming never made you think otherwise?"

Kayla's gaze filled with venom as she stared at Dan. TJ walked to the window and found Sara's suitcase. He tucked in a few stray items and started zipping it. "Is this everything of hers?"

"Um, her toothbrush is in the bathroom. It's the blue one." Would Kayla's death glare actually work to neutralize Dan?

After stuffing the toothbrush into her suitcase, he finished zipping it. He grabbed it, and her guitar, before pausing. "I suggest you stay away from Sara."

"She's all yours," Dan snarled. "Don't know what you see in the uptight bitch, but a few good fucks might loosen her up."

Red seared across his vision. Dropping the items in his hands, fists flew. The left into the soft flesh of his gut, then the right into the smug bastard's face. Dan crashed to the floor with a heavy thud, then struggled to his feet and growled. "That's assault, you know. I should call the cops."

"Go ahead. You fill out the complaint while Sara has you arrested for attempted rape. She came to the store last night petrified and with her clothes ripped. It's on my security tapes. Here, it's your word against mine."

Glancing at Kayla, the slime had to know he'd get no help from her.

"If you ever touch Sara again, I'll rip your heart out and feed it to you. Just a friendly warning."

Picking up Sara's luggage, he left. The sound of yelling and items being thrown echoed down the stairwell after him.

Sara anxiously stared out the window, unlocking the door as he approached. Stashing her things in the cab, he got in and took her hand. "Let's get back, and you can change into your own clothes."

"Thank you." She held his hand for a second longer, then looked at it closer. "What happened? The skin here is broken and red."

Smirking, he pulled his hand from hers to shift. "I…bumped it on something."

Sara looked away, but her lips curved up. Good. The smile was starting to grow on him more than he'd ever thought it would. Now to find a way to keep it there.

The afternoon proved futile in finding Sara a new place to live. He called a friend, Ted, who was in the real estate business but no luck. Not for anything cheap enough or close enough for Sara.

"He'll let us know if he sees anything."

"Thanks for asking…and for letting me stay here last night and getting my suitcase…and for punching Dan."

"Who said I punched the bastard?"

Sara blushed and stuck her nose back in the computer, her expression forlorn. Would any of the people from work have space? Not likely, or if they did, they'd be totally inappropriate for her to live with.

"You can stay in the guest room for a while if you want." Where had that thought come from? No way she could stay here. She'd have him twisted in a knot in no time. "Just until you find something."

"Really? Thank you. I can ask around when I go to The Melody Tent tonight. There are lots of girls my age. Maybe one of them needs a roommate."

"I'll give you a ride when you go."

"Are you sure? It's only about a mile. If I leave earlier, I can get there easy enough."

"I'm heading nearby anyhow. What time are you done?"

"Sometimes close to one if the concert is sold out, and this one is."

"I'll be there by twelve-thirty. Finish your job and come out when you're done."

"You don't have to do this. You aren't responsible for me, you know."

Standing, he closed his laptop. "No, but if something happened to you, I'd feel guilty. Plus, I'd need to find someone else for Story Hour. I hate interviewing people."

"Is that why you were such a grouch when you interviewed me?"

He'd never tell her the real reason he'd been out of sorts. She'd thrown him for a loop and left him breathless.

"I'm always a grouch. Now get ready for work, and we can grab a bite on the way."

Sara took a few steps closer, and he held his breath. "You're not always a grouch. I woke you up in the middle of the night last night, and I didn't hear a single snarl."

He narrowed his eyes.

"Thank you." Placing her hands on his shoulders, she touched her lips to his, then bounced up the stairs.

He stood rooted to the spot for a few minutes. The kiss had been innocent and short, but it was like nothing he'd ever experienced in his life. Her lips were soft and tasted like ambrosia. And they were off limits. *Keep reminding yourself.*

Running his tongue over his own lips, he hoped to get a taste of hers again. Was this one more addiction he'd have to fight off?

Chapter Eight

The pounding in his head woke TJ up, but his eyes refused to open. Then he realized it wasn't his head, but someone knocking at his door. Loudly. He glanced at his clock. Eight-thirty. Still early by Sunday standards but not an ungodly hour. No pun intended.

Throwing the covers back, he peeked through the window facing the front porch. Two men stood there. Who? They better not be selling anything or trying to convert him to some strange religion. It was definitely too early, especially as Sara hadn't gotten out of work last night until well after one.

He walked to the door in only sleep pants. Good enough for people who woke him on his day off. As he pulled it open, one of them started pounding again.

"What?" No sense hiding his irritation.

"Where's Sara?" the one on the right growled. They were around TJ's six- foot height and both blond with similar features.

TJ folded his arms across his chest. "Who wants to know?"

"I'm Alex Storm, her brother. This is Luke. What the hell are you doing with our sister?"

Her brothers. Shit. Not who he wanted to face at this hour of the morning, but maybe they could help her out better than he'd been able to.

Taking a step back, he opened the door wider.

"Come on in. She's still asleep. We had a late night."

Both men wore scowls. Had Sara told them what happened? Maybe they'd come down to dole out their own brand of justice to dirty Dan.

"Luke? Alex? What are you doing here?" Sara stood at the bottom of the stairs, looking sleep tousled and far too sexy in her skimpy shorts and another snug tank top.

As he turned back to the brothers, Luke's swinging fist impacted, and he staggered back.

"What the fuck!"

Automatically, he put his hands up, but Alex got in on the fight and swung, coming in low. The blow glanced off his ribs, and he lashed out with his clenched right hand. It struck the side of Alex's head, but within seconds Luke had gotten behind him and had him in a choke hold.

"Stop it!" Sara screamed, pouncing on the fist Alex was about to hurl at his face. "Knock it off. What the hell do you think you're doing? This is my boss you're beating up, you stupid idiots."

Alex dropped his arm, but Luke continued to hold TJ in a grip he wasn't sure he could get out of.

"Lukas Storm, let him go." Sara's voice was low and dangerous. He'd never heard her so angry, not even after Dan had attacked her. Then she'd been petrified.

The arm around his neck eased, and he pulled away. Positioning herself between him and the still fuming men, she breathed heavily, her fists clenched.

"What the hell? Answer me."

"What were you thinking, Sage, shacking up with your boss?" Alex yelled. "Are you crazy? Do you know what it would do to Mom and Dad, if they found out?"

Before TJ could object, Sara took a step forward. "I'm not shacking up, you twit. What gave you that idea?"

Crossing his arms over his chest, Luke glared at TJ while Alex glared at Sara. Finally, she glanced at him, and he could tell when she realized he was only wearing a pair of pajama pants, and they were riding low. He tugged them up as she looked down at her own attire. Her face turned red, and she crossed her arms over her own chest.

"How did you know where I was?"

Alex pulled out his phone. "Sofie texted me. Kayla told her you'd moved out to live with your boss. Must have been sometime last night, but I didn't see it until I was about to go for my run this morning. I grabbed Luke, and we rushed down here."

"How did you know where he lived?"

"That GPS app we put on your phone last year after you got lost coming back from the fair."

Sara rolled her eyes. "Didn't you think to call and ask what was up before you wasted gas coming all this way?"

"We didn't want you being taken advantage of." Luke said. "We know how naïve you can be."

TJ finally had to speak up. "No one's taking advantage of your sister. She stayed in my guest room the last two nights. It's upstairs, and my room is down here."

"Why is she staying here?" Alex challenged. "What's wrong with Kayla's place? Sofie made the arrangement, and it wasn't that expensive."

Sara's face fell, and she wrapped her arms tighter around herself. "I can't stay there anymore."

Both men looked at her curiously, then turned their critical gazes at him. Luke took a step closer, and his arm tensed like he was ready to take another swing. TJ touched her shoulder above where the bruises had darkened. “Sara?”

Sniffing, she walked to the bottom of the stairs where she leaned her head on the banister. A tiny sob escaped, causing TJ’s stomach to tighten. He glanced back to where her brothers still glared at him. They needed to know, but apparently, she couldn’t talk about it yet.

“Kayla’s boyfriend, Dan, attacked Sara Friday night and tried to rape her. I brought her here to keep her safe from the bastard.”

“What?” Alex was at Sara’s side in seconds, pulling her into an embrace. She curled into him, whimpering into his chest.

Luke snarled. “We can’t stand the thought of anything bad happening to our baby sister.”

“I know.” TJ said. “Neither can I.”

Luke scrubbed his hand over his short hair, then down the back of his neck. He glanced at Sara, then stuck out his hand. “Thanks for helping her. Sorry we beat on you.”

He shook the offered hand, then touched his face where there’d most definitely be a bruise. “If she was my sister, I’d probably have done worse.”

Alex whispered into Sara’s hair and rubbed her back. TJ glanced at Luke who shrugged. “Alex is the better man for that job. He’s way more touchy-feely than I am.”

Sara pushed Alex away, swiping a hand across her face.

"I'm fine. And if everyone stops talking about it, maybe I can forget it."

"How about breakfast?" TJ suggested, wanting to alleviate the tension in the room. "I'm starving."

Sara looked nervously at her brothers. They both nodded.

"Alex dragged me down here without any coffee," Luke complained.

"You were the one who refused to stop for anything."

"Sara, why don't you get dressed while I start breakfast for all of us."

Luke smiled, and TJ saw the similarity between siblings. "He cooks. Maybe I can move in."

"Hey, I cook," Alex griped.

Shaking her head, she trotted up the stairs. "Try not to kill each other while I'm up here, please."

Once in the kitchen, Sara's brothers surrounded him. "What exactly happened, and have you killed this scumbag yet?"

TJ rubbed his bruised knuckle. "I didn't kill him." They both glanced at his hand and grinned. "I'm not too sure about his girlfriend when she learned what he did."

"Did you go to the police?"

Quickly, he explained how he'd come across Sara at the store, and what she'd said. "I mentioned filing charges, but she kept freaking out she didn't want the whole world to know. It's possible this guy was so out of it he didn't realize it wasn't Kayla. I'm not convinced. I put a little fear into him. I think Kayla will put even more."

It was obvious they wanted to say more, get the slime bag's address, and go after him. But Sara would hate it. He put coffee on, then said, "Let me throw on some clothes, and I'll start breakfast."

A few minutes later, he took out bacon, eggs, and started mixing batter for pancakes.

Alex sat on a stool, but Luke paced a bit, looked to where the stairs were, then stopped. "Exactly how far did this guy get?" His face was hard as granite.

"I don't know. She was crying so hard when she told me, it was a little disjointed. But her shirt was ripped, and she's got bruises on her arms where he grabbed her and pushed her down."

He gripped the spatula in his hand tighter. "This guy is huge. Just having him hold her down must have been terrifying. She's lucky she managed to get away. Apparently, she kneed him in the groin."

Luke looked smug. "I taught her that."

Alex shifted in his seat. "Listen, I'm sorry about earlier. Sagey's a bit naïve, and we thought you were taking advantage of her. She's our baby sister, and we get a little defensive around her."

"Sagey?"

"Her name is Sara Jean. It's what we call her. She hates it, but we're her brothers. We're supposed to tease her. And protect her."

"She says *overprotective*." He flipped the bacon, then poured batter on the griddle. "She came down here for a little space this summer."

Both men looked sheepish.

"I'm glad you look out for her. She's a sweet girl and a hard worker. I hate what happened to her."

Alex narrowed his eyes, "A sweet *girl*? You've never noticed anything beyond that?"

He laughed. "You don't have to point out she's

beautiful, but she's also way too innocent, and I'm not in the market for any kind of relationship right now. Especially not with someone like your sister. But she's a good employee, and I want to help her if I can. She didn't have any place else to go."

"She can come home with us," Alex said.

"Probably best." Definitely for his inactive libido that had been pulsing back to life lately.

He busied himself with breakfast, and soon Sara came down as he put food on the table.

"And she arrives just as it's all ready," Alex teased. Sara scowled, but her cheeks tinted a lovely shade of pink.

She took a few bites, then glanced cautiously at her brothers. "You guys aren't going to tell Mom and Dad what happened, are you?"

"We should be going to the police and having this slime bucket arrested," Luke growled.

"No!" Her face grew pale. "You remember what happened to Shelbie? No one else saw it. They'll just say I wanted it, then changed my mind. Or I was stoned, too."

Both men stared but didn't say anything.

"If you tell Mom and Dad, they'll make me come home. They won't let me out of the house until I'm thirty."

"Maybe you should come home."

"Alex, no!" Tears welled in her eyes again, and TJ wanted to comfort her.

Luke patted her hand. "Listen, Sage, we only want what's best for you. We can't be around to protect you down here."

Sara dropped her fork. "You don't need to protect

me. I'm twenty-three years old. I need to do things by myself. I'll never become independent if I don't have a chance to get out on my own."

"Sage—"

"No, Luke, I need to stay here. I've got a job, two actually, and if I leave it will be irresponsible of me. Right, TJ? You'll be short-handed if I leave."

God, he hated doing this, betraying her, but she was a threat to his sanity. "We could manage."

The hurt and disappointment in her expression made him feel like a traitor. She'd trusted him to back her up, and he'd let her down.

"What about Story Hour?"

"I could get Darcy or maybe Hunter. We'd be okay."

Anger and disbelief raged across her face. "Are you kidding me? Darcy thinks they're all brats. And Hunter, please, she'd be flirting and trying to pick up the dads. The kids would get a crash course in female anatomy."

True. He'd never let Hunter read to the kids. "You need to be safe."

"See?" Alex pointed out. "Even your boss thinks you'd be better off home. You aren't ready for this big step yet."

"Not ready? First of all, nobody had to rescue me. I got myself out of this predicament all by myself. TJ only came along when I was already safely in the store."

The men looked at TJ who shrugged. "She did get away by herself. But she was—"

"Scared, yes, I was," Sarah interrupted. "I had every reason to be scared. But the fact remains, I didn't need some white knight riding to my rescue to pull me away from the evil dragon. I managed to take out the dragon and get away myself."

The room fell silent as Sara fumed. Not that he blamed her. He'd betrayed her.

Alex folded his hands on the table. "Listen, maybe you can do this next year. Maybe your boss…"

"TJ," he supplied.

"Maybe TJ will hire you next summer." Alex glanced at him, and he nodded. Maybe he'd take an extended vacation next summer.

Sara shot daggers at them, but Alex didn't seem affected. "We'll make sure you have a better, safer living situation. You can save what you earn at the library and afford someplace not so cheap."

Narrowing her eyes, she snapped, "All well and good, Alex, but I don't have my job at the library anymore. I quit, remember? They've hired someone else to take my place. And I don't care where I stay. I'll sleep on the beach if I have to. I'm not coming home right now."

"Sage?" It was Luke's turn to try. "We only want what's best for you. Can't you understand?"

"I do, and I love you guys for it. But I'm never going to be able get anywhere in life if I let you fix all my problems. Can *you* understand?"

Luke and Alex made eye contact but remained silent. Finally, Alex turned to Sara. "Where do you plan on staying?"

"I don't know. Maybe with one of the girls from The Melody Tent."

"And if that doesn't work out?"

"I'll find a place," Sara snarled. "I'm not coming

home."

Alex turned to TJ. "You said she could stay here for a few days, right?"

He nodded.

"Can you do us a favor? If, and when, she finds a place, can you check it out and make sure it's okay?"

"Be happy to."

Crossing her arms, she huffed but didn't say anything.

"And…" Luke fidgeted. "You'll be a gentleman while she's here."

Sara slammed her hands on the table. "Cut it out. He's not interested in me that way. Stop being an ass and embarrassing me."

Luke and Alex's expressions held disbelief. Was the longing he felt written on his face, or had they seen him get hard when she walked into the kitchen?

"I have the utmost respect for Sara." He couldn't say much more truthfully. It seemed to satisfy them. "Now, if you don't mind, I usually go to church on Sunday mornings. You're welcome to stay and visit."

He stood and so did Alex. "Thanks for breakfast and for helping Sara." Digging into his pocket, he pulled out his wallet. "Here's my business card with my cell number. Call me if you have any questions, or if there's a problem."

TJ glanced at the card. *APS Designs. Alexander P. Storm, architect*. Sara mentioned her brothers had all been popular and successful growing up. It seemed they still were. More reason to try and make something of herself.

"I'll let you know if there's something Sara can't handle."

The smile she threw him was warmer than any he'd seen so far. Yes, he'd said he wanted the smiles back, but this one, meant only for him, might do more damage to his tightly held control.

"Finish eating, and I'll clean up later."

Now her brothers had relented in letting her stay, Sara dug into her food as if starved. Luke took a piece of bacon from his plate and threw it on hers. A peace offering?

"We'll clean up," she said, after swallowing the food in her mouth. "Actually, I'll make them do it to atone for their sins."

He headed to his room and jumped in the shower. Sins, yeah. Maybe if he rushed to church, father would still be hearing confessions. And the way his thoughts had been regarding Sara, he'd need a whole lot of time to get them out.

****

"You won't tell Mom and Dad what happened, right?" Sara pleaded as she sat on the porch swing overlooking the ocean. "Because you know I have blackmail stuff on both of you."

Alex looked unsure, but Luke looked petrified. Alex had always been perfect. Luke, closest in age to her, was a bit wild, and she'd seen more of what he'd done when their folks weren't home.

"Stay away from people like this bastard, Dan."

"I will, believe me. He was totally wasted and didn't know what he was doing." *Convince them it wasn't a big deal.* "Mostly he scared me. He never even got it out of his pants."

"Oh, crap, my ears are burning," Alex yelled as he put his hands on the side of his head. "My sister did not just say that."

"Okay, guys, I'm not stupid. I know how it works, the body parts involved, even if I've never actually done it before."

Luke dropped his head into his hands. "Sage, you need to stop talking. We're your brothers, and we have to pretend, for our own sanity, you have no idea how any of this stuff works. Can you please keep that image intact for us?"

She chuckled. "Maybe if I hadn't heard you with Taylor Markham, the night you snuck her in when Mom and Dad were away for the weekend. The groaning and yelling made me curious. I went online to get details of what you were doing."

"Holy shit, Sage. You heard us?"

"Kind of hard to miss with the way the bed kept banging against the wall for like an hour."

"Taylor Markham?" Alex gagged. "Seriously? What were you thinking, and did you get yourself checked after? God knows how many guys she's had crawling all over her."

Luke shrugged. "I was sixteen, and she was willing. She knew what to do. I needed someone to teach me."

Standing, she paced the width of the porch. "Okay, now who's providing TMI? You were sixteen and I'm twenty-three. No more crap from you, Lukas Storm."

Alex smacked Luke on the side of the head. "We don't discuss this in front of the sister. Did you *not* get the memo?"

Sara laughed at her brothers. She did love them immensely. They were lots of fun, most of the time, when they weren't trying to run her life. Even with rushing down here to 'save' her, Alex appeared as if he'd ironed his clothes and groomed thoroughly. Luke was the opposite. He obviously hadn't shaved in a few days, and his clothes looked like he'd slept in them. He might have, knowing him. Up all night with some engineering project he needed to finish or prowling with the boys…or with some girl.

"What do you know about this boss of yours?"

She frowned at Alex, knowing this topic would come up.

"He owns a book store/coffee shop. He does as much work as his employees even though he could just have them do it. He has a spaniel named Freckles." Leaning down, she scratched the dog who'd stayed by her side all day.

"He's read lots of the classics and likes to debate them with me."

Alex chuckled. "Getting you riled up in librarian mode, huh?"

She glared at him. "I think he plays the piano considering what he's got in the music room, but he's never said, and I haven't had time to ask him. We spent yesterday trying to find a new apartment, then I had to work."

"Not a lot to know about someone you're living with."

"No, Luke, it isn't. And I'm not actually living with him. I'm staying here a few days until I find another place. All his employees respect him. He actually worked for Mary for a few years, then she sold him the store when her husband died. I don't think Mary would have done that if TJ wasn't a decent person."

"He hasn't hit on you or shown any interest in…you know?"

"Look at this place." Sweeping her arm, she indicated the huge house steps away from the ocean. "And did you see the piano he's got in there? It's a Steinway. The man has money from somewhere. Mary says he's not even thirty, and he already owns his own business."

Alex waved his hand. "Hey, I'm only twenty-seven and I own my own business."

"Yeah, but you're the only employee, and aside from your drafting board, you don't need a whole lot of supplies. TJ has essentially two stores and a dozen employees."

"And you're like a fifty-year old in mentality anyway," joked Luke.

Alex smacked Luke in the head again.

"The point is," Sara reminded them, "someone like him wouldn't want someone like me."

"Why not?" Alex asked. "What's wrong with you?"

She loved her brothers standing up for her, but she was also realistic. "Someone like TJ isn't going to be interested in the librarian from Small Town, Cow Hampshire."

"I like our small town in Cow Hampshire, thank you," Alex quipped. "There's nothing wrong with the Granite State."

"Especially not for a block-head like you." Luke chuckled.

While her brothers bantered back and forth, she thought about TJ. She didn't know him well, but she wanted to. Wanted to know why he had a huge piano and a whole room dedicated to an instrument. Wanted to know how he could afford an ocean-front house on Cape Cod and a downtown business at his age. Why he lived by himself and seemed to spend most of his time at work when he had people to do the job for him.

But she also wondered why he'd been so sweet when she'd burnt her hand. And again when she'd run away from Dan. He could have been mad she'd used the store as her safe spot. Or her predicament had made him protect her. He hadn't even been upset when her brothers had shown up and started whaling on him.

Then she remembered his arms as he'd held and comforted her. Safe. But they'd started other emotions deep within her stirring and growing. Like nothing she'd had with Robby.

She looked out over the ocean and wondered the most important thing of all. Would someone like TJ ever be interested in someone like her?

Chapter Nine

Sara stood in the doorway admiring the Steinway yet again. It had been four days since she'd been here, and she hadn't moved any closer to touching the piano. It cried out for her to run her fingers along the keys. She folded her hands into fists to keep them from itching.

"You want to give her a try?"

She jumped at TJ's voice behind her. "I didn't realize you were home." Damn, she'd said home, like this was her home, too. Had he noticed? He'd been so patient she hadn't found another apartment yet.

"Are you serious? Could I play her?"

He grinned. "That's what she's for. I've neglected her the last few days."

Because of her. "I'm sorry. You should play her then. I'll watch."

Walking over, he took the sheet music from the bench, tossed it on the piano, then lifted the cover. "I'll warm her up, then let you have a turn."

As he ran his fingers over the keys, she sighed. Incredible, and he was only warming up. A few runs up and down the keyboard, and Sara knew why he had this instrument. He was born to play.

"Your turn."

She stared at him. "You want me to play after that? Your warm-up is better than anything I practiced for months. Where did you learn?"

Looking back at the keys, he stroked them like he was caressing a lover. "My parents played, so I picked it up from them."

He slid off the bench and motioned for her to sit. She'd never play like him, yet she couldn't resist. Once settled, she stretched her fingers for a few seconds, then placed them gently on the keys.

"You have to press down if you actually want them to make any sound."

She giggled. "I know. I'm just savoring the moment. This is a far cry from the fifty-year-old upright my brothers and I practiced on."

"You all had lessons? Do they still play?"

Finally getting up the nerve, she depressed her fingers. The most amazing sound came out, and it was perfectly in tune. "Not as much as I do, but when they visit the house, Mom'll sometimes coerce them into playing."

"They don't live with you?"

"No, Alex and Luke rent a house on the other side of town. It's where Alex has his business. My oldest brother, Erik, is a Marine stationed in the Middle East right now."

Pressing down on the keys, she began a few classics she'd had drilled into her from a young age. A few songs later, she finally remembered TJ watched her. His beaming face told her he'd enjoyed it. You couldn't fake a look like that.

"It's not as good as you, but I love to play."

TJ sat on the bench next to her, and she held her breath. She'd have to let it out at some point, but his proximity made her more aware of him than ever.

"You have nothing to be ashamed of. You have a nice style that's easy to listen to."

Exhale so you can answer. "Thank you."

"Want to play something together?" He lifted his eyebrow.

"Sure, what are you thinking?"

"Just play something, and I'll jump in."

He could do that? What was the most difficult arrangement she could remember? He listened as she played a few bars, then started a complementary tune on his side of the piano. It was so incredible Sara almost forgot to continue playing her part.

"Unbelievable. You obviously have an ear for music. Why do you own a bookstore? You should be performing on a stage somewhere."

Getting up, he shuffled through the sheet music he'd thrown on the piano. "I don't like being the center of attention. The shop is calm and undemanding. And I get to read any book I want."

Shy? Not a word she'd equate with TJ, but he must like his privacy. One day, maybe she'd be brave enough to stand in front of millions who wanted to hear her sing.

"You've got lots of music from James True. I love his songs."

His head tipped to glance at her sideways. "You've heard of James True?"

"Yeah, I took a Music Comp class, and we studied lots of contemporary composers. James True was one."

"Really?" He looked pleased. "Did your professor like True's work, too?"

"Loved it. He made us all love it. He's got more hits in the Top Forty right now than any other songwriter ever has."

"I'm aware." He started playing a song she recognized right away as one of True's. Without sheet music. As he played a few more, she sat back and enjoyed the mini concert. She found herself singing softly along as TJ sang, too.

"You must have an amazing memory if you know all of these by heart." Scooping up a few of the song sheets, she scanned them. Something was different about them, and she shuffled through a few more before she realized what it was. These were written in pencil, and the words were in TJ's bold script.

She held one up. "Why do you have handwritten sheet music?"

He ignored her question and played some more. Confusion filled her when she noticed one of the pages wasn't finished. The lyrics were on the back, but the music was only half done. It was a song she'd never heard of before. But it had James True's name written on the top. Again in TJ's handwriting. Why…? An idea formed in her mind. It couldn't be but…

"Holy crap!" Hopping off the seat, she waved the paper in the air. "You're James True. This is a new song you're writing, isn't it? And how you can afford this house and a Steinway. *Tea and Tales* is just a cover up."

His eyes grew cold. "It's not a cover up. I love the store. I told you, it's calm and undemanding. Unlike many people in the music industry."

A warmth inside her blossomed and kept growing as she realized who sat in front of her. "So, you admit you are James True. I can't believe I'm standing here next to you, and I just played your piano."

"Sara, sit." He tugged on her hand, and she plopped onto the bench beside him. "I'm simply TJ Bannister, owner of *Tea and Tales*. I happen to write a little music on the side."

She shook with excitement. "A little music? You won four Grammys last year, and every singer in the country wants one of your songs."

His eyes narrowed as he looked down at her. "You're going all fan girl on me, Sara. A few minutes ago, I was boring TJ, your boss. Now, all of a sudden, I'm exciting."

His expression was resigned. Was his lack of public appearance because he wanted to be seen as a regular person?

After stacking the sheets of music on the holder, she settled on the bench with one foot under her, giving her a little extra height, then touched TJ's shoulders.

"First, there's nothing boring about my boss, TJ Bannister. He's a great guy who's been there for me over and above what's needed. He can debate classic literature, even if he does have ridiculous opinions." She winked.

"He works as hard as his employees when he could easily order them around. And he's patient with squeeing little fan girls when they get out of control."

Go for the potent pout. The one that always got her brothers to do her bidding, even Erik, who was immune to every little sister ploy she tried. "Forgive me for my star struck moment. I'll try and control myself from now on."

He took her hands and held them in his lap. "You're forgiven, Sunshine. But one of the reasons I don't advertise my identity is I can never tell if people like me for me, or because I've won fifteen Grammy Awards."

She squeezed his hands. "I know what you mean. I've never won a Grammy, but I've had lots of girls want to be my friend because they wanted an introduction to one of my fabulous brothers. I hated it. Made me cautious about choosing friends."

His face was solemn as he nodded.

"You don't have to worry with me. I liked you even before I found out your secret identity. TJ Bannister is a great guy. A little grouchy at times but really sweet and helpful when you burn your hand, or get in a sticky situation with a doped-out idiot, or need a temporary place to stay. He doesn't even get mad when irate brothers pop out of the blue and beat him up."

"I'm guessing Alex might have some coloring on his face, too."

His smug expression made Sara go all gooey inside. Reaching up, she touched where Luke's fist had made contact. The swelling had eased, but the bruise was still obvious. "I'm sorry. Luke texted to make sure you weren't too angry. I told him he owed me big time."

"Playing the guilt card, huh?"

"You know it. Does it still hurt?" When she ran her finger gently across the bruise, he took a deep breath. Was it the pain or the feeling of her touching him? *Her* hands were tingling where they brushed across his skin. On a whim, she leaned over and touched her lips to his cheek where it had been damaged.

****

Sara's lips on his skin sent jolts of electricity

through him. He wanted to pull her close and turn his head so their lips connected. *Resist.* Keeping a tight hold on his control, he allowed her to lean back, her smile bright. The smile alone could warm him through a New England blizzard.

Her eyes sparkled, and her fingers continued to caress his cheek. “Does it feel better? My mom always kissed the boo boos away.”

A motherly fashion wasn’t exactly how he saw her but let her think that. One of them needed to remain sensible.

“Does that work?”

Sara gazed at him strangely. “Your mom never kissed your boo boos so they didn’t hurt anymore?”

His mother never did much in the way of being a mother. Except maybe give birth. Before Sara could drive him to complete distraction, he captured her hand in his.

“No, not really.” *Not ever.* “But you must have the magic touch because it definitely feels better.”

“I’m glad.” Her cheeks tinged and her eyes lowered as she pulled her hands away. Facing the piano again, she peeked at him sideways. “I’m all done fawning over James True and back to being friends with TJ Bannister. Just so you know.”

She was something else. But were they friends? More would be nice, but for now friends seemed a good place to start. *Friends with a woman?* Not something he’d ever desired before. It could be interesting.

“Do you want to sing some of my songs?”

Sara’s eyes lit up. “James True songs with James True accompanying me on the piano? Are you kidding? Of course.”

Swinging around, he faced the instrument. His fingers danced over the keys, and Sara sighed. He wasn't sure whether to be annoyed or thrilled at her fan girl ways. Then she began to sing, and he forgot all about the way she'd been fawning over him.

Of course her voice would be angelic. Everything else about her was nearly perfect. But her sweet tone was like melted honey swirled together with rich cream. Intoxicating. Not a good thing for an addict. He'd want this all the time. Swiftly, he realized Sara was something he wanted, too. In many ways.

As he played, he simply listened to her sing. So much talent. If some music promoter heard her, he'd be stupid not to sign her.

But then she'd leave him. And be thrust into the lifestyle he'd run away from. Even living far away from Los Angeles in New England, he still hid from the media and publicity to the point of dealing only through his manager. No way would he take the chance of relapsing back into his old bad habits. He might not live through it this time.

When she finished the song, she glanced up. Excitement wrapped around her like a second skin.

"Can I convince you to keep the whole James True thing under wraps? I don't want people to know."

"Does anyone know?"

"Some people at work know I write songs, but I'm pretty vague if I mention it. I'd like to keep it on the down low. Can I count on you?"

"Most people wouldn't know the name James True so spilling that wouldn't mean anything. Mentioning the songs you've written would be another story. But yes, I'll keep your little secret." Her eyes twinkled. "For a price."

His stomach twisted. Was Sara greedy like everyone else in the world, only looking for what she could get out of a situation? Had he misjudged her like he'd done with others?

As she ran her fingers over the keys, her eyes gleamed with mischief. What was she up to?

"Actually, two things. First, I get to use this piano when I'm here. And second, if you have time, maybe you could help me get better at playing. I'd love to have a fraction of your talent."

His muscles relaxed at her demands. Hardly demands. "You're welcome to play, and I'd be happy to give you a few tips."

"Thank you, thank you!" She squealed and clapped her hands. Was she back in fan girl mode or just happy he'd agreed? Whichever it was, her excitement and attitude was contagious.

"You're welcome. But you can't play if you're bouncing up and down." When he rested his hands on her shoulders, she immediately stilled. She let out a small laugh, then wrapped her arms around him in a warm hug.

"Thank you." Her soft voice tickled his ear, and he did his best to hide the shiver it caused. "I would have kept your secret whether you agreed or not."

He allowed himself a few minutes in her arms. Maybe he could add giving him a hug before and after every lesson into their deal. It wasn't something he was used to, but he found he liked it far more than he thought he would.

****

"Ohmagawd! Guess what happened?"

Sara turned to see what she called The Ponytail Platoon gathered in their typical clique. Three brunette girls, about her age, who always wore stylish ponytails with a pouf on the top. Trina sidled over to Bianca and Skyler, gesturing wildly. She shouldn't judge. The girls had been nice to her since they'd all started at the same time at The Melody Tent. Not much in common with them, though, always talking about parties and the guys they picked up. Was she the only loser not with the times?

The concert was in full swing, so they had a little down time in between collecting tickets, showing people to their seats, and cleaning up the trash after. They were hanging around behind the stage area in case the stage managers needed any assistance.

"Sara," Trina called and waved her over. "You might be interested, too. I met the manager for the band, and he said they've rented a house on the beach for a few days. The band's going to wrap things up by eleven, and they're having a party after the concert tonight. He asked me to go and said I could invite some friends. You guys up for it?"

"Are you kidding me?" Bianca squealed. "I am so there. I've been eyeing the drummer since they got here. Think I could get his attention?"

"As long as you change out of this dumpy shirt," Skyler chimed in. The polo shirt with the Melody Tent insignia wasn't the most flattering, but they'd gotten it for free, and it was conservative the way Sara liked.

"We can stop at my house, and you can all borrow something of mine." Bianca said. "Are you coming, Sara?"

"I don't know. Where is this place? I don't have a

car.”

Trina flapped her hands in excitement. “It’s right near the Kennedy Compound. It must be huge.”

“We can take my car,” Skyler offered. “I’ll bring you home, too. Don’t worry. It’ll be amazing.”

Should she? She’d love to discuss music with the band, but big parties weren’t her thing. Bianca pulled her close.

“You have to come, Sara. You said you wanted to be a singer. Here’s your opportunity to play with the big boys. Find out how they got noticed and get advice.”

“Yes,” Trina said. “Their manager represents other performers, plus he said Jerry Tonaway, the rock promoter, was stopping by. Cozy up to both of them and maybe they’ll offer you a singing contract.”

Right, like little librarian, Sara Storm, would be offered a music contract simply by going to a party. But it certainly wouldn’t hurt to talk to these people and get some tips on making it in the business. It was what she wanted, wasn’t it? The reason she’d come to the Cape this summer. To prove she was good enough to be a singer. Handing out tickets and cleaning up popcorn wouldn’t get her there.

“Okay, as long as someone can bring me back. I need to text my friend and let him know I don’t need a ride.”

“Your friend? Him?” Bianca smirked. “Who is this? Someone who’ll be upset if you hook up tonight?”

Rolling her eyes, Sara said, “I’m not planning on hooking up and no, he won’t be upset. He’s just a friend. My boss, actually, from my other job. He’s letting me stay with him until I find a new apartment.

Remember I told you I was looking?"

"Your boss, huh?" Trina wiggled her eyebrows. "Cool."

"Intermission's in ten minutes. You better go now," Bianca pushed her away from them. "Go into the ladies' room so management doesn't see you using your phone."

Sara followed their advice and entered a stall to text TJ. Why was she nervous? This was what she wanted. It could be her big chance to get noticed. If she backed down now, then she might never get the opportunity again.

—No ride tonight. Going with friends. Be home later, don't wait up. Thanks.—

It was only a few moments before her phone vibrated.

—You sure? Everything ok?—

She loved his concern and had to admit she was a little concerned, too. But this was something she needed to do.

—Meeting the band. Possibly a music promoter. Wish me luck.—

The text was immediate.

—Good luck. Be smart. Here if you need me.—

After texting back her thanks, she shut off her phone. She wasn't sure if the butterflies in her stomach were due to who she'd be meeting tonight or the fact TJ said he'd be there for her.

****

Sara shifted her wine to one hand and tugged on her shirt again, but it only made her boobs stick out from the top more. There was no happy medium. Bianca had provided a top for each of them after the concert, but Sara wasn't comfortable in the cropped crocheted thing she'd been given. The whole shirt was loosely woven, and you could see right through to her skin, except for the sewn-in lining in small triangles around her chest. They'd made her take her bra off, too, since it could be seen through the holes. Luckily, it was snug enough it gave her some support. But it only had two buttons right between her breasts, and it kept flapping open as she walked, showing off her stomach.

Which wouldn't be bad, but the shorts she had on were lower cut on her hips. They were fine when she wore the polo for work, but with this top she felt very exposed. It was still the most conservative of the shirts Bianca had offered. The Ponytail Platoon all wore material barely holding in their much more endowed chests. And they were working the crowd.

Well, Bianca worked the drummer while the other two narrowed down their prey. Sara moved through the crowd talking with some of the band. They were dedicated musicians who wanted to make it bigger. She'd made sure to mention her music background and interest in becoming a singer. When asked where she'd performed, she'd been embarrassed to say she had no experience singing in public other than high school and college performances.

"You need to set up some gigs in public, sweetie," Troy, the lead singer of the band suggested. "Maybe even sign up for that Summer Star Contest thing they've got going at the big fair here in a few weeks. I know Celia Muñez is performing, and rumor has it they've asked her to be a judge in the contest."

Celia Muñez was a big name and becoming as well-known as her would be a dream. But performing in front of someone of her caliber, scary. Did she want this bad enough? *Yes.*

"Great idea, Troy. I'll check it out. Thanks for chatting tonight. You're very talented."

Troy grimaced. "Unfortunately, it's not always about talent in this business. Sometimes it's luck and who you know. But thanks. Right now, I need to make a phone call. My kids are ready for bed back home on the west coast, and I promised I'd talk to them before they went down."

"It was nice meeting you."

"You, too, sweetie. Oh, hey, there's Jerry. Let me introduce you. He's got lots of contacts." Troy walked off and talked to the rock promoter for a few seconds, then pointed to her. Oh, God, what did you say to someone like him? Please, don't let her sound stupid.

The man walked over and held out his hand. "Jerry Tonaway. Troy says you've got an amazing voice, and I should listen to you."

A laugh burst out of her mouth before she could stop it. "I'm sorry, so sweet of him, but he didn't hear me sing. I don't know how he could judge."

"She's honest." Jerry winked. "But you do have a sweet voice and a nice lilt to your tone. Can you sing?"

"Yes, and I'd love for you to hear me sometime."

"What kind of music do you like, um…?"

"Sara Storm and anything, really." Did he promote more one kind of music than another? She didn't know much about him though she'd certainly heard his name. If she'd known ahead of time, she could've done some searching on the internet. Thinking of TJ's music, she blurted out. "I love anything written by James True."

"Well, who doesn't? The man has magic fingers.

Everything he composes turns to platinum. What I wouldn't do to get a few of his songs."

Troy said sometimes it's who you know. Could she? If she was careful?

"He's got a new song he's writing and it's absolutely beautiful." It was. He'd played it for her this week and actually asked her opinion on a few different options.

"You know James True?" Suddenly, Jerry seemed a lot more interested.

She couldn't break her promise to TJ, but this could be her big chance. "Not really, but I met him through a friend. He mentioned his new song and played a little for us." Not too much of a lie.

Jerry looped his arm over her shoulder, steering her away from the party. Grabbing a bottle of wine from one of the coolers, he poured some in her now empty glass. "Drink up while we discuss your future."

Sara did but lightly. If this man was willing to give her a shot, she wanted her wits about her. He guided her near the water in sight of the house.

"Wanted to get away from the noise. How about you sing for me. Let me hear this amazing voice Troy bragged about."

Flamingos did a tango in her stomach. Would she screw it up? "What would you like to hear?"

A shrewd look came into Jerry's eyes. "How about the new James True song."

Panic settled in the spaces between the flamingos. *Don't break TJ's trust.* "I don't remember much. But I can sing one of his earlier hits."

They were near a breakwater and Jerry settled back against a large rock, then tipped his head. She broke into a cold sweat but needed to do this. If she couldn't sing for one person, how could she do it for thousands?

Taking a last sip of her wine, she handed the glass to Jerry, closed her eyes, cleared her throat, then started singing. It was an early song from maybe eight or nine years ago. TJ must have been very young when he wrote it. Obviously, his talent had come early. It was a song of despair and losing someone you loved. As she sang, she wondered if he'd gone through what the person in the song had. And who was it he had lost? The song was called *Everything,* and the words spoke of losing everything and being left with nothing. Had it been his mother? The one he said hadn't kissed his boo boos? The thought of him in pain made her voice quiver with emotion.

When she was done, she took a step back and stared at Jerry. It was dark, but the moon was high and bright enough to see. He was smiling. Good, right?

"Lovely, Sara. Troy was correct. You do have an amazing voice. And the emotion you put into the song feels real."

He liked her singing. Did he like it enough to help her become a professional singer?

"Thank you."

"Have some more wine, dear, and we can talk about music."

Sara took another sip, and Jerry plied her with questions about her favorite musicians and what singers she wanted to emulate. The conversation was enjoyable, but her anxiety grew as he stepped closer, putting his arm around her shoulder.

"Bit chilly near the sea, isn't it? Need to keep you warm."

"Thank you." For some reason, she didn't feel like his holding her was as altruistic as he made it sound. Especially when he started running his hand over her back and along the exposed skin above her waistband. The wine had mellowed her a bit, but she was still aware enough she felt uncomfortable with what he was doing. And where he might want it to go.

They drank more wine and talked a good deal, but when Jerry's hand slid inside her shorts, she jumped and pulled away. Her breath was shallow and rushed, and her first thought was to run as fast and far as she could go. *Don't burn your bridges.*

"Thanks so much. I enjoyed our conversation. But I think my friends are ready to go. They're probably looking for me."

"I understand, dear. You go run and find them." Pulling a business card from his pocket, he held it out. "Listen, if you get a chance to speak with James True, give him my number, huh? I'd love to talk with him about his music. And you know, if you were to sing one of his songs, it could make you the next big thing. Think about it."

Sara shoved the card in her back pocket and ran back to the party on the patio. Trina, Bianca, and Skyler were nowhere to be found. She went inside the house, but the people there were all snuggled up together or drinking heavily. Too much like the night Dan—

"Do you need something, sugar?" It was the drummer. Apparently, Bianca hadn't hooked up with him like she'd wanted. But his eyes, glued to where her boobs pushed out of the shirt, made her decide he wasn't one she wanted to ask for help.

"All set, thanks." She turned to find the bathroom,

then splashed water on her face. What should she do now? Not go back out to the party, and it was freezing by the water. Checking her phone, she grimaced. It was almost two.

TJ said he was there if she needed him. *Try texting first.* If he was asleep already maybe he wouldn't hear the tone.

—Are you awake?—

She looked out the bathroom window, wondering what she'd do if he didn't answer. Considering the time, he probably wouldn't. She wouldn't call and wake him. Could she get a taxi? When her phone sounded, she let out a huge sigh of relief.

—You okay?—

Had he really been awake? It was late, but sometimes he worked on his music after she'd gone to sleep.

—Yes, but could you come get me, please?—

—Where?—

After sending the address, she told him she'd be out front. He hadn't even asked why, just where, and he'd be there soon. As she made her way back through the house, she avoided Jerry, who was hitting on another young girl. Would he ask her to sing, too?

She left the house and walked down the long driveway to the street. The air was brisk, so she rubbed her hands up and down her arms wondering how long it would take TJ to get there. The ocean breeze had kicked up, and her skimpy top didn't cover much.

Ten minutes later, she considered walking in the direction of TJ's house, but she hadn't paid close attention when they'd driven here. Pacing back and forth, she jumped up and down to stay warm, but the alcohol she'd had made her dizzy. Finally, lights came down the street, and TJ's truck stopped in front of her.

She grabbed the handle and swung herself up into the seat. Freckles sat in her usual spot in the middle.

"Thank you for coming. I'm sorry it's so late."

"You okay?" No anger, only concern.

She felt stupid for getting herself in this predicament. "I'm fine. Just cold."

Shrugging out of his sweatshirt, he tossed it at her. He wore no shirt under it.

"But you'll be cold."

He pointed to the dashboard. "Got the heat on. Wear it until you warm up."

She slipped the top over her head and snuggled into it. It smelled like him; salt air and Irish Spring. As he pulled onto the road, she peeked at his muscled arms and firm shoulders. Her brothers had physiques like this, but somehow this was different. TJ wasn't her brother.

"The girls I came with, and who promised me a ride home, disappeared. I should have known since they kept talking about hooking up with some of the band members. I just felt weird and didn't want to be around all these people who were only interested in getting stoned and hooking up."

"Not your thing, huh?" His lips twisted as he drove down the street.

"Not really."

"Did you meet anybody interesting?"

"Yeah." Her eyes struggled to stay open. *Way too much wine.* More than she was used to. Pulling Freckles toward her, she rested her head on the dog's soft fur. "I'll tell you tomorrow. Not sure I can stay awake long enough to get home." Home. *Why did she keep calling it that?* TJ made it feel like home.

Her eyes drifted closed and didn't open again until TJ was at her door, lifting her into his arms.

"What, no, I'm okay." But she snuggled against his broad chest instead of trying to get down. Chuckling, he carried her into the house. The hair on his chest felt strange against her cheek, and she twirled her fingers in it. Nice. And with her nose to his skin, she inhaled. Yup, the scent of TJ. They should bottle it. Best seller, for sure. Could she taste him, too? Using all her senses would be very scientific.

Before she could, they entered her room, and he placed her gently on the bed. After slipping off her shoes, he pulled down the covers, then adjusted them over her. When he moved to leave, she reached out and grabbed his hand.

"You're too good to me. I wish I could be good to you."

TJ leaned over, placing a kiss on her forehead, then whispered, "You're good *for* me, Sunshine. Better than anyone else has ever been. Sweet dreams."

What did he mean? But too much wine and the late hour took its toll and sleep claimed her swiftly.

Chapter Ten

"That's Sara, huh?" Jim commented as he and TJ stood at one end of the court, while Ted and Ernie discussed their strategy at the other end. "I see why she's got you twisted in knots. She's gorgeous."

His gaze roamed to where Sara sat on a swing in the public playground, looking like a little kid with her cute top and shorts. You couldn't hide the mile-long legs and curvy figure though.

"She still staying with you?"

Bouncing the basketball a few times, he shrugged. "She hasn't found another apartment yet. Ted mentioned a couple, but they weren't in a good location."

"A little proprietary with her, are we?"

TJ tossed the ball to Jim, who caught it and threw it so it swished right through the hoops. For a man of sixty, he was in damn good shape.

"Shouldn't we be discussing how we're going to cream those two in basketball?"

"Nah. We'll just beat them like we always do. I want to know what you've done in the Sara department."

"What do you mean, what I've done?" Grabbing the ball from Jim, he swooped in for a layup, the ball rolling around the rim before it went in. "I'm letting her stay with me until she finds another place."

"Have you had a real date yet? Taken her out anywhere?"

"No, I uh…no."

"What are you waiting for? You like her, and it seems she likes you. Ask her out."

When he turned, Sara waved, wearing one of her million-watt smiles. Lifting his chin, he returned the greeting with what he assumed was his own ridiculous grin.

"You are so whipped, and you haven't even gone on a date yet," Jim said, stealing the ball. "Ask her out for Pete's Sake."

Ernie and Ted walked toward them, so TJ stepped close to Jim. "I don't want her going out with me because she's grateful. And you should talk. Take your own advice and ask Mary out. It's been two years since her husband died. You don't come hang around the shop because of my charming personality."

The other players moved in, and the game began. As usual, he and Jim had no problem outscoring their friends. He even tried a few shots he'd never have dared before. Was he showing off for Sara? It wasn't like he typically had someone cheering him on.

Her swing swayed as she left it to sit on the grass surrounding the courts. She clapped and yelled whenever he or Jim got a basket, but never booed or jeered when Ernie and Ted got points. The perfect spectator.

When the game was over, they'd won by ten points. After agreeing on next week at the same time, the others took off. Jim gave him the eye before he got into his car. Trotting over, TJ dropped on the grass beside Sara, sweating and breathing heavy from the exertion.

"You're really good." She plucked grass from the lawn and dropped it onto her legs.

Collapsing onto his back, he chuckled. "The others are out of shape. Plus, I'm the youngest. It'd be embarrassing if I couldn't beat a couple of guys who have at least ten years on me."

"You still played well." This time she plucked more grass and sprinkled it on his leg. It tickled and he brushed it away. Her silence had him looking up.

Her gaze focused on his right thigh, now exposed. Damn. His tattoo stared her right in the face. Sitting up, he pulled the shorts down, but she leaned over and swatted his hand away.

"You have a tattoo." She actually giggled. Not the reaction he'd wanted when he got it at sixteen.

He tugged again. "Yeah, stupid teenage rebellion."

"It's a snake. Hmm, I would have thought some sort of music note, maybe. Why a snake?"

He made a face. "Like I said, stupid. And not quite sober." Not far from the truth.

Folding up her legs, she faced him. "I almost got a tattoo once. I was eighteen and my girlfriends thought it would be cool."

"You didn't get it though."

"No." She shook the grass from her lap. "My brothers got wind of it and stopped us. Then they took turns following me around for the next three months. A bit embarrassing since I had a boyfriend."

"He didn't last long, huh?"

Her smile was wry. "We dated for five years. But Robby and I were more like friends. We still are."

How could anyone go out with Sara for so long and

only be friends with her? Pushing at his shorts again, she squinted at the ink.

"Why a snake? It looks familiar, like what that band uses. The hard rock one. It's a snake name. Do you know which one I mean?"

Did he know? Intimately. Thankfully, she wasn't more familiar with the group. Could he give her a little truth without blowing his whole cover?

"Python."

Her eyes lit up. "Yes, that's it. Did you get it because you like their music?"

Like their music? Lots of their music was his music. Even though he didn't see his dad often, he still gave them first choice at many of his songs. If it hadn't been for Abe and his contacts, he never would have made it as far as he did as a composer.

"Python has used some of my music. More early on. They don't buy much from me anymore. I've kind of mellowed with age and they haven't."

Her expression was thoughtful. "You're right. Your music has gotten calmer. And I do remember a few of your early songs by them. Is it why you have their tattoo? They bought your early work?"

"They bought my first two songs." It was the truth. Hopefully, she wouldn't ask how he'd managed it.

"I guess I might get their symbol tattooed on me if that happened, too."

She got quiet and looked around. "I have a confession to make, and I hope you won't get mad."

His muscles tensed.

"Yesterday, Troy, the lead singer of the band playing, told me sometimes success wasn't about talent but who you know."

Too right.

"When I met this promoter, Jerry Tonaway, I mentioned how much I loved James True's music."

Tonaway. He knew him. Big in the industry and a bit of a sleaze. Known mostly for auditioning singers on his couch. God, he hoped the douche bag hadn't touched his Sunshine.

"He said he'd love to get some of True's music. So I told him you had a new, great song coming out."

"You told him who I was?" A knot formed in his stomach.

"No." Her eyes widened. "I told him I'd met you, and you'd played your new song for us. I didn't tell him who you were or anything else. He was more interested in hearing me sing once he knew I'd met you."

"Did he listen to you?" Or do more? The thoughts running through his mind were not good ones. For his own sake, he hoped all promoters were stupid and couldn't see her talent. It wasn't the kind of life for an angel like Sara.

"He did. He wanted me to perform the new song you'd written, but I told him I didn't remember it."

Chuckling, he reminded her, "You sang it with me the past few nights."

"I know, but I promised I wouldn't tell your secret. I sang another one of your songs. He seemed to like it. We talked about music for a while. Then…" Sara's gaze flitted from tree to swings but never landed back on him. "It got cold by the ocean, and he tried to warm me up, but I…well it was late, and I thought I should find my friends."

Tonaway had put the moves on her. His smart girl had known enough to get away when she could. TJ patted her hand. "Then you called me. I'm glad you did." But not before the man had plied her with alcohol. The smell of it had been strong last night when he'd picked her up from the party. Luckily, she'd been able to keep her wits about her.

Her anxious stare raked his face. She'd kept his secret and still managed to get the man to listen to her.

"It's fine, Sara. The music industry is all about name dropping. You did it without revealing my secret identity. Thank you." He winked, and she gazed at his tattoo once more.

His throat caught, and he swallowed hard as her hand ran over it again. Her fingers felt heavenly against his skin, but it made him have all sorts of thoughts he shouldn't be having.

When she looked up, she caught him staring. "You don't like people knowing about the tattoo, do you? You seem uncomfortable."

More uncomfortable because of her hand caressing his thigh and the reaction other parts were having.

"It's part of my past I like to keep private."

Patting his shorts into place, she leaned over, so close he could kiss her if he shifted even a fraction. "Your secret is safe with me. I won't tell a soul."

How would she feel about his other secrets? Like his early years and the fact he allowed his sister to die because he was too busy getting wasted and screwing some groupies? Or he was a drug addict and alcoholic? Would she be as understanding with those secrets?

Jim's words of *putting it in the past and moving on* rang through his head. Maybe he should try. Ask her out on a date. Easy, right? Baby steps.

"I'm hot. How'd you like to get ice cream before

we head home?"

Sara chewed on her lip. "I didn't bring my purse. Are you paying? I'll pay you back later."

"My treat."

Jumping to his feet, he took her hand and hauled her up. They were going out for ice cream, and it was his treat. Could that count as a date? He thought it could. Even if she didn't know.

****

Sara closed the book and looked around the shop while Elliot chose the next one. It took him longer because he was meticulous. Reminded her of Alex. Elliot was definitely in training to be as OCD as her middle brother. She sang a song with the other kids until he'd picked one.

A couple came in, maybe in their fifties but definitely trying to look younger. The man's hair was shoulder length, and he wore faded jeans fraying at the bottom. His paisley print top opened halfway down his chest, showing off the large metal decoration he wore around his neck. His tattooed sleeves were in plain sight below the rolled-up arms of his shirt.

The woman, in contrast, had on skin-tight Capri leggings with four-inch Jimmy Choo's, and her lacy blouse caressed her figure flatteringly. Her large, expensive jewelry complemented the outfit nicely. Burgundy highlighted the dark hair piled in a complex knot on top of her head. Enormous sunglasses perched on her nose, and her make-up was professionally applied.

They stood in the doorway for a short time, then the woman sat near the front window while the man approached the counter. Elliot handed Sara his choice, and she gave her attention back to the children.

As she read, she was aware of Darcy hustling around the couple, waiting on them. Since when did they provide table service? Who were these people? The woman looked familiar, but Sara could only see her from the side, and she still wore her glasses, even in the store.

Hope picked out the book for her turn, and luckily it was one where the children all said the words together, and Sara basically turned the pages. The couple had started attracting attention, and she wanted to know who they were.

It finally dawned on her who the woman was. Celia Muñez, the singer. What was she doing in Hyannis? Yes, she was performing at the Barnstable County Fair, but not until the end of July. The month had just started.

And who was the guy? There was something familiar about him, but she couldn't place him. What did she know about Celia Muñez? She was divorced from the lead singer in some big rock band, but she couldn't remember which group. It wasn't one she listened to. Was this guy another rocker? The look was certainly there.

Story Hour ended, and Sara allowed the children to sit and read their favorite books. Eddie snuggled on one side of her, and the quiet Hope had been brave enough to sidle up to her other side. Freckles had his head right in her lap.

As the children read, TJ came down the stairs and froze, staring at Celia Muñez and her friend. Was he star struck even though he wrote songs for people like her? Sara had gotten the impression his manager handled all his music deals.

His face turned to granite, and his eyes grew cold. After tipping his head in their direction, he went into the back room. Strange reaction. Like he knew who they were but didn't care. Darcy followed behind him, but he turned and gave her a look, the one he usually reserved for Hunter when she was flirting. Darcy's eagerness dimmed, and she went back to work.

A few minutes later, TJ came out and headed toward Celia and her friend, but he was about as enthusiastic as someone walking to the gallows. He sat and engaged in conversation, but he wasn't happy with what they were saying.

Parents started collecting their children, and Sara spent the next ten minutes saying goodbye to the kids. Walking behind the counter, she began to make lunch for Jasmine and Eddie who were still here.

"I wish you would go with us," Celia was saying to a tense TJ. "It's not like you need this job."

"It's not a job. I own this place," TJ growled. "Stop talking about it like it's a hobby?"

"You make plenty from your music, True," the man said. "Get rid of it and do more composing."

The man had called him True and knew he was a composer. She shouldn't eavesdrop, but they were only two tables from the end of the counter where the peanut butter and jelly were stored. TJ's back was to her, so she couldn't see his reaction.

"Abe, he likes his little store, and we need to respect that," Celia said.

Abe. The name rang a bell, and she tried to remember why it sounded familiar. It took a few seconds, but it finally came to her. It was the name of Celia's ex-husband. Abe…Abe…Abe Bannister. That was it.

Holy cow! Seriously? Bannister? No, it couldn't be. TJ would have said something. He'd told her about being James True, and she'd kept his secret. Well, actually she'd discovered his secret, and he'd admitted to it. But still, he trusted her, right? Maybe it was only a coincidence.

Standing up, TJ leaned on the table. His tones were low, but she heard him clearly.

"Cut the doting parent act. I'm not buying it. You didn't know how to be parents when I was a kid so don't try and make up for it now. Take your vacation on Martha's Vineyard and leave me alone. But thanks for the offer. Mom. Dad."

He turned and stopped cold when he saw her standing there. Color leeched from his face, and she realized he hadn't wanted anyone to overhear. But there was no denying it now. It wasn't just coincidence, having his songs sung by Python, his Python tattoo, his music ability.

TJ Bannister was the son of Celia Muñez and Abe Bannister, king and queen of the rock world.

Chapter Eleven

"Sara?"

Sara's expression told him she'd heard what he'd said. Shit. He hadn't wanted this meeting with his parents to get out of control. But his mother was insisting he leave the store for a month and go with them on their vacation to Martha's Vineyard.

"Sara, I um…"

Pasting on a fake smile, she grabbed the plate of sandwiches and practically ran to the children's section, then called Jasmine and Eddie to eat. Great, he was finally getting somewhere with her, and his parents had come along and blown everything to hell. He and Sara had actually gone on a date.

Okay, maybe Sara hadn't realized it was a date, but he'd pretended it was. Opened her car door and helped her with her seat belt. She'd laughed, but he'd still been an absolute gentleman. He'd let her choose her flavor and which picnic table to sit on. There'd only been two empty ones, but still he'd let her decide.

Maybe it wouldn't go down in history as the best date ever, but he'd enjoyed himself, and if the amount of laughing they'd done was any indication, she'd had fun, too. Next time, he figured he might even let her know it was a date.

Now his plans had been flushed down the toilet. Turning, he stared at the people who had once again taken something nice in his life and turned it to shit.

"When you're done, I'd appreciate if you left. You're starting to cause a commotion." They weren't really. Some people had recognized them but most were being polite and giving them privacy.

After walking into the back room, he kept busy organizing napkins, coffee filters, and sugar packets. None of which needed to be done, but he wanted to appear busy if anyone came looking for him.

"Holy Rock Star, Batman." Darcy was the first to seek him out. Not surprising. "You know Abe and Celia, boss. You holding out on us?"

"I'm sorry I snapped earlier, Darcy. It can be exciting to see famous people."

Darcy shrugged. "No problem. But I gotta know, what's the connection? You were sitting with them for like…forever. Is it that song writing thing you do on the side? Do they want to buy one from you?"

Damn, Darcy had been a loyal employee for two years, and he hated lying to everyone. She deserved to know the truth. Maybe.

"I don't usually advertise, and I'd appreciate if you didn't either. You've probably figured it out with the name similarity."

Darcy's eyes grew huge. "You're shittin' me, right? I mean Bannister is pretty common, but seriously…you're Abe and Celia's kid? Hot damn!"

Dropping his head, he closed his eyes. "Darcy."

"No, it's cool, boss. I can do nonchalant. And I'm great at keeping secrets. I haven't even told anyone you've got the hots for Sara."

His head snapped up. "Where'd you get that impression?"

Darcy chuckled. "Please, I've been working here for two years, and you've never showed interest in anything even remotely female. I was honestly starting to wonder if you swung the other way. I've got a few guy friends I'd thought of bringing here to meet you."

"Whoa, wait, you thought I was—"

"Don't sweat it, boss." She held up her hands. "I know now you're not. You just aren't into chicks who put all their assets on public display. I respect that. And I like Sara. She's pretty decent."

"What makes you think I've got the…am interested in Sara?"

Darcy shrugged. "Don't worry, it's nothing overt. Although maybe if you let people know, Hunter might stop shaking her boobs in your face."

Good thought.

"I just noticed you pay a little more attention to where Sara is in the store. You always make sure she's got a ride to work or home."

So Darcy didn't know Sara was staying with him. Well, temporarily anyway. But it had been over a week since she'd moved in, and TJ wasn't in any hurry to have her find a new place.

"And it's the way your face kind of lights up when you see her. It's really sweet, boss. And just so you know, I think she's into you, too. With her though, she blushes like a freakin' virgin. It's the scourge of people with light skin."

He cleared his throat. "Well; thank you, Darcy, for your observation. I'll try to keep my…interest better under wraps in the future."

"Oh, don't, boss. I think it's really cute. You deserve to be happy and have someone. Being the son of those two out there." She flipped her thumb in the direction of the coffee shop. "It might be cool for a while, but I bet it gets a little crazy at times."

TJ laughed. "You have no idea, Darcy, no idea."

****

TJ fiddled with supplies in the back room. He needed to speak with Sara. What did she think of his famous parents showing up? Or the fact he'd hidden it from her? He moved to where she cleaned up the kids' lunch. When she turned and saw him, she froze.

"Sara."

The fake smile appeared again. He hated it.

"I thought I'd restock the postcards while the kids are here. Unless you need me for something else."

Her voice was calm and professional. The way he'd always tried to be with his employees and what he wanted back from them. Until Sara had come along and wrapped her rays of sunshine around his heart and squeezed until it pumped with life again. The way it had when Sonni'd been around.

"Sara." The store was too crowded for any kind of conversation. It was Tuesday at noon for cripes' sake. Why was it so packed?

Because word had gotten out his parents were here. A few brave souls had gone over to talk to the superstars and get autographs. God help him. They better not be charging.

Sara stared, waiting for instructions? Or something more? God, don't let what had been growing between them wither and die. And something had been growing. More than he'd ever felt for a woman. And not only sexual. He liked Sara. Liked so much about her.

"Yeah, the postcards are good." The tourists posed

with Abe and Celia as Darcy took their picture. Surprisingly, Darcy hadn't dug out her phone to snap a shot, too. His gaze turned back to Sara. "Can we talk later?"

Avoiding his stare, she picked up the kids' plates. As she passed by, she murmured, "Of course."

His shoulders dropped as he sighed and walked over to the book store register where Mary bagged some items. The customer left, rubbernecking as he walked out the coffee shop doors instead of the book store doors which were closer.

"Is the crowd buying anything or simply gawking?"

"It's a good day."

Maybe for business, not for him.

"I take it you didn't know they'd show up here today." Mary touched his arm, her eyes filled with the motherly concern he'd never gotten from Celia.

"I'm not privy to their itinerary and honestly don't care to be. They want me to go with them for a month-long vacation to the Vineyard."

She eyed him curiously. "I thought your parents were divorced."

"They are. I think sometimes they forget. Apparently, this is some harebrained scheme to see if they can fall in love again. Like they even know what that is."

Mary squeezed his hand. "Do you want to take off? Darcy and I can handle it, and Cam's stocking shelves upstairs. I can get him down here to work the floor."

His gaze moved to his parents as they charmed more customers and chatted amicably. Their picture would be posted all over social media by tonight with reports of how nice and polite they were. Sure, they knew how to work a crowd, even a small one in a coffee shop.

“Thanks, Mary, but I’ve got paperwork to do in my office. I only came down to—” Damn, he’d almost said it out loud.

“To watch Sara read to the kids.” Mary’s grin was huge. “She’s wonderful with them. She should have a whole passel of kids herself.”

Images of Sara surrounded by kids, all blond little rays of sunshine, entered his mind. Was he in the picture anywhere? Kids had never entered his mind. His own childhood had been so transient with hordes of people enlisted to watch him and Sonni. Always plenty of volunteers. People who wanted to do something nice for Abe or Celia, and hopefully get in good with the stars. But none had ever wanted to be there with him or his sister.

Sara would want to be with her children. She loved kids and was good with them. Her children would grow up in a caring family, always together. Would he ever be able to live that way? Or was he too damaged because he had no idea what a loving family was?

When Gabby walked in, he was still staring across the store. Scooping up Eddie, she smiled down at Jasmine hugging her legs. His cousin knew what family meant, but she hadn’t grown up with Celia as her mom. His grandmother and Gabby’s grandmother were sisters, and she’d been raised here in New England, not in the land of Hollywood.

As he walked toward where Sara and Gabby chatted, he noticed Celia and Abe heading in his direction. Finally tired of the common folk and their simple ways?

“We’re leaving, True. Are you sure we can’t convince you to come with us? Maybe even for a week. Bring a friend.” Celia shrugged her dainty shoulders as if the suggestion could sway him.

“Or we could provide you with a friend.” Abe winked. “Always plenty around.”

Yeah, he knew this all too well. Saying it in front of Sara sent ripples of embarrassment and shame through him. God, what she must be thinking right now.

“Tia Celia? I didn’t know you’d be here today.”

A perfect bow of surprise formed on Celia’s mouth. “Gabriella? How lovely to see you. Mami mentioned you lived on the Cape near True. What are you doing here?”

“TJ keeps any eye on my two darlings during Story Hour a few times a week, letting me work without paying for a sitter. He doesn’t have to, but I’m grateful.”

Celia stepped toward him and patted his face. Seriously. Why must she act like the devoted mother in public when she’d never done it in private?

“How wonderful of you, sweetheart, helping your cousin. I’m performing at the big event here later this month, Gabriella. You must come and bring your family. They give me lots of free tickets, so I’ll send you some.”

Celia gave Gabby an air hug, then turned to him. “If I send you the tickets, you’ll make sure Gabriella gets them, won’t you, dear?”

For Gabby’s benefit, he pasted on a smile. “Of course.”

“Must go,” Celia called out, like she was

announcing it to the whole store. "I'll email you the details of our Vineyard trip, True, darling. In case you change your mind and decide to come." His mother swept out like an ocean wave, his father following behind in her wake.

Kissing Gabby on the cheek, he said, "I'm not sure about those tickets Celia promised, but I'd be happy to take you and the kids to the fair, and Big Eddie, if he can get the time from work."

"You don't have to pay for us, but I'd love to go with you. Maybe we can treat you. Perhaps Sara could come as she's been the one taking care of these brats the last few weeks."

Sara looked up at Gabby's suggestion and waved goodbye to the kids. He'd love to take Sara to the fair, but first he'd have to get her speaking to him again.

****

Gabby was TJ's cousin. That fact had never come up. Or who his parents were. Even though she should be upset, she was actually a little thrilled. The kisses TJ and Gabby shared were nothing more than their way of saying goodbye.

Freckles started pacing. Maybe she'd take the dog home and use the time to wrap her head around this new information. Yes, TJ wanted to talk, but she wasn't ready yet, so she made her way upstairs and quickly popped her head into his office.

"TJ." Glancing up, he removed his glasses. "I thought I'd walk back to the house when I took Freckles out." *Do not call it home this time.*

He stood and shuffled the papers. "I'll drive you."

"No, we'll walk. She might like a dip in the ocean. You do your work."

It was obvious he wanted to argue, his Adam's apple bobbing up and down. His eyes closed for a second, and when they opened, Sara could see resignation in them. "Okay, but be careful on the road."

"We'll be fine."

Should she tell him she'd see him later? Honestly, she wasn't sure what she'd do. Maybe look harder for a place to stay. There were a few options. None any better than what she'd had with Kayla and Dan.

By the time she got to the house, she was ready for a swim. After slipping into her bikini, the one her cousin Sofie had talked her into, she led the dog into the surf. So wonderful she soon lost track of time.

She called to the dog, and they ran to the back of the house where the outdoor shower was located. Freckles got rinsed first, then she stepped under the spray and shampooed the salt from her hair. Her back started to sting, and she feared she may have been out too long in the sun. The sunblock had been forgotten with the turmoil in her mind.

In her room, she gazed in the mirror. Yup, she'd be hurting tomorrow. Putting on loose clothes, she grabbed her laptop and settled on the porch swing overlooking the beach. Freckles padded around but finally curled up at her feet.

Sara checked her email and social media accounts and wasn't surprised Abe Bannister and Celia Muñez's appearance on the Cape was a top story. There'd been lots of camera phones clicking away while the couple had been chatting with the customers.

More interesting was their son. A little digging and she discovered TJ stood for True Jam. Somewhere in the back of her mind, she'd known, but had never connected it. Why would she?

Skimming through sites and articles about the famous couple, she found some with pictures of TJ and his sister, Sonata, as babies and small children. They were always hugging or holding each other. Like the picture in TJ's room.

Something niggled in the back of her mind, and soon she discovered what it was. Sonata Bannister had died of a drug overdose when she was twenty-one. The date? Ten years ago. TJ would have still been a teenager. God, how devastating. But now she knew who the song *Everything* had been written about. The words made perfect sense.

Scrolling through, she found more articles showing TJ as a teen, with long hair and trendy clothes, at parties and concerts and tons of Hollywood events with his parents. The pictures she saw and the articles she read were in such contrast to the man she knew.

She began to feel like a stalker and was about to close the browser when one headline caught her eye. *'Abe and Celia's son, five years after the death of his sister; How the tragedy changed him.'*

It was written by someone named Kerri Sanborn. She claimed to have dated True for a few months and gotten to know him. The story was all about how sad he'd become and was now living a quiet life working at a book store. It spoke of his struggle to get his drinking under control. The author hinted it was only a matter of time before it all started boiling over and he was back to the wild lifestyle of a child of rock and roll legends.

The article was written five years ago. Clearly this Kerri whatshername didn't know what she was talking about. The TJ she knew wasn't anywhere near what she described. His sister's death obviously had a huge impact on his life. His parents today offered him a trip to the Vineyard for a month, and he wanted nothing to do with it.

Of course, with the money he made as James True, he could buy a place on the Vineyard. Maybe he already had one, and she just didn't know about it. There were things he'd apparently never told her. Lots of things. The question was, what would it mean to their relationship? And was she being naïve to think they even had a relationship?

Chapter Twelve

"Oh, you're here."

TJ turned from removing a carton of eggs to see Sara standing in the doorway. Her hair was sleep tousled, and a loose nightgown ended just below her hips. The outline of her curves showed through the thin material. *Look away.*

"Omelet?"

"Um, sure. I didn't expect you here this morning. You're usually at the store."

After pulling out more ingredients, he cracked eggs into a bowl. "Mary kicked me out. Said I needed a day off, and if I showed up today, I'd be in big trouble."

Sara chuckled. It almost sounded normal except for her staring at the salt and pepper shakers. Big elephant right here in this room.

"You know you own the store now, right? Mary works for you."

In order to use the island burner, he had to face her. "That's what she lets me think anyway. I'm still not too sure, but I'll humor her. I could use a day to unwind."

Silence fell over the room. The first omelet he gave to Sara, then started on his own. Could he stretch it out longer, so they didn't need to sit in discomfort too long? Wouldn't make it any easier. The few bites he took gave him pause. His stomach wasn't in the mood for eggs now Sara was here.

"So…about my parents." He eyed his plate like his eggs would do a little dance or something. "Surprise."

No laugh or smile from her.

"Look, Sara, I'm sorry I never told you about them. It's another one of those things I don't go around advertising. Believe me, lots more people know who Abe and Celia are than James True. The things people do once they find out…it's something I try and avoid at all costs."

"I understand." Her hurt tone indicated otherwise.

He played with his food. She did the same.

"How mad are you? Scale of one to ten?" Might as well get a reading on it.

Her eyes softened, and she granted him one of her genuine, Sara Sunshine ray of happiness smiles.

"I'm not mad at you, TJ. You have every right to your private life. I guess it was stupid thinking you trusted me with all your secrets. I've only known you a month, and this friendship thing only started a few weeks ago."

Reaching out, he covered her hand. "You don't want to know all my secrets, Sunshine. Believe me. Most of them are not pretty."

"But they're part of what made you, you. And I think I mentioned I like you. TJ Bannister-you. Not Celia Muñez and Abe Bannister's son-you, or James True-you." Her mouth quirked into a grin. "Although, I do like the songs of James True. I can't lie."

She was so freakin' honest. He wanted to grab her, kiss her, and wrap his arms around her. He wanted to be the recipient of one of her amazing hugs and maybe learn how to give them back. Give her back even a fraction of what she'd given him. Hope. The possibility of a future. The damn Happily Ever After of one of his ridiculous romance novels he couldn't stop reading because he wanted life that way.

"Damn, you are amazing."

"I know." Her smile turned cocky, and he couldn't stop the laughter bubbling out of his mouth.

"Maybe we should take a day for ourselves. No shop talk, just fun and frolics. And if you're good, maybe I'll share a few more of those secrets I mentioned. I'm warning you…they're not filled with sunshine."

After putting down her fork, she leaned closer. Too close. This woman had no inkling of personal space. If he shifted his head just a smidgen, he could kiss her. She reached out and touched his face. It almost stopped his heart.

"Nothing you can tell me will change the way I feel about you. I know what you're like *now*. What happened in the past is where it should be. In the past."

As he sat back, he hoped she was right. She had no clue how messed up he'd been—still was. A person who didn't deserve anything as good and pure as Sara. No matter how much he wished he did.

****

"TJ, could you give me a hand?"

Sara stood in the doorway of his bedroom with her shirt held up in front of her, but not *on* her. His lungs stopped working. What exactly did she want him to do? It couldn't be what he wanted to do with Sara and no shirt. Because that would involve no pants or clothes for him either.

"I spent too much time in the water yesterday and forgot sunscreen. My back is killing me." When she turned around, he saw the red skin marred only by a thin white line across the middle of her back.

"I have some Aloe Vera, but I can't reach my back and it's the worst part. I'm sorry to bother you, but Freckles isn't very helpful, and she's the reason I went in the water."

"Yeah, her claws would do more harm than good. Where's the gel?"

Sara slid a bottle out of her shorts pocket and handed it over, then stood with her back to him, still clinging to the shirt in front of her. He tipped the bottle into his hand, then placed it on the bedside table. Before applying it, he rubbed his hands together to warm the lotion. When he finally touched her, something between a groan and a sigh escaped from her mouth.

"Did I hurt you?"

"No, it's just cool on the burn. Keep going."

Moving his hands, he spread the gel over her back. Even burned, her skin was like silk. Okay, *this* was the real torture. With the pretense of applying therapy, he allowed his hands to wander. He was even so bold as to glide up her sides so his fingertips were within touching distance of her breasts. If he curled them inward a bit he might…

Shifting, she tugged on her drawstring shorts, and he saw the burn went down lower. What had she been wearing, and why hadn't he been here to see it?

"Can you get my bathing suit line? It's really sore where the burn starts."

She was pushing it. Pushing him to the limit of his control. With anyone else, he'd suspect it was a ploy to get him into their pants, literally. But with Sara, he had doubts. Not that he'd turned down many opportunities to get into a woman's pants. Since Sara, though, he had no desire for hard and fast sex. With her, it would need to be slow, sensual, and gentle. The images in his mind sent the blood rushing to his groin.

"Good enough?" He handed her the bottle, then went to wash his hands, hoping she'd put her shirt on. If he had to watch, he'd be done for. The only choice would be pushing her on the bed to seduce her or take a cold shower.

The shirt was on when he came back, but it was this sleeveless, lightweight cotton thing and practically see-through. God, no bra. Sensibly, he knew a bra would be excruciating on her tender skin, but it was playing havoc with the libido he'd been trying to ignore for so long.

"Since I don't think hanging out in the sun is the best choice for today, but it's too beautiful to stay inside, how about we sit on the front porch. It gets shade most of the day."

"Sounds perfect."

They gathered some iced tea and settled on the bench swing. Sara leaned her head back and sighed. "This is gorgeous. I don't know how you go to work every day. If I lived here, I'd sit on this swing and stare at the ocean all day."

And he'd stare at her blissful face.

"I sit here a lot. Unfortunately, not as much in the summer because it's the busy season at the store. And I have to tell you, January isn't as nice as it is today."

Sara laughed, her feminine tone like music to his ears. They sat and sipped iced tea, then she shifted to face him, her expression serious.

"I have a confession to make."

"Another one. You already told me how you threw out the James True connection to make points with that sleazy promoter."

"How did you know he was sleazy? I never said he was, did I?"

"You didn't need to. The fact you wanted to leave while he was interested in what you had to say told me plenty. I also know Tonaway. He's a good promoter, but his recruiting process is intense, and not many make it past the bedroom interview. Although, he certainly has a lot who make it there."

Her face paled and she sat back, winced, then leaned forward again. Peeking up, she smiled guiltily.

"I looked you up on the internet yesterday."

He laughed. "That's your confession? I'm pretty sure 'Thou shalt not stalk thy boss online' isn't one of the seven deadly sins."

Sara crossed her legs on the seat in front of her. "I wanted to know more about you and your parents. I can't imagine having your family."

Family. It wasn't really a family. Had never felt like one anyway. Maybe when he and Sonni would be together and make forts in the tour bus or play games in some empty amphitheater. But then someone would come by and make them stop. Shove them in a little corner somewhere and tell them to be quiet. Sonni would pull him into her lap and read him a story. That was the family he remembered, and it had absolutely nothing to do with his parents.

"What did you find out?" There was lots of information online, but some was obscure and hard to find unless you knew where to look.

"Your sister, Sonata, died when you were a

teenager. I'm sorry, TJ. I don't know what I'd do if I lost one of my brothers." She leaned her head on his arm and wrapped her hands around his. It was the most comfort anyone had given him regarding his sister's death.

"Thank you." Nothing else would come out. Even after ten years, he still had a hard time talking about it.

Sara stroked his hand and brushed the hair on his arm in a soothing manner. If he'd had someone like her when Sonni had died, maybe he would have been able to get his shit together quicker.

"Can I ask you a question? You can tell me it's none of my business, if you want."

Reveling in the caress of her fingers, he nodded. She seemed unaware of what she was doing.

"The song you wrote, *Everything*, was about losing Sonata."

The song had been so personal he hadn't wanted to sell it. But his manager had shown it to a top vocalist, and they'd begged him for it. It was still his highest grossing song to date. It had bought this house.

"Yeah, Sonni was the world to me. When I lost her, I lost everything."

His voice hitched at the last word, and Sara held his arm tighter. Her eyes were damp, and he hated he'd made her sad.

Blinking the moisture from his own eyes, he said, "She hated the name Sonata. Wanted everyone to call her Sonni. I only called her Sonata when I wanted to piss her off." Yeah, lighten the mood. It was getting too somber.

"That's why my brothers call me Sagey or Sage. I hated it for so long, but it's kind of grown on me. I've actually thought of using it as my stage name if I ever become famous."

He didn't want fame for her. Not because he didn't think she had talent. She had more than most performers. But she didn't belong in that world. They'd strip away her innocence and naivety in no time and leave her as jaded as the rest of the music industry. And as much of a user as all of them.

She wasn't a user. Here she was, having learned she was friends with the son of major rock stars and instead of sucking up to his parents yesterday or trying to get an introduction from him, she'd backed off. Had actually been upset he hadn't told her. Getting all she could wasn't what she was about. It's what made her so different from them.

"Can you tell me about Sonni? Is it still too painful to talk about her?"

"She was my sister, and I loved her. More importantly…she loved me." The lump in his throat wouldn't allow anything else to come out. He pressed his lips together to stop the bottom one from trembling. What the hell was wrong with him? It was ten years ago, damn it. Hadn't he mourned enough by now?

Sara kissed his arm and snuggled closer. Her warmth almost undid him. Tears pooled in his eyes, and he clamped them shut, trying to keep the emotions at bay. He inhaled deeply, but the release breath was shaky, embarrassing him.

"I'm sorry." His voice hitched again. "I don't know what the hell is wrong with me. It was a long time ago. I think you're being too nice, and I'm not used to it."

"No one's been nice to you in ten years?" A tear streaked down Sara's face, and he lost it. Pulling her close, he held her, careful of her back. Her warmth and presence worked to soothe him. When she rested her hands on his chest, her lips touched the side of his neck. It was sweet and not at all sexual. How did she do that?

They stayed close for a while, how long he wasn't sure, but finally his control returned. Easing back, he grinned. "Well, if I ever need comforting, I'll know who to come to. You're very good at it."

"I used to take boo-boo kissing lessons from my mom, and even though I was the youngest, I always took it upon myself to help my brothers when they got hurt. And they always indulged me. Until they became teenagers anyway. Then they were too macho and didn't want me to see them cry."

TJ cocked his head at Sara. "You saw my mother. I'm not sure she realizes you can kiss a boo-boo to make it go away."

She glanced at him, then lowered her eyes. "One of the articles said you'd done some rehab. Did you start drinking after Sonni died?"

Leaning forward, he rested his elbows on his knees and steepled his fingers together. This was the big secret. He needed to tell her. The truth. All of it. Stumbling upon some information tucked somewhere would have her running in the other direction. Might anyway after he told her what he was. What he'd always be.

"No, I didn't *start* drinking then, Sara. I'd already been drinking, for years. Way too much and far too often. And it wasn't only alcohol. You've heard the saying, 'Sex, Drugs, and Rock and Roll,'…well, my life in a nutshell."

Sitting back, he looked Sara straight in the eye.

"I'm a drug addict and an alcoholic."

She sat up tall, her eyes wide. Emotions ran across her expressive face he couldn't interpret. Was she horrified? Would she run in, pack her bags, and call her brothers to come get her? Darcy would just shrug it off and tell him no sweat. But Sara wasn't Darcy. And she probably hadn't come across someone like him in her sheltered life.

Confusion darkened her face. "Still? Because I've never seen you drink anything stronger than tea."

Leave it to Sara to have questions. "Once an addict, always an addict, Sunshine. There's no halfway about it. Do I still drink or do drugs? No. I've been clean and sober for seven years, five months, and twenty-two days."

Her eyes crinkled with humor. "Very precise."

"Jim, my friend from basketball, is my AA sponsor, and we meet every week. It's the first thing he asks me every time."

"Is he an alcoholic, too?"

"Twenty-five years, nine months, and eight days."

"Wow." Her eyes held confusion. "You were only a teen when your sister died. How is it you were drinking already?"

"When you're the son of a celebrity, you can do anything you want, and it all gets overlooked. My parents didn't care. Once I was old enough, they let me come join all the parties they had at the house.

He stared at his hands again. "When I was younger, I'd wait until my parents were tanked, then I'd sneak down and grab some of the half empty champagne or wine glasses. The guests thought it was funny to get the little kid drunk, so they'd give me glassfuls."

Horror lit Sara's features. "And my parents laid into Luke because he let me try some champagne at my high school graduation party. Of course, he wasn't drinking age yet, either, but he'd snuck it from my uncle who wasn't looking."

"Because your parents cared, Sunshine. Don't ever take your family for granted."

"What made you stop drinking? Sonni's death? I read it was a drug overdose."

He closed his eyes, guilt rampaging through every cell in his body. Could he tell her this part? Reveal what a twisted mess he was? He'd seen the revulsion when he'd said people had given him drinks when he was little. What would this bit of information do to her? But he needed to be truthful.

"Yeah, it was Sonni's death. But more the fact…I was responsible."

Chapter Thirteen

Sara heard his words but couldn't quite believe what he said. How could TJ be responsible for his sister's death? It had been an overdose. He'd loved his sister. When he'd talked about her earlier, there'd been real tears in his eyes, even though he'd tried to hide them.

"Why do you say that?"

"Because I wasn't there for her. I didn't stop her from taking the damn drugs. I should have been there." His voice quivered with regret.

Rubbing her hand up and down his arm, she wondered how a seventeen-year-old boy was supposed to stop what had happened. "You can't blame yourself. You didn't make her take them, did you?"

"Not those, no, but I'd noticed she'd started using them and was happy she was finally loosening up. I didn't realize how much she was taking. I'd been partying harder and had pulled away from her. It had been a while since we'd spent time together, just the two of us."

"TJ, you were a teenager. Teenagers are self-centered and egotistical. You weren't responsible for her."

"Maybe I should have been. She was always responsible for me. She'd been nagging me to drink less and think about going to college. I had Abe and Celia's money and had sold two of my songs to Python. What did I need college for?"

She sat and listened as he unburdened his guilt.

"They said she'd only been dead a few hours when I found her. If I'd gotten to her earlier, maybe they could have saved her, pumped her stomach, and gotten the drugs out before they killed her."

TJ had found her. Found his sister dead. She couldn't even imagine the horror if she found one of her brothers that way. "You had no way of knowing she'd taken those drugs."

"If I'd been a better brother, maybe she wouldn't have needed to take them. We should have been together while everyone else partied. Instead, I was doing my own thing."

"TJ."

Shrugging her off, he stood, then paced the length of the porch. "Do you know what I was doing? What was so important I didn't have time for my sister, the only person who ever really loved me?"

His rough, scratchy voice struggled to speak. He looked out over the ocean, then turned slightly in her direction as if he couldn't fully face her. "I was downing a bottle of Chivas Regal and screwing the two girls who'd given it to me. What a brother, huh?"

He turned completely away, and the rigid set of his shoulders told more than his words. No, she couldn't imagine Luke or Erik doing it, definitely not Alex. But then they'd been raised by warm, loving parents who'd taught them right from wrong. Given them a moral compass so they could make their own decisions, but always stay steered in the right direction. One luxury TJ hadn't been given.

How to help him wasn't clear, so she let the cool breeze from the ocean swirl around them, hoping the sound of the waves lapping on shore might soothe him somehow. Seagulls screeched overhead, crying as she felt like doing. But he needed someone to be strong right now. Her parents and brothers had always been there for her. TJ had no one.

His shoulders moved up and down, and his breathing grew more relaxed. Sara finally stood and gently touched his back. "The Chivas Regal in the kitchen? For a reason?"

He nodded but remained facing the ocean. "It's proof of my guilt and a reminder I can't hurt anyone else because of my own selfishness and stupidity. It keeps me sober."

"If it helps you not want to drink, then it's good it's there."

When he turned around, his face was pinched and hard. "Oh, the desire to drink is always there, Sunshine. Some days it's stronger than others. The bottle is a reminder of what happens when I drink."

"But for seven years you've fought it and won, right?" She'd always tried to look on the bright side of things. Maybe TJ needed some lessons.

"Yeah, but it took more than a few years of fighting to eventually win. You sound like Jim."

"Jim's a smart man. Maybe you should listen. What else does he say?"

"He says I should let it go and move on."

"Good advice. What would you like to move on to?"

Picking up her hand, he stared at her. Her lips curved into one of her winning smiles. She'd been told they were contagious. He smiled back. Yup, guess they were right.

"It sounds ridiculous, but I want a happily ever after."

"You mean like at the end of fairy tales?"

His smile was crooked and his eyes embarrassed. "Fairy tales, chick flicks, romance novels. Sappy, I know."

To keep herself from laughing, she bit her lip. "It's not sappy. It's a nice dream. Like the romance novel I found in your room."

Closing his eyes, he turned partially away from her. "Pretty silly for a guy like me to read them. Can I convince you I'm doing research to see what I want to purchase for the store?"

"Sure, I'll buy that."

"Of course you would, Sara Sunshine. Does anything ever get you down?"

Images of Dan, and his rough hands holding her to the bed, rushed through her mind. Chills ran over her. "Yeah," was all she managed to say.

"Oh, Sunshine, stupid, I shouldn't have said it."

"No, it's fine. I feel kind of silly for all the fuss. It's just…I'm not as experienced as you people who start having sex in your teens."

Sara sat back on the bench, and TJ joined her, his leg touching hers. The shorts he wore today were longer than his basketball ones and thoroughly covered his tattoo.

She ran her hand over his thigh. "How old were you when you got this? It wasn't because of the songs, was it?"

His hand held hers tight. "No, this was a present

for my sixteenth birthday."

"And you didn't have three brothers trailing you for months after."

"Maybe I should have."

"Tattoo at sixteen, having sex at what…seventeen?"

His gaze sought the ocean again. "It was a different world than what you're used to. Abe arranged for my first experience. Thought it would be a great present for when his boy became a teen. He hand-picked the groupie himself. Said she'd show me how it was done."

Wait, became a teen…Was he serious? "You become a teen at thirteen. Please tell me it was later."

He inhaled deeply. "I had no clue what to do and was nervous as hell. I needed to suck down half a bottle of Tequila before I could even get in the room with her."

Bile rose in Sara's throat. How could any parent do that to a child? Teens might brag about doing it young. She had brothers and they certainly talked. But to actually provide your son with the opportunity. No wonder TJ drank and did drugs as a child. He needed to escape from his life.

Thinking of her own lack of experience caused a nervous laugh to come out. "You were thirteen, Luke was sixteen. God knows when Erik did it. And here I am twenty-three and still haven't—"

Shit! She slapped her hand over her mouth. Had she said it out loud?

She stared at TJ. His lips trembled as he tried not to laugh. Damn him. God, how embarrassing. Pulling her knees up to her chest, she hid her face in them.

"Forget I said anything."

"Someone else have a little secret they've been hiding?" His voice sounded closer.

It was the first sign of humor she'd seen in him since they started this conversation. And it was at her expense.

"You can just leave me here while I crawl into my hole."

"It's not a big secret, Sunshine. Darcy said you blush like a freakin' virgin."

Sara snorted in a most unladylike fashion. Darcy would say that. When she peeked through her hands, TJ wore a huge smirk on his face.

"Do I have like this big scarlet V pasted on my forehead?"

"Oh, Sunshine, it would never be scarlet. It would have to be pure white."

Groaning, she lowered her head again.

"What I don't get," TJ mused, "Is how you managed to stay that way. Didn't you say you had a boyfriend for five years?"

"Yes." Robby, and her failings in that department, were not what she wanted to discuss right now.

"In all those years, he never managed to get to home plate?"

God, awkward conversation. "You've met my two big, masculine brothers, right? Well, there's a third one, too, and believe me, Erik makes Alex and Luke look like little girls. He's not much bigger in height, but he's mean and tough. Did I mention he's a Marine?"

"They went out on all your dates with you?"

She glared. "No, but Robby never tried too much."

"Seriously?" His expression said he didn't understand. Did she have to tell him the truth? After sharing so much of his past, it was only fair. But it was damned embarrassing.

She stared at her hands. “Robby wasn’t interested in that stuff with me.”

His confusion upped a notch.

Swallowing her pride, she said, “Robby is gay.”

A little laugh escaped his mouth and understanding lit his eyes. “Okay, now that makes sense. But why go out with you? Was he using you as camouflage?”

“No, we’d been friends since we were kids and decided to go out before my senior year of high school. We dated until my last year in college. It was fun, and we always had a great time. My friends all talked about going further with their boyfriends, but I thought Robby was being a gentleman. And maybe he was afraid of my brothers.”

TJ rubbed the cheek Luke had punched. “Yeah, sure, for a while.”

“We never had much passion between us. I didn’t know, maybe I made him gay.”

Bursting out with laughter, he shook his head, then tucked a strand of hair behind her ear. “Oh, Sunshine, it doesn’t work that way.”

“I know,” she said and rolled her eyes. It had still gone through her mind. “But he only realized, or maybe I should say acknowledged, he was gay after we’d been seeing each other for so long.”

TJ’s face lost the grin. “Listen, you’re either gay or you’re not. It has nothing to do with choice. It’s genetics. You didn’t cause Robby to become gay. Take my word for it.”

Yeah, she believed him, but it was still ridiculous she’d spent five years with the guy and never suspected.

When he'd told her, and they'd broken up, she'd been a little relieved. The spark people talked about getting with the right one was never there. Now, as TJ rubbed his thumb over her hand, it was more than she'd ever felt with Robby as they'd kissed. One tiny touch from TJ sent shivers through her whole body. They settled somewhere low in her stomach, in a place that had no business feeling anything right now.

"Darcy thought I was gay."

Her head whipped up. "What? Why on earth would she?" There was nothing about this man even pointing in that direction. Like she was a good judge.

"Since she's been at the shop, I've never been interested in anything remotely female. Her words."

"Did you tell her—?"

"She knows now."

"How?"

"I started showing interest."

What had he been doing of late? "Who?"

Pressing his lips to her knuckles, he asked, "Think you can figure it out?"

Her? Seriously? Why would someone like TJ, from his extensive background, have any interest in Sara, the librarian from East Podunk, New Hampshire?

Her gaze glued to his face. The man had his first sex at thirteen for Pete's sake. His parents were famous rock stars. He wrote music every singer in the world wanted and lived in a million-dollar house on the beach. Why was he interested in her?

When she looked into his eyes, she saw regret, big and fierce.

"Yeah, but the whole Big V thing," she held her fingers in a V up to her forehead, "has got you freaked.

No biggie. I understand. It freaks me out, too."

"That isn't what I was going to say. But you're right, we're not a good match."

And why not? Anger and a sliver of bravery peeked out, smacking her in the head. "You want to explain it to me?"

Standing, he paced the porch again, then leaned back against the railing facing her. "Part of it is your innocence, Sunshine."

She wanted to object but remained silent, letting him talk.

"But it's my problem, not yours. You heard what my life was like growing up. Sex, drugs, and rock and roll, baby. I don't have an innocent bone in my body. Everything I did was hard and fast and way too young."

The pain in his eyes as he spoke filled her with sadness. His past haunted him, but he hadn't been able to do anything about it. Until recently.

"You're so sweet and innocent, Sara. Like a ray of sunshine fallen to earth, blossoming into this beautiful young woman."

He thought she was beautiful. She shouldn't be happy, especially since he'd told her why they couldn't be interested in each other, but…he thought she was beautiful.

"My past is filled with filth and degradation. I'd only bring it into your life. I don't deserve anyone as wonderful and pure as you."

"What are you talking about? You make it sound as if you're some horrible person."

"Sara, have you not listened to what I've said today? I'm an alcoholic and a drug addict. People with addictions always have addictions. They don't go away.

They might get pushed aside for a short time, but the longing is always there, right around the corner, ready to sneak up on you and bite you in the ass. Usually when you're already feeling down and weak. I can't take the chance of taking you down with me."

Standing, she moved right into his face. "You're telling me I don't get any choice in this matter. And you're still talking about yourself like you're going to start drinking tomorrow. Do you have plans to start drinking tomorrow?"

"No."

"Good. Now think about this. Your friend, Jim, has been sober for over twenty-five years. You've been clean for over seven."

"Seven years, five months, twenty-two days."

His lips twitched, and she thought maybe she was getting through. Her brothers always said she was a tenacious little bug when she wanted something. Did she want TJ?

"Right, so if you can go this long, you can go longer. You have the support of great people like Jim and Mary and even Darcy. And you've got my support. Do I need to reiterate my support is for the TJ Bannister—you, not the child of rock stars—you."

"Or the James True-me?"

Sara swatted at him. "Right, so what's your problem? You don't have one."

His eyes sobered. "The thing is, Sunshine, you're a nice girl."

"Yeah, we've established this whole innocent thing." She placed the V on her forehead once more. "We can deal later. It's not like we're talking about getting married. Just an interest in each other."

Reaching up, he held her shoulders. "The problem is you're a nice girl. Stop, let me finish. I've never dated nice girls, Sunshine. In fact, I've never dated anyone really."

She flashed him a disbelieving look. The man had sex at thirteen.

"Never *dated*, I said. I've had sex with plenty of women. But my typical *date* consisted of meeting someone in a bar, or at a party, finding a convenient place to screw, then saying goodbye. It's different from what you and Robby had."

Shit! Seriously? What a crappy idea of a date. He needed help.

"What I'm saying is I have no idea how to treat a nice girl. I don't know what constitutes a real date, and I have no intention of only using you for my sexual gratification."

Her lack of confidence came flooding back in with his comment. He had sex with girls he didn't even know, yet she didn't turn him on enough to get him in the mood. Maybe she did turn Robby gay.

"Oh, don't go there, Sunshine. I can see in your face exactly what you're thinking. You're as desirable as any woman. I've been walking around with a hard-on ever since you entered the shop. Might be another thing Darcy noticed but had the couth not to say."

Her eyes slipped lower, then whipped back up when she realized what she'd done. She bit her lip, and TJ chuckled.

"Earlier, when you asked me to put gel on your back, you know what I was thinking? I wanted to move my hands to your front and continue caressing and—you get the picture. You're gorgeous and sexy, but you're also a beautiful person, and I would never disrespect you with my crude ways."

Moving to the edge of the porch, she stared at the beach. Freckles got up from her nap and trotted to the stairs, hoping someone would take her for a walk. Maybe she would soon.

"So, we simply remain friends. You can stay here as long as you need to, Sunshine, and I promise to be a perfect gentleman. You're safe with me."

Yes, she *was* safe with him. He'd always treated her well, like he was a gentleman. Sometimes a grouchy gentleman, but he'd always been polite and well-mannered. Even though he said he'd desired her since the beginning, he'd never acted on it.

She understood where he was coming from, but his thought process was flawed. It wasn't that he didn't know how to date, or she was too innocent for his brand of sexual activity. She was, but not the point. He didn't know how to treat a nice girl. And she was a nice girl. Maybe he just needed to be taught. The right ingredients were all there; patience, control, respect for her. She could work with that.

Turning, she planted her hands on her hips. *Take the bull by the horns*, whether he liked it or not.

"Seems to me, you're going about this the wrong way."

"Sara, please don't argue."

"No, you shut up and listen." Her brothers had needed some treatment like this, but she'd never used it on anyone else. It made TJ close his mouth and stare.

"You've got a great opportunity here, and you're not utilizing it. You say you want the happily ever after in the storybooks, right? No, don't answer, just stay quiet."

When he did, her confidence grew.

"Well, to get a happily ever after, you have to do more than screw strange women in bars."

"I haven't done that in a—"

"No talking. If you want the romance novel ending, you need to find a nice girl. Well, I'm a nice girl. Not that I expect you to marry me, but it's a way for you to get experience."

When it looked like he would say something, she held up her finger. "As I said, I happen to have extensive experience dating. The sweet, nice-girl kind of dating. I know you say you're too rough and crude to be able to do it, but I disagree. You admitted yourself you find me attractive to the point of…well, let's just say you find me attractive."

Heat covered her face again. TJ smirked but remained silent.

"Now, even with your finding me attractive, and dare I even say desirable, you still never acted on it. You have self-control, TJ, and you have lots of it. You can be a sweet and caring guy when you want to be. I've seen it. You helped me when I had my whole Dan issue. You gave me a place to stay when you obviously didn't need to. And you even allowed my brother to punch you in the face for completely false reasons."

His expression was suspicious. *Get to the meat of the proposal.*

"So, I'm suggesting…we start dating. I'll teach you how to treat a girl and act on a date. I'm only here until the end of the summer, then you can kiss me goodbye and say good riddance. But at that point you'll be an expert. Perfect plan."

She folded her arms over her chest. “What do you think?”

****

What did he think?

She was crazy. The plan had merit, but he hated the thought of her degrading herself to go out with him. Yet, when she got all spunky in her bossy little sister way, she was adorable. The quiet, little angel layer had been peeled back to reveal a determined young lady. This one appealed to him as much as the innocent ray of sunshine.

She’d teach him how to treat a nice girl, show him the types of places you went to, and what you did on a date. In the bargain, he’d get to spend more time with her. Quality and alone time, without Darcy or Mary horning in on their interaction.

The part of him expecting the worst of people reared its ugly head and poked him in the chest.

“What do you get out of this deal? Because I get dating lessons, but I’m not sure you get anything out of it.”

“I get to spend time with you, TJ. The whole *I like you* thing we’ve discussed ad nauseum. I get to practice dating a little more, too. I hate to admit, Robby and I kind of got into a rut after a while.”

“When would we start these lessons? And should we tell anyone at work?”

She touched her finger to her lip and bit on the end. *Don’t do that.* Not with dating possibilities on the horizon. Maybe he could teach her a few things, too. Nothing intense enough to damage the Big V but introducing her to some new experiences might be fun. If she allowed it.

"We should do the first date soon," Sara declared.

"You're working Friday and Saturday night, so that's a no go."

"For a first date, we should start smaller. Something during the day."

His lips twitched. "Like getting ice cream after a basketball game."

"Yes, exactly—wait, we did that last week. Did you consider it a date?"

He shrugged. "Jim told me I needed to ask you on a date. I just…didn't tell you. Was that kind of a nice-girl date? I had fun."

Her smile turned on full power. "Yes, it was. See, you already know how to do this."

"A fluke. But if we already went on our first date, can we jump to the part where we have sex?"

"It's a good-girl date, remember, good girl."

"What date do we get to have sex?" He grinned.

Her expression turned pensive. "Well, Robby and I dated for five years, and we hadn't gotten there yet, so…"

"Forget I asked."

"How about tomorrow after my morning shift?"

"For sex?" He wiggled his eyebrows.

Sara narrowed her eyes. "No, for our first date. I get off at noon."

"I bet if I spoke to the boss, I could get you off earlier." His eyebrows went up and down again making her laugh.

"No pulling strings. Besides I've got to watch Eddie and Jasmine until Gabby gets there. We can go after. And telling people at work…I don't like to lie, but maybe we don't need to put out a sign either."

“Lunch after your shift is over tomorrow? Where should we go? Someplace fancy?”

“No, a light lunch, casual. Maybe where we can eat outside if the weather’s nice.”

“A few doors down at the café,” he suggested, then glanced at his watch. “We’ve got lots of time before I need to drive you to work. Any suggestions?”

Rolling her shoulders, she grimaced. “I could use another application of Aloe Vera, if you’re willing.”

As he rubbed his hands together, he grinned. “We are officially dating now, right?”

“On my back, TJ, just my back.” Sara walked into the house, her sweet ass swaying temptingly.

TJ followed behind. “Spoilsport.”

Chapter Fourteen

“Where are you heading so early?”

Darcy’s question stumped Sara for a minute. She glanced at her watch. “It’s twelve fifteen. I get off at twelve.”

“I know, but you never actually leave until almost one.”

“I didn’t realize you kept close tabs on my schedule.”

“I keep track of everything around here. It’s a hobby. So, where are you going? You’re rocking the look today, and you even put makeup on.”

The geeky teenage image came back to haunt her. “Do I usually look bad?”

“Hey, don’t freak out, you look gorgeous. You always look gorgeous. It’s why the boss man can’t take his eyes off you.”

Her nerves jumped as she looked around, but no one payed any attention to them. “I wish I was brave enough to do some of the things you do with your makeup, but I don’t know how. I’d probably end up looking like a clown.”

Darcy ran a finger under her darkened eye and made a duck face in the mirror behind the counter. “Nah, you don’t need anything like this. It’s my image, not yours. You gotta do your own thing. Don’t let anyone tell you otherwise.”

"Good advice, Darcy." Peeking in the mirror, Sara finger-combed her hair.

"If you ever want tips on makeup, I'd be happy to show you. Not my stuff, but stuff that would look cool on you."

"Would you? I'd love it."

"No prob. Now, where you going? Looks like a hot and heavy date."

Heat crept up Sara's neck and into her cheeks. "It's just lunch."

When TJ walked past, Sara smoothed her skirt.

Pausing, he said, "I need to check something in my office, then we can go."

Her face grew warmer. Darcy's lips turned up in a grin.

"Lunch with the boss man. Nice. When did this start?"

Sara scanned the room. "This is kind of our first date. I mean, we went out for ice cream on Sunday after his basketball game, but it wasn't an official date."

"He let you watch him play basketball? Pretty intimate, isn't it?"

Was it intimate? They'd been out in public. Darcy pursed her lips, trying not to laugh. "You're kidding, right?"

Raising her eyes to the ceiling, Darcy snickered. "You're such an easy target. Now, make sure you be good to him. He deserves nice things, and I know he likes you, but…he's got a lot of crap in his past. I don't really know what it is, although seeing who his parents were the other day, I can guess. Just remember, people with crap in their backgrounds sometimes have a harder time doing normal things."

Sara stared at Darcy's many piercings and dark makeup. Was she speaking from experience?

"How do you know he has crap in his past?"

Darcy gave a wry smile. "I just know. I'm good at reading people. He's coming down the stairs now. How's your breath smell?"

Her heart raced. "I don't know."

TJ stopped to chat with Mary, so Sara stepped closer to Darcy and exhaled. "Is it okay?"

"You'll do. But this'll make it better if you want." Reaching for her bag under the counter, Darcy pulled out a pack of cigarettes. Sara eyed her skeptically. Until she got a closer look at the carton. They were candy cigarettes.

"Is this what you use when you take your cigarette breaks?"

Guilt filled Darcy's expression, then she made a face. "You don't think I'd smoke real ones, do you? Those things can kill you. And they make your breath rancid. No one wants to kiss a chick with rancid breath. These are minty flavored."

A flicker of mischief flared inside Sara. Reaching out, she grabbed a candy cigarette. "I'll take one. Maybe I can shock the pants off TJ."

Darcy laughed. "I love it when I can corrupt a new victim." Shoving the box of candy in Sara's direction, she said, "Here, take the whole thing. I have tons. I've got a three pack a day habit. I really need to cut back."

After grabbing her own purse, she slid the candy inside. Darcy winked and went to wait on a customer. Why was she nervous? It was a simple date. A casual lunch with TJ. They'd eaten together a lot the last few weeks. But it had never been an actual date. Would this be any different?

****

"Mary, I'll be back in a few hours. I'm just running out for lunch. You've got my cell if you need anything."

"I ran this store before you did. I think I can handle it."

TJ cringed at the maternal tone, but deep inside he loved it. Mary had been more like a parent to him than his own. She'd given him guidance and support and even discipline when he needed it. His success with the shop endeavor was mostly her doing.

"Yes, ma'am. Do you need anything while I'm out?"

"I'm good. Who are you meeting? Jim?"

Mary's curiosity was higher than usual, and TJ suspected it was due to the man she just mentioned."

"No, just a lunch date." Mary's face fell though she hid it well.

"You're all dressed up."

Glancing down at his clothes, he frowned. Nothing special. Khakis and a button-down shirt. Too much?

"Who's the lucky date? Anyone I know?"

Mary's gaze wandered across the store, and she stared where Sara and Darcy chatted. Should he say anything? It would be apparent soon enough when they walked out together.

"I'm taking Sara to lunch."

Mary tried to hide her delight, but her eyes gleamed.

"What? No comment? No push to try and hook us up and get us married."

"If you're taking her to lunch, I don't need to push,

do I? Seems you managed it on your own. Finally. And you shouldn't get married this soon. I'd suggest at least a few more dates."

"You're hysterical, you know that. I'll see you later."

"Take your time."

TJ narrowed his eyes and turned to see Sara walking his way. Holding out his hand, he followed her to the door. When he closed it, he glanced back. Mary and Darcy stood in the middle of the floor whispering to each other. Great. The topic of gossip again. At least they didn't work for a tabloid magazine.

Placing his hand on Sara's back, he guided her down the sidewalk. "Have you been here before?"

"No, I haven't done much exploring on the Cape."

"We'll have to change that. I've lived here for six years. I'd love to take you around and show you some of my favorite places."

"Sounds great."

The café was busy, but he'd called the owner earlier and mentioned he'd be by. Carlos said he'd save them a table for lunch. And true to his word, they were shown to a small table outside, with an umbrella, in a private corner of the patio. When they had iced tea sitting in front of them, TJ leaned forward and ran his fingers over Sara's.

"How am I doing so far, teach?"

Her gaze wandered over the outside terrace and the tall, frosty glasses. "So far, I'd give you an A plus. You pulled out my chair and everything. Where'd you learn that? A former teacher?"

Was there a touch of jealousy in her voice? "You're the first person to give me instruction of this kind, Sunshine. And the chair thing I got from movies. I try and brush up if I can, but there's nothing like field work to understand how it's done."

The waiter came, took their order, and TJ leaned back in his chair. "What's the first lesson?"

Pink slid onto her cheeks, and he quietly chuckled. Yesterday, she may have been bold as brass when she'd suggested this, but he'd guess she was as nervous as he was.

She leaned forward. "Usually on a first date, you get to know the other person, if you didn't already know them."

"Well, we met about a month ago. Does that count as knowing each other? What did you and Robby do?"

She shrugged. "Robby and I met in first grade."

"You've never done this first date, getting-to-know-you thing."

"I've dated other guys." Sara huffed, then her shoulders slumped. "Well, one other guy. And it was only one date."

"Was this before or after Robby?"

"After."

"And you did the getting-to-know-you thing?"

"Yeah." Her voice sounded resigned. "Unfortunately, he wanted to get to know my friend, Shelbie, more than he wanted to get to know me. She's the one who set us up on the date."

Were the guys in her town idiots? Couldn't they see what a precious gem she was? He patted her hand, then rubbed his thumb over her soft skin. "I'm glad it didn't work out. Left you available for me."

Taking a sip of her drink, she looked up as the waitress brought their plates. The roast beef sandwich piled high with meat and cheese made his mouth water, but he waited for Sara to have her lobster roll set in front of her before he took a bite.

“Tell me about life in Squamscott Falls, New Hampshire.”

Sara took a delicate bite of her roll, chewed, then sipped her tea. “There’s not much to tell. It’s a small town, and most people know each other. I’m guessing it’s different from where you grew up.”

“I grew up in Los Angeles. Hardly small town. But everyone wanted to know my parents.”

They spent the next hour swapping stories from their childhood. He enjoyed hearing about her brothers, and how she used to always get in their way. And the jokes they used to play on her. It reminded him of what he and Sonni had done to keep themselves occupied on long road trips when their tutor was too busy with one of the stage crew. He shared some of these with her, glad to be able to remember them with fondness.

When the sun moved across the sky, he decided they needed to go. He didn’t want to. Sara was a joy to talk to, nothing new there. They strolled to the store but went around back to his truck.

“You know there’ll be a million questions from Mary and Darcy, but I’d like to put it off as long as possible. If I drive you home, Mary should be gone by the time I get back and hopefully I can avoid Darcy. Maybe she’ll be on one of her infamous cigarette breaks.”

Scooting into the truck, Sara dug in her bag, pulling out a pack of cigarettes. She opened it and took one out. What the hell?

“Don’t tell me Darcy corrupted you. You know

smoking is terrible for you."

Sara put the cigarette in her mouth but sucked on it instead of lighting it. When they stopped at the light, he took a closer look. "A candy cigarette? It looks like the brand Darcy smokes."

Her eyes twinkled. "Yep, it is what Darcy smokes. She gave them to me."

He shook his head. Should have known Darcy was too smart to inhale real smoke, especially considering how health conscious she was. Sara continued to lick and suck on the cigarette as they drove, distracting him to no end. It was gone by the time they pulled into his driveway.

After helping Sara out of the truck, he walked her to the house, unlocking it. Her eyes skittered around the yard as she twisted her hands together.

"Now what, nice girl?"

Her teeth sank into her bottom lip. "I think this is where you say you had a great time and want to see me again. Or you can lie and say it was fun, and you'll call me, but then don't."

He pulled her closer. "I had a nice time, Sara. I'd love to do this again. Can we set a time, so you can't back out?"

She laughed. "I had a great time, too. I'd love to see you again." So nice she played along.

"What do you suggest for a second date?"

Closing one eye in thought, she said, "We could do a picnic on the beach. What day do we both have off?"

"Sunday. I know you clean at night, and I have my game at two, but we could do it after my game. I'll make sure we beat them fast. It'll be easy if I have motivation."

"I like being motivation."

"Now, how do we say goodbye? I'm pretty sure it's not by having sex." Even if he really wanted to.

She glared. "No, but even good girls can get a small kiss on the first date. This isn't a historic novel where one kiss will ruin my reputation."

Stepping closer, he slid one hand around her back to draw her near. This kiss needed to be out of this world. It wasn't something he ever spent much time on. Not when he'd had willing women ready for the good stuff. But he wanted this kiss to mean something.

Reaching up with his free hand, he tucked a strand of hair behind her ear. Her eyes were wide and anxious. As nervous about this damn kiss as he was? As he caressed the side of her face, he lowered his mouth, stopping just before it touched hers. Her breath wafted across his lips, the minty scent pleasant and tantalizing.

Touching his forehead to hers, he kept their lips apart, inhaling her strawberry fragrance and closing his eyes. He'd remember this moment forever. Finally, his mouth skimmed across her lips, like a dragonfly touching down on the water. Light and sweet, playfully pulling back, then drifting near again.

A soft whimper floated from her throat, and he was lost. The desire to devour her was strong, but he didn't want to scare her. This teasing he found more erotic than anything he'd ever done. He didn't want it to end.

His tongue stroked along her bottom lip, and another small cry escaped. Opening his eyes, he found hers closed, and her face filled with rapture. Her open lips were an invitation to plunder, but he didn't. Couldn't. This innocent kiss was absolutely perfect, and he wanted nothing to ruin it.

He pressed his lips to hers again, softly, gently, lovingly, running his tongue over her top lip, then back to her bottom. Timidly, her own tongue poked out, and he nearly lost it. His arms drew her tighter as her hands slipped into the hair at the back of his neck, clutching and pulling.

Delicious swirls of heat radiated through every cell at the connection between them, but he held back. How could this one chaste touch be more passionate than the dozens of sexual encounters he'd had? He was drowning, going under for the third time, yet he had no desire to even try and reach the surface. Only wanting to prolong this contact.

The ache in his groin radiated through him. How had something as simple as a kiss gotten him so hard and ready? But Sara wasn't ready, no matter how her lips tried to convince him otherwise. It was time to stop.

Reluctantly, he eased back, still holding her flushed body next to his aroused one. Her breathing was as shallow and fast as his, and he allowed them time to recover before he released her. Her dreamy eyes focused on his face, and the tiniest of smiles lingered on her freshly-kissed lips.

"A simple goodbye kiss, Sunshine. Nothing more for today."

"Simple, yeah." Her voice was throaty and deep, making him crave her lips again. "Certainly, nothing to ruin the young maiden."

TJ stepped back before his arms decided to grab her and ravish her. "I'll see you later if you're still up when I get back tonight."

Sara's tongue slipped out and ran across the lips he'd just worshipped. Could she taste him there? As he backed toward the truck, she only nodded, still standing at the door. When he pulled onto the street, her hand touched her lips. Lifting his own, he waved. God, what an incredible experience.

Yes, she might not be ruined, but for sure, he definitely was.

****

"How was lunch with the boss man?"

TJ peeked from the back room to see Darcy talking with Sara as they rinsed out coffee pots at the sink.

Blushing, Sara lowered her eyes. He loved how natural it was.

"Nice. He's easy to talk to now he's not grouchy all the time."

Darcy's eyes grew mischievous. "I think he was grouchy because once you started working here his pants were always too tight."

Sara's head turned quickly, and she glanced around. He took a step back, so he couldn't be seen. This wasn't a conversation he should allow to continue as he hated to be gossiped about, but he wanted to know what Sara truly thought.

Silence made Darcy chuckled. "I notice there's no denial. He came back here in a happy mood. Did he kiss you?"

Sara busied herself drying the pot. "Yes."

"And?" Crossing her arms, Darcy stared.

"And he kissed me."

"Don't ever become a writer. Your skills with details are seriously lacking."

Sara glared at Darcy. "What exactly did you want to know?"

"How was the kiss? How did it feel? That man has

some pretty hot lips. I was wondering if he knows how to use them."

Sighing, Sara nodded her head. What did that mean? Did she like the kiss? Was she going to answer?

"You ever been kissed before, Sara?" Darcy cocked her head to the side.

"Yes, I had a boyfriend for five years. We did lots of kissing."

"And the boss's kiss?"

"Why are you interested, Darcy? You must go on plenty of dates."

"I'm participating in girl talk. It's what friends do. And yours is much more romantic than Hunter and her stories of boinking a different guy every night."

Sara stepped closer to Darcy. "TJ's kiss was better than anything Robby ever gave me. I honestly think if he hadn't stopped, I would have melted into a puddle on the ground."

Warmth spread inside at Sara's words. He'd almost melted, too. It was why he'd stopped, yet it was the last thing he wanted to do. Darcy's expression turned mushy and emotional, something he'd never seen in his employee before. Who knew she had a romantic streak? The words Sara spoke made him feel that way, too.

Backing further into the room, images of the kiss surfaced. Over the last few days they hadn't spoken much about the date other than saying they'd both enjoyed it. Work had been busy for both of them.

His gaze drifted out to the store where Sara was setting up Story Hour. The children swarmed around her, vying with Freckles to get in her lap. He didn't blame them. Her lap seemed a great place to be.

"Day dreaming, boss?"

Darcy stood in the doorway with her pack of candy cigarettes. How had he never noticed they weren't real?

He cleared his throat. "I had a local artist ask if we could stock some of her watercolor paintings. I'm thinking where we might put them."

Darcy's dubious expression let him know he hadn't fooled her. Not much did. She may not have a college degree, but she was smarter than most people he knew.

As Darcy walked toward the back door, he gathered the invoices he'd set on the table. Before she opened the door, she paused. "Did you enjoy your lunch date, boss? Sara did."

"Yes, I did. I like Sara, and for some strange reason I think she might like me, too."

Darcy raised one eyebrow. "You're a pretty nice guy, boss. Cut yourself some slack. Apparently, you have mad kissing skills."

"One kiss, Darcy, that's all." No way he wanted rumors flying around. "Don't—"

"Chill, boss, I know. There wasn't time for you to do anything else unless it was 'Wham, Bam, thank you ma'am'. A kiss was about all you could've done."

"Good to know you're keeping track of these things."

"I know you respect Sara too much to take her out for a quick screw."

"Darcy,"

"I know, I know, this is a *family friendly* store." She used her fingers to make air quotes.

"It is. But you're right, I respect Sara a lot. She deserves respect, from all of us."

Darcy pulled a cigarette from the box and stuck it in her mouth. "You won't get an argument from me. I respect the hell out of her."

As she left for her break, he shook his head. The girl was an enigma, and he was glad he wasn't responsible for trying to figure her out.

Taking the invoices, he climbed the stairs to his office, lingering a bit longer than he should at the top to watch Sara with the kids. It was something he could do all day. But then he'd never get any work done. It was the exact reason he hadn't wanted to hire her to begin with. Now he was glad he had.

Around noon, he shoved aside his paperwork and went downstairs to spend a few minutes with Gabby and the kids before they left. Sara was coaxing Freckles to the back room, most likely to take her out for a walk. After saying goodbye to his cousin, he headed to the back room himself. Sara looked up as he entered.

"I thought she might need to go out."

"Probably." He stepped closer until Sara was backed against the wall. "I was wondering about this dating thing."

Her eyes opened wider. "What about it? You don't want to do it anymore?"

"Oh, I definitely want to do it." Exactly what he'd like to do would scare the crap out of her. Her skin would flush crimson from head to toe. "About the kissing…I know it's okay to have a kiss at the end of the date, but what about if you happen to run into the person at some other location? And it's not an official date. Can you kiss?"

"Sure. Robby and I didn't always have official dates. Sometimes we simply hung out, either alone or with friends. And we'd kiss, although not in public. Not my thing."

His mind wandered to some of the places he'd screwed girls. Maybe not completely out in the open but certainly not private. Something he'd never do to Sara. He respected her far too much. And was dying to kiss her again.

Placing his hands on either side of her head, he leaned in. Her pupils dilated. "This isn't exactly public. Would it be okay to kiss you now?"

Glancing around, she gave a quick nod.

He leaned in, loving how her eyes closed, and her mouth opened slightly. *Slowly.* He skimmed his lips across hers, then stroked his tongue around the edge of her mouth.

When she lifted her hands to his chest, he pressed closer to imprison them. He slid his fingers into her hair and caressed her cheek with his thumb. How he'd love to explore her silky skin further. This was hardly the time or place.

"You might want to get a room or at least go to your office." Darcy's sarcastic voice was like plunging into the Arctic Tundra. He reared back as Darcy walked through the door, putting her cigarettes back in her purse, then sauntering past without saying another word.

"I should, um…take Freckles out." Sara's cheeks colored as she fiddled with the dog's leash.

TJ walked closer. "I'm sorry, Sara. I shouldn't have kissed you back here."

She only smiled, her embarrassment showing. When she started to open the back door, Darcy poked her head in and held up Sara's purse. "I think your phone is ringing. Did you want to get it?"

"No one calls me when I'm at work." Grabbing her

bag, she dug around for her phone. Her eyes widened when she looked at the screen, then at him. “It’s my mom. I’m sorry. I need to make sure there isn’t a problem.”

Sara walked out the back door. “Hello. Mom, is everything okay? I’m at work.”

Her expression grew concerned as she walked away from the building. He stayed in the doorway in case she needed him.

A few minutes later, she lowered the phone, but didn’t move. Taking Freckles’ leash, he walked outside. When she turned, tears glistened on her lashes.

“Sara, what happened?” He put his hand on her shoulder, lowering his face to hers.

“My mom wanted to let me know my brother, Erik, is coming home tonight.”

“That’s a good thing, right? He was overseas in the Middle East.”

“Apparently, he was in some bombing almost a month ago and has been in the hospital since then. He wouldn’t let them call my parents.”

“What’s his condition?”

She shrugged. “My mom didn’t know. Erik was the one who called to say he was flying into Hanscom Air Force Base this afternoon.”

Rubbing her shoulders, he tried to ease her tension. “If he called, it means he’s fine, Sara.”

“I know. But he asked them to bring the SUV because he’s using a wheel chair. Something about his leg being messed up. He wouldn’t give Mom any more details.”

He pulled her into his arms. “Did you want to see him? Assure yourself he’s okay?”

Sara's liquid eyes gazed at him sadly. "I do, but I don't have any way of getting there. If I take a bus, it'll take all day, and I can't leave now since I have to work at The Melody Tent tonight. And I have to be back here to clean tomorrow night."

Pressing a soft kiss to her lips, he said, "Don't worry about the cleaning. The dirt isn't going anywhere. If you want, I can drive you home tomorrow morning, then bring you back here if everything seems all right."

"But tomorrow's your day off."

"Right, so I don't need to worry about the store."

She leaned against him, her cheek on his chest. Perfect.

"I can't ask you to drive two hours to bring me home, then back."

"You're not asking, Sara. I'm offering. I'd be happy to take you home to see your brother. Gives me a little alone time with you. Not quite the beach picnic I expected, but we'll still be together."

Tilting her head, she looked at him. "You don't mind? I haven't seen Erik in a long time, and I'm kind of worried."

"I'll go to the early mass, and we can leave right after. That's not too late is it?"

"It's perfect. You're perfect. Thank you so much."

Perfect? Hardly. But with Sara holding him, he felt much closer than he'd ever been before.

Chapter Fifteen

"So, this is downtown Squamscott Falls, New Hampshire?"

Sara pointed to the water rolling under the bridge they were crossing. "This is the Squamscott River. The actual falls are up river a short distance."

She checked TJ's expression. What was he thinking? It was nothing like L.A. The downtown was barely a half mile long and consisted of some old brick buildings holding a variety of stores.

"It's nice, Sara. Quiet and homey."

Okay, not disgusted, unless he was being nice. Which he obviously was, having driven her all the way here on his day off.

She pointed again. "At the band stand, you need to take a left, before the town green. My parents live just up the street."

Following her directions, he maneuvered through the light traffic. It was nothing compared to the Cape, but for Squamscott Falls anything more than five cars was a lot. Except weekends, when shoppers from neighboring Massachusetts and Maine came to the boutiques and novelty stores downtown.

After the town center, they passed the campus.

"That's Brookside Academy. It's a private high school, and it's where my mom works as a bookkeeper. Luke got a full scholarship to go there because he's brilliant."

TJ glanced at her briefly. "You didn't go there?"

"No, it's wicked expensive. Unless you're rich or a brain like Luke, you go to the public high school. I didn't mind 'cause all my friends went there. It's down that road, about a mile." She pointed to the right after they'd passed the academy. "And we're taking the next left."

They pulled onto the short street.

"Our house is the blue Victorian on the left. My Uncle Nick and Aunt Luci live in the one on the right, with my cousin, Greg and his son, Ryan. Mrs. Mazelli lives in the Victoria in between."

TJ pulled into the driveway as Alex exited his silver Volvo in front of them. Jumping out of the vehicle, she walked around to greet her brothers. Her mom came down from the porch and hugged the boys.

"Hi, Mom. How's Erik?"

"Oh, sweetie, you managed to make it back. I'm so glad." Her mom's gaze flicked to the house, then back to them. "Erik will be fine, I think. He's just a little banged up right now, and he's dealing with some…issues caused by his accident."

"It was a bombing, Mom." Alex, succinct as always.

Her mom simply nodded and took a deep breath, then pasted on a smile as she hugged Sara.

"Hi, sweetie, who gave you a ride?"

Gasping, she spun around to look where TJ lounged against the truck, waiting casually. She ran to him and grabbed his hand, pulling him toward her mom and brothers.

"Mom, this is TJ Bannister. He owns the bookstore

I work at."

TJ held his hand out. "Nice to meet you, Mrs. Storm."

"Oh, please, call me Molly. We're not very formal around here. These are two of my sons, Alex and Lukas."

The men shook hands. "We met when they came to visit Sara a few weeks ago."

TJ looked at Sara and his eyebrow rose. "Tell me what time you want to be picked up, or you can call if you decide to stay."

Taking his arm, her mom began walking toward the house. "Nonsense. We've got lots of food, and you're more than welcome to join us. I'm sure we'll have friends and neighbors dropping by throughout the day."

The site of TJ being led off by her mom made her chuckle. Until her brothers each grabbed an arm and held her in place.

"Have you had any more trouble from the slime bucket who attacked you?" Luke's voice was cold and deadly.

Sara sighed. They meant well, and she did love them. "No, I haven't even seen him. TJ got all my stuff while I waited in the truck."

Alex hugged her as they walked up to the house. "We never got any word about where you moved. Do you have a new address for us?"

"And is it safer than where you were?" Luke chimed in.

"I'm still staying in TJ's guest room. He took you seriously when you said I couldn't stay anywhere less than perfect. He's just as anal as both of you and won't let me live in some of the places I've found." Not likely she'd be telling them she hadn't looked very hard. Living with TJ was fun. And his kisses…yeah, best not think about his kisses when with her brothers. They could sniff out a crush from ten miles away.

Alex stopped on the front porch. "He's still being a perfect gentleman?"

Shaking them off, she rounded on them. "Don't embarrass me with him here. I swear I will exact revenge."

When she entered the living room, her mom was showing TJ the pictures scattered around. A formal portrait was the focal point of the room, and TJ examined it. Unfortunately, the picture had been taken when she was about thirteen and in the height of her geekiness. Many of the pictures surrounding it weren't much better. The Wall of Shame.

"Mom, please, TJ doesn't want to see old pictures of us from ten years ago. You need something newer. This one is majorly embarrassing."

Her gaze went to the picture of her with new braces, thick rimmed glasses, and her hair in stupid banana curls her mother had insisted on. Like she belonged in the Brady Bunch. And TJ, the guy she was currently crushing on, stared at it, grinning.

"You look adorable. Most of the girls I knew at that age looked like they were twenty-five. The hair, makeup, and clothes looked ridiculous on them. Kids need to be allowed to be kids. No one should force them to grow up too soon."

Her mom smiled in approval, but she didn't know where TJ's comment came from. Didn't know he'd had sex so young and was already living the life of an adult in many ways.

"Mom, where's Erik?" The reason she'd come was to see her brother and assure herself he was okay, not dwell on the difference between her past and TJ's.

When her mother smiled sadly, her heart raced. How bad was it? Her mom pointed to the back of the house. "He's on the deck with your grandparents."

Touching TJ on the arm, she said, "I'll be out back. Don't let my mother pull out any old photo albums. You'll be here for a week."

Racing past the dining room and through the kitchen, she pushed open the screen door. Alex and Luke had gone down the hall and beaten her there. They stood near the railing in front of what she assumed was Erik. Her Gram and Gramps, her father's parents, sat on the cushioned bench under the shade of the umbrella.

"Sara, honey," her grandmother crooned. "We haven't seen you all summer. It's nice you managed to get back here to see your brother."

Her grandparents got a quick hug and kiss, then she focused her attention on Erik. Alex and Luke stepped back, and there was Erik, sitting in a wheelchair near the railing.

"Erik, I missed you so much." She launched herself into his arms. He attempted to rise, but she pushed him back. It didn't take much, which surprised her. Erik had always been solid and strong. "Don't get up. It's not like you ever did when we both lived here." Could her teasing take the grim look off his face?

His arms tightened, almost desperately. Tears welled in her eyes, and she pressed kisses to his cheek until she had her erratic emotions under control. *Don't let him see you cry. He'd hate it.*

"Missed you, too, Sagey. How's the Cape?" Stoic and in control, as always. Diverting attention from himself and thinking of others.

Slipping into the chair beside him, she reached for his hand. As she told him about her jobs, she took a closer look at his injuries. The most obvious was the left leg, bound tightly around the knee in a huge brace and resting on an extension of the wheelchair. Erik wore shorts, and his other leg looked fine. His arms held some scratches and scars but were still muscled and toned.

Her heart dropped when she saw his handsome face dotted with pink, tender wounds. The worst, on his right temple, started at the hairline of his short, sandy-blond strands, then sliced through his eyebrow, giving him a rakish appearance. Another ran along his jawline and under his left ear.

Erik must have noticed her concerned expression because he squeezed her hand tighter. "I'm fine, Sara. It's nothing you need to worry about."

"Yeah, and maybe with you banged up and ugly now," Luke joked, "Alex and I can get some girls looking at us instead of simpering after you all the time."

When Erik laughed, it was real. He'd be okay. They'd all make sure of it.

The back door opened, and her dad came out carrying a tray loaded with a large pitcher and glasses. Rushing over, Alex gave him a hand setting it on the table. Erik's arms pushed on the side of the chair to rise, but Sara stroked his hand. "I think you can let others do a few things for you now. You'll be good as new in no time."

His eyes turned cold, and his jaw tensed as his gaze roamed the yard. Would he be good as new? Or was there more to this injury? Would Erik be forthcoming or simply blow it off, so he didn't ruin his tough guy image?

"What's with the leg? Mom said you were in an explosion."

"Yeah," he said, his voice low as his gaze flickered to Gram and Gramps. "Fractured pelvis and the knee cap is shattered. I had a few surgeries to glue it together. Kind of like Humpty Dumpty. Luckily, our King's horses and King's men did a much better job. They needed to attach a metal plate in there to keep everything from shifting."

"But it's going to be fine, right?"

Avoiding her question, and her eyes, he gave a half-hearted shrug. "Can you get me some iced tea, Sage?"

She jumped up and returned with a glass in seconds. "Can I get you anything else?"

"Hmm, let me think. I could get used to this kind of service."

She glared but stayed close. "I'm glad you're back. I missed you."

"Sara," her mom interrupted. "Why don't you introduce TJ to everyone? He was nice enough to help me get the fruit and vegetable platters finished and out here."

Sara rose and took TJ's elbow. "This is my friend, TJ Bannister. He owns the shop I work at in Hyannis." It didn't seem right to introduce him only as her boss, but she didn't want to get into the fact she and TJ had started dating. The whole story behind why was kind of strange.

She pointed around the porch. “These are my grandparents, Hans and Ingrid Storm. My Dad, Peter, and this is my brother, Erik. He’s the one who liked to put frogs in my bed when I was little.”

Erik chuckled. “I didn’t realize she liked frogs and would breed them in the back pond. She constantly collected polliwogs and kept them in a jar in her room.”

TJ’s eyes sparkled with delight at the information.

“I wanted to make sure they were okay until they could get to a bigger water source. One year the pond dried up, and it took me forever to lug water to keep filling it so they didn’t dry out. I still lost so many of them.”

Luke sighed. “God, the crying was unbelievable. You’d think someone had killed her puppy.”

“I remember you dragging buckets of water back there, too, Lukas Storm. Seems to me you didn’t want them to die, either.”

His mouth twisted. “I only helped so I didn’t have to listen to you whine all day.”

Sara stuck one hand on her hip, but the tender look in Luke’s eyes told her he hadn’t minded doing it. He’d been as worried about the pollywogs as she’d been.

As TJ greeted each person politely, he kept his arm tight to his body where her hand was tucked. She didn’t mind. His insecurity was endearing.

“I’m going to get the grill started,” her Dad announced. “Alex, I’ll need your expertise, please.”

“Dad, I can help,” Erik stated, his face tight. “I can stand, you know. I only need the chair so my leg is elevated while I’m sitting.”

"I know, Erik, but you're the guest of honor. You have the day off."

Luke grinned. "Yeah, and if Alex burns the burgers and dogs, we can rag on him."

Alex looked skyward. "Oh, like I don't get enough grief from all of you about my neatness or organization."

When Alex and her dad went down into the yard to get the grill ready, everyone else grabbed some finger food from the table to nibble on. Her gram asked TJ about his store, and while they chatted, Sara got a plate of fruit and veggies for Erik.

Erik took the plate but pulled on her hand so she'd sit. Leaning in close, his gaze wandered to the others. "So, your boss, huh? Awfully nice of him to drive you home for the day."

"Yes, he's a nice guy. And a friend, too. He knew I wanted to see you and offered to bring me."

"That's it?" Erik looked at TJ. The quick glance TJ threw her didn't go unnoticed.

"Why do you ask?"

"Just wondering. He keeps looking over here to make sure you haven't taken off."

She rolled her eyes. "He doesn't know anyone here, and he wasn't even planning on staying."

"Do you like him?"

Erik's words caught her by surprise and snapped her head back from where she'd been staring at TJ. How to answer that question.

"He's a great boss and a good friend, so yeah, I like him."

"That isn't what I mean, Sage, and you know it." Erik narrowed his eyes. "You and Robby broke up over a year ago. You haven't gone out with anyone since then. You aren't still upset over his revelation, are you?"

"No, I'm fine. Robby and I are still friends. I know now that's all we ever were, and I'm okay with it."

Erik flicked a carrot stick in front of her face. "You haven't answered my question, yet. You can't keep your eyes off the guy, Sage. You got a thing for him?"

Heat rose up her neck and spread through her face. Blushing had always happened far too easily. "Maybe a little thing." No way she could lie to her brother, he knew her too well. "But I'm only there for the summer, and he's way out of my league." This was true but not for the reasons she hinted at now.

Erik's voice softened. "Why do you say that? You're beautiful and smart enough to get any guy you want. My only concern is if he's good enough for you."

"He grew up a big city boy in Los Angeles. I'm a little too country bumpkin."

"He said that?"

"No, he'd never say anything mean. He's a nice guy. But I'll only have to leave him behind when I get my big break in the music business."

When she wrinkled her nose, Erik laughed. "You still have those big dreams, huh? You keep reaching for them, Sagey. Don't let anyone take them away from you." He was serious.

This was the first real support she'd gotten from her family about her singing career. Exactly what had Erik gone through, and how much had it changed him and his perspective on things? More questions rose in her mind, but her brother wouldn't reveal any secrets. Nothing too personal anyway.

Sara made sure to sit near TJ during lunch to deflect any personal questions that came their way. Holding his own, he made small talk like a pro, charming her parents and grandparents. Even her brothers had lightened up grilling her for information on their relationship. As the afternoon slid by, Erik relaxed, too. The family hadn't treated him any differently, except maybe getting him food and beverages so he didn't have to get up. The teasing, banter, and lighthearted conversation was exactly like it always was.

Her uncles, aunts, and cousins dropped by. Some only came for a quick visit, while others brought more food and settled in.

Her cousin, Sofia, found her in the kitchen, refilling the iced tea pitcher.

"The gorgeous hunk out there is your boss?" Leaning in close, Sofia hugged her. "Can you get me an application for a job?"

Sara laughed. "You're an interior designer. What would you do in a bookstore or coffee shop, Sofie?"

Putting her hands on her hips, she exuded attitude. "Anything he wanted me to, sweetheart."

Sara looked skyward and shook her head. She missed seeing her cousin so often. Sofie was Sara's age and her sister, Leah, a few years older, but the girls had always been close.

"Seriously, Sara, the man is hot with a capital H O T. Do you have something going on with him? Your mom wasn't sure, but she did say she liked him and would approve."

"She did?" That was good, wasn't it? Her mom approving of TJ. Would she still if she knew of his background? Probably. Her mom didn't hold grudges and believed in second chances.

"Mm hmm. Now answer my question, dear cousin. Your tall, dark, and handsome chauffeur? Is he doing more than driving you around?"

Busying herself adding ice to the pitcher, she hoped her cousin wouldn't see the color washing over her face. It didn't work. As Sofie sidled closer, she crossed her arms over her chest.

"Ooh, there is more. So, what kinds of places has he been taking you? And how far have you gone?"

Sara groaned and made a face at her cousin's double entendre. Glancing around, she made sure no one lurked nearby. "We've only been on one date so far. But I haven't told anyone here yet. We were supposed to have a day on the beach today, then Mom called yesterday about Erik, and TJ offered to drive me home."

Sofie's face softened. "Sweet. So, he's a good guy? And he doesn't have the same problem as Robby?"

Closing her eyes, she snickered. "Yes, he's a super nice guy and no, believe me, he isn't anything like Robby."

Her eyes lit up with mischief. "Is he a good kisser? You did let him kiss you, right?"

The memory of TJ's lips on hers made her stomach flip. "Incredible. Oh, my God, Sofie, it was like nothing I ever imagined. He was so sweet and gentle and didn't push. I almost wanted to cry."

Sofie hugged her again. "I want to cry with you. I hope it all turns out the way you want it to, sweetie."

At her words, Sara paused. How did she want it to turn out? She didn't want to come back home and live with her parents. She loved them, but she needed more independence. Could she stay working at *Tea and Tales* even though she was only summer help?

"Why haven't you told anyone you two are dating? Is it a big secret for some reason?"

"No, but you know I moved out of Kayla's, right?"

"Oh, my God, yes, and I am so sorry." Another hug. "Alex told me the details and no, I didn't tell my folks or yours. I never met Dan. Kayla wasn't seeing him when we roomed together a few years ago."

"It's not your fault. You didn't know, and you managed to get me a place to stay for a short while. Now I have someplace better."

Sofie eyed her suspiciously.

Lowering her voice, she said, "I'm staying at TJ's house in his guest room. Alex and Luke know but think TJ has no interest in me and vice versa. If they knew we'd started dating, all hell would break loose. My folks don't even know I've moved or what happened. I told my brothers I'd exact revenge if they tell on me. But they might not care if they think TJ's got a thing for me. You know how overprotective they are."

Sofie sighed. "I don't know how you do it with three older brothers. I only have Greg and he's bad enough. Wants to make sure I don't make the same mistakes he did."

"I hardly think you'll get a girl pregnant."

Sofie rolled her eyes. "No, but I suppose I could get knocked up ."

"Luckily, we have supportive families who love us no matter what."

Sara thought about TJ and his lack of a loving family. He and his cousin, Gabby, got along well, but he'd told Sara they'd only connected a few years ago, once he'd moved here and managed to get his addiction under control.

"I should get this outside." Sara lifted the full pitcher. "Mom will be wondering where I got to. And I have to make sure she isn't grilling TJ or telling him stupid little Sara stories."

"Okay, but keep feeding me details of you and hot stuff. I need to live vicariously through someone. My love life is stuck on stall."

"I will." Sara walked outside to see TJ and Erik discussing the finer points of grilling. Alex hadn't burned the burgers, but Erik still gave him a hard time about them not being juicy enough.

"What are your plans now, Erik?" she asked, settling next to him in a chair.

Erik glanced over at their grandparents. "Since I won't be able to get up and down stairs for a while, Gram and Gramps said I could move into the Maine beach house. It's all on one floor, so I don't have to adapt anything."

Her mom's brow furrowed. "What will you do up there? It's a two-hour drive from here and not exactly close to anything? What if you need something?"

"Mom, I'm twenty-nine years old," Erik pointed out. "I think I can take care of myself."

"When do you plan on moving there?" As she always did when her children were concerned, Mom looked worried.

"Next week maybe. I need to get the house ready. I have another little announcement, and it might come as a bit of a shock."

As she glanced around the deck, her family all

stared at Erik, anticipation in their eyes. All except TJ who looked at her, his expression concerned.

"I'm adopting two children from Kandahar. A three-year-old boy and one-year-old girl. They were in the collapsed building with me, and I got to know them pretty well. Their mother didn't make it, but before she died, she asked me to bring them here and give them a better life than they'd have there."

"Two children? And little ones? Erik, kids are so much work. You can't even walk yet."

Erik's face tightened. "I know, Mom. They won't be coming for a few weeks. There are all sorts of health clearances and paperwork to be taken care of first. I have to show I have a place for them to stay before they'll release them to me. I got to know these kids while we were trapped, then at the Military Base in Germany once we were rescued. They know and trust me. I made a promise to their mother. I won't go back on it."

"You care for these kids, don't you, Erik?" Sara asked. Her brother wasn't one she'd immediately think of as a kid person. Heck, he'd been in the military since college, but he was a good man and would make an excellent father.

"Yeah, I do. I think some peaceful time spent near the ocean will be exactly what we all need."

No one argued. They had no idea what Erik or the kids had been through.

Alex broke the silence. "Mom, Dad, should we make our announcement, too, since it seems to be a good time?"

When she turned to face her parents, they looked slightly guilty. Her dad cleared his throat.

"Your mother and I have decided we want to move to one of the smaller houses at the fifty-five plus community near the hospital. This house is too big for us now you're all going in different directions." His gaze landed on his eldest son.

"You're selling the house?"

Her emotions fluctuated. It wasn't fair for her parents to hold onto it just so she could visit. Making it in the singing world was her goal, even if she had to move to another state to do it. But what if it didn't happen? It wasn't like opportunity had knocked on her door lately. Unless you counted Jerry Tonaway. His business card was burning a hole in her purse. Could she get him to help her without having to participate in the bedroom interview TJ hinted was a requirement?

Alex moved near and placed his hand on her shoulder. "Don't worry, Sage. You can still live here. I plan on buying the house from Mom and Dad. I'm going to move my business here with an office in the front parlor and my drafting area in the back parlor."

Luke cleared his throat. "With OCD Alex buying the house at least Mom'll know it'll stay neat and clean."

Alex smacked Luke on the side of the head, something he'd been doing to his little brother forever. It broke the tension, and they began to discuss details. Sitting back, she absorbed the information. Everything was changing so fast, like she spun inside a kaleidoscope.

TJ's hand crept into hers and squeezed tight, reminding her he was here.

The tingling in her fingers traveled all the way to her toes, yet held her in place, making her feel grounded.

She smiled up in silent thanks.

Chapter Sixteen

The smile on Sara's face couldn't hide the turmoil in her eyes. TJ shouldn't have been here for this family conference, but Sara's hand wouldn't let go now he'd taken it. It was nice to feel needed. Something he hadn't experienced since Sonni had been alive. And during the last few years, he hadn't been there for her, especially when she'd needed him most.

He watched as Sara's family chatted about the moves and changes happening, yet they all supported each other unconditionally. Molly's concern was for Erik moving to Maine and raising two children. Yet instead of trying to talk him out of it or telling him he was an idiot, she started listing the supplies he would need and how they could get them all to Maine. Alex and Luke came up with names of people who had trucks and could help move everyone. Even their grandparents suggested people who might be available to help Erik with the children.

"You know that sweet, little girl, Tessa Porter, still lives next door," Ingrid informed them. "The Millers left her the house when they passed. Well, after she took care of them during their last years, it's only right. She works from home and might be available to help you when you're at the restaurant, Erik."

Sara laughed, and his insides lifted at the sound. "Little girl, Gram? Tessa's a year older than I am."

Luke smirked. “Which makes you an infant, Sagey.”

Sara glared back, but there was no venom in her stare. None of these people harbored any ill will or anything even remotely negative toward each other. They might tease and taunt, but the love they had for each other blazed brighter than the hot sun beating down on them right now. What would it be like to be part of a family like this? Would he ever belong to something this loving and supportive? Could he keep up the pretense long enough, or would he be found out for the damaged soul he was?

“All right, my butt’s getting numb in this damn chair,” Erik complained a while later. “Think any of you wimps could give me a hand getting down the stairs? We can go shoot some hoops in the driveway.”

Alex made a face. “You’re going to play basketball? Seriously?”

Erik’s lips twitched. “No, you and Luke are. I’m going to watch. And maybe TJ here can play, too. You said you played b-ball.”

Nodding, he put his hand out for Erik to take. The man had pride but also needed some help getting up. Erik settled his good leg on the floor, and Alex moved in behind him while Luke grabbed the crutches. Erik maneuvered pretty well, and between them they managed to get over to the driveway where a basketball hoop was attached to the side of a shed.

Ducking into the small building, Luke returned with the ball, then tossed it to him. After dribbling a few times, he pushed it through the air. It slid through the hoop without even disturbing the net.

“Yes!” Erik pumped his fist in the air. “I want this

guy on my team."

"I thought you weren't playing," Luke complained.

"I obviously can't run around, but I get a special proviso. I shoot without you gorillas surrounding me."

Alex and Luke groaned but agreed. Luke passed Erik the ball, and he lobbed it in the air right to the rim of the net. It rolled around the edge for a few seconds, then dropped inside.

"I am still the king!" Erik shouted and almost fell over in his excitement. The three of them tensed but didn't move to help him. A man needed some dignity and pride.

They continued to play for a while, and more people stopped by to welcome Erik back and mingle with the crowd. It turned into a party but one unlike anything TJ had ever been involved with. The only similarity was the beer sitting in a cooler Luke dragged near them.

Alex pulled a Sam Adams from the plastic container and popped off the top, offering it to TJ. The sound of the fizz called out to him, and the amber liquid waved hello. He gritted his teeth and shook his head.

"I'm good, thanks."

Luke narrowed his eyes. "You don't drink?"

How to answer this question so he didn't spill his little secret. Would they expect everyone to have a beer with them?

"Do you want me drinking if I'm driving your sister back to the Cape later?"

"Oh…no," Alex admitted. "Smart boy. How about you, Erik?"

Erik snarled. "Wish I could, but I'm on some heavy meds right now, and they don't mix with alcohol too well."

Luke grabbed the ball from Erik's hands and dribbled along the driveway. TJ noticed Sara standing in the backyard with a group of people. One was her cousin, Sofia, who had been introduced to him earlier, but there was a young guy next to her, hugging her with too much familiarity for TJ's liking.

"Oh, hey, Robby's here," Alex said, dribbling. "He's got his new boyfriend with him."

Erik and Luke looked in Sara's direction, and TJ watched as the young man gestured enthusiastically toward the cousins. It was fairly obvious his feelings toward the girls wasn't romantic in nature. Especially when his arm wrapped around the shoulder of the guy next to him, pulling him close.

Crossing his arms over his chest, TJ continued to stare. "Seriously, none of you guys figured out his little secret during the five years Sara dated him? Kind of hard to believe."

The brothers all wore guilty expressions.

"She told you, huh?" Luke said.

Alex kicked at a rock on the ground. "Well, maybe we had an inkling. But we figured Sage was safe since he wouldn't take advantage of her."

"We would have mentioned it, eventually." Luke grimaced. "Once she was a little older and not so naïve and innocent."

"You know she thinks she turned him gay."

"What?" All three men stared, horrified.

"Why would she think that?" Erik asked, his gaze following his little sister and her ex-boyfriend as they chatted.

"Like you said, she's incredibly innocent and

doesn't see herself as desirable enough to keep a man interested."

"Stupid," Alex grunted. "Do you know how many guys we needed to strong arm away from asking her out or putting the moves on her? Way too many."

Easy to believe. Sara was a beautiful young woman, and he couldn't imagine too many guys would look past her. Basking in her sunshine warmth was where he wanted to be.

Shuffling in his direction, Erik mumbled, "You're not jealous of Robby, are you? They're only friends. That's all they'd ever really been."

TJ snorted with an *are-you-kidding-me* look. "Him? No, I'm not jealous of *him.*"

Erik's sly expression made TJ realize what he just admitted or at least hinted at. Shit. He didn't need Alex and Luke figuring it out, too. They'd have Sara moved out faster than a speeding bullet. And he needed to avoid said bullet right now. He liked Sara in his house.

Pulling the ball out of Alex's hands, he dribbled along the hot top, then threw it toward the net. It bounced off the backboard, and Alex grabbed the rebound. The game was back on, and TJ had successfully diverted attention from his interest in the youngest Storm sibling. Erik smirked at him every now and then during the rest of the game, especially if he caught him staring at Sara, but he never tried to warn him off. It was encouraging.

As the sun drifted toward the horizon, TJ finally managed to get Sara nearby to ask what she wanted to do.

"Are you staying? I'd be happy to come get you in a few days if you wanted to spend more time with your family."

When she placed her hand on his arm, heat seeped into his skin where her fingers made contact. "You're sweet. Thank you. But I think Erik's going to be fine. He's got some issues to work out, I can tell, but he won't be sharing them soon. It's the kind of guy he is. We can leave whenever you want."

"Take your time and say goodbye to your family first, Sunshine. I'm in no hurry." Glancing around, he noted no one in earshot. "I may have to stop before we hit the highway so I can kiss you. My control isn't as strong as it should be. You look too damn sexy in your cute sundress."

Sara's breath hitched, and her eyes twinkled. "We should go now. I'll say goodbye quickly."

She kept her promise, and they were soon heading south. As the miles flew past, he thought back on the day. It had been fun, yet he'd felt a bit like a party crasher at times. Her family had treated him great and welcomed him as one of their own. But she'd kept their dating a secret.

Erik suspected, at least a little bit, and didn't seem bothered. But he probably didn't realize Sara was living with him at the moment. Maybe once Alex and Luke filled him in, he'd have a change of heart. If they continued dating, would she eventually tell her family, or did she not want them to know?

He'd seen a little taste of family life today and it was something he could definitely live with. The question would always remain; would he ever truly be good enough to fit in and be accepted?

****

"Your reward for being such a trooper, Sunshine."

Sara gazed up as TJ handed her a chocolate frappe he'd whipped up in the blender. The thick ice cream and milk concoction looked heavenly after the last few busy days. They'd come back from New Hampshire on Sunday night, and the July Fourth celebrations were in full gear on Monday. Today had consisted of lots of restocking and taking care of the leftover tourists who hadn't departed yet.

As she closed her lips around the straw, she shut her eyes. "Mmm!" The crash of the incoming waves was like music as she leaned back against the porch swing.

"This is perfect."

TJ settled next to her, his own frappe already half gone. Using his foot, he pushed against the floor to make the swing glide back and forth, easing her tension.

"Thanks for putting in extra hours yesterday and today, even though you weren't scheduled."

"Happy to do it. I'll need some time off for the Summer Star contest next week. I hope poor Hunter feels better soon. It's terrible how she caught the flu in the middle of the summer."

TJ growled, "The flu, seriously? Save the sympathy for when I kick her sweet, little ass out of the store."

"You think she has a sweet, little ass? I always thought it was kind of big."

Chuckling, he placed his empty glass on the porch floor. His gaze was territorial. What did he want from her? But more importantly what did she want from him? They'd shared more kisses the last few days but had kept things low key. Each time his lips touched hers, Sara's stomach did flips and back turns, and her legs liquefied. She wanted to explore more, but she was afraid at the same time. The phrase 'too hot to handle' might apply here, and she didn't want to get burned. Or did she?

"The only ass I'm interested in, Sunshine, is the perfect one sitting next to me."

After she took her last draw on the straw, TJ removed the glass from her hand, setting it next to his. He pulled her against his body, draping her legs over his.

Her heart beat double time. His heartbeat wasn't any slower. His lips touched her hair, and she looked up and smiled.

"Thanks for not tossing *me* out on my ass. I know you didn't plan on letting me stay here this long."

He kissed her nose. "I'm not in any rush to have you leave. I've gotten used to you being here, and I think I kind of like it. Especially, when I have you in my arms."

As he lowered his head, she closed her eyes. His kiss electrified her as always. It was sweet and gentle, but her nerve endings tingled, sending a current all the way to her toes.

Slipping his hand under her baggy sweater, he caressed the bare skin of her back. Her breath grew shaky as longing curled inside. What kind of magic spell did TJ have over her to elicit such desire and behavior? She wanted to crawl further into his lap and melt into him.

"Your skin is like satin. If you want me to stop, you need to tell me."

No, don't stop. If he took his hands away, she

might expire right here. “God, you aren’t wearing a bra. Did you do this on purpose to torment me?”

“No,” she whispered against his lips. “They aren’t comfortable.”

His hands moved from her back around to her sides, and Sara’s breath hitched. Sinking her hands into his hair, she touched her forehead to his. His eyes gleamed wickedly as he nipped at her lips.

When he cupped her breasts in his hands, colors swirled behind her eyelids, and the world tilted.

A groan escaped her lips, and TJ’s mouth drifted lower along her jaw line, then to her throat. More sensations assaulted her, sending shocks to her inner core. Dropping her head onto his shoulder allowed his lips to roam freely over her neck.

When he shifted, she panicked, thinking he was going to stop. But he only adjusted her position so she sat with her back to his chest. He brushed her hair aside and nibbled on her neck again. At one spot, electricity surged through her body. What the heck was happening to her? Goosebumps covered her arms, and she shivered.

“You like that, huh?” His chuckle tickled her ear, and she could only nod weakly.

His lips returned to torment her, but his hands crept under her sweater and caressed the skin of her stomach. They shifted higher, and Sara held her breath. Would they keep going? Should she tell him to stop? She’d allowed Robby to touch her before, but he’d only squeezed hard, and it hadn’t been pleasant. TJ’s gentle caress sent tremors rushing through her.

He was doing something with his hands, causing all sorts of activity in her stomach…and lower. His fingers stroked the underside of her breasts, then he tilted his head so his scratchy stubble rubbed against her cheek.

"You're gorgeous. I could sit here and touch you all day long."

"Okay." Her voice shook. How would he take her reply? *Keep going. Don't stop.*

He laughed softly in her ear. His lips whispered along her cheek and temple. His hands continued tempting her, enticing her to give in to her desire. This was so new. How could TJ have the ability to make her want to do far more than she'd ever done?

"God, you are perfect."

"I'm not very big." Right now, Sara wished she had boobs like Hunter's. TJ would like those better.

"You're exactly the right size, Sunshine. Don't ever think otherwise."

"I thought guys liked big-breasted women. They all go to places like Hooters and strip joints, right?"

His arms held her in a reassuring fashion. "I can't say they don't. But feel this." He cupped her weight. "They fit perfectly in the palm of my hands. Anything more is a waste. This is what pleases a man. The way you react to my touch…you have no idea what it does to me."

She wiggled her rear against him. "I might have some idea."

TJ groaned. "You're killing me. Just lean back and let me enjoy this."

She did as he asked. TJ skimmed his hands from her breasts to her rib cage and down over her stomach, then back up. When his fingers flicked her nipples, she twitched in his arms. The sensation sent shock through her. And when he pinched the tips, heat flowed all the way to her core.

"The little sounds you're making are driving me wild."

"I'm sorry."

He stilled his hands. "Don't be sorry. I love knowing I'm the one causing them."

One of TJ's hands drifted lower, lingering near the waistband of her shorts. Heavenly. Her insides twisted and between her legs started to throb. She'd explode if she had more. But she wanted more. Such conflicting desires?

Her fuzzy mind registered when TJ's hands slid inside her shorts. God, she wanted this, but was she ready? She'd been on sensory overload for the past hour, and she needed to pull away. Her body begged to let him continue.

Common sense overrode her desire, and she pushed off his lap and stood, her breath shaky. "I'm sorry. It's getting late. I should go to bed. It's been a busy few days."

Smiling pleasantly, he kissed her hand. "Good night, Sunshine. Sweet dreams."

Sara pressed a light kiss to his lips. "You, too."

She practically ran into the house and up the stairs. What had she been thinking allowing TJ that kind of intimacy? What happened to her giving him dating lessons? Tonight, she'd been the one on the receiving end. And the lessons she'd learned were scorching and hot. There had been no nice about them.

As she readied for bed, she imagined TJ's hands on her again. She was twenty-three years old. It was about time she let herself experience what could happen between a man and a woman. She liked TJ. He was honorable. He'd never consciously hurt her. Maybe while she taught him how to date a nice girl, she could be learning other things from him. Tonight's lesson had certainly been an eye opener.

Chapter Seventeen

"My breakfast isn't ready yet?"

Sara turned quickly from rinsing out a glass at the sink as TJ entered the kitchen.

Making a face, she opened the fridge. "What would you like? Eggs, pancakes, French toast, or we could go light and have cereal?"

Breakfast wasn't what he wanted, not looking at Sara in her night clothes. Delicious as any food. Her snug shorts exposed her long, trim legs, and today's tank top had small buttons down the front begging him to undo them. If they asked nice enough, he might have to oblige.

"Cereal is good. I'm having lunch with Jim, so I don't need much now."

As Sara got the milk, he pulled out some sugary cereal she liked. They grabbed bowls and spoons, then sat at the counter. After pouring his cereal, he reached for the milk at the same time she did.

"I'll wrestle you for it." Her eyes twinkled.

"Or, I could just take it from you."

"You could try."

Leaning in, he aimed his mouth straight for her delectable lips. They opened for him, and he took what she offered. God, he wanted more. He wouldn't take it. Not yet. She needed time, and he'd give her whatever it took. A few nights ago, he'd moved too fast and scared her, so he needed to take it slower. But he couldn't stop kissing her. It was becoming yet another addiction.

Her grip loosened on the container, and he pulled it away, grinning. "See, no wrestling involved."

No reply, simply heavy breathing. *Love the reaction I get from her.*

"Here." He poured the milk onto her cereal, then put it away. When he returned, she'd managed to recover, though her cheeks were still pink.

Conversation was general as they ate. They'd gone to an early movie last night, before she needed to clean, and TJ had gotten another lesson in dating. Sitting next to Sara, he'd watched the movie and simply enjoyed her presence. Yes, he'd been allowed to put his arm around her shoulder, but nothing else had happened during the date.

His control had been shot to hell by being the epitome of a gentleman. The awareness of her sitting so close had caused him to miss most of the movie. The good night kiss had lingered longer than any previously, and sleep had been long in coming. Too many thoughts of Sara swirling through his mind. But the fact he'd enjoyed simply being with her had him confused. You got together with a woman to satisfy a need. Now he found maybe he had other needs. And they didn't include sex.

With breakfast over, TJ followed Sara as she rinsed off the bowls and put them in the dishwasher. Moving up behind her as she turned the water off, he trapped her against the sink. Sometimes, he still thought about sex, especially with her gorgeous ass swaying in the skimpy shorts.

He brushed aside her hair and planted kisses along

her neck and shoulder.

"I'm sorry if I scared you moving too fast the other night."

Turning in his arms, she placed her hands on his chest.

"You didn't scare me. I think I scared myself. The lack of experience thing. It got a bit overwhelming. I was afraid if I didn't stop…I wouldn't."

"I'll never do more than you want me to. I hope you know that. Seemed like you enjoyed it."

She rested her head on his chest. "I did."

"Good, you're supposed to enjoy it."

He gently tugged on her hair until she raised her face to his. He kissed her nose, forehead, cheeks, and finally her lips.

He feasted on those. She was no slouch in the kissing department. Jealousy reared inside thinking about the five years she'd spent with her ex, and all the practice she'd obviously gotten. And the poor bastard hadn't even known what to do with her. He knew.

Slipping his hands under her sweet ass, he lifted her onto the counter. Her eyes widened in surprise and apprehension, yet she didn't release her hold on him. She trusted him. That fact delved deep into his soul, making him want her even more.

"Are you prepping me to serve for lunch?"

God, yes! "I wouldn't mind a taste here and there."

Pressing his lips to her shoulder, he nibbled down her arm and back again. He stroked her neck and throat and let his fingers drift down toward the edge of her top.

"I like the view from here." His fingers drifted lower over the rounded fabric, and when they found the peak, her reaction was obvious.

When he flicked his thumbs over the tips, he reveled in the shudder going through her. “I love how I can make your nipples tighten so quickly.”

Crimson washed over her and seeped from her face down into her chest.

“I’m sorry. Did I embarrass you? My background’s a bit crude. I’m trying to clean it up.”

“I’ve overheard tons of guy talk from my brothers, even though they try and shelter me from it.”

The buttons on her shirt screamed out again. Reaching for the first, he slipped it through the hole. The second and third quickly followed. Sara watched mesmerized but didn’t object. When the final button was released from its confinement, TJ slowly separated the sides. He’d touched her a few nights ago, but it had been dark, and she’d still worn her sweater. Now she was displayed in majestic brilliance for his viewing pleasure.

“Beautiful. And absolutely perfect.”

Caressing her breasts, he played with the nipples making them hard and erect. They weren’t the only things getting that way. But he wanted to give her pleasure. It was his only thought at the moment. When had he suddenly become such a giver in this department? Pleasing someone else had never been a priority in the past. All he’d needed was to get a woman ready enough, so he’d never bothered much with foreplay. It hadn’t been important.

He wouldn’t get his release, yet he still wanted to make Sara feel good. As his hands kneaded their prize, his lips got jealous and soon joined the fun. When his tongue circled one nipple, Sara gasped, her hands digging into his hair. She didn't pull away, actually held him tighter. So he couldn't escape? It was the last thing he wanted to do.

Her soft moans incited him to continue worshiping her. Sucking harder on her nipple, he almost fell over when her legs slid apart and wrapped around his waist. Her grip never loosened on his head.

He caressed the soft skin of her back and wanted desperately to slip his hands inside her shorts to grab hold of her delicious ass. A few days ago, she'd been frightened off by something similar. *Slow. Go slow.*

"What are you feeling, Sunshine?" She liked it yes, but what was she thinking? "What do you feel when I do this?" He sucked on a nipple, then swirled his tongue around it sensuously. Why did he suddenly care?

Breathing deep, Sara looked at him still nestled between her breasts.

"It sends shock all the way down to—"

Her eyes opened wide like she'd realized what she was about to say.

"Down where? Down here?" He stroked the back of his hand down her stomach, then brushed his knuckles against the apex of her thighs.

Her knees tightened around him, and she rested her head against his, nodding weakly.

"It's supposed to feel good there. I'm not sure you're quite ready."

When he moved his hand, her hips shifted like they wanted to follow.

"You don't want to?" Her voice was unsure.

"Oh, there are lots of things I want to do to you, Sunshine. You have no idea. You'd be shocked if I actually told you what they are."

Her shoulders straightened, and her expression grew determined. "Shock me."

Easing away, he checked her expression.

"Tell me, don't do anything, just…tell me."

Heat ran through his blood. "The good girl wants the bad boy to talk dirty to her. Huh?"

She sucked on her bottom lip, and he almost flew over the edge right then. The movement alone had him twisted in knots. Of course, her shirt hanging open may have contributed as well.

"Tell me."

He skimmed his hand up her front and slowly buttoned her shirt. No way he could talk dirty while he stared at her naked chest. Well, he could, but he might explode.

"I'd love to continue sucking on those perfect nipples. See your head thrown back while I flick my tongue over them and lick you. It makes me rock hard."

Her eyes never left his, but she was stained from head to toe with color.

"Then I'd carry you to the kitchen table and lay you down to touch every last inch of your skin. I'd slowly peel these ridiculously skimpy shorts off you and end the teasing they've been doing for weeks."

A few more buttons. His pants grew tighter every second. But Sara seemed mesmerized by his words.

"Then I'd spread these gorgeous legs and taste you." He rubbed his fingers against her shorts again. "You'd be so ready for me. I can feel the heat from you even now." After rubbing against her panties one last time, he removed his hand.

Closing her eyes, she sucked in her bottom lip. "Is

that it?"

"Not by a long shot, Sunshine. After I teased you with my lips and brought you right to the edge, I'd wrap your legs around me, thrust inside, and make you mine. I'd—"

The words, *I'd fuck you until you screamed,* formed in his head, but he couldn't say them. Not because she was a virgin and wasn't used to such things. Not because he wanted to treat her with more respect, although he did. The act had never been anything other than screwing or fucking or some other vulgar term. It's how he'd thought if it. Always.

Suddenly, the idea of having sex with Sara was more than just the act of shoving his cock inside her. With Sara, it would be so much more.

"Then you'd what?" Her voice was soft and hesitant. But the curiosity in her eyes bore into him.

"I'd make love to you for as long as you could take it."

After slipping the last button into its hole, he stepped back. His hands shook, so he shoved them in his pockets. The realization of what he'd said haunted him.

He helped her off the counter and straightened her straps. She looked lost.

"Did I do something wrong?"

Her anxious tone stabbed into his heart.

"No, you're amazing." He ran his thumb down the side of her face. "I need a few minutes to get myself back under control. You're potent stuff."

After kissing her on the forehead, he walked toward his room, leaving her standing in the kitchen looking so damned sexy and desirable. But he needed to get away from her and think.

He'd said he wanted to *make love* to her. It was a term he'd never used before, ever. Not how he thought of it. But when he imagined doing it with Sara…it couldn't be called anything else.

****

"How long has it been?"

Jim's question usually irritated TJ, but suddenly he looked at things differently.

"Seven years, six months today." Puffing his chest out, he inhaled like he'd won a race. Jim eyed him curiously.

"Twenty-five years, nine months, and sixteen days. What's going on?"

TJ shrugged, trying not to grin. "What do you mean?"

"You always get surly at that question even though you know it's coming. Today you seemed eager to answer it. Any special reason? Or maybe I should say any special person causing the change?"

He couldn't lie to Jim. The man had done more for getting him to straighten out his life than anyone else. When things got tough, he'd kept TJ from falling back on his old habits.

"Maybe there is."

"The pretty blonde who works for you? The one living in your guest room? You missed our game this weekend because of her."

He took a bite of his fried clams. "I told you her brother returned from Afghanistan, and she wanted to see him. I offered to drive her."

Nodding, Jim dug into his seafood plate.

Past the picnic tables, the traffic on the street was

busy. It had been lunch time for the kids when he'd left. Too many curious eyes had looked in their direction, so he hadn't given Sara the kiss he'd wanted to. Their morning make-out session was still fresh in his mind. It had been so much more than kissing.

His revelation came back to haunt him. What did it mean? He didn't have any experience dealing with emotions during sex. It had always just been sex. Why had it changed?

His sigh echoed in the air as he stared at his plate, wondering if it would provide any answers.

Jim chuckled. "You've got it bad, my friend."

"What have I got?" He honestly needed to know.

"You want Sara. It's pretty obvious."

"That's just it. It's more than wanting to have sex with her. I want to do stuff for her. Be with her. Make her happy."

"You do stuff for lots of people. Makes you a nice guy."

"It's more than that. I want to keep her smiling. It's never been enough for me in the past. I always needed something out of it, too."

As he took a few more bites of his lunch, Jim grinned.

"It's nothing new. You care about her in a way you've never cared about any other woman. Most people call it love."

His face pinched. Love? Ridiculous. He'd loved Sonni, and she'd left him. He thought he'd loved his parents, but they'd never been there for him. Love was fleeting. It didn't stick around.

"I don't have much luck with love." No need to elaborate. Jim knew his history.

"Maybe your luck is about to change. Or maybe you've changed."

Had he changed? Over the past ten years, sure. No more drugs and booze for the last seven, and he'd made a whole new life for himself. People respected him, and he was successful. Not only as James True, the songwriter, but as TJ Bannister, owner of a thriving business in a popular Cape Cod town. It felt good.

Now he had Sara. But did he have Sara? Yes, it was obvious she desired him. But was it because she'd never had real passion before? Or because she cared for him, too?

"Sara's helped me see things differently. Her sunny disposition brings out the good in me."

"Maybe you need to keep her around. What are her plans?"

"I don't know. She wants to be a goddamn singer. She's good enough to make it if she had the right contacts."

Jim's shrewd eyes stared him down. "But you won't help her with *your* contacts?"

Pain lanced through his heart. "No, I won't. How can I set her up to become everything I used to be? They'd destroy her. I can't be part of that."

"You could go with her and make sure she doesn't get destroyed."

Ice trickled through his veins. Go back to that life? The one that almost killed him? Had killed his sister?

"You know what that life did to me, Jim. I'd be right back where I was ten years ago. And maybe Sara would be the one I'd find dead from an overdose." The image of Sonni's lifeless body flashed through his mind. "No, I can't do it."

"Isn't she only here for the summer? What then?"

It was a question he'd asked himself. "We've got over a month left. But she doesn't have a job to go back to. Maybe if things keep heading in the same direction, she might consider staying."

"Have you mentioned it to her?"

"Are you crazy? We've only been dating a week. Give us some time to get to know each other."

"What does she know about you?"

"Lots."

Jim looked surprised. Yeah, he rarely shared his past with anyone.

"Your addictions and family history?"

"She's okay with it. Sounded like you, saying it's in my past. It's her damn optimistic outlook on life."

"There's nothing wrong with optimism. You should try it sometime."

Jim was right. He should look on the brighter side of things. Yet optimism had never been his strong suit. But with Sara in his life, he might finally have something to look forward to.

Chapter Eighteen

"Just up ahead is what I wanted you to see."

Freckles nosed around in the bushes as Sara followed the tree-lined path along the hill overlooking Quisset Harbor. It was another date after TJ's basketball game. He and Jim had actually lost. Only by a few points, but TJ had spent more time looking at her and not the ball. Jim had laughed and shaken his head.

"Stay home next time, Sara, huh?" he'd joked. "Then TJ can give all his attention to the game."

There'd been some good-natured teasing from the other guys as well, but she hadn't minded. The game had been quick, and they were now alone on a trail in what TJ called The Knob.

"Right through there," he directed and held aside a branch so she could pass. It led to a large clearing with a massive tree in the center. Hanging from the tree was a rope swing with a board tied to the end as a seat.

TJ's eyes twinkled with mischief.

"You brought me here to swing? There are swings at the high school we just left."

Taking her hand, he walked toward the tree. "But this is the coolest tree to climb, and it's a *tree swing*."

Like a kid in a candy store. Should she tell him she'd had a tree swing growing up? Nah, why spoil his fun?

"This is better than a swing set?"

Looking down, he scratched Freckles on her head. “I don’t know. I haven’t been on it.”

“I thought you’d been here before?”

“I have. I just never tried the swing. I didn’t want anyone catching a grown man swinging all by himself. It seems kind of lame.”

“But it’s okay for me to appear lame?” She glared, trying to appear stern. *Fail.* He was so darn cute.

“I’ve seen young couples here swinging before, and for some reason it’s okay. But a guy, by himself, no, not cool.”

Her lips twitched, and she crossed her arms over her chest. “So, you didn’t actually want to be with me. You only wanted to go on the swing, and I’m here to keep you from looking stupid.”

His eyes got wide. “No, I want you here. I thought—”

“It’s okay,” she interrupted, brushing a lock of hair from his forehead. “I’m teasing. I take my cousin’s boy to see Disney movies, so I don’t look ridiculous going by myself. But I also like being with Ryan.”

He glanced around the clearing. “We don’t have to go on the swing.”

“No, I think it’d be—”

“We could climb the tree.” His lips curled into a smirk.

The tree. It was big and twisted and had a massive branch jutting out low to the side, then turned back up. It would be kind of cool to climb it. He tried to hide it but was chomping at the bit to do it.

“Have you climbed it before, or it’s too uncool for a solitary guy?”

“I’ve climbed it. Later in the day, like now, so it’s

not as busy. Most people come earlier to enjoy the beach."

TJ tugged her hand and pulled until they were standing near it. Grabbing hold of a branch, he swung up onto another one nearby. She followed. They spent the next hour climbing up the tree and sidestepping onto the low twisted branch. Then one would bring the rope over while the other managed to grab hold, step onto the board, and fly over the ground. It was a blast, she had to admit.

"I feel like I'm ten again," she confessed as the swing slowed, and TJ helped her off. Freckles wandered back from searching the area.

"I wish I'd known you when I was ten." TJ's voice was wistful. "You and Sonni would have gotten along great."

"What was she like?"

Taking her hand, he led her away from the clearing where another path opened up to the ocean on one side. He called the dog to follow. "Sonni was amazing. She was the best sister and friend anyone could have."

His smile dimmed. He needed happy memories.

"Tell me what she was like. What did she like to do? What was she good at?"

"Sonni loved to read. She read to me all the time. It's one reason I love books so much. It reminds me of her. Makes me feel closer to her." He touched his chest where his cross rested. Had it been Sonni's?

When she leaned in to kiss his cheek, he kissed hers back, then led her along the path. The large wooded area they'd come from tapered dramatically, and the ocean flanked them now on both sides. Up ahead the land rose in a series of steps formed by planks inserted in the ground. It was so narrow they had to walk single file until they reached the top.

The view was breathtaking. Water in every direction glimmered as the light of the sun danced along its surface. The waves crashed on the shore, joining the cries of the seagulls.

The small hill they were on was rounded and slightly larger than the strip of land they'd crossed. This was why it was called The Knob.

Reaching for her hand again, TJ pulled her close to his side. Tingles skittered up her arm each time. Would it ever stop? Hopefully not.

"This is breathtaking."

"Like every time I look at you, Sunshine. I figured with you here…nothing could be more perfect."

Her heart melted. He'd said things like this before, but she had a hard time believing it. Too many snide comments from nasty teenagers in high school had damaged what little self-esteem she'd been able to build up. He was slowly helping her believe in herself again.

Wrapping her hands around his arm, she burrowed into his shoulder.

"You were telling me how Sonni loved to read."

A smile appeared on his face, and his eyes grew warm. He stepped back and settled them on the small bench overlooking the bay while Freckles sat at their feet.

"She always had her nose in some book or at least had one nearby. She basically taught me to read."

"You didn't learn at school?"

"Not a traditional one. My parents traveled so much we weren't in one place long enough. We had tutors most of the time. Unfortunately, my dad liked to hire sweet young things with big boobs and a tiny moral code. If they weren't giving my father some one-on-one instruction, they were giving lessons to one of the crew."

"I'm sorry." She rubbed her hand up and down his thigh. He slung his arm around her shoulder and placed his other hand on hers.

"Keep it up, Sunshine, and my moral code will shrink to nothing. And don't be sorry, I always had Sonni growing up. We didn't need anyone else. We had each other."

It was sad his sister was the only one he could turn to. The girl had only been a few years older but had taken on the responsibility for her little brother's happiness. Perhaps she felt guilty TJ had become so wild. Enough to start taking pills? Lord knew TJ had enough guilt eating away at him.

"When we were younger," he said, gazing off into the horizon, "Sonni loved reading The Hardy Boys and Nancy Drew Mysteries. She'd read them to me, and we'd go off looking for some grand mystery. On the road, we'd pick someone from the crew or hotel and pretend they were a criminal trying to smuggle diamonds into the country or selling secrets to some foreign government. We'd sneak around, following them, taking notes, and trying to find clues."

"It sounds like fun. Luke and I used to go creeping through the woods behind our house, pretending we were lost in some jungle and had to survive on our own. We'd build a little shelter and store food and stuff for us to eat. It was only sticks and leaves, but we thought we were cool and clever."

"My parents would plunk us in front of the TV

most days to keep us quiet. But Sonni created her own games or read. She got me interested in reading, too."

Looking at the sky, he chuckled. "Well, at least until she discovered romance novels. It's where we parted ways with our choice of books."

"But you read them now."

"They remind me of her. Sonni believed someday she'd be rescued by a white knight on a fancy steed and whisked away to a beautiful house with a white picket fence, and they'd live happily ever after."

"Not you?"

"My parents had a revolving door on their bedroom. There are no white picket fences in Los Angeles. But Sonni lived vicariously through those books. She truly thought she could have it all. I guess since moving here and seeing the slower pace, I've started to wonder if it could happen."

Sara turned to face him. "It can, TJ, it can. My grandparents have been married for close to sixty years. They had three sons, my Dad, my Uncle Nick, and my Uncle Kris. They're all happily married with kids, too."

"And the next generation?"

"Well, Nathaniel and Greg have gotten rocky starts, but they could still find true love someday."

"What about you, Sara, what do you want?"

Why had he called her Sara, not Sunshine? Was he asking for a reason or simply curious?

"I want my own home and family someday but not yet. I want something different for now. A singing career and to be noticed and respected for being me, Sara Storm."

His mouth tightened and he loosened his grip on her hand.

"Sonni had a beautiful voice. She could have been bigger than Celia. She had that much talent."

"She didn't want to sing?" Oh, to have those connections.

He shook his head. "She wanted the simple life. Our childhood was constant frenzy and traveling. She wanted to stay in one place."

"I've been in one place my whole life. It's kind of boring. Especially when it's a small town like Squamscott Falls. You've seen it. Not much happens there."

"How about when you went to college?"

"The University of New Hampshire is only thirty minutes, so I commuted. Mostly to save money since I was the fourth Storm kid to go through college. Many of the kids from town also went there." Same old, same old.

"What about you? You were in Boston. Must have been exciting. A lot more exciting than anything in New Hampshire."

As Sara said this, his jaw clenched, and she realized maybe excitement wasn't what TJ had been looking for or needed at the time.

****

TJ looked out over the ocean at the rolling waves and setting sun. The crash of the surf and the hiss of the wind should have been relaxing, but his body stiffened. Sara craved excitement. Exactly what he was running from. Had been running from for over ten years.

"I went to a college in Boston because my mother had some connections there, and it was the only place to let me in. I told you about my tutors, and I pretty much tanked my SATs. But Abe and Celia made a sizable donation to the music department and voila, I was accepted."

"You majored in Business?"

"I took some music classes, too. Mostly to satisfy my parents who paid my tuition. The Music Comp class was a breeze.

Sara laughed, and his heart thawed even more. It shouldn't. He had to keep his wits about him and his heart protected. Her desire was to go out and do all the things he'd already done. The things that had nearly destroyed him. Pushing her away would be smarter, yet he wanted to pull her closer. His fractured heart was in danger of breaking off into small pieces. Could he take a chance with her? Damn, he wanted to, but fear and the pain of Sonni's death crept through him.

Snuggling into his arm, she looked up with her hypnotic blue gaze. *Totally lost.* Maybe she had to be the one to pull away since he was too weak. Would more of the truth head her in that direction?

"My college years were hardly ideal. I didn't start when everyone else did."

"Why not?"

Time for the unvarnished truth. She knew of his addiction but didn't know the nitty gritty details of how bad it had been.

"Sonni died in the spring right before I turned eighteen. I needed to get away, and my grandparents were willing to let me live with them…with a few stipulations. I needed rehab before they'd let me in the house.

Her body stiffened, but she listened. Freckles must have sensed the tension because she sat up and placed her head in Sara's lap.

"I went to a residential facility because they didn't trust me."

Her lips turned down, her eyes sad.

"They had good reason not to trust me. I was a mess. Even more after I'd lost my sister. But I didn't want to stay in LA. I was afraid I'd end up just like her. Sonni had done so much for me, there was no way I was going to let her down. So, I cleaned up my act."

Sara nodded acceptance he didn't deserve.

"I tried to anyway. The first rehab was the hardest because I'd been on drugs and booze for so long."

"The *first* rehab?"

"Yeah, six months the first time. I was okay for a while, but the stress of classes started weighing on me. There were parties everywhere I turned. I thought one drink or joint wouldn't hurt. Just to relax, you know."

Listening, she searched his face. What did she see?

"I spent another month in rehab the next summer after my freshman year. My grandparents were pissed, especially since my grades had been horrible, and they weren't sure I'd be admitted back. But another big donation made it happen. It makes me sick to think how much money the school made off my addiction and stupidity."

"You must have done okay in order to graduate."

Always the optimist, his little Sunshine. It was what he loved about her. "I straightened out and managed to get my grades up. I stayed away from the parties but replaced them with another vice."

Confusion crossed her face. Would this further information be the thing turning her away?

Taking a deep breath, he sat back, looking out at the yellow disk lowering in the sky.

“I never hid the fact I was Abe and Celia’s son. Lots of people wanted to hang out with me. If they had pot or beer or some other drug, I was all for it. I wasn’t getting any money from either my grandparents or my parents. After my second stint in rehab, I tried to be more selective. But I replaced my addiction for substances with sex.”

Sara eased away, only slightly, but he felt it. Felt the loss of her warmth.

“The girls on campus didn’t care if I had cash to spend on them. They only wanted to be with the son of Abe and Celia. And who was I to deny them the thrill?”

Easing back even more, she leaned closer to the dog. Yeah, he didn’t always want to be near himself either. Still, she hadn’t said a word.

“I basically screwed any girl on campus who wanted me. What a guy, huh?”

Glancing at Sara as she stared off into space, he slid his hand along the bench and touched the side of her leg. Nothing big but a subtle reminder he was still there. Like she could forget with the past dribbling from his mouth.

She glanced sideways at him. “Are you proud of that?”

“Hell, no. I hate thinking how many girls I used.”

Her hand slid from her lap to rest on his. “It sounds like they used you, too.”

Her voice was soft, and he had to strain to hear, but she defended him. Why? Her words sent regret slashing through him. Yeah, they’d used him, too.

His gaze roamed the horizon, absorbing the scene of boats and seagulls frolicking on the waves. It was the abuse of his weakness that finally got through.

"They had a list, you know. Making bets."

When she leaned closer, her strawberry scent tantalized his senses, and he forgot what he'd been saying. "What kind of bets?"

"To see how many girls could have sex with me. And they had a contest to see who could do it the most. I was such a sleaze, I honestly didn't remember if I'd done someone or not. And then there was the big prize."

Venom crept into his tone, though he tried to keep it light. "They actually had money riding on who could sleep with me, all night long."

"But you just said you slept with all of them?"

Turning, he faced her full on. So damned innocent she had no idea the difference. "No, Sunshine, I fucked them. I never *slept* with anyone. It was one thing dear old Dad taught me from the time I was old enough to do the deed. Have your fun, then shove them out the door. Nice lesson, huh? I always thought he should get Father of the Year."

Looking away, he checked the view so he didn't see the horror, or worse, pity, on her face. He didn't expect the sniff. Was she crying? For him?

As he turned back, she wiped a tear from the corner of her eye. Reaching out, he stroked his thumb along her face. "Oh, Sunshine, don't cry for me. I'm not worth it. I was a slime, and I know it. But at least finding out about the bets finally made me get my act together, for good."

Her eyes closed for a moment as she held his hand in place on her face. Emotion, strong and deep, rushed through his blood. Why did he turn to mush when she was around?

When she opened her eyes, they were filled with warmth. “How’d you find out?”

“I overheard some girls talking. Seemed several of the sororities had a competition going. Some stupid trophy was involved. It made me realize I didn’t like being used. I hated the fact I didn’t know who liked me for me, and who was only in it for the fame it brought them.”

“What changed?”

“I cut myself off from the college social life. Got an apartment away from campus, so I wasn’t constantly surrounded by the parties and girls. I started going to AA meetings and buckled down and began studying for real. I even took summer classes, so I could graduate within a reasonable amount of time.”

“Weren’t your grandparents proud of you then?”

“It was a little too late. I’d spent eighteen years living the life of a musician, then a few more acting like the spoiled, pampered brat I was. They went through a lot when I was drunk or stoned. Two years of trying to stay sober hadn’t convinced them, especially since they never saw it. I didn’t visit too often. My royalties had started coming in for some of my music, and I could afford to live on my own.”

“What about now? Don’t they see how far you’ve come? You own a successful shop and haven’t had a relapse in over seven years.”

Slowly, he shook his head. “They don’t lecture anymore, but I’m not sure they trust me yet. I think they’re still waiting for the other shoe to drop. For me to fall off the wagon and go back to my old ways. I can’t guarantee it won’t happen.”

Sitting up straighter, Sara placed her hands on his

shoulders. “Look here, TJ Bannister, you stop this negative talk right now. You *can* guarantee it. Why? Because you aren’t the same person you were before. You made a conscious decision to pull yourself together and make something of your life. And you *have* been successful. You won’t go back to who you were before because you don’t want that life anymore. And you have control over it. Stop doubting yourself.”

“Yes, ma’am.” The fire in her eyes and the determined look on her face amazed him. “Whatever you say, ma’am.”

Her eyes twinkled, and one side of her lip turned up. God, she was adorable.

For years, he’d been like his grandparents, always waiting for the other shoe to drop. Waiting for the time something happened so overwhelming he couldn’t resist the bottle. But with Sara staring, her full lips in a smirk and her cute nose wrinkled, he finally started to believe it. She forced him to see beyond his addictions to the man he was underneath. Made him want this normal life more than ever. Made him stronger.

With her near him, he could finally see the future. And it was filled with sunshine.

Chapter Nineteen

"Um, I had an unexpected arrival while you were working."

Sara closed the truck door and fastened her seatbelt. "Unexpected arrival?"

TJ grimaced. "Abe and Celia showed up a few hours ago. Seems they came back from Martha's Vineyard early, and their hotel doesn't have a room for them."

"She's performing at the fair tomorrow."

"Right. And in her infinite egocentricity decided she could come back an hour beforehand. Then it dawned on her she might want to shower and get ready somewhere other than the fairgrounds. But the hotel is booked because of the fair. They decided my house would do for the night."

"Oh, are they up partying?" Just what she needed was a reenactment of Kayla and Dan.

After pulling into the driveway, he cut the engine. "No, they already went to bed. I guess the reunion is still going strong."

She followed him into the house. "So, is there a problem?" The way he'd spoken of his parents, she wasn't sure.

Freckles greeted them with a wagging tail. "I wanted you to be aware in case you bumped into them in the middle of the night. I also thought it would be a good idea for you to sleep in my room tonight. They're in the room diagonal from yours, but I know they can get loud when they're *in the mood*."

Sara held her breath for him to continue. Was he expecting to sleep with her? The thought scared her and excited her at the same time.

"I'll sleep in the other front bedroom upstairs."

Disappointment seeped into her veins. It shouldn't. She was a nice girl and didn't go around sleeping with guys at random. TJ was hardly random, and her feelings for him had been growing stronger every day. What did he feel for her? Desire, yes. It was apparent every time he looked at her. But was there more? Did she want more? Her life was mapped out, and right now it didn't include a devastatingly handsome bookstore owner.

"I'll get my stuff."

It took her only a minute to run upstairs, grab what she needed, and slip into TJ's bedroom. He was just coming out of the bathroom, pulling on the drawstring of his pajama pants. His chest was bare.

Sara sighed. The sight of him always took her breath away.

"I'll get out of your way in a minute. Let me throw on a T-shirt."

"Not on my account." The words slipped out of her mouth before she could grab them and shove them back. What had possessed her? Besides the fact she didn't want him to cover his gorgeous chest. Her parents had raised her to be truthful.

As TJ picked up a notepad, a grin covered his face. Was he laughing at her or glad she was loosening up?

"Are you composing tonight?"

"There's an old Doris Day and Rock Hudson

movie on cable, and I wanted to watch it. I like a notebook handy in case I get inspiration for a song."

The notepad had been in his bedside table. She was displacing him from his typical movie spot since she knew the upstairs bedrooms didn't have TVs. Could she talk him into watching here? Snuggling up next to him with an old classic sounded perfect. Was she brave enough to ask?

Sara went into the bathroom and got ready, spending extra time on her teeth. A long good-night kiss from TJ always gave her sweet dreams. She found him filling Freckles' water dish in the kitchen. Glancing at her attire, he grinned. The desire in his eyes was obvious. Poker wouldn't be a good game for him. Unless it was strip poker. God, again with the sassy, sexy thoughts. What was up with her?

Taking a deep breath, she bolstered her courage. "Did you want to watch the movie in your bedroom? It might be more comfortable for you, and we can close the door, so we don't disturb your parents."

"I thought you'd be tired. Did you want to see it?"

"I love old classics. I'll probably drift off, but I wouldn't mind watching if it's okay with you."

A few minutes later, TJ joined her in the bedroom, closed the door, and sat next to her. "Are you sure you want me here? I might hog the covers."

When she made a face, he leaned in and kissed her nose, then grabbed the remote and set it to the right channel. "Ready?"

Looking at her outfit, she said, "Pajamas, check." She blew out a puff of air. "Teeth brushed, minty fresh breath, check."

His head tilted. "Hmm, maybe I should take it out

for a test drive. To make sure you did a good job."

Her heart rate picked up. This was what she wanted. Why was she nervous? His gaze centered on her. What was he looking at? Oh, the question. She hadn't answered it.

"Test drive. Sure."

When he scooted closer, she slid into his arms willingly. *Too comfortable with this. I want it far too much.* Playfully, his lips skimmed along hers, teasing and tempting, then pulling back to make her go after him for more. And she did. Sliding her hands into his hair, she tugged him closer as their lips feasted on each other.

The movie came on, and TJ stopped to watch but never let go of her. He angled them so they could both see but were still snuggled together. Resting her head on his shoulder, she became bold enough to swirl her fingers in the hair on his chest, something she'd been dying to do for weeks but never had the courage.

He moaned softly. "Feels nice, Sunshine. I love when you touch me."

"This is okay, then." Her lack of experience rose to the surface, along with her insecurity.

"You can touch me anywhere you want."

Did she dare explore?

"Anywhere?"

"Nothing's off limits to you." He chuckled. "Some places might have consequences attached."

"Like if I tickle you?" She put her hand under his arm.

He nuzzled his nose into her neck, while his hands skimmed to her ribs. "Sure, you might get tickled back."

Steeling her nerves, she allowed her hands to drift across his chest again. She played in the mat of hair around his nipples, then followed the arrow down the middle of his belly to the edge of his pants. When her fingers circled his navel, he sucked in a huge breath of air, watching her intently. His muscles tensed, yet he remained silent. Was he waiting to see what she'd do? Would he stop her if she went further? Did she want to go further?

Hell, yes. She was dying to see a real man. Her fingers itched and slipped slowly under the waistband of his pajamas.

"You really want to go there, Sunshine? Any further and there'll be some definite retaliation."

As Sara watched, the mound under his pants grew and twitched. She hadn't even touched him yet.

"That's what happens thinking about you."

When she caressed along his waistline and over the material quickly, his breathing came out shallow and fast. He was hard and long, and Sara wanted to explore more. Noise from the TV distracted her, and she jerked her hand away, then looked up. Could he see the indecision in her eyes? Did he think she was ridiculous?

"Little too hot for you to handle right now? It's okay. Every time I touch you, I get third degree burns."

He kissed her hard and deep, letting her know he still wanted her. Then he spun her around so her back rested against his chest. Good, less temptation.

They focused on the movie, and her eyes began to close with the comfort of being held. They popped open again when TJ's hands roamed over her torso, playing with her breasts. Closing her eyes, she simply enjoyed it.

As his hands grew bolder, his erection grew also. It pressed against her backside, taunting her, as if to ask to be touched again. *Ignore it.*

When his fingers flicked over her aching nipples, groans slipped from her mouth.

"I love the sounds you make when I touch you." His breath warmed her cheek, and his lips skimmed down the side of her neck until they stopped to nibble on her shoulder.

Sensory overload. The sounds from the television and slapping of the surf on the sand, along with the fresh ocean scent, all combined with TJ's hands and lips, sent her into a spin. She floated along on waves of ecstasy, simply feeling.

His hand on her breast headed south, and she stopped breathing, waiting to see where it would go. And if she would allow it. Her body screamed out for the hand to continue its journey. Her mind told her she should stop it. Her body was louder.

The fingers playing with her nipples now slipped under the loose waistband of her shorts. Had she worn this old pair with the stretched-out elastic on purpose? Subconsciously, did she want this to happen? Did she want to make it easier on TJ?

Moving his hand from one hip to the other, TJ dipped lower, making her forget where she was and who she was. The sensation of his fingers sliding into her curls caused awareness she'd never experienced before.

The naughty girl buried deep inside her, one she hadn't even known existed, gave a hearty yell and poked her head out. Sucking in her stomach, she allowed his hand to slide in deeper. His other hand joined the first, smoothing across her hips, then lowering to caress the juncture of her thighs.

To hell with being good, this felt amazing, and she'd been curious too long. As she sank into his arms, his length poked her backside. When she wiggled her butt, he groaned, low and deep.

"Oh, you definitely need to be punished. You're killing me."

"What kind of punishment?" What the hell? She should be pushing him away and running for the hills, not flirting with the devil himself. But this devil's hands felt like heaven. How could she walk away?

He bit down on her shoulder, then licked the spot he'd nipped. Electricity coursed through her, and goose bumps dotted her arms. When his fingers skimmed lower still, she arched her back and spread her thighs wider. Touching the folds between her legs, he slid one finger inside her opening.

"Shit, Sunshine."

"I'm sorry. I—"

"Shh, it's all good." His mouthed touched her ear. "I've got you worked up. The same way you've got me worked up rubbing your cute little ass across my lap."

"This is my punishment? What you're doing now?"

"Do you like this?"

She could barely nod her head. This time, he dipped one finger deeper, and she involuntarily clenched her muscles. His groan was long and almost painful.

"TJ?"

"I'm fine. Imagining something else where my fingers are. I hope you're enjoying this."

"Are you?" Her voice was small, but she needed to

know.

"Oh, no worry there. I'm getting plenty out of this. But I think it's time you learned what the big payoff is."

What did he mean? Sex? She wasn't ready yet. What he was doing now was more than she'd ever imagined.

When she stiffened in his arms, he whispered her name and kissed her neck until she relaxed, his fingers still working their magic. Sliding one inside again, he didn't immediately remove it. As he thrust in and out, she saw colors swirl across her eyes. More playing this time with the nub, and she almost flew out of his arms.

Faster, harder, the pressure built up so high, she didn't know if she could survive it. She was flying through the sky, soaring, and needed to get somewhere. Where, she didn't know, but God, she was so close. Almost there.

The rainbow of colors burst open, and she found herself shuddering, then floating back to earth. Shattered. But warmth and serenity took over as she sprawled against the firm body behind her.

The rumble in TJ's chest tickled as he held her tighter. "Your little cries nearly sent me over the edge myself." His chest heaved as if he'd run a marathon.

"I'm sorry, I didn't mean to be loud. I didn't realize I'd said anything."

"Sara, stop apologizing. The noises you make let me know you got pleasure from what I did. Right?" His typically confident tone stalled for a moment. Did he not know if she'd liked it?

"It was unbelievable. I've never—I mean obviously, you know I've never—but not even that. Is it always…even when you…" The words wouldn't come out.

"Sometimes it's even better. You only got a small taste."

Settling back more comfortably against the pillows, he kept his arms around her. "Now let me watch the rest of this movie. I already missed the best part."

She whipped her head around, ready to tell him off. His eyes twinkled with mischief, and he bit his lip to keep from laughing.

What had just happened? God, she should have stopped it, but some part of her wanted it so badly. And it had been worth it. Never had she imagined it could be so powerful and explosive. And they hadn't actually had real sex. Not the full-blown kind she'd seen pictures of on the internet. Of course, she'd never admit to anyone she'd looked it up.

And he'd said he'd gotten plenty out of it, but she could still feel his erection against her back. She'd read enough to know it shouldn't stay hard. He seemed engrossed in the movie, so she didn't ask. No sense in showing how ridiculously innocent she was.

But he'd given her an amazing gift. And he'd given it selflessly, holding himself under strict control, never asking for anything in return. She'd heard the talk. Most guys were selfish. TJ himself said he'd been a real bastard about sex when he was younger. He'd come so far. It filled her with joy to realize he'd let her come along for the ride.

****

The tantalizing scent of strawberry shampoo brought TJ out of his slumber. Sara curled against him, her head on his shoulder, her hair spilled across his chest. Sunlight drifted through the windows telling him it was later than usual.

He glanced at the bedside clock. Half past eight. They had to be at the shop by ten, so they had time. Time for what? More of what he'd done last night? The memory of Sara's enraptured face and little cries of satisfaction echoed through his mind, making his cock hard. Better tone it down. He had his parents upstairs at the moment. Hadn't stopped him last night.

His arms tightened around Sara as he watched her sleep. Like an angel. His sleep had been amazing, too. Must be the woman in his arms.

He froze. He'd actually slept with a woman. In bed. All night long. And he hadn't even gotten laid. Whoa! It had been a first for both of them. Pretty sure Sara had never had an orgasm before. It was most likely what she'd started to say before she'd blushed bright red.

Never before had he given so unselfishly to a woman. Sure, he'd played with them a bit but mostly to make sure they were ready. Then he took his pleasure, not actually caring if they got anything out of it. Wasn't being the son of Abe and Celia enough reward?

His old attitude was long gone. Sara had helped banish it to a point it wouldn't ever return. It surprised him to realize how much he'd enjoyed simply giving to her and making sure she was satisfied. He never even finished himself off. She'd fallen asleep soon after, and he hadn't wanted to let go. The discomfort eventually faded. When the movie ended, he'd shut the TV off, sliding under the covers so he could hold her a bit longer. Sleep came in minutes.

Her warm skin nestled along his had such a relaxing effect. Like all his cares had flown out the window, never to come back. Not true, but right now it didn't matter. He'd take every second of this and store it away for later.

A soft sigh slipped from Sara's mouth as her hand inched across his torso. Fingers played with the cross around his neck, and he didn't dare move in case she woke up. When her leg slid within striking distance of his growing arousal, he held his breath until it paused in its movement.

His turn. The thin tank top outlined her breasts, her nipples apparent. Would they tighten into little nubs even when asleep? Lifting his free hand, he gently circled a finger around the peak. Immediately it hardened and stood at attention.

He didn't stop even as a tiny whimper escaped from Sara's mouth.

"Oh, my God, what are you doing?" Her throaty voice was raw and deep.

"Waking you up. Thought this might be nicer than slapping you in the head."

Her laughter had a groan mixed in as he rubbed her nipple again.

"Definitely nicer."

He sat back, admiring the view.

"As much as I'd like to continue, we need to get ready for work."

The disappointment in her eyes almost had him heading back for more. But she sat up and sighed.

"Do you want the shower before me?" Images of Sara and him entwined under the spray washed through his mind. Bad question to ask.

Slipping off the bed, she shook her head. "No, I'll take a shower after work. I don't want sticky kid stuff on me while I sing tonight. You go ahead."

TJ quickly showered, and Sara was already dressed in shorts and a T-shirt when he came out. Moving to the dresser, he grabbed clothes as she brushed her hair into a ponytail. She turned her back and pretended to be busy, but her gaze flickered to the mirror every so often. Good, he wanted her to be familiar with his body. Hoped to become even more familiar with hers.

After slipping his feet into shoes and towel drying his hair, he opened the bedroom door. "What are you in the mood for?"

Waltzing past, she glanced over her shoulder. "Maybe more of what you woke me with."

Shit, she'd be the death of him. One minute all sweetness and innocence, then out strutted the sassy, sexy twin whose only purpose was to drive him insane. Clenching his fists, he followed her.

Cereal at the counter was easiest. When his was gone, he reached over and grabbed a sugary ring from her bowl. She slapped at his hand.

"Hey, go get more if you're still hungry. This bowl has my name on it."

Grabbing another ring, he tossed it in his mouth. "Wrong, everything in this house belongs to me."

Sara raised her eyebrow. "I'm in this house. Do I belong to you?"

"Hmm, yeah, I'm thinking you do. Especially those gorgeous lips. I know those are mine."

Leaning over, he nipped at her bottom lip. Sara gravitated toward him until a throat cleared.

"That explains the girly stuff upstairs." Abe stood in the doorway, a smug grin on his face. "Your mother noticed one of the bedrooms had lady paraphernalia in it. Figured you had some chick stashed away."

Sara was not *some chick*. She was far more and only recently had he begun to realize his feelings for her. He cared and wanted the best for her, regardless of what it brought him.

"Where's Celia?"

"Still sleeping. Needs her beauty rest after all we did last night. Man, we—"

"Abe," TJ cut him off cold. "We don't need details. This is Sara. Sara, my father, Abe Bannister."

Abe assessed Sara, and TJ could tell when she passed muster. His father's smile grew creepy, and his eyes lit up as he held out his hand. She took it but pulled it away quickly. Because of all he'd said about his childhood?

"We're going to work. I assume you and Celia will see yourself out. She's performing around four, right? You'll be able to get into your hotel by then."

"Yeah, yeah, no problem. Thanks for letting us shack up here last night. Are you coming to see your mother sing?"

He'd planned on taking Sara to the fair early so she could enjoy some of it before her performance. Watching Celia was a different matter. "Maybe. We'll have to see how things go at work."

"It was nice meeting you, Sara," Abe called as TJ ushered her through the back door.

Sara smiled back. TJ took a step out, then swore. "Go ahead. I forgot the keys."

Reaching inside the door, he grabbed the keys hanging on the hook. Abe looked out the window as Sara walked to the truck.

"She's mighty fine, True. Is she good in the sack?"

His vision clouded, and his hands clenched so tightly around the keys, pain slashed through his palm. “Get the filthy thoughts of her out of your mind.”

“Okay, okay.” Abe held up his hands. “I’m trying to get this thing with your mother off the ground anyway. So, no side hanky panky. But I’ll tell you, she’s got some nice equipment. Understated but there. Hope you’re getting something out of it.”

As he huffed out the back door, he glared at his father. Yes, he was getting something out of his relationship with Sara, but it wasn’t anything Abe would understand. It was his self-respect back. And control over his addictions and emotions. The most important thing, though, was his heart. The part of him, frozen and lifeless for so long, was finally thawing and coming back to life.

Chapter Twenty

"Deep breath, sweetheart, you'll do fine."

Mary's reassuring voice helped calm Sara's nerves, but the fluttering in her stomach didn't dissipate. Only fifteen minutes until she needed to be in the tent behind the stage. She and the other dozen contestants.

"Need a cigarette to chill you out?" Darcy asked, smiling at their little secret.

So many friends had shown up to support her. TJ, Darcy, Mary, and Jim. Gabby and her husband and the kids were here also, along with a few of the other Story Hour children.

Earlier, she and TJ had walked the fairgrounds, and the fried dough enticed her. Although she didn't relish puking it back up with the nerves dancing in her stomach. Nibbling on TJ's pulled pork was about all she could manage. Her hands wouldn't stop shaking.

"I'll be okay." She took a slow, deep breath. "I hope I don't fall off these shoes."

Her gaze roamed to the three-inch heels Darcy had insisted she wear. Along with her snuggest sundress. TJ could barely keep his eyes off her, so it must look decent. But she didn't want them judging her on clothes. If she won, she wanted it to be because of her voice.

"You'll be fine." TJ's arms wrapped around her from behind, and she leaned into his embrace. She didn't care others watched. She needed his comfort and support more than anyone else here. "You have the most beautiful voice I've ever heard. Even if you don't win, know it's not because you aren't a beautiful singer."

They were being judged on stage presence and audience interaction, as well as their vocal talent. Her experience performing for large groups wasn't extensive. Luckily, the crowd on the lawn in front of the main stage wasn't too big yet, but the show didn't start for a while.

"Did you invite your family down?" Mary tried to be solicitous, but it was another reminder her family wasn't as supportive of this career choice.

"I mentioned it to them, but it's Thursday night, and they all have to work tomorrow. Long drive for one song."

"Or two," Darcy added smugly. "You've got it happening, girl. You'll get in the top three, no problem. I know two of the other contestants, and they suck."

TJ glared at Darcy while Sara checked to see if the kids had heard, but they scampered around in front of the stage oblivious. Darcy looked chagrined and covered her mouth.

"Oops, sorry. Don't always remember my filter. My bad."

Gabby laughed. "I'm sure they've heard worse."

Checking his watch, TJ tilted his head at Sara. "You should probably head into the tent now. You don't want to be late."

Everyone gave her hugs, and Darcy held her especially long, whispering, "Give 'em hell."

TJ walked her to the tent and hugged her. "You're

a beautiful person, inside and out. You have an amazing voice, and I can't wait to see you up on stage showing everyone here what you're capable of. Remember the pointers I gave you about using a microphone."

"I will. Thanks for helping me practice the songs. I hope I do them justice."

"You will, Sunshine. Knock their socks off."

He kissed her, soft and gentle, but with strength and courage woven in. She'd need it.

The next couple minutes she spent introducing herself to the other contestants. A few seemed nervous, but several had cocky attitudes and confidence Sara longed for.

The contest started and the MC announced the judges. The applause was especially loud for Celia Muñez. They'd watched her perform this afternoon, and it was obvious where TJ got his musical talent from.

As each contestant left the tent and returned, her fear grew. She could hear them sing but couldn't actually see what they were doing. Were they wowing the crowds? The redhead with the huge chest and spunky personality sure got lots of response.

Soon it was Sara's turn, and her knees turned to jelly. Could she do this? Would she fall flat on her face? And not just because of the shoes? Was she making a fool of herself? Delusional she actually had the kind of voice people wanted to listen to?

They announced her name and her steps onto the platform felt like walking to the gallows. The bright lights blinded her, but she focused on taking the microphone from the MC and answering the few questions he asked.

"I'll be singing the song *Everything*." Now she

knew the story behind it, she hoped she'd get the needed emotion into it.

"Good luck. Here you go."

The stage lights overshadowed the darkness beyond, but Sara could see a few of the people near the front of the stage. Jasmine and Eddie still ran around but stopped to wave enthusiastically. She smiled at them, then looked around as the music began. TJ stood to one side, but his gaze remained strictly on her. When he nodded slightly, she knew everything would be okay. She would sing this for him.

****

When Sara crossed the stage, TJ knew she'd be okay. Yes, she was nervous, but her sunny disposition glowed bright. When she looked at him, her confidence visibly grew. Because of him? Had he helped her become more sure of herself?

Her performance was fifth out of thirteen. So far two of the contestants had been good, while the other two didn't have a chance. Maybe at home or with a karaoke machine they might wow the crowd but not on a full-fledged stage. That wasn't Sara.

The first notes floated from her mouth, and he sighed. Perfection. The mic was held not too close, letting it project her voice instead of yelling. As the words he'd written echoed through the air, he fought the emotion threatening to choke him. Sara's version was far better than the original and held deeper meaning.

"When I lost you…I lost everything."

Tears formed in his eyes, knowing he still hadn't gotten over Sonni's death. His grief and pain echoed across the stage for the whole world to hear. Well, the world here in Barnstable County. Reaching up, he grabbed the front of his shirt to see if his heart had fallen out.

"How can I go on...knowing you won't be there for me? Knowing everything is gone."

Tears rolled down his cheeks, and he let them. He didn't want to miss one second by wiping them away. Her voice mesmerized him. Her gaze, connecting with his as she sang, held him captive. He was falling deeper and deeper under her spell, and there was no chance of getting free. *I don't care. I want to be right here.* Completely linked to her.

At a break in the vocals, he checked to see Celia's reaction. His mother knew what the song meant. Doubtful it did anything. She'd left on another world tour only three weeks after her daughter died. The show must go on.

But Celia dabbed her eyes, holding her hand in front of her mouth as she stared intently at Sara. Would this go against Sara in points? When she belted out the last poignant tones of the song, Celia nodded and smiled sadly. It had touched her.

It was good to know his mother had some feelings hidden under all the expensive clothes and jewelry. He'd often wondered.

When Sara left the stage, he began to breathe again. It would be a while before they announced the finalists.

"Sad song, boss, but I never expected to see you crying over it. Or did you get a little fair dust in your eyes?"

TJ glanced at Darcy, who eyed him curiously. "If you knew the meaning of the lyrics, you'd understand."

"How do you know what they mean? Did you ask the composer?" She blinked. "Holy shit! Is that one of your songs? It's a mega hit. It topped like all kinds of records."

TJ glanced around, but no one seemed interested in their conversation. The next singer butchered a perfectly good Bruce Springsteen number. Didn't he know wearing ripped jeans and a tight T-shirt didn't automatically get you a voice to go with it?

"It's about my sister."

Darcy stepped closer. "I didn't know you had a sister. What happened to her?"

"She died." It was all he could say. His emotions were already stretched thin. "I'm going to get some air before they announce the finalists."

"Sure, boss, go get some air." As he walked off, she muttered, "Not like there's any air here…outside."

He didn't go far, just walked along the edge of the stage grounds, wondering how Sara was. Calmer now she was done. Her performance had been flawless. The audience may not have been clapping and cheering like some of the others got, but she'd certainly engaged their emotions. The applause had been real and strong.

A small break was called after the last song, and TJ strolled near Mary and Jim, who'd brought lawn chairs and sat to the side away from the speakers. They held hands, and Jim leaned in causing Mary to giggle. Like she was a little girl again. It was good to see. Her husband's stroke had devastated her. They'd needed each other then, and he'd never forget what she did for him as well.

"Should you two be chaperoned?" he teased, coming up behind them. Their hands sprang apart, and they looked guilty.

"What are you doing sneaking up on an old couple? You should know better, young man," Mary scolded.

"Yes, mother." His tone was snarky, and Jim laughed.

"What did you think? I thought Sara was the best, but I'm not in the music biz. What's your professional opinion?"

Jim would ask for his unbiased opinion. It wasn't something he could give. The song had moved him too much. "I think the composer of the song should win a Grammy Award."

Jim snorted. "You're hysterical."

The MC returned to the stage, bringing all the contestants back on. They announced the top three, and when they called Sara's name, a huge cry and wolf whistle went out. Darcy. You had to love her exuberance.

TJ clapped along madly as well, then excused himself from Mary and Jim to move back to his spot near the stage. He wanted Sara to know he was here, cheering her on.

"I knew she'd get this far. The other suckers had no chance once she belted out the long note at the end."

Putting his arm around the outspoken girl, he said, "Thanks for being here to support her, Darcy. Appreciate it."

"It's cool, boss. I like Sara, a lot."

He did, too. A lot. Maybe more than a lot. Now wasn't the time to process it, so he let it slide and waited for her to sing her second song. It was the one he'd been inspired to write when he'd met her. It was still slow but more upbeat than *Everything*. The crowd responded well. Good news for whoever bought it from him. Within the next week, he planned to get it to his manager.

The final notes faded away, and it took only a few minutes to get the results this time. They announced the third-place winner first. It was the girl who'd gotten everyone clapping to her country beat. The fact her breasts had bounced up and down as she pranced around the stage might have had something to do with it. She'd brought her own entourage of guys who'd enjoyed her show.

The MC made a big production of announcing the winner. Lots of smoke and lights flashed around the stage. Sara bit her bottom lip, and TJ wanted to hop on stage and pull her into his arms. Finally, the name was called out.

"Sara Storm is our first-place finalist and winner of the thousand-dollar check. Come on over here and take a bow."

Jasmine and Eddie screamed and danced in circles in front of the stage. Harrison, Benson, and even shy Hope joined in the ruckus. Sara blew them kisses, then accepted her prize. As the MC offered his congratulations, she turned to glance his way. Dancing around like the children or blowing her kisses was what he wanted to do, but he merely grinned and nodded.

When she finally got off stage, she ran right into his waiting arms. Twirling her around, he planted kisses on her neck, then set her back on her feet. The others came over and gave her quick hugs, then excused themselves. The kids needed to get to bed, Darcy had had enough of the county fair, and Mary and Jim had other plans.

Embracing her again, he kissed her and didn't give a shit who saw him. It was what he needed and she deserved.

"True, I wasn't aware you knew this girl."

Celia approached, and TJ let Sara slide from his arms but kept his hand over her shoulder.

"She's a friend. Sara, this is my mother, Celia."

"Congratulations, dear. You have an amazing talent. I hope you know."

"Thank you." Sara leaned in closer. Was she intimidated by Celia?

"True, your father mentioned a young woman at the house this morning. Is this her? I hadn't realized you were seeing anyone."

"You're hardly around enough to know my personal business. But yes, Sara's been staying with me. She had some problems with her old apartment, so I offered to let her use one of the guest rooms."

Celia's mouth quirked, and he waited for her to point out Sara hadn't stayed in the guest room last night, but she remained silent on the subject. She looked at Sara instead.

"Are you planning a career as a singer? I think you have the talent to make it."

Excitement radiated from Sara as she stiffened in his arms. "Yes, I'd like to. I figure this contest gets me one step closer to achieving my goal."

Celia kissed TJ on the cheek and congratulated Sara once more. When they walked back to the truck, Sara looked tired. But this contest had given her more confidence and experience performing. And more hope one day she would achieve her goal. It had definitely brought her one step closer to her dream.

And if she attained her dream, it would bring him one step closer to having his heart ripped out of his chest.

Chapter Twenty-One

"Are you kidding me? When did this happen?"

TJ shook the water from his hair while he stood in the pool. Sara looked shocked as she talked on her cell phone. Who had called? It was usually some family member. Her parents, brothers, or often her cousin, Sofia.

Floating around the deep end, he didn't want to appear to be eavesdropping. Except he was. Not being nosy, just making sure she was okay. As she listened, her face went through a variety of emotions. Confusion, happiness, excitement, and disappointment.

After she hung up, he gave her a minute, then swam over to where she sat on the edge of the pool, her feet dangling in.

"You okay?"

Her gaze darted around the enclosed yard, then settled on him. When she held her hands out, he sloshed closer until he was right in front of her. Sliding her arms around his neck, she rested her head on his shoulder. He returned the embrace, letting her take what she needed from him.

"My brother, Erik, is getting married."

As he examined her face, she seemed conflicted. "Not a good thing? Did I meet this girl at your house? I don't remember her."

"He wasn't seeing anyone at the time."

"Oh, so he's only known her what…a few weeks, a month at most." TJ had only known Sara a few months, but there were times he wanted to chain her to him permanently.

"It's Tessa Porter, and we've known her since we were teens. She lives next door to my grandparents' place in Maine, which is where Erik lives now."

"You don't like her? Don't think she's good enough for Erik?"

"No, she's really sweet, and I get along with her great. It's just…they're getting married next Sunday. One week from today. One week."

"What's the rush for?"

"My mom was a little vague. Remember Erik said he was adopting two kids from Kandahar. Apparently, this is to make their lives more stable."

"So, they're doing it for the kids?"

She shrugged, and he rubbed his hands up and down her arms.

"My parents went up a few weeks ago to visit Erik and meet the kids. Erik's still not steady on his feet, so Tessa's been helping him out. Mom thought they might have a thing for each other because of their interactions. But it was only a few weeks ago. Now they're getting married."

"Is the wedding in Maine?"

"No, it's at my folks' house in Squamscott Falls. But they want me there Saturday to help get the house and food ready."

TJ tucked a strand of hair behind her ear as she nibbled on her bottom lip. Looking up, she patted his shoulders.

"Oh, you're invited, too."

“Me, why? Is it a big wedding?” They only had a week to prepare.

“No, it’s just us and the cousins, but my mom liked you when she met you. Plus, I’d have a ride home.”

He pressed a kiss to her lips. “Happy to drive you home. How early Saturday? It’s my day to open the store, and Becca doesn’t come in until eight.”

Sara’s smile filled him with warmth. With her around, he’d never be cold.

“We could leave after Story Hour. I told my mom I’d do some baking here to save time.”

He moved his face next to hers. “Will there be any free samples with this baking?”

“Maybe, if you help me.”

“That could be arranged.”

“Oh, and I need to find a dress. Tessa doesn’t have any family, she was a foster child to the Millers next door, and she wants me to be the Maid of Honor.”

“You have tomorrow off. You could go to a few places and see what you can find. Darcy doesn’t work until five. Take her along to help you pick something out.”

“Yeah, I can picture what Darcy would choose. Black, short, low cut, and way too tight. Along with four-inch heels and a spiked dog collar.”

He ran his fingers down her throat. “I don’t know about the dog collar, but I like the low cut and too tight features of this dress.”

He settled between her legs and allowed his hands to drift across her back, playing with the string on her top. One little tug and she’d be free for him to explore.

Sara did her own exploring, her fingers twirling in his chest hair, then playing with the cross around his neck. It drove him crazy. He lowered his head, planting his lips firmly on hers, while her fingers slid into his hair and held him close. Damn, he loved kissing her. The art of kissing was never anything he'd appreciated. Always in too big a rush to reach the finish line, he'd never taken the time to enjoy the route. Now he was. Sara was teaching him to be patient and celebrate the act of giving as well as receiving. The foreplay he'd zipped through, or ignored before, was becoming a heady trip and showing him how pleasurable using all his senses could be.

Her heavy breathing, and the little whimpers she made when he nipped her neck, sent streaks of desire to his growing erection. Tasting the berries she'd eaten at lunch, with a hint of the chocolate he'd seen her sneak afterward, made him want to suck on her lips all day.

The tie on her bathing suit kept taunting him, and he finally pulled it loose, then dragged the triangles to expose her beautiful breasts. She grabbed at the fabric, but when he skimmed his lips down her neck and latched onto one of her nipples, the material was forgotten.

Her nipples puckered, and he wanted to devour them, devour her, get so close they became one person. How had this woman gotten under his skin so far he had no chance of ever getting her back out? Did he want her out? No, he wanted her here with him, keeping his days warm and sunny.

When he licked at her breast, her legs clamped tighter around his waist. He was a goner and wanted to bury himself so deep inside and show her exactly how he felt. Was it time? Was she ready? Still so innocent and he'd never push it.

For now, he could touch and taste her. Maybe he could taste even more of her. Show her the pleasure his tongue could bring to the parts his hands had thrilled the last few days. The night Celia and Abe had stayed here, he and Sara had slept in the same bed. Together, but apart. The last four nights he'd coaxed her to stay with him, too.

He'd been good and stayed in control…to a certain extent. His frustration level grew, but he wanted everything good for her. Wanted her to understand her own passion and desires before he took any back.

Her hands wandered over his chest and lowered to his navel, dipping into the waistband of his bathing suit. The head of his erection peeked from his shorts, and Sara stared as if mesmerized. Would she take the initiative to explore further?

"You do this to me, Sunshine."

Her fingers skimmed lower, then a tone sounded, pulling them back. Her phone. Who the hell was calling now?

She shook her head, as if waking from a spell. She wasn't the only one in a spell. Pulling herself from the pool, she grabbed her phone from the chair, shooting him an apologetic look. "It might be my mom with more details about the wedding. Sorry."

"Hello…oh, hi." She balanced the phone as she retied her top. Her expression grew serious as she listened, then her eyes lit up as the other person spoke.

"Are you serious? What do I need to do?"

Her head bobbed up and down, and her body bounced in excitement. What was going on? Something more exciting than his kisses apparently.

"Okay, I can play my guitar. No problem. How

many songs do you think?"

Her hand flew up to cover her mouth, and she looked about ready to cry. What the heck? It had something to do with music. But what?

"Thank you. Thank you, so much. I really appreciate the opportunity. I'll see you then."

Disconnecting the call, she placed the phone back on the chair, then started hopping up and down. He hauled himself from the pool and walked closer.

"I'd say you're excited about something. Care to share."

She took a few deep breaths. "That was the manager at The Melody Tent. The backup band for Friday night had to cancel. He saw I'd won the Summer Star Contest and wondered if I was interested in performing. It's hard to find someone on short notice."

TJ's heart fell to his toes. One more step toward losing her. But it was only the local venue. It wouldn't amount to anything, right? Some bands played local clubs for years and never went any further. He could be excited for her.

He pulled her in for a hug. "Awesome. You'll be fantastic. What are the details?"

She continued to bounce. So cute.

"I go on at seven and perform for about thirty-five to forty-five minutes. He said maybe six or seven songs should do it if I chat with the audience in between. I have to have my own music, but I can play my guitar. He said they have a piano I could use, also. And they're going to pay me two hundred dollars for doing this."

More bouncing. "My first paying gig!"

"You'll be amazing. I'll be in the front row, cheering you on."

Her eyes widened. "Oh, I don't know who the main act is. They might be sold out. I really want you there."

TJ touched his lips to hers gently. "I could always be your pianist."

"You would?" The look in her eyes was worth getting in front of an audience again.

"Although, I think I can manage some tickets. Friday night's group is Python. Abe left some tickets when they were here last week. I tossed them in a drawer in the kitchen since I hadn't planned on going. I think I'll pull them out and use them."

Sara froze in place. "I'm opening for Python. Holy shit. What kind of music can I sing to go with that?"

"I can help. I happen to know a good composer who has access to lots of top hits. If you're nice, he might let you get away with not paying royalties."

When she threw herself further into his arms, he picked her up and her legs automatically wrapped around his waist. He carried her into the house and into his bedroom.

"You're a bit wound up, Sunshine. I think we need to find a way to relax you. We could celebrate your first singing engagement."

He placed her carefully on his bed. "We won't do anything you're not comfortable with. I promise."

Sara grinned. "I think I'm getting a little *too* comfortable with some of what we're doing."

Taking the silk robe she'd used before from his closet, he handed it to her. "Never too comfortable. Put this on and let me get out of my wet suit."

TJ stripped off his suit and grabbed a pair of cotton boxers. He turned to face Sara as he slid them on. If her eyes got any wider, they'd pop right out of her face.

Wrapping the robe around her, she turned her back before slipping her bathing suit off. Soon enough he'd see what was under it. He was patient.

"Let's celebrate. You're still excited, right?"

"I am. You'll really play the piano for me? At the Summer Star contest, I kept looking at you to make sure you hadn't gone anywhere. You made me feel grounded."

"It's how you make me feel, too." He brushed her hair away from her shoulders. "Like I'm finally capable of reaching my dreams." Hopefully, those dreams were with Sara.

This time, Sara was the aggressor. She pulled his head down and pressed her lips to his, opening her mouth to allow him entry. No need to wait for a second invitation. He thrust his tongue inside and a battle ensued. There'd be no loser. They were both getting what they wanted.

As he followed her down to the bed, he slipped his hands under her ass and her legs wrapped around his waist. He nibbled his way down her neck and nudged aside the robe. Sara arched her back as he found and licked her nipple. When he took it into his mouth and sucked, a cry of delight echoed through the room.

"You like when I do that, huh?"

"Oh, yes." Her voice was raw and shaky, sending shivers of desire straight to his groin.

"Anything else you like?"

Nodding, she closed her eyes, her face blissful.

"Come on, Sunshine, let the naughty girl out and tell me what you want."

Her eyes opened, and he smiled to ease her discomfort. But she surprised him and smirked. "I want you to touch me." Her hand trailed down her torso to where the robe covered her thighs. "Here. Like you did before."

She still couldn't say it. He adored her.

Settling next to her, he caressed her leg, then slid his hand under the robe, playing in the curls on her mound. Whimpers floated to him and her hips moved, indicating what she wanted.

"I'm getting there. Be patient."

When his fingers got more intimate, her legs parted. She gasped but settled back for the ride. And he planned on giving her the ride of her life. Or as far as he could go without getting certain parts of him involved. Shit, he should get sainthood for this.

Her moans and whimpers got louder as his fingers caressed and stroked. He wanted her writhing. And knew exactly what to do. Kissing his way down her chest to her stomach, he let his fingers work their magic. Keep her close to the edge but not so close she'd go over. A delicate balance. How had he never realized how erotic this could be? He was ready to go over himself.

Pulling the tie of her robe, he spread it apart. Her beauty made his heart stop. When his lips got to the juncture of her thighs, she gasped and grabbed his head, not pushing him away but not pulling him closer either.

He slipped off the bed and tugged on her hips until her legs hung off the edge. Lifting them, he draped them over his shoulders. Her body stiffened, and she stared at him.

Reaching up, he touched her breasts, then caressed down her stomach again. "Relax, Sunshine. You'll enjoy this."

He nipped and licked along her thighs to get her used to the feel of his lips below her waist. As he slid his finger back inside, her head fell against the bed, and her hands clenched in his hair. *Can't wait any longer. Need to taste her.*

Stroking his tongue over her folds, he flicked the tiny nub. Her back arched, and she screamed, "Oh, God! Oh my God!"

"Told you you'd like it. I'm not done yet."

As his tongue got busy, licking, stroking, flicking, along her sensitive skin, her fingers tightened and her cries escalated. He had her so close it wouldn't take much to push her over the edge. He kept his eyes on her as he sucked on her most sensitive nerve.

Her hands nearly ripped his hair out as her body convulsed and her mouth opened. No sound came out. Only a strangled breath, followed by shallow panting. Her body shook as he crawled back up and rolled her to align with him.

"Holy shit. That was…I don't even know what it was."

Kissing her nose, he snuggled her to his chest. "Such language. I think you put the nice girl away for a while, and the naughty one came out to play."

Her impish grin killed him.

"It got me turned on. Not a hard thing to do with you around. Especially when you're all naked and warm in my arms."

Sara touched her forehead to his, so he couldn't fully see her face.

"Are you okay? You've still got the Big V, if you're worried."

Her laugh lightened the mood. "I'm afraid you

might have created a monster. I like it too much."

"You're meant to. It's essentially for procreation. If no one did it, the population would die out."

She touched his face. "Ever the sensible one."

"Yeah, me, sensible. Finally."

When her hands wandered down his chest, he warned, "Not such a good idea. Seeing you fall apart got me pretty worked up. It wouldn't take much to push me over the edge."

"Why aren't you allowed to go there? You sent me." Her fingers continued to walk south.

"You're sure?" Was she serious…and ready for this?

"I don't know what to do. But, yeah."

"God, you're beautiful. Give me a second." Running into the bathroom, he grabbed a towel, then settled next to her again.

"Do I just touch it?"

"Yeah." If she wanted him to explode. Tentatively, she stroked him through the shorts, then lifted the waistband to find his cock already jutting out. Pushing his shorts down, he let her explore.

"How?" Her hesitant tone tore at his heart.

Taking her hand, he wrapped it around the shaft, then slid it up and down. Once she got the rhythm, he let go. Her look of wonder kept him humble. She trusted him so much.

"Do I use my mouth, like you did with me? Some of my friends mentioned it."

"A lesson for another day. I'm"—He closed his eyes as ripples of pleasure overtook him—"very close now."

Watching her stroke him, and the lack of sex he'd

had lately, sent him spinning. He grabbed the towel and twisted on the bed. His body trembled, but Sara spooned up behind him, holding him as he exploded, then floated back down.

Turning back, he pulled her close. “Sorry it was so quick, but it’s been a long time.”

Her smug expression hit him in the chest. Thank God she was the one to break his dry spell. If it was up to him, he’d never look any further than the gorgeous woman in front of him. Thinking about her news from The Melody Tent, he realized it wasn’t up to him.

****

“What about this one?”

Sara looked at the dress Darcy held. Lime green with slits in places Sara didn’t want slits. Maybe bringing her had been a bad idea.

“I don’t think so, Darcy. It’s not exactly my color.”

“Not for the wedding, for the stage. You need to stand out.”

“This’ll make me stand out all right. They might even use me for a lamppost.”

“Well, how about this one, for the wedding?”

Did she dare look? It would be bad. They all had been so far.

Turning slowly, she was startled by the lace and soft colors of the dress Darcy held. She checked the price tag. Of course. It was far more than she wanted to spend, especially since she needed to get two dresses. One for the wedding and one for the stage. Darcy had told her, in no uncertain terms, could she wear a sundress when opening for Python. Something edgy and hot was needed. Sara didn’t do edgy and hot. She did sundresses in pastel colors.

"Don't make that face. You just got a thousand bucks for the contest last week. You can afford a small amount on a dress for your brother's wedding. Think what a real bridesmaid dress would cost."

True. Tessa hadn't been picky about colors or styles. Or so her mom had told her. Sara hadn't actually spoken with Tessa. Her mom was taking over and doing all the planning for the event. How did Tessa feel?

"Okay, let me try it on."

"Excellent. I'll see if I can find something a little less bright for the stage."

When she tried on the dress, she actually loved it. It was a soft peach cotton sheath covered by an ecru lace overdress with tiny sleeves and a sash belt. She had some off-white shoes at home to match.

"How does it look?" Darcy's voice called through the curtain.

"It's nice. I think I'll get it. Thanks."

"Don't thank me yet. I've got a few more things for you to try on. These are your stage outfits. One of them should work."

As Darcy shoved her hand through, three more garments appeared, and Sara groaned. Taking them, she muttered what she hoped was a heartfelt thanks. It *was* nice Darcy had come along. They just had very different tastes in clothes.

Her gaze perused what Darcy had picked out. At least the colors were more subdued than lime green. When she tried them, she actually liked one. It was a lightweight dress in muted shades of purple and gray and belted low on the hips. It was shorter and snugger than what she typically wore, but her ass wouldn't show if she bent over. Not much anyway.

Darcy approved of her choice, then Sara paid, an they headed for lunch.

"I still can't believe you talked me into the thigh high boots. They were way too expensive, and I'll never wear them again."

"Once you make it big, you'll wear them tons. And when the boss man gets a look at you in them…he'll be paying plenty of attention."

He already paid her plenty of attention. And yesterday she'd paid him back. *I still can't believe what I did.* It had never gone so far before. She was glad TJ had been the one to initiate her into it.

"You're blushing again. Because of the boss, huh? He makes you blush. How come?"

Sara rolled her eyes. Why was she having this conversation with Darcy? She liked the girl, but she was way more vocal about sex than Sara was comfortable with. *Like the naughty girl who told TJ where she wanted him to touch her yesterday*? Damn, the little voices in her head were becoming quite pesky.

"I'm not very experienced, so I'm not comfortable talking about it."

"You seem way more comfortable around the boss now than you did at the beginning of the summer. Hopefully, he's helping you with the experience thing."

Her face heated and Darcy smirked. "Thought so. Boss man was so chillaxed when he stopped in last night to drop you off for cleaning. Glad you guys are working out."

TJ *had* seemed calmer after she'd…well, after they'd…Damn, why couldn't she even think it? This good girl image had to go. Good thing Darcy had insisted on the boots. They were what she needed to

make a better impression than her sundress and flats.

As for what Darcy said about she and TJ working out, she wondered. Did the fact TJ offered to be her accompaniment for the performance Friday night mean he was taking to the idea of her singing. With his background, it was understandable why he was leery of the music life. But with enough encouragement, and maybe her in the deal, would he be singing a different tune?

Chapter Twenty-Two

"You look so hot." The ponytail platoon gathered around Sara. Yep, the boots had made the outfit. The figure-hugging dress didn't hurt.

"And your makeup, omagawd, it's amazing."

"I did her makeup, hair, and picked the outfit." Darcy stepped between them. "So back off, paparazzi, and let my girl have some breathing space. She needs to be jazzed to go on stage and be amazing."

The girls fawned one more time, then scurried off to their jobs. They looked back with longing as TJ sauntered into view and sidled up to Sara.

"How are you feeling? Nervous?"

She nodded, fiddling with her belt.

TJ put his arm around her shoulder and whispered in her ear. "Do we need to relax you again?"

"It'd be easy enough tonight in this dress," she mumbled.

TJ's eyes lit up and his mouth twisted wickedly. "Ooh, you left the good girl home tonight. Should be fun."

"I needed the one with more confidence. I still don't feel totally comfortable with what I'm wearing."

He stood back, and his eyes gleamed with admiration and desire. "You look stunning. I'm not sure I want people seeing you like this. They might get ideas."

"You getting any ideas, boss? 'Cause it's one of the reasons I picked this outfit."

TJ raised his eyes thoughtfully. "Hmm, yes, I'm getting the idea to fire one of my longtime employees."

"Too bad. We'll miss Mary."

"Go sit down, Darcy. I didn't get the best seats in the house so you could miss the show."

Darcy gave her a hug and wished her luck. Sara thanked her as she scurried off.

"Almost ready, Sunshine? The audience is still filling up but most don't come for the back-up band. Don't take it personally."

"I know, but I have everyone here from the store. I still can't believe you closed it for the night, so they could all come see me."

TJ kissed her nose. "You're important to all of us. Very important to me."

Throwing her arms around his neck, she squeezed tight. How had she deserved someone as great as TJ? Her own family hadn't come. Yes, she knew it was because of the wedding. They were all in a frenzy getting the house ready for the ceremony. She just wished someone had taken the time to see her.

"Hey, if it isn't baby True Jam himself." Sara turned as Stevie Hirsch, the drummer for Python, entered the ready room she was in. "I heard you might be here. Look at you, boy. All grown up. What's with the short haircut and office clothes? You look like a freakin' lawyer." TJ wore jeans and a button-down shirt. Hardly dressy. Gorgeous as always.

"Stevie," TJ greeted, but his face was like stone. Moving closer, she wanted to show TJ her support.

"I'm Sara Storm. I got called in to perform after

your back-up band cancelled."

Stevie frowned. "Yeah, stupid idiots, trying to drive after a party. Three of them in the hospital. They were lucky no one got killed."

TJ took Sara's hand. "She's got to get on the stage in a minute. Take care, Stevie."

"Come back to our ready room. We're getting warmed up with a bottle of scotch. Your old man's back there. It'll feel like old times."

TJ's lips tightened into a smile. Sara could tell it wasn't real. Had his whole life been this way growing up? With these kinds of people?

"Can't, I'm her music tonight. Thanks for the offer."

Stevie waved as they walked out. "You're coming to party after, right?"

TJ shrugged. "Maybe." Taking her elbow, he guided her to the back of the stage.

Elephants tap danced in her stomach as she stared at the stage and all the people sitting around it. Could she do this? Singing at the fair had been a success, but this was tons more people. The reassuring presence of TJ at her back helped.

"You'll be terrific. Never doubt it."

When she glanced up, his deep brown eyes were filled with emotion. Yeah, she'd be fine. Because of him.

The announcer, introducing her name over the loudspeakers, startled her, and she held TJ's hands in a death grip. He pressed his lips to hers for only a second, but it was enough to settle her nerves and help calm her.

"Ready?" He held out his hand so she could go up the stage stairs before him. A deep breath and squared shoulders and she was ready. She took that first step, wondering where it would lead her.

****

TJ sat at the piano as Sara took the microphone and introduced herself to the audience. She was nervous, but her optimistic personality took over, and the crowd soon warmed to her. It wasn't typical of what Python usually had as back-up, but once they heard her voice, they'd love her. Just like he did.

Like he did. Shit. He did. Love her. Jim had suggested it, but he hadn't wanted to believe it. Hadn't thought he was capable of love any more. Sara had done this to him. Made him believe in love. Made his heart thaw and open up, so he could feel again.

Should he tell her? Obviously, not right this moment. When she finished talking about the first song, he took his cue. The love thing he'd have to figure out later.

Flexing his fingers, he played a short run on the piano, then started the first song. Sara joined on the right note, and he let the music take him. Autopilot kicked on as Sara's angelic voice drifted lovingly around the arena.

The applause was thunderous as she finished the lyrics, and he took note of her face. It was flushed with excitement, and her eyes shone with pride. Tonight, she'd be perfect.

And she was. Her interaction with the audience was natural, and her voice rang out beautifully. A few songs were upbeat and energetic, while a few were soulful and filled with emotion. The emotion found its way inside his heart and expanded the love he felt for this incredible woman.

Exquisite in every way. And, God, how sexy did she look in that outfit? A far cry from her usual sweetness. Her dress didn't show much skin with the mid length sleeves and round neck. It wasn't much more than a glorified long T-shirt with a low-slung belt, but it fit and emphasized her curves and showed off her mile-long legs. Her hair was all curly and pinned up in spots, while it fell over her shoulders in others. And those boots. God, those high-heeled boots rising all the way past her knees and up to her thighs…they were giving him some luscious ideas. Ideas involving her in nothing but those boots.

"Thank you for being so kind and making me feel welcome. My last song of the night holds special meaning to a friend of mine, and I hope you enjoy it."

Taking a deep breath, he started the notes for *Everything.* It was always hard to get through this one.

"*You were everything to me, I was everything to you.*"

Sara walked around the stage, connecting with the audience. Her eyes filled with tears, and she sang as if she had lived through the pain herself. So tangible he could feel it. But as she poured out his agony all over the stage, TJ's heart seemed lighter for some reason. Losing Sonni still sliced through him, but somehow it didn't hurt as much. Listening to the words, he focused more on how much they'd cared about each other and done for each other. Not on the loss. One more thing Sara had helped him accomplish. Was he finally coming to terms with Sonni's death and ridding himself of the guilt? Not all, he'd always feel responsible to a point. But maybe he could allow himself to move past it and get on with living.

"How can I go on…knowing you won't be there for me? Knowing everything is gone."

The last haunting notes died away, and the crowd roared. The shop crew stood and cheered furiously. Darcy's whistles echoed through the tent.

Turning around, Sara waved to all in the circular theater, and he saw how moved she was by the reaction. She loved it. And he loved her. If there had been even the tiniest bit of doubt in his mind before, it had been erased. This woman had stolen his heart, and it would never be the same again. He'd never be the same again.

"Wasn't she fantastic?"

The familiar voice echoed through the speakers. Abe appeared at the back of the stage, waving to the audience. TJ would kill him if he ruined Sara's night.

"I wanted to thank this beautiful, young lady for stepping in at the last minute to help us out."

The crowd roared to life as Abe stood beside Sara and placed his arm around her shoulder. Sara smiled shyly at him.

"Let's all give her another round of applause to show our appreciation for her and her outstanding performance."

The audience clapped wildly, and Sara's face turned pink. Abe was working up the crowd, but he allowed her to have her moment, too. TJ wouldn't interfere.

"Can I introduce your pianist?" Her gaze flew toward the piano, and she nodded.

"The lovely, and extremely talented, Sara Storm was accompanied today by none other than my son, True Bannister. True, take a bow."

He rose slowly, hating the limelight. After lifting

his hand for a quick wave, he walked toward Sara. She slipped her hand in his and held tight.

Abe kissed Sara's cheek and thrust out his hand to TJ. After shaking his father's hand, he guided Sara off stage. As they left, Abe chuckled into the microphone. "Taught him everything I know."

The audience roared to life again as the rest of Python bounced onto the stage. Seriously, he was surprised any of these guys could still bounce at all. Within seconds, the first strains of their biggest hit echoed through the arena. Satisfaction ran through his veins. It was a song he'd written for them.

He'd barely pulled Sara into the alcove behind the stage area, when the Ponytail Platoon descended on them.

"Omagawd, Sara, you were amazing." They fawned over her first, then one turned on him and hung on his shoulder. Too many years ago, he would have been all over it. All over her. Times had changed and so had he. The only one he wanted touching him in any way was the wide-eyed beauty standing in front of him.

"You're Abe Bannister's son. And is Celia Muñez your mom? I love her."

"Sara, you didn't tell us you were living with Abe and Celia's son. How could you not tell us?"

Sara looked overwhelmed, and he stepped in, pulling her close to his side. "It's not something I advertise, for obvious reasons. If you'll excuse us."

Steering her away, they bumped into the bookstore crew. After spending a few minutes congratulating Sara, Mary shooed them all away.

"Let the poor girl have some air."

TJ gestured to the arena. "The tickets are for the

whole concert so feel free to listen to the rest. I hear Python's a popular band."

Darcy rolled her eyes. "Don't give up the day job to go into comedy, boss. But you've got mad piano skills. Who knew?"

"I think Mary and I will cut the night short," Jim said. "It's not really our kind of music."

TJ thanked them for coming. The others wandered away as the noise ramped up with Python's music. "You want to stay and listen, or are you done for the night?"

When she slid into his arms, he held tight. Her whole body shook. With excitement, nerves, or fear? Didn't matter. Someplace quieter was what she needed, and he had just the place.

"Come on, I'm going to take you *home*."

Chapter Twenty-Three

Tonight had been unreal. The applause still thundered in Sara's head, making her thoughts swirl and dance. Subconsciously, she knew the people had gone to see Python. But they'd clapped and yelled for her. It was heady stuff, and she was still shaking.

"Sit here, and I'll get you something to eat." TJ guided her into the chair at the kitchen table. "You haven't had anything since breakfast."

"Thanks." She sighed and allowed TJ to put together a sandwich. Her stomach couldn't handle anything heavier.

"You're floating on cloud nine right now. I'm going to fill the Jacuzzi so you can wind down a little. I'll be right back."

Floating on cloud nine. Yeah, she was floating all right. What a rush. She'd gotten a taste of what it felt like to sing in front of a large audience. Maybe not the thousands she wanted, but it was more than she'd experienced before. And she liked it.

Her mind whirled as she picked at her meal. When TJ returned, he sat next to her and stared.

"What?" Did she have the make-up Darcy'd insisted on running down her face?

"You're simply amazing." He took her dishes to the sink. "You need some pampering. After your outstanding performance, I think you deserve it."

Leading her through his bedroom, where one small lamp was on, he continued into the bathroom. The sight took Sara's breath away.

Jets churned the water filling the tub. The rest of the bathroom had been transformed into a romantic dream. A dozen candles flickered on multiple surfaces. The mirrors reflected the light, making the room appear alive. It was magical.

She slipped into TJ's arms. He'd done this for her. "I love it."

A muscle twitched in his face, then he kissed her. A soft, gentle kiss, but it promised more.

"We need to get you wound down, or you'll never sleep tonight."

She tried for a coy smile. "I like how you relaxed me before."

Throwing back his head, he laughed. "Oh, we'll get there, Sunshine. Don't you worry. But I've got a few other things planned. First, we need the jets to work off any lingering tension from your earlier anxiety."

Her gaze went to the tub, then back. Did he expect her to strip in front of him, or would he leave while she did? Or…would he join her? The thought sent delicious heat rushing straight between her legs. This man made her feel in more places than she'd even known existed.

"Let me help with this belt."

Question answered. The belt slid off, and he dropped it behind him. When she bent to unzip her boot, he stopped her.

"No, those stay on till last. I've been having some wicked fantasies involving those boots."

Darcy had been right. She said they'd drive TJ crazy. Reaching for the hem of her dress, he slowly lifted it over her head. Biting her lip, she stood before him in only the boots and lacy underwear Darcy had forced her to get. Thank God, she hadn't worn her white cotton.

TJ's eyes glowed with desire, and she had the urge to cover herself. But the naughty little girl she'd hidden away her whole life pushed past the nice one and took charge. Pulling out the elastic holding up part of her hair, she shook her head.

"I should put it all up, so it doesn't get too wet." Turning slightly, she bent over and spent a few moments scooping her hair together. More time than needed, but she could tell TJ was getting an eyeful of her behind covered only by a wisp of lace. When the second groan left his mouth, she figured he'd been tortured enough. Quickly, she twisted her hair into a knot and secured it.

TJ stepped closer and ran a finger over the lace of her bra. It was black and pushed her up, making her look larger than she was. Would he be disappointed when it was off? Could she wear it in the tub?

He rubbed his thumb over where she'd bitten her lip.

"I've seen it already, Sunshine. I approve."

Still reading her mind. Some of her thoughts were not of the nice-girl variety. She better be careful.

Sara waited for him to remove the rest of her clothes, but he didn't. Standing there, he simply stared, hunger in his eyes.

He trailed a finger down her throat to rest between her breasts. "I want to memorize this moment so I'll never forget."

Was he doing this because he thought it wouldn't

last? Would he take what he wanted, then kick her aside, like he had so many others? No. It wasn't who he was anymore. It wasn't only what he wanted, it was what she wanted, too. She wanted it all. Wanted all her questions answered. TJ was the perfect person to answer them. Her feelings had never been this deep for anyone else.

"You should probably get in the tub before the candles burn down."

"I guess I need to remove this, then," she whispered, her voice rough and throaty. Where had the seductive tone come from?

Reaching back, she unhooked the bra and let the straps slide down her arms but held the cups for a moment before letting it fall. TJ's Adam's apple bobbed up and down as he swallowed.

"These need to go, too." Slipping her thumbs in the waist of her lacy black panties, she twisted her hips from side to side as she lowered them. When they got to her knees, she turned slightly and bent over, showing TJ the same sight he'd groaned over earlier. This time sans lace.

As she sat on the edge of the tub, she struck a pose. Was it seductive? Like she had any experience with seduction. But she wanted TJ to think of her as sexy and not some innocent little virgin to be pitied and comforted.

"I almost want you to stay in those boots for a while longer," TJ growled, his eyes fierce and hungry. "But I imagine they were expensive and—"

"Darcy would kill me if I ruined them."

When she reached for the zipper, he knelt in front of her. "Let me…please."

Running his hands up her legs, he kissed along her thighs. The sensation of his stubbled cheeks moving over her skin sent shivers up her spine. It made her crazy, but she wanted so much more. When he leaned back, and his gaze roamed over her exposed body, she stiffened. Her instinct was to cover up, but she wanted him to see her. To know what his touch did to her. To invite him to do more. It seemed to take forever for him to unzip the boots and peel them off. As he kissed his way up each leg, she held her breath, wondering if he'd keep going to the soul shattering end.

When he stopped right above her left knee, she could have cried.

"Time to get in and relax." He helped her slide in, and she sighed as the jets pulsed against her back. Wonderful in a completely different way than TJ's lips on her.

She glanced up to where he stood watching her, then lifted her hand from the floral-scented water and motioned for him.

"Are you joining me?"

Desire flared in his eyes, making her warmer than the heated water.

"If you want me to."

She did. Wanted him very much. Could he see it in her eyes, the way she saw his need and passion?

At her nod, TJ kicked off his shoes and socks, never letting his gaze leave her. Now it was her turn to watch, as he unbuttoned his shirt and let it fall off his shoulders. His lean, muscled chest heaved in and out as he undid his belt and opened his snap. The sound of the zipper seemed louder than normal. Her breathing did, too. The pulsating water and the scent of jasmine mingling with roses from the candles, caused her senses to heighten. And the unique smell that was TJ. Heady. Like knowing he'd soon be joining her.

His pants slithered down his legs and his boxers followed.

"Last chance to change your mind."

She couldn't tear her gaze away from TJ's arousal. It was huge and practically quivering as he stood there waiting for her answer. He said he'd never do more than she was ready for, right? So, if she wasn't ready, he'd stop. He was giving her time to back out.

Moving aside, she crooked her finger at him. As he climbed in, he grinned but stayed on the other side of the tub, resting his head and letting the jets pulse against his back. Would he do more? Confusion set in, so she sat back and allowed the water to relax her.

It wasn't long before something slid by her leg. She opened her eyes when his foot ran along her skin. Okay, so it wasn't just a bath tonight. Good, she'd been hoping for more.

She slid her own foot up and down his leg. As it got closer to his middle, he caught it and pulled. Squealing, she flailed her hands, splashing water all over the place.

"Are you trying to drown me?"

"Drown, no," he answered, his arms now around her, her back to his front. "Trying to save myself from rogue feet. They were getting a bit too close to some delicate parts. Didn't want any damage done."

As she snuggled into him, his erection pressed against her back. "I wouldn't have done any damage."

"Maybe not, but I like you here better and it's safer for my goods."

“Are you sure your goods are safe here?” She wiggled her butt.

TJ moaned. “You do know how to torture a man, Sunshine. Now be still, or I’ll—”

“You’ll what? Retaliate? I liked your retaliation last time.”

“Mmm, so did I. Maybe I’ll have to come up with something worse.”

She shifted her behind again. “I can’t wait.”

“Oh, you’re getting awfully sassy. You’ve released the naughty girl and didn’t put a leash on her, did you?”

“Do you like the naughty girl better?” What did she want him to answer?

His nose nuzzled into her neck. “The naughty girl is fun, but the sweet one, the girl filled with sunshine, is the one I fell in love with.”

She froze. He’d fallen in love with her? Really? They’d only known each other a few months. Could people fall in love that fast? And how did she feel? He’d released her passion and made her aware of her sensuality. Certainly, she cared for him and trusted him more than anything. Would she be sitting naked in a tub with him otherwise? But love?

“You love me?”

“I do, Sara.” He used her name. Shit, what did she do? Say?

“I, um…”

“It’s okay. You don’t have to say anything.”

His arms stiffened, but he didn’t let her go. Damn. How the heck would she know what love was? She loved her family, and she thought she’d loved Robby. But it was a very different kind of love. Not like what TJ was talking about.

"I don't know…I've haven't…I've never been in love? How do you know if you are?"

When he sat up straighter, she missed his skin against hers. But he turned her around to face him and stroked her cheek. "Sometimes it takes a while to realize. I think I've been fighting it ever since I met you."

"Why?"

He shrugged and pulled her closer. She settled on his lap, enjoying the feel of his legs under hers.

"You were perfect, and I didn't think I deserved something so innocent and beautiful."

"But, you—"

"Shh." When he placed his fingers against her lips, she drew one into her mouth, causing him to groan. "You made me see I'm not the horrible person I thought I was. I hate who I used to be and don't ever want to go back there, but I know now I've changed. Become a better person. Because of you. You've healed my heart and taught me to love again. I didn't think I could."

A tear slipped down her cheek, and he caught it with his finger, then kissed where it had landed. Sliding closer, she pressed her lips to his, wrapping her arms around his neck. He ran his hands over her back, his fingers scorching a path wherever they touched.

"You are my Sunshine…" TJ's words penetrated her brain. He was singing an old children's song.

Sara leaned her forehead against his. "Do I make you happy?"

"You do. No matter what kind of sky we have."

"You make me happy, too."

"I like making you happy. I can't believe how good it feels to not be totally self-indulgent all the time."

"You're not self-indulgent. What are you talking about?"

He kissed her cheek, then traveled to her earlobe. "I was for a long time. Even after Sonni died. I just indulged myself with different things. Even the bookstore was an indulgence. I had the money, so I bought it."

"You bought it to help Mary financially, then kept her working on after. Hardly self-indulgent."

His lips twisted. "Hmm, maybe you're right. But I do feel kind of self-indulgent right now. I want to indulge myself in you. Any objections?"

"None at all."

She straddled his lap to get as near as possible. Indulging never felt so good.

Their mouths met and soon a battle ensued. She loved kissing him. It was intense and made parts of her tingle she hadn't known existed.

Part of her was tingling right now. Especially with the tip of TJ's erection teasing her opening. What would it be like to have it inside her?

As they kissed, she wiggled until she had him right there. Would he even notice? Could she move a little and feel more of him inside her? Not much but just more. The part of him rubbing against her was driving her crazy. She needed more.

When she eased down a tiny bit, he started to fill her. Oh, God. Unbelievable. Just a little more.

TJ pulled on her arms and settled her farther away. "What are you doing?"

"I'm sorry." All her old insecurities flooded back. "It felt good. I thought…"

Framing her face with his hands, he kissed her

tenderly. “Of course it feels good. It’s supposed to. But if you really want to go there, we need to do it right.”

****

Sara’s innocent face fell. “I did it wrong?”

Damn, he loved her so much. Loved teaching her about her sexuality. She was an apt student. Almost too good today. When she’d wiggled her cute ass onto his lap and started impaling herself on his cock, he’d almost thrust inside out of shear habit.

“No, but since it’s your first time, we should do things a little differently. We can do the bathtub sex later.” He winked outrageously. “Let’s dry off before we start to prune.” When he stood, Sara gazed at him, her eyes sparkling.

“Isn’t it good to be wet?”

The naughty girl would kill him. “Yes, in certain ways. Not right now.”

Taking a fluffy towel, he wrapped it around his waist, then took another and helped her from the tub. The sight of her all dripping and glistening with fragranced water made his cock twitch. If he didn’t find release soon, he’d burst out of his skin.

He took his time, patting her damp skin, then tucked the towel under her arms. After picking up a candle, he led her into his bedroom and placed it next to the bed, grinning. “Ambience.”

As she sat, she twisted her hands together. When she tried to ride him a few minutes ago, she certainly hadn’t seemed nervous. Hopefully, he could get her back there.

“Come here,” He pulled her to lie next to him. “Let me hold you for a minute. We could take up where we left off in the tub.”

As he pressed his mouth to hers, her body softened and relaxed again. Soon she wiggled against him, and they'd be right back to where they were in the tub if he didn't do something.

"When you make love to someone, you have to be careful. You never know who they've also…made love to." It felt strange using that term, but what he planned to do to Sara was definitely making love.

"Oh, my God, like STDs. I totally forgot. Do you—?"

He shook his head. "No, I'm clean. It's been a while since I've done this, but I was always careful, and I get checked every year. But don't ever forget, Sunshine." The thought of her with any other man twisted his gut into a knot. He couldn't imagine his life without her.

TJ kissed her again, then reached in the bedside table to retrieve a few packets he'd stored there earlier. "I wasn't sure if I'd need them, but with the way we've been getting closer, I bought some just in case."

"I'm glad you did." She still looked nervous. Kissing her again, he slid his hands over her arms, then loosened the towel, so he could trail his lips down her throat to nibble and lick. As she arched her back, tiny whimpers started the moment he made his way to her pebbled nipples.

Damn, he could do this forever. Touching, caressing, tasting this incredible woman was heaven in so many ways. She became braver, and her hands roamed his torso, then untucked his towel. Her eyes widened when she saw his arousal.

"It's awfully big."

TJ kissed her again. "You're so good for my ego.

It'll be perfect, you'll see. But we need a little prep work first."

He wanted her ready and squirming when he entered her. Inching his hand down her flat stomach, he twirled through the trimmed hair on her mound. Her hips twisted at his touch, and he let his fingers slip lower. His mouth soon followed.

When she opened her legs to accommodate him, he nearly exploded right there. Did she have any idea what effect her actions had on him? He caressed her for a minute, then stopped to pull on the condom. She watched curiously, her eyes wide, her teeth nibbling her bottom lip.

He stroked his tongue through her sensitive skin, eliciting whimpers. With his fingers taunting her opening, he slid them inside to prepare her for what was to come. Reaching down, she grabbed his hair and held tight. Her hips twisted as his tongue and fingers worked their magic.

So close. Her cries escalated, and her frenzied movements grew. But he wanted to be inside her and watch as she came apart.

Crawling back up her body, his lips nibbled along the way. Her whimpers of protest got to him, so he skimmed his hand down to where he'd been playing before and rubbed along the sensitive nub.

"Ready for the big time, Sunshine? You need to be sure." One last chance to back out. *Oh, God, don't let her take it.*

She wrapped her arms around his neck and her legs around his waist. His tongue tangled with hers as he kissed her soundly. Then he shifted positions, so she was across his chest, her legs draped on either side of his hips.

"I'm putting you in the driver's seat. Take as much time as you need. I may explode in the meantime, but I want you to move at your own pace."

Panic crossed her innocent features. "What do I do?"

Running his hand across her back, he pulled her closer to where she needed to be. "You were doing fine in the tub."

Sara wiggled her gorgeous ass around his hips and soon found right where she'd been before. As she pushed forward and he entered her, her eyes closed and her mouth opened. When she rotated her hips, he nearly died from the torture. Tight, though not in as far as he wanted to be. But she was in control. It was all her.

"Feel good?" Her expression told him it did.

Her forearms rested beside his head, and her nipples teased the skin of his chest. The pressure built, but he wouldn't rush her. This had to be perfect.

A tiny nod, then she kissed him, her tongue running over his bottom lip. Nipping at it, he pulled it into his mouth.

"This is…so good. Darcy said I shouldn't be a writer. I guess she's right. But it feels amazing. I thought it hurt."

Damn, so innocent. "I'm not all the way in yet, Sunshine. We've got a bit to go. I've heard there can be some pain. This is my first, too. My first virgin, so I haven't actually seen it in action." He may have been a slime, but he'd never taken an innocent before. He'd drawn the line at that.

Sara bit her bottom lip. "A first time for both of us."

Caressing the side of her face, he tucked a strand of hair behind her ear. “Take your time. Go at your own pace. I’ll simply lie here, enjoying the look of pure ecstasy on your face.”

As she twisted her hips, he sucked in a deep breath. It was going to kill him. But he’d die a happy man. Slowly, agonizingly, he filled her. At one point, she paused, her face intense, then continued until they were pelvis to pelvis.

“That’s it, huh? I’m deflowered now?”

God, he could cry. Why had he allowed her to do this? He should have had more control. Did she regret it already?

Her breath rushed out, and she stared at him, passion flaring, her hips moving again. “This feels unbelievable.” As she pushed herself to sitting, rapture filled her expression. “There’s more, right? You still feel really hard. Aren’t you supposed to get soft after?”

Precious. “We aren’t done quite yet. Remember how you felt when I touched you the other day? We still need to get there.”

Her eyes lit up, and she looked like she’d stolen a cookie and gotten away with it.

Running his hands over her hips, he rocked her away slightly, then pulled back again. Soon she seemed to get the idea and began rocking back and forth, her eyes wider with each thrust. He sat up until he could surround her nipple with his mouth. When he sucked and licked, Sara’s breathing sped up, and her hips gyrated faster.

He couldn’t do anything but watch her face, filled with awe. Closer, closer, anticipation apparent in her every muscle. And he was right there with her. The sight of her gently swaying breasts and twisting hips made him grab control and hold on until she found her pleasure. He sucked on her nipple again to help her out.

Suddenly, her shoulders hunched and tremors racked her body. Her head fell back as she cried out his name. Damn, so gorgeous. Flipping her over before she could recover, he thrust inside, deeper and harder. He didn’t want to hurt her but needed release, and she was the only one to give it to him. It would only ever be Sara.

Tremors rocked as his orgasm ripped through him. It was like nothing he’d experienced. The emotion running through his veins and into his heart was more powerful than ever. It was the first time he’d truly made love.

He eyed her, his breathing quick and heavy.

“You okay?” When had he cared about his partner’s wellbeing? Never. Until now.

The stolen cookie expression returned. “Now I know what the fuss is about. But it’s not always this way, is it? My friend, Shelbie, said it wasn’t so great.”

“If you’re with the right person…and they take your needs into account…” How many times had he simply taken what he wanted, regardless of what the girl got from it? Too many to count. His face must have shown his disgust because Sara gave him a sweet kiss and ran her hand over his cheek.

“You took my needs into account. It was more than I could have ever imagined. Thank you.”

“No, thank you, Sunshine.” There was so much more he wanted to say, but he was afraid of scaring her off. These feelings were still new and confusing, and he’d give her time to figure them out. It had taken him a while to admit his.

TJ got up to blow out the candles in the bathroom and clean up, then slipped back in bed, pulling the covers over them. Sara curled into his arms and within seconds was asleep. Holding her, he couldn't help think how much this tiny woman had changed his life. Changed him. There was nothing more he wanted than to stay here by her side, snuggled up and content. They might threaten to take away his man card if he ever admitted how much he liked cuddling with her, but he didn't care. With Sara in his arms, he could conquer anything.

Chapter Twenty-Four

"We did some checking on your boss," Alex announced as he and Luke surrounded her in the kitchen. Sara glanced around quickly, relieved TJ and his truck had been commandeered as soon as they got to New Hampshire.

Luke tilted his head. "Do you know who he is? Or maybe I should say who his parents are?"

Sara shook them off. "Yes, I know. They were in the shop about a month ago."

Both men looked deflated. Alex narrowed his eyes. "Did you know he has a history of drug and alcohol abuse?"

Clamps tightened around Sara's heart. "Yes, and I also know he's been clean for over seven years. He still sees his AA sponsor every week. What's your point?"

Luke crossed his arms over his chest. "We're just watching out for you. We don't want you hurt."

"He told you all this stuff?" Alex looked doubtful.

"Yes, he also writes music under the name James True. For full disclosure, in case you planned to hire a private detective to follow him around and dig up all his dirt."

Alex sighed. "We only want you safe. We didn't know if this guy was hiding information from you. Why does he write under a different name if he has nothing to hide?"

"When his sister died of an overdose, he wanted to get away from that life, so he moved here. He still wrote music but didn't want anyone knowing who he was as reporters can get pretty bad. He wants privacy and to live quietly."

Luke and Alex nodded at each other. When would they stop fussing over her? She was a grown woman now. Although she wouldn't share that fact with either of them. They'd chase TJ down with a hatchet.

"Don't you boys have anything better to do than bother your sister," their mom asked as she entered the kitchen. "We have a wedding here tomorrow with about twenty-five people coming. I'm sure your father has a list of things needing to be done."

The list was probably her mother's, but Sara silently thanked her for the interruption. No more interrogations from her brothers. She turned to load the dishwasher as her mom scolded the guys and shooed them out of the house.

"Thank you, sweetie, for helping out." Her mom kissed her cheek, then pulled out some casserole dishes. "I appreciate your getting here early. I know you were up late last night and must be tired."

Her gaze whipped to her mom. How did she know they'd been up late? Did Sara have a big sign on her forehead? One replacing the pure white V she'd worn forever?

"How was the concert? We were all disappointed we couldn't get down, but I've been out straight with this wedding. I don't know why Erik needed to do it so soon."

She sighed. Okay, no sign reporting the incredible sex she'd had last night. *Be careful. Mom reads you like a book.* And this book was now a sexy romance novel, thanks to TJ.

"The concert was excellent. I only performed for a half hour, but the crowd was so great. I think they liked me."

"Wonderful, honey. Of course they loved you." Her mom gave her a quick hug on her way to the fridge, then handed Sara some eggs. "Can you crack half a dozen of those and whip them up."

They worked alongside each other for a while getting food ready. Her dad and TJ returned with chairs from the VFW, and Sara stared out the window for a few minutes, hoping TJ was okay. Luke and Alex were also out there, and she didn't want them giving TJ a hard time. He meant too much to her.

"Mom?"

Her mother was in the middle of cutting chicken for the Alfredo dish and lifted her brow as Sara picked up a knife to help. Did she have the courage to ask?

"How did you know you were in love with Dad?"

Her mother's smile was all knowing as she glanced toward the window, then back to her cutting. Damn. Had she given herself away?

"Your father and I were pretty young. I liked him right away, but it took a while before I realized I was in love with him. Is there a reason you've asked?"

Carefully slicing the knife through the white meat, she said, "Not really. I mean, no, I just…I've never been in love before, and I wondered if it was something you just knew when it happened. Someone told me it took a while for them to figure it out. I didn't know if it happened faster for some, or if it always took a while."

Damn, that sounded lame. "With Erik and Tessa

getting married, I started thinking of it. Nothing more."

Her mom scooped the chicken and put it in a large dish, then washed her hands in the sink. She stared out the window, then turned back. "There are people who fall in love right away. Your Uncle Nick said he knew the second he laid eyes on Aunt Luci she was the one. Now your father, we had to break up and be apart for a few months before he came to his senses and realized he loved me."

"Did you break up because you said you loved Dad and he didn't say it back?" Her stomach clenched. Would TJ not want to be with her if she didn't say she loved him?

"No, we were young, and your father got scared. He did love me. He just didn't know it yet. Those feelings frightened him. When I wasn't around for a while, he missed me, then he knew."

"So, he came crawling back to you?"

Her mom grinned. "Not quite crawling, but he came back. He asked me to marry him a few months later."

Marriage? Marriage wasn't anything she'd thought of except in the future. Fulfilling her dreams needed to come first.

"You know, sweetie, you seem much calmer, less anxious today. Maybe living on your own down the Cape has been a good influence on you."

Living on her own, hardly. And the relaxed part was mostly TJ's doing. Oh, shit, she couldn't think about this with her mother standing right here.

"Maybe I needed to spread my wings and see what flying was all about." She looked out the window to hide the red cheeks those thoughts were causing. Her mom simply nodded, so Sara got cups and the pitcher of iced tea and carried it out to the yard. The men were setting up a large tent to protect everyone from the harsh sun during the ceremony.

"Mom says you can take a break. A short break."

"It's a good thing you brought TJ along," her father said. "Not only did his truck come in handy, but he doesn't argue when you give him a task."

"I'm not arguing, Dad," Alex called back. "But you have to measure these things or they come out lopsided. Do you want the tent falling down on the bride and groom?"

"I don't think a quarter inch will make much of a difference."

Luke grimaced. "If I engineered something with so much leeway, I'd get fired."

Her dad took his drink, then went back to help her brothers adjust the side of the canopy. TJ finished hammering a stake into the ground, then walked over.

"You surviving?" she asked as she poured him a glass.

"I'm fine, but I really need to kiss you."

Her brothers watched them like hawks. "My guardians might get upset. Maybe we can sneak away later and do something…relaxing." *Holy shit. Had she actually suggested this?* The naughty girl was running amok.

After downing the liquid, TJ held out the cup for more. "I don't think we'll get much chance to do anything, especially not something…relaxing."

Sara tried not to giggle at their code word.

"Alex informed me the sleeping arrangements for tonight were women at one house and guys at another."

"What? Where are you sleeping?'

TJ glanced back at the men. "Not with you, Sunshine, unfortunately. I didn't expect to, but I hoped for the same house. We're staying at Alex's for the night."

Reaching over, she touched his hand. He squeezed back, rubbing his thumb over her skin. *Enjoy this now. It's all you're likely to get until you're alone again.*

****

"Your dress is beautiful, Sara."

Sara looked at Tessa as she pinned the woman's long walnut tresses into loose ringlets.

"Thanks, Tessa, but today is your day. No one's going to notice me. You're the bride. They'll all be looking at you."

Tessa fiddled with the lace on her dress. "I really wish they wouldn't. Maybe you could keep them distracted while the ceremony is going on."

Adjusting a small flower in Tessa's hair, she scanned to make sure all of them were placed a nice distance apart, then held the mirror for Tessa to see the back. Her future sister-in-law didn't seem interested, so Sara sat in front of her and took her hands.

"Are you okay? Is there some reason you aren't as excited as I thought a bride should be? Did Erik do something to get you upset?"

"No." Tessa shook her head, curls bouncing. "Erik's been great. I guess I'm a little nervous. You know I've never been one for the spotlight."

It was true. Tessa was about Sara's age and had moved in with the Millers, her grandparents' neighbors in Maine, when she was fourteen. The shyness had been extreme, and she hadn't interacted much at first with all the cousins who hung around the Storm house. Slowly, she'd come to hang out with Sara and her cousins, but even then, she was the quiet one of the group.

Why are these two getting married and so soon? "I know my mom can be a bit like a steamroller when she has things to do. Did you want something different for a wedding?"

Standing, Tessa gazed at herself in the mirror. A tiny smile lit her face. "Your mom's been great. She helped me pick this dress and even asked what I wanted for flowers and decorations. It doesn't really matter. I never figured I'd get married, so I didn't have anything special in mind. What she's planned is beautiful. I love it."

"Do you love Erik?" Maybe she shouldn't have asked, but he was her brother, and he deserved someone who loved him.

Tessa's eyes closed for a moment. "This marriage isn't really about love. It's about helping Erik so he can keep the children. He needs them, you know."

Tears filled Tessa's eyes. "He needs me, too. Even if he won't admit he needs anything."

Sara chuckled. "Yeah, that's my brother, the big strong guy who won't ever ask for help. He can do it all."

Now Tessa's smile was real. "And he *can* do it all. But not right now and not without some help. I'll be there for him and make sure the kids are safe and taken care of. Make sure they have a family. And I'll do anything else he needs me for. I do care for him, Sara. Erik's always been nice to me, even when others haven't been. He's a good man."

One tear slipped down Sara's cheek hearing Tessa

talk about her brother. Yes, Erik was a good man, and Tessa was lucky to get him. But it seemed like Erik was getting a great deal with Tessa, too. Maybe, like her, Tessa and Erik only needed some time to realize they were in love.

Wiping her cheek, Sara looked around the room. "Do we have everything? I think it's time to head downstairs."

Tessa pulled Sara in for a hug and held tight. As she let go, Sara kissed her cheek. "I'm glad I'm finally getting a sister. I've been outnumbered too long in this house. Welcome to the family."

Squaring her shoulders, Tessa nodded, as if trying to convince herself of something, then they walked downstairs. The next few minutes flew by as Sara walked down the makeshift aisle, her grandfather escorting Tessa behind her. When Erik saw the bride, his face lit up. Yeah, maybe there wasn't love yet, but it was close.

As Tessa and Erik said their vows, Sara peeked at TJ, who sat in the second row, next to Sofie. His eyes were glued to her, and he smirked as he saw her turn. Facing forward again, she thought about TJ and what they'd done the past week. He'd introduced her to her passionate side, and she didn't think she could ever ignore it again. But did she want to?

The answer was no. Friday night had been spectacular. Her imagination hadn't even come close to picturing what her first time would be like. A few of her friends had mentioned the back seat of cars or cheap motels. She'd gotten a candlelit Jacuzzi and king-sized bed with an ocean breeze.

But she'd missed TJ's arms around her last night.

For the past week, she'd slept in his bed every night and woken to him kissing her every morning. It was something she could get used to. Would he want her to? Or would he say goodbye when summer was over and send her back home? *He said he loves you.* The problem was her and her uncertainty. Living with him for a few months, while she was doing a summer job, was one thing. Living with him permanently was something very different and a much bigger commitment. It was too soon for something so deep.

The priest declared Erik and Tessa husband and wife, and Sara paid closer attention. Erik caressed Tessa's face, then lowered his head to kiss her tenderly. They looked beautiful, exactly like a bride and groom should. Her brother's Marine dress uniform emphasized his good looks while Tessa's lace dress was simple yet elegant. Erik couldn't hide the fact he thought she looked amazing.

Tessa might say this marriage was only for the kids, but the way she and Erik looked at each other, Sara would place bets more would grow very soon. Her heart hoped they found happiness. They deserved it.

Applause let Sara know it was time to bring the food out. The guys repositioned the chairs around tables, leaving a small space for an impromptu dance floor. There was no band or DJ, but Luke had hooked his phone up to speakers with appropriate music for dinner and dancing. Erik's new children, Matty and Kiki, frolicked in the empty space.

With the food placed on long tables, and the guests getting their meals, Sara nodded to TJ, ready for their little present.

"Can I have everyone's attention? TJ and I

prepared a little gift for the bride and groom. This is a new song he wrote this summer, and we've been practicing it all week. Congratulations, Erik and Tessa."

Sara picked up her guitar, and TJ sat behind the keyboard Alex had moved into place. TJ started playing, and she joined in.

"*Gray skies filled my world as I passed through yesterday*," TJ's deep vocals joined her higher ones. "*Never knowing which path I should take along the way.*"

"*But you stepped into my life, and the sun began to shine. I see the path I need for happiness to be mine*."

Sara looked around to see her family smiling. They'd heard her sing but not often. Except for her brothers, who always complained she sang too much.

"*You said, 'Put the past behind you and live for today,' you taught me how to love and see beauty along the way. Now we're walking hand in hand down a road I've never known. With promise of tomorrow, you have given me a home.*"

The words moved Sara, and she thought of how tender TJ had been when they'd made love. He glanced at her now, and desire lingered in his eyes. Would they do it again tonight, once they got back to the Cape? Her body was still tender is spots, but she wouldn't let that stop her.

The song ended, and Sara walked over to hug Erik. As he held her tight, he whispered, "That was beautiful, Sagey. The best gift ever. Don't take what you have for granted."

Tessa had tears in her eyes as Sara embraced her new sister-in-law. "Be happy with him."

Tessa gave a small nod, then kissed her cheek. TJ

was behind her shaking Erik's hand. Her family clapped, then her mom stood and ordered everyone to eat. Laughter floated through the air, and Sara walked back to her table with TJ at her side.

"Is the food any good in this joint?" he teased, lifting a forkful to his mouth. Oh, the things his mouth had done recently. Heat rose in her cheeks as his hand slid onto her thigh under the table. He gave a squeeze, then took a sip of his iced tea.

"It should be good. I slaved over it all day yesterday. You better eat every bite on your plate."

He looked down, but not before she saw the glint in his eye. "Yes, ma'am."

"You've got him trained well." Sofie sat on Sara's other side and gave her the look. The 'we'll discuss this later' look. Sofie knew her too well and knew something was up.

It wasn't until much later, when they were in the kitchen cleaning up, they had an opportunity to talk alone.

"What's with your gorgeous hunk?" Sofie pretended to wash silverware as Sara scraped out casserole dishes into plastic ware. "And are you guys taking that act on the road? The song was spectacular. You said he wrote it?"

Nodding, Sara stuck the dish into the sudsy water. "TJ's done well with his songwriting." She wouldn't tell Sofie how much he earned. Her cousin got a little money happy at times, saying if she could be as happy with a rich guy as a poor one, then she'd like rich.

"You know he's in love with you, right? The way he looks at you, there couldn't be any doubt."

"I know. He told me."

Sofie did a double take. “He told you he loves you? Shit, when did this happen? Details, girl?”

Lowering her voice, she said, “Friday night, after I sang at the Melody Tent.”

Her face burned with embarrassment at the memory. TJ peeling her clothes off, her in nothing but thigh-high boots. The soak in the tub, and then…

“What were you doing when he told you?”

“We were in his Jacuzzi.”

Sofie’s eyes bugged out. “Wearing?”

“Nothing.”

Her cousin’s gaze whipped around the room, then back to Sara’s face, which had to be fire engine red at the moment. “You slept with him? Oh, my God! How was it? Better than my first time, I hope.”

It wasn’t like she could hide this fact since Sofie knew her little secret. Closing her eyes, she smiled. “Mind blowing. He was so gentle and kept giving me time to change my mind.”

“But you didn’t.” Sofie’s face was only inches from her own.

“No.”

“How do you feel about him?”

Doubt spread through her again. “I’m not sure, Sofe. He means a lot to me, or I wouldn’t have…you know.”

“I know, honey. So, what’s next?”

She shrugged. “Taking it one day at a time. We’ll see what happens by the end of the summer.”

Sofie looked about to say more when Sara’s mom trotted through the back door, TJ in tow. “TJ has graciously agreed to play the piano for us. And sing. But only if you sing with him, Sara. Let’s go.”

After wiping her damp hands, she hugged Sofie, then dragged her along to the family room. Some of the cousins had drifted off, but a few joined them inside. TJ sat at the piano, running his fingers along the keys. When she walked in, he tipped his head in the direction of her guitar which had made its way inside.

"Thanks," she whispered as she sat next to him on the bench. "You couldn't have refused?"

"Have you met your mother? Refusing didn't seem an option."

Sara chuckled. He was right. When Molly Storm got something in her mind, it happened. But was TJ okay with it, or was he horrified he was now the center of attention?

****

"I've heard all you Storm men took piano lessons," TJ mentioned after he and Sara had a mini concert. "I bet your mother would love to hear you play while I get something cold to drink."

"Yes, Luke, play something for us," Sara coaxed, and her youngest brother shot her a deadly look. After refreshing himself, TJ went into the kitchen. Sara's voice rang clear from the other room, but the piano skills were hardly practiced.

Molly followed him in. "Would you like something a bit stronger than iced tea, TJ? We have beer. I'm surprised Alex or Luke haven't offered it yet. I don't know where their manners are?"

"I'm fine with tea, thanks."

"We have wine. Or I could get Peter to give up some of his good Scotch if that's more to your liking."

It was very much to his liking, but he merely smiled. This family, the extended family as well, had been accepting and welcoming. Not once had he felt like an outsider today.

"I don't drink, Molly, but thank you." Big lie. Would she buy it?

"Oh, okay." Her voice gave away her curiosity. "Um, let me get you some ice in a glass."

As he poured, he debated whether to say anything. He wanted Sara in his life, and this was her mother. Certainly, she had a right to know his past. Some of it anyway.

After taking a sip, he said, "I don't drink anymore. I'm an alcoholic."

Molly's eyes widened, and he wondered if her warm welcome would be rescinded. "Oh," she repeated, only now with concern instead.

Her gaze bounced around the kitchen. Damn, why did his past always have to ruin everything?

Molly put her hand to her mouth. "I'm sorry. I didn't know. We've had alcohol here all day. If Sara had said anything, I would have kept it away."

Seriously? She was apologizing for having alcohol out? "Molly, its fine. I don't expect people to change things for me. I haven't had a drink in seven years, so I can be around it without too much trouble."

Her shoulders sagged with relief. Because he wasn't going on a drinking binge?

Reaching out, she patted his arm. "Thank you for telling me. I'm sure it's not something you shout to the world. I'll keep it to myself."

"Pretty sure Luke and Alex know. They kept offering drinks last night. Test of my strength maybe? Luckily, Erik wasn't drinking and appreciated a sober friend."

“Yes.” Molly frowned. “Erik is still on some heavy medication. Those two boys, I should think of something devious to pay them back.” Her eyes gleamed, and he fell a little bit in love with her, too.

“Don’t do anything on my account. Though they both mentioned some sauerkraut dish you make they aren’t too fond of.”

“Ha, perfect.” Her eyes lit up again. “I can make it this week. You, TJ Bannister, have a devious soul. I like you.”

“Thanks. I’ve enjoyed being here. You have a lovely family, and I appreciate how welcome everyone has made me feel.”

“As a friend of Sara’s, you’re always welcome. I couldn’t help but notice maybe there’s a bit more than friendship there?”

Don’t lie to the mom. “I care for Sara deeply.” He wouldn’t use the L word yet. Sara knew, that was good for now. “She has a way of making everything seem better, no matter how bad it looks. I’ve been more optimistic with her around.”

Straightening her shoulders, Molly smiled proudly. “Yes, Sara’s always been upbeat. It’s one of her best assets. And her smile.”

“Her smile could stop wars.”

Molly pulled him into a hug. This is where Sara had gotten the skill. Molly’s hug was warm and comforting, so he returned it with vigor.

“I’m glad you came today.”

“I am, too. Thanks for inviting me. This family is wonderful, and Sara’s extremely lucky.”

A very wrong note sounded from the other room, and Molly winced. “Not lucky Luke hasn’t touched the piano in years. Maybe you can take pity on her and get back in there."

After she gave him another quick squeeze, he followed her back to the others. If he played his cards right, maybe he could be part of this family, too. Someday, if his luck held out.

Chapter Twenty-Five

"Nice melody," TJ commented, stepping onto his porch where Sara played her guitar. "Are you trying to give James True a little competition?"

Sara blushed and continued strumming her fingers over the strings. "I'm just experimenting with some notes. I doubt James True has anything to worry about."

Leaning against the porch railing, he watched as Sara played. She'd already changed into her night attire after they'd come back from work and eaten. The sun was low in the sky, and the warm breeze drifted over them like a caress. It didn't get more perfect than this.

Well, kissing her would make it more perfect. He placed his hands on the back of the swing on either side of her head. When she looked up, her eyes filled with laughter.

"Did you want something?"

"You."

"Me?" Her lips quirked. "What could you possibly want with me?"

When he skimmed his tongue over her bottom lip, her eyes closed and a happy sigh escaped her mouth. He'd caused it. Him. TJ Bannister was the reason Sara was happy. It lifted his heart and sent fulfillment coursing through his veins.

"To love you, be with you, spend every second with you. Is it a problem?"

Had he come on too strong? Her feelings were still uncertain. Obviously, she cared. Sara wasn't the type to jump into bed with a guy without some emotion involved. *Give her time. You have plenty.* Her job at the store was there for as long as she wanted. All he had to do was keep her happy here with him. Easy enough, right?

Sara's eyes crinkled with warmth. "No, no problem at all."

"Good." He lowered his head to feast on her lips again. Maybe they should take this inside. His gaze roamed the beach. No one around. Maybe the porch would be fine.

The sound of a car engine shook him from his sensual thoughts, and he glanced toward the noise. A Mercedes pulled into his driveway. Who could it be at this time?

Sara stood putting her guitar on the bench. Abe and Celia exited the car. Damn. Why the hell were they here now? He'd seen them more in the past month than in the last few years. His quota was certainly filled for a long time.

"Who's with them?"

At Sara's question, he noticed a man dressed in a stylish suit with a shaved, shiny head and dark, square-rimmed glasses. He looked familiar. Earl something.

"True!" Abe's voice boomed toward them. "Glad to find you home."

"Abe, Celia." He kept his voice neutral. Find out what they wanted first.

They approached the porch and started up the stairs. "Darling." Celia kissed his cheek, and he tried not to snarl. Such a good mother in public. Why couldn't she have given him a few more kisses when he was a child and needed them most?

"You remember Earl Rawlins. He's in the industry. We ran into him when your father was performing at The Melody Tent."

Rawlins? Yeah, now he remembered. A music promoter, big into concerts and tours. Why was he here?

"Sara, it's lovely to see you again. I enjoyed your singing at the fair, then again at the concert last week." Celia strolled toward Sara and kissed the air near her cheek.

Her smile was strained. "Thank you."

Abe grinned at Sara, and TJ wanted to slug him. It wasn't anything overt or sexual, but he knew his dad and figured he was checking her out. So was Rawlins. His gaze roamed Sara's skimpy outfit, and TJ wished she'd stayed in her sundress. They hadn't expected company.

"Hi, Sara, I'm Earl Rawlins. Nice to meet you."

Taking the man's hand, she glanced nervously around. "Can we get you something to drink? We have iced tea and lemonade."

"Lemonade would be lovely, dear," Celia answered. "Should we go inside?"

After following them in, he helped Sara get the drinks. Earl looked around. "Great place."

TJ didn't respond. What the hell did these people want? Sara motioned for them to sit at the counter. Standing next to her, he placed his hand on her shoulder.

"Was there a reason for your visit?" *Done with small talk.*

Earl took a sip, then placed his glass on the counter. "I wanted to meet Sara. I was at The Melody Tent last week. I'd thought of signing on Hooligan, the canceled band. They'd been doing well, and I had big plans for them. I was pleasantly surprised to find Miss Storm performing instead."

Sara's expression was apprehensive, but a sliver of excitement flickered behind the fear. His chest tightened and his fists clenched. He didn't like where this was going.

"I ran into Abe and Celia and after chatting, realized they knew you." He spoke exclusively to Sara now. "I was quite impressed with your voice and how you interacted with the audience. I have to say the response you got from them was overwhelming."

"Thank you." Her hands twisted in her lap.

"I have a proposition for you."

Oh, God, no. Here it comes. The man was about to kill TJ's dreams.

"I'd like to sign you to a contract. I have a band I think you'd be perfect to open for. They're up and coming and at the top of the charts."

"Seriously?" Sara's voice quavered.

"What band?" The knot tightened around his heart.

"Ammunition."

Ammunition. Damn. They were big time party boys. He might have been out of the loop for ten years, but he still saw the tabloid covers.

"They're not exactly Sara's type of music?" Ammunition was hard core rock.

"She has the voice and the look to sing anything. I think they'd eat her up."

It's what he was afraid of. They'd eat her alive.

Then spit her out. She'd never be the same.

"What do you think, sweetheart, are you interested?"

Excitement visibly danced on her skin, but her eyes held doubt.

"What exactly does this contract entail?" *Good girl, ask questions. Find out it's not for you.*

"The tour starts the beginning of September and runs until right before Christmas with a short break at Thanksgiving. We'd need you as soon as possible in Los Angeles for rehearsals. This leg of the tour is Chicago and West. There's a few months hiatus, then we do the Eastern part of the country."

Earl dug in his coat pocket and withdrew a folded packet of papers. Shit, he already had a contract drawn up. He meant business. TJ's dinner threatened to come back up.

"I have the details right here."

As Earl showed her the document, she listened intently. How much she'd be paid, where she'd stay while on tour, and what she got for food allowances.

It all sounded wonderful. Except he knew better. Often you slept on the tour bus and ate fast food along the way. And socialized with the hardcore party crowd.

Tension wound its way through his body, making him feel like he might explode any second. It wasn't like he could start spouting the horrors of tour life with Abe and Celia present. Yes, they knew his feelings, but he'd never embarrass them in front of someone else.

"What do you think? Ready to sign? I can have a car here for you tomorrow."

His lungs stopped working. Tomorrow? Not so soon. He needed time to talk Sara out of it. To tell her how much he loved her and needed her here with him. She'd want it, too, wouldn't she?

"Can I have time to think about it?"

Yes. Relief surged through his blood. She was being sensible. Waiting to really check things out.

"Of course, sweetheart. And you should get a manager once you sign the contract. I have a few I could recommend. This contract is only for the first leg of the tour. There's a clause to extend it to the second half, if we both agree. I have a feeling the crowds will love you, and we can move forward with it."

When Sara took the papers, her eyes glazed over.

"Your manager will want to get a recording contract underway. If you start with a small CD, they can be sold at the concert venues which always helps with promoting the rest of the tour."

Sara bit her bottom lip, and he wanted to assure her everything would be fine. But would it? Not for him probably. As he placed his hand on her shoulder, she looked up, anticipation written across her features.

"Here's my business card." Earl presented her the card, then patted her hand. "I look forward to working with you. Don't take too long getting back to me. There are lots of things to do before the tour starts. If you say no, I'll need to find another act."

"Thank you. I'll call soon. I promise."

Celia finished off her drink, then stood regally. "True, your father and I are heading back to Malibu tomorrow. Maybe when Sara comes out, you could come along and visit. We'd love to have you back home. It's been a long time."

Home. California hadn't been his home in forever. He tried to smile but didn't think he got more than one side of his mouth turned up.

Earl stood as well and stuck his hand out toward TJ. “Any time you’d like to come back into performing, you know I’d be more than happy to sign you.”

A snarl threatened to escape, and he pushed it aside. Luckily, no one except his parents and his manager knew his James True connection. Surprisingly, Abe and Celia had kept his little secret.

Once they’d left, TJ turned to see Sara practically jumping out of her skin. When he stepped toward her, she launched herself into his arms. *Don’t let go. Not for any reason.* Definitely not to go on tour with some hard rock band of party boys.

“I can’t believe it! I just can’t believe it!” She couldn’t stay still and slipped from his arms.

As she looked at the contract sitting on the counter, he put his arms around her again from behind. Her body vibrated with energy.

“Pinch me so I know I’m not dreaming.”

He lightly squeezed her nipples. They immediately puckered.

“TJ.”

“What? You said pinch you.”

Sara turned in his arms. God, why couldn’t he be excited for her? No matter how much he tried, he couldn’t muster up any enthusiasm. If she went on tour, he’d lose her forever.

“You have a great talent, Sunshine. It’s not hard to believe.” He swallowed the compliment. Every word was true, yet there was no joy in saying them.

Sara leaned back, a glint in her eye. “Did you have anything to do with this? Ask your parents to talk to Mr. Rawlins?”

"No." TJ caressed the side of her face, then slipped his fingers into her hair. "I try and talk to my parents as little as possible. Especially about music."

"Good. I don't want this because someone did me a favor. I want to be known because I have talent."

"You do have talent. Never doubt it."

He hugged her tighter, feeling the pent-up energy trying to get out. Easing away, she bounced up and down again. How would his sweet, innocent angel survive in the world she wanted to be in, the world she'd gotten a first-class invitation to?

"I don't even know what to do next? I should call my parents and tell them. I need to tell Sofie myself. She'll be ticked if she hears it from anyone else. And I need to…I don't know what I need to do."

Her confused stare haunted him. Yes, he should help her figure things out, but he just wanted to lock her up and keep her here. Tell her she shouldn't go.

"My advice is…you should kiss me."

Sara giggled. It was great seeing her giddy with excitement, but he hated the reason for it. Skipping over, she held her face up for a kiss.

"Great advice. I like it."

He closed his mouth over hers. *Wish she would take all my advice. Would listen to me when I tell her she shouldn't go*. Could he say those words? Destroy her dream? Or let her go, and in the process destroy the one chance he had for happiness? Because if Sara left, he'd never find anyone to replace her.

As her lips moved under his, TJ began to hope maybe she would choose to stay with him. She had to love him, didn't she? She was a nice girl who'd want a husband and family of her own. He never thought he'd get married. Was convinced he'd never find someone to accept him. Sara had proved him wrong. After hearing his story, she hadn't run in the opposite direction.

"You make me forget everything else, TJ. I could stand here kissing you forever."

"Sounds perfect. Forever can start right now."

She laughed again, still giddy at the offer. "I guess I should probably look at the contract. Would you go through it with me?"

Sure, and point out all the reasons why she shouldn't sign it. "Why don't we sit in the living room?"

They settled side by side, and Sara spread the contract over her lap, then leaned into his shoulder. He focused on the papers so he wouldn't grab her and ravish her instead.

It was a standard contract, and he read it out loud spending a few minutes telling her what it meant and interpreting some of the terminology.

"This says they have the right to final decisions on your stage wardrobe. Which means they can dress you up any way they want, and you can't argue."

"But it says they'll pay for the wardrobe, so that's good, right? I'm thinking it'll be nicer stuff than I can afford. Although what they're paying me is awesome. I can take a nice chunk out of my college loans with it."

"If I pay you more, will you stay here instead?" The words slipped out, but he didn't want to take them back. Sara batted at his arm as if he'd made a joke. Leaning in, he pressed his lips against hers

"I'll pay off all your college loans if it'll get you to stay."

Kneeling up, she stared, then tilted her head. "You

really don't want me to do this. Why?"

Touching his forehead to hers, he whispered, "I love you, Sunshine. I want you here with me."

"Oh, TJ, this doesn't mean we have to stop seeing each other." She kissed him, stroking his cheek. "We can talk on the phone and Skype and text. And I'm sure Mary and Josh will help out, and you can come visit me."

"No. I can't." He swallowed hard.

Her shoulders sagged. "You've got plenty of money. You can hire someone else to help at the store. And the big summer crowd will be leaving in a few weeks. Then it'll get easier to take time off."

"I won't do it, Sara." He couldn't. Not even for her.

The disappointment in her eyes tore at his soul. "Why not?"

Tell her the truth. "I don't want you to go, not simply because I'll miss you, and I will. But because that type of life isn't for you. I've been there, Sunshine. I know."

"Yes, I'm still a little innocent and don't like the party scene, but I'm a lot tougher than you think. Three older brothers got me ready to tackle anything. I want this, and I can do it. I've wanted it so long. How can I turn it down?"

"You don't have to go all the way across the country to sing. I love you. I want you here. I thought maybe you cared for me a little, too."

"That's not fair." Her eyes darkened.

No, he wasn't being fair. But love wasn't fair.

"I do care for you, and you know it. I never would have done"—she waved her hand between the two of them—"if I didn't care for you."

She still couldn't say it. How would she survive in the music world? Grabbing her hand, he held it to his chest. Could she feel how fast his heart thumped with the thought of her leaving?

"I don't want to lose you. If you stay here, you can sing at the shop every weekend. I'll write dozens of songs only for you."

Tears filled her eyes, and she reached for him. Had he convinced her? "You won't lose me, I promise."

Pulling her in, he ravaged her mouth. Tasted her lips and skimmed his hands down her back. Her fingers slipped through his hair and gripped tight. She didn't want to let go. Neither did he.

TJ shoved his hands under her top and pulled it off. Her response was to lift his T-shirt over his head. Slipping her hands inside his drawstring pants, she tempted his arousal to life.

Slowly, he drew her shorts over her hips and down her thighs revealing the porcelain skin of her cheeks. "You ready for more, Sunshine."

Her breathy, "Yes," was enough answer for him.

TJ pulled her around to straddle his lap. God, he needed to be inside her right now. Needed the release only she could bring. Her breasts swayed in front of his face, and he licked one, then sucked on her nipple. Holding his head tightly, she lowered her hips until they found their mark. As his erection slid inside her, he remembered the condom he'd put in his pocket earlier. He'd had hopes of a blanket on the beach and a naked Sara in his arms.

Placing his hands on her hips, he planned to stop her when a thought nudged its way into his mind. If they didn't use protection, she could get pregnant. If she was pregnant, she'd have to stay here with him. But could he betray her? God, he was desperate. *I can't lose her.* When she wiggled again, he let her.

Then she froze. And lifted up. "Do you have a condom? I almost forgot."

"In my pocket." Heat seared through him, anger at her or at himself for his deceit.

Soon, the latex was on, and she returned to slide onto him. Heaven.

"It's your move, Sunshine. I'm only here for the ride. I'll enjoy every minute."

As Sara lifted and lowered herself on his arousal, he watched. Saw her face burst with rapture, her breasts bounce up and down, her slim hips rotate back and forth, her flat stomach tighten and release. The strawberry scent of her hair tantalized his nose, and he leaned forward to taste her once more. The whole picture had him spellbound, and his desire soared as she threw back her head and cried his name. Shuddering, he drew her close to his chest, and she snuggled there, sagging with fulfillment.

"Relaxed?"

She chuckled softly. "Boneless."

"Then I guess you don't want to enjoy the Jacuzzi with me."

"Mmm, sounds wonderful." Her voice purred.

"I'll get the water going." He shifted her to the side.

"Not sure I have enough energy to move. You might need to leave me here. I can't feel my toes."

After carrying her into his room, he dropped her on the bed. Her hair spread out around her, her expression one of extreme satisfaction. Leaning down, he kissed her swollen lips. Completely uninhibited, she lay there naked and seductive without knowing how sexy she looked.

Taking a deep breath, he started the water in the tub, then stood in the doorway gazing at her perfect form. They'd spend the next few hours making love and exploring each other in every way he could think of. If he was lucky, by morning, she would be so addicted she'd never want to leave him. It was his only hope.

Chapter Twenty-Six

The whisper of minty breath across her cheek woke Sara from her delicious dreams. TJ sat on the bed beside her.

"I'm heading to work in a minute. It's my morning to open."

The clock read six-fifteen. Too early to be up yet. As she stretched her arms above her head, the sheet shifted, and she realized she had nothing on. Oh, yeah, after what they'd done last night, she hadn't enough energy to slip her night clothes back on.

When she pulled the sheet up, TJ laughed, a sexy smile on his face. "Too late to cover up, Sunshine. I've seen it all."

He kissed her, but she didn't prolong the contact. Her teeth hadn't been brushed.

"I know you're anxious to make a decision on the contract, but promise me you won't do anything until we can talk."

What was there to discuss? This was her golden opportunity. "You're going to try and talk me out of going?"

Pain filled his eyes, and her heart ached. This didn't have to be as hard as he was making it.

"Yes, I am. I don't want you to go."

"Don't you understand, this is my big chance. Why can't you be happy for me?" Her tone grew angry, and she regretted it immediately. But he was being unreasonable. He made it sound like if she took this opportunity, they were done. Stupid. He loved her. They wouldn't be done.

TJ stood and paced in front of the bed. She couldn't talk about this naked. One of his shirts hung on the edge of the hamper, so she scampered out of bed and slipped it over her head. Slightly better.

His gaze followed her as she rose, desire evident in their brown depths. Lifting her chin, she repeated, "Why can't you just be happy for me?"

"Because I can't." His voice was harsh and raspy, and his eyes hardened. "I told you, I'm self-indulgent. This is one more example of my selfishness."

He *was* being selfish. This was her time to shine, and she deserved it. How could she simply throw it all away? Didn't he understand?

"Come with me." She held out her hand.

He took a step back, and his Adam's apple bobbed up and down. "I can't. I can't go back there. That life killed my sister. It almost killed me. I love you too much to watch it destroy you, also."

"You don't know what'll happen. I wasn't raised the same way you were. I was taught morals and values you never had. I'll be fine. You'll see. Or come with me and make sure it doesn't happen. We can do it together."

He closed his eyes, and her stomach clenched at the agony she saw in him.

"I can't go back. I won't become who I used to be. You're so innocent and sweet, they'll eat you alive."

Why did everyone think she was such a goody two shoes? Yes, she'd been a virgin until recently, but that didn't mean she had no clue about life and how to get through it. Did no one have any faith in her? Not even TJ?

"I'm not as innocent as everyone thinks." When she touched his arm, he stared at her hand, his body tensing. As she ran her fingers up and down his skin, his shoulders relaxed.

"I'm not as innocent in some ways, thanks to you."

TJ jerked his arm away. "Is that what this was about? Losing your virginity and getting experience?" His face was like stone. Damn. She hadn't meant the insinuation.

"The bad boy comes in handy for something, huh? Why? So you can go and fuck someone more famous. Someone who'll actually use their connections to get you the stardom you want?"

She reeled back as if slapped, holding the impending tears at bay.

"Is that what you think? I used you. Like one of those college girls you slept with…oh sorry, fucked."

His face visibly crumpled. He scrubbed his hand over his eyes, then through his hair. Turning abruptly, he shoved his fists in his pockets, his head bowed. His shoulders rose and fell with a few deep breaths. When he finally faced her, his eyes were wet.

"No, of course not, Sara." He glanced at the clock. "Shit, I have to go. I'll be back as soon as I can. I've got deliveries at ten, but I'll be home right after. Promise me you won't sign anything until I get back."

The lump in her throat prevented any words. TJ stroked his thumb down the side of her face and kissed her sweetly. "Remember, I love you."

He walked out the door. She stood until her legs

turned to jelly, then collapsed on the bed. Tears sprang to her eyes, and she let them fall unheeded this time. What should she do?

TJ loved her and wanted her to stay. By his own admission, he was being selfish. Being here with him had been wonderful. But did she love him? How could she be sure? This summer, she'd been happier than she could ever remember. But if she stayed, she could kiss her singing career goodbye.

Yes, she could sing at the shop every weekend, but it was hardly the same thing. Signing the contract with Earl Rawlins was a dream come true. It wouldn't be immediate fame, but she'd never expected that. Touring with Ammunition would be a boost to her career. All their fans would hear her sing. If even a small fraction of them loved her voice, she'd be on her way.

Turning her head, she inhaled TJ's scent from his pillow. She wanted to stay, but she couldn't. All she'd be was a clerk in a bookstore, nothing more. Why did he refuse to give in and come with her? He'd be an asset in helping her adjust to the music world, but his own fears were too great. Maybe he didn't love her enough to actually try.

If she stayed here, she'd begin to resent him and what he'd kept her from. The fight they'd had would be nothing compared to what might come. Angry words and hurtful thoughts. They'd come to hate each other, then she'd have flushed her career down the toilet for nothing. This was something she needed to do.

Knowing she wouldn't be able to go back to sleep, she pulled herself from the bed. Pack first, then call Earl Rawlins. He said he could have a car here today. Hopefully, he'd let her go home to New Hampshire first to talk to her parents and pack more of what she needed.

Digging in her purse, she found his card and set it aside. It was still too early to call. But she could have all her things packed and ready to go. TJ had asked her to stay until he got back, but she hadn't actually promised him. If she waited, they'd have more harsh words and tears. Then she'd have to say goodbye for real. When it came to TJ, she didn't want to admit it was goodbye.

****

"Sara."

TJ walked in the back door and placed his keys on the hook. Standing still, he listened, but the house was silent. It was later than he'd wanted thanks to a delayed shipment. Was she mad he hadn't returned when he'd said? Freckles trotted through the kitchen door and wagged her tail begging for attention.

"Hey, girl. Where's Sara?" Holding the dozen red roses he'd bought tighter, he stalked toward the bedroom. Was she still asleep? They hadn't gotten much last night.

His heart pumped faster as he approached the door to his room. As he looked in, he held his breath. The bed was made and her clothes gone from the floor where they'd been tossed last night. He swallowed hard and closed his eyes, leaning against the door frame. The roses fell to the floor.

Keep it together. Check upstairs or the music room. No music sounded, so he dragged his feet up the stairs and down the hall to the room she'd used until last week. When she'd started sleeping in his bed. And holding him tight while he slept. He'd never realized how nice it was to have someone hold you as you slept. His damn father had told him not to. Of course, the kind of girls he'd been screwing wouldn't have been the right kind to snuggle with anyway.

Her bedroom door was open, and TJ peeked in. The top of the dresser was empty, but then she'd brought much of her stuff into his bathroom downstairs. Damn, why hadn't he looked there first? He walked in farther, fear slowing his steps. She wouldn't have left. She promised she'd stay until he got back.

Did she promise? The nagging voice echoed in his head. She hadn't. Hadn't said anything. Had simply stared like he'd killed her kitten. Couldn't blame her. Rotten things had spewed from his mouth, because he didn't want to lose her. If she loved him, wouldn't she feel the same?

If she loved him. Damn voice. Why couldn't it leave him alone?

"Sara?"

Still no sound, except the cry of seagulls flying over the incoming tide. He understood. Crying seemed good about now.

Taking a deep breath, he moved to the dresser, opening the drawer. It was empty. So was the next one and the next. No! She wouldn't have just left. Not without saying goodbye. Running to the closet, he pulled it open. A few bare hangers hung there taunting him, laughing at his foolishness in thinking he was capable of being loved. Of having someone like Sara actually care for him and want to be with him.

As he leaned against the closet door, waves of desolation and agony washed over him, pulling him out to the sea of unhappiness. Why had he allowed himself to love her? Love was fleeting. It never lasted. He knew this. Why hadn't he remembered? Saved himself the heartache and pain?

He had no idea how long he stood there, trying to breathe, attempting to get his heart beating again, instead of hardening back into the block of ice it had been a few months ago. Shit. How had she gotten past his defenses? *Never should have let her in.* Her damn sunny smile and angelic face had fooled him. Lulled him into believing he might have it all. Finally. *Stupid.* He should have known better.

He dragged himself downstairs, his limbs like concrete. What did he do now? His feet automatically brought him to the music room, and he slogged over to the piano. Music had always allowed him to get lost in it. Maybe it would work today. Except Sara was music. His inspiration and his song, and every part of this room reminded him of her.

A sheet of paper on the bench caught his eye, and he picked it up. Sara's fancy cursive decorated the page. For a split second, his heart soared, wondering if she'd run to the store, but when he saw the first line, it plummeted back down further than before.

Dear TJ,

I'm sorry I didn't wait until you got back, but it would be too hard saying goodbye to you. I know you don't want me to go, but I need to. I need to prove to myself I can make it in this world. That I can be more than just the youngest of the Storms. If I don't take this chance, I may never get another one. Then I'll regret it for the rest of my life. I hope you understand and don't hate me for leaving. You've taught me so much about having confidence in myself, and I'll always be thankful for it. And you. This summer has been the best of my life. I've loved every single minute of it. I'll never forget it. I'll never forget you.

Sara

The last few lines blurred, and he blinked trying to see them clearly. *I've loved every minute.* Every minute. She just hadn't loved *him*.

He sat on the bench, crushing the paper in his hand. His head lowered, resting on his clenched fists, and he struggled to find the control and indifference he'd been such good friends with for so long. It was nowhere to be seen. A blanket of despair wrapped around him, cloaking him in darkness, crushing his chest, and strangling his heart.

"Damn!" He banged his hands on the keys, and the sound vibrated through the large room. His fingers slid along the black and whites and began subconsciously plucking out a tune. It started as simple notes but somehow segued into the children's song he'd had stuck in his head all summer.

"You are my…" He couldn't say it. Couldn't say the name he'd called her since the first time he'd set eyes on her.

"You make me…" Happy? Right, what did he know of happiness? If you found it, it would be ripped from your grasp before you could truly enjoy it.

His fingers moved up and down the keys, the tone dour and bleak. It was just a stupid children's tune. Why was it affecting him so much?

"Please don't take…" His head fell onto his hands, and he pummeled the keys as if they were responsible for his distress.

Slamming the cover over the offending ivory, he

shoved away. Somehow, he found himself in the kitchen, the walls wavering and hostile. It suddenly came into focus as he turned around slowly. It called to him. Whispering his name. Tempting him with its seductive power. How could he resist? Why should he even try?

His hand lifted of its own accord and wrapped around the smooth glass, releasing it from its dusty prison. TJ grabbed a tumbler from the shelf and wandered to the counter. Removing the cap, he inhaled. Mmm, the spicy, woodsy aroma was like an old friend, welcoming him home. After filling the glass, he lowered the bottle and held the drink aloft. The scotch swirled around the glass, mesmerizing him.

He knew this. Was intimately familiar with it and its healing powers. Closing his eyes, he brought his old friend closer as the amber liquid whispered to him, promising everything would be okay.

Chapter Twenty-Seven

All alone in a crowded room.

Sara looked around the fancy house Earl Rawlins had rented for their last few performances and beelined toward an empty corner. Smoke from cigarettes and other substances floated through the air as laughter mingled with the music blaring from the speakers.

'*You came into my life and made me believe in love, my dreams were of you.*'

The passionate lyrics drifted across the room and hit Sara like a sledge hammer. It was the newest hit recorded by one of music's superstars. Written by James True. Another notch in his Top 40 belt.

'*Yours were different. You followed your true dreams, and I let you because I loved you.*'

Sara hated the pain behind the words.

'*Now I'm afraid to close my eyes because my dreams are all gone—they left with you.*'

Over the past four months, she'd tried to contact TJ but had gotten no response. No answer on his cell or her texts. Calling the store had been a thought, but she hadn't wanted to risk Mary picking up the phone. The woman probably hated her for leaving TJ. She was like a mother to him.

'*Gone, you're gone. Everything left with you. No light, no air, no hope. All I've got is despair, tangled in the memories of how we used to be. The past can't soothe me 'cause when I run back to you, you're gone.*'

Wiping her hand across her face, she got rid of any signs of the wetness threatening to fall. *Get control. And have a good time.* Vivienne, her manager, had encouraged her to enjoy herself and the benefits of the job.

Another glass of wine should help, so she walked toward the makeshift bar. Not strong by anyone's standards, but it helped give her the courage to mingle a bit more. And maybe ignore some of the bad habits many of these people had. TJ hadn't been kidding when he told her about sex, drugs, and rock and roll. It was rampant.

She sipped her drink, knowing she wouldn't do this if TJ was here. But he wasn't here, and he wouldn't be. Obviously, the love he claimed to have hadn't been enough to help her on this new journey. It was scary doing this on her own. A friendly face or a hand to hold would have been nice.

TJ hadn't answered any texts, but Darcy had sent a few. And in typical Darcy style, they were totally non-judgmental. She'd congratulated Sara on getting the contract and wished her the best. And mentioned the boss had been more than a little surly lately. Jim had been in more often and seemed worried about TJ. That made Sara nervous.

"You're dynamite, Sage, darling!"

Sara looked over her shoulder at her manager, Vivienne Ashford, as she barreled across the room toward her. The woman was a godsend and had helped Sara maneuver through this new music world.

"Hey, Viv." She lifted her drink to the mature woman who smiled, probably glad to see Sara partaking of the free booze. Shaking her wild gray curls, Viv slid her red, square framed glasses back on her head and beamed.

"Sweetie, the concert tonight was fabulous. You were amazing, as usual. You look spectacular."

Another outfit provided for her. A hip-hugging denim mini skirt with a few pounds of rhinestones running along her hips to look like a belt. This was paired with a skin-tight leather vest attached with a few frog enclosures between her breasts. The snugness pushed her boobs up and out as did most of her stage outfits. This one left her stomach bare as well. The thigh high boots she'd gotten with Darcy covered her feet.

The boots reminded her even more of how much she missed TJ and what they'd done with her in only the boots. She lowered her eyes, hoping Vivienne would think her high color was a result of her compliments.

"Thanks, Viv."

"You sold another few dozen CDs. I know it's only got four songs, but it's a great start. People like you enough to fork out money to hear you sing. We'll get you there yet. Earl is excited about the crowds and wants to go ahead with the clause for the second half of the tour. I'll make sure we get it signed in blood before you head home for Christmas."

Why did the thought of more concerts not thrill her like it should? Maybe she was just tired and needed sleep. After a month of being home in small town, New England, she'd be raring to go again. Wouldn't she? Home. Most days she was so busy she didn't have time to miss home, but when she was in the midst of a chaotic party like this, the thoughts of her serene hometown called to her.

Her manager's green eyes lit up, and she grabbed Sara's hands. "I haven't told you the best part yet."

Viv waited as if for dramatic effect. Not a performer, she still knew how to work it. Sara attempted some form of excitement. It was the least she could do for the effort Viv put into her career.

"I managed to get the most amazing deal for some new songs. You'll never guess who the composer is."

Again the pause. The first composer coming to Sara's mind was always TJ. No one else could compare.

"James True. Can you believe it? I actually made a deal with his manager for him to write you some songs. Exclusive, darling. We don't have to bid on them or anything. Do you know how long I've been trying to get a James True song for one of my clients? And *you* get a handful."

Breathe. Don't forget to breathe. The rest of her wine went down fast. TJ had agreed to write songs for her. Did he know his songs were going to her, or had it simply been a deal between managers?

Vivienne's laughter tinkled through the air as her hands waved. "And you didn't even have to sleep with him." More laughter rang out.

Sara didn't laugh. Biting her tongue to keep from crying, she tried to push the shame back deep inside. Is that why he'd done it? As a thank you for the gift of her virginity?

"Oh, sweetie, when his manager called saying True had heard you sing and wanted to do an exclusive, I couldn't believe it. I wish I knew what concert he'd heard you at. The man is elusive. I'd love to know his identity."

What was he up to? No returning her calls or texts, and he had downright refused to come with her or even visit. Then all of a sudden, after four months of silence, he wanted to write some songs exclusively for her. What did it mean?

"Oh, and I have a few right here." Viv dug into her enormous bag and pulled out some sheet music. "I had this faxed to me just this afternoon. They're fabulous. I think you'll love them."

"They look great, Viv." The words blurred with the tears gathering in her eyes. Why had TJ written songs for her?

"All yours, sweetie. As soon as we get someone to do the arrangement, you can start performing them. For now, you need to have a good time."

Viv took the sheet music, stuffed it back in her bag, and dumped the bag on a table by a doorway. "You can check them out later. Here, have another." She plucked a drink from a passing waiter, shoving it in Sara's hand.

"Thanks, Viv. I won't let you down with the songs. I'll make them amazing."

Viv took her own glass of champagne. "Everything you do is amazing, darling. With the magic of a James True song, now you'll be even more so." Viv was good for her ego. Earl Rawlins had been right when he said Vivienne would be a perfect fit.

After kissing her cheek, Viv toddled off to socialize, and Sara's gaze followed her. No one cared if she was here or not. Yes, people had been nice, especially the guys. Most of them just wanted to get in her pants. They'd certainly tried enough. The backup band had been a good fit, and they'd become friends as well as gotten into a nice rhythm. She enjoyed singing with them. But right now, even they were partaking of the freebies and looking for the stress relief they needed after so many days on the road.

Wandering around the room, she chatted and drank, but avoided the drugs being passed around like candy. She wasn't that stupid. The alcohol she'd had gave her more than a buzz. But it helped her relax enough to mingle. Which made her think about TJ again and how he helped her relax. Why couldn't she get him out of her mind?

She glanced at the bag holding a few of TJ's songs. Viv had pulled them out and shown them to a few people tonight, bragging she'd finally snagged the deal of the century. Sara wouldn't take that away from her by revealing her relationship with James True. But did she even have a relationship with him anymore? Certainly not lovers. But could they even be considered friends? She had to know.

Catching Viv's eye, she gestured to her purse, then held her hand up to her ear like a phone. Viv got the message and waved her away, nodding. After pulling out the song sheets and Viv's phone, she slipped into the room around the corner where the noise was slightly lower.

She took a deep breath and punched in TJ's number. It wasn't her phone, so maybe he'd answer.

It rang a few times, then picked up.

"Hello." The familiar voice caused her heart to race and her stomach to clench. God, she missed him.

"TJ, it's Sara." The alcohol made her feel bold and bubbly. But silence followed, and she swallowed, wondering what it meant. “You haven’t answered any of my messages.”

“Didn’t have much to say.” His voice was cold and strained, reminding her of their first days.

“How’ve you been?”

A pause and then, “Fine.” Nothing else. No return greeting or question asking how she’d been. Her heart sank, and the lonely feeling grew.

“I, um, got some songs today from my manager. She said James True wrote them for me.” Why wasn’t he saying anything? “I was wondering…”

“Have to sell them to somebody. Why not you?”

Business as usual and that was it? Was there anything she could do to bring back the camaraderie they’d shared before she left?

“Sara, I—”

“Babe, you were smokin’ hot tonight.”

Sara whipped around as Judd ‘Bullet’ Ryker, lead singer for Ammunition, strolled up behind her. She’d been around the band for four months but still couldn’t get over her star-struck reaction.

“Thanks.” Why was he talking to her now? He’d never paid her any attention before. Now he concentrated his dimpled smile straight at her. It was lethal.

“Guess you’ve got company.” TJ’s voice grew frigid. What had he been about to say before Judd walked in?

Sara held up one finger as Judd ran his hand down her arm. “No, um, there’s a party.”

“Of course. Lots of booze around? How many have you had?”

Her mind swirled, counting the drinks she’d

consumed. “Uh, only, um, a few. Not too many.” Liar.

“Right. Well, you go have fun at your party.” He’d called her bluff.

“Babe, lose the phone. You and I have things to do. Good things.” Judd ran his hand over the bare part of her back, and she squeaked at the contact.

“Getting more experience, Sara? Finding someone else to help you…relax?” The chill in TJ’s voice could cause frostbite.

“No, it’s not—just wait, Judd. I’m talking.” He sidled up close and ran his hand over her ass.

“Oh, the big man himself, huh, Sunshine.” The nickname dripped with sarcasm, and she hated hearing the tone from him. “Better not keep him waiting. I’ll bet he can do a lot for your career. Good thing you’re not so…innocent anymore.”

“No, TJ, I…” but the line was dead. He’d hung up. Damn.

She turned to Judd, who now leaned against the wall. Easing his lean body away, he walked toward her, his eyes undressing her.

“Killin’ the look, babe.”

She stared as the rock star got closer. He wore his sex appeal like a badge of honor, his tattoos up and down his arms and across his chest, and his blond hair as long as hers. His crooked smile aimed her way, and Sara admitted she wasn’t immune. Especially when he called her hot. Tugging on the short skirt, she smiled. Once she talked to Judd, she’d call TJ back and explain.

His gaze zeroed in on the exposed skin between her vest and skirt. “I’ve got to tell you, doll, you have got the crowd jumping every time you sing. You just grab ’em by the balls and don’t let go until you hit the final note. Definitely the way to play ’em.”

He thought she was good. Seriously? Someone like him.

“Thanks, Judd. I love singing, and I hope it shows in my performance.”

“Oh, it shows. And call me Bullet. All my friends do.”

Bullet took her elbow and led her in front of a couch, then reached down and held up a bottle of champagne. How had she missed that when he’d come in?

After refilling their glasses, they chatted about the concert, and she consumed her drink. Perhaps she should slow down, but after the disapproving tone in TJ’s voice, she needed this. The champagne was excellent and helped sooth her nerves. Talking to someone as famous as Bullet Ryker made her anxious.

He finished his drink and refilled both their flutes. “I foresee a bright future for you. You’ve got some major talent.”

Her heart swelled with pride, yet she still had many doubts about herself. If she was so wonderful, why wasn’t she happy?

Bullet closed the door, then resumed his place in front of her. Apprehensive, she took a step back.

“No worries, babe. I just wanted to have a private conversation about your future. You’re going to make it big, and I want to help. Let’s celebrate, huh?”

He lifted his glass and indicated Sara should do the same. Her head spun with all the excitement of the concert and actually speaking with such a big name musician. Taking a few more sips, she closed her eyes as the room wobbled. *Yeah, drink, slow down.*

"When we start the rest of the tour, I'd love for you to come back on stage after Ammunition gets on, for a duet."

Had she heard right? Bullet Ryker wanted to sing with her, Sara Nobody.

Bullet moved in closer, and she smelled the expensive cologne he always wore. He ran his hand up and down her arm as if trying to warm her up.

"Is this only for one specific concert?"

"No, babe," he replied as he tossed her curled and teased hair over her shoulder. "I'm thinking the rest of the tour. If it's well received, I'd love to record it."

"Record it, really? For Ammunition's next album?"

Bullet pulled her close. "You like the idea? You and me, babe. We could go places. You want to make it big, you stick with me, be seen with me. It'll get you noticed." Which is what TJ had just said. His suggestion hadn't sounded as nice.

Sara realized she was leaning against Bullet's chest, but it wasn't as firm or warm as TJ's. His hands weren't as gentle either, as they ran over her back and the bare skin between her vest and skirt.

Putting his lips near her ear, he said, "Don't say anything yet, but I'm thinking I'd like to branch out and do a solo album. The duet would be on that one. You and me…and a really great song. We could make tons."

His lips tickled her ear, then glided to her neck. What was he doing? It felt kind of good, but did she really want to be doing this? With him? And what had he said about the album? Her mind was too fuzzy.

"A solo album?"

"I chatted with Vivienne earlier, and she mentioned you've gotten your hands on some chart-topping James

True songs. One had definite duet potential."

If the lead singer of Ammunition did a song with her, she'd become a household name.

Bullet nibbled on her shoulder. What was he… God, why couldn't she think straight? Removing the champagne flute from her hand, he set it on a nearby table. That's why. The champagne. It had made her brain all woozy.

"What do you think about working with me? We on for it? I'm ready to start now." His arms wrapped around her from behind.

A duet with a famous singer? How could she say no? She closed her eyes and nodded as the room spun. "I'd love to sing together. Thank you."

"There are lots of ways you can thank me. I've got a few ideas."

Bullet's fingers undid one of the closures on her vest. The garment loosened, and he slid his hands and grabbed her breasts. This wasn't what Sara had in mind. But, oh, why was her head so befuddled? One hand slid lower and skimmed up her leg while his lips sucked on her neck. She'd loved when TJ did this.

"This duet is going to rock, babe, you'll see. I'm already rockin' it."

When he pressed against her back, his evident arousal shocked her. Is this what he meant by duet?

"I thought you wanted to sing together." Would this get her noticed? His fingers pinched her nipples, then slid over her panties, between her legs.

"Yeah, babe, sing. We can start right now for practice. I'll have you singing my name. Come on." Did she want this? Her foggy brain made her responses slower than usual. Bullet turned her and kissed her, hard and fast. TJ said this world was hard and fast.

"Singing together. On stage. For an album. Not this." Sara's less than eloquent words stammered from her mouth.

"Yes, all those things." Bullet slid his hands under her skirt to squeeze her ass as his mouth attached to hers again. He paused only long enough to say, "But this kind of duet is also excellent. It'll solidify our agreement."

He backed up, and Sara fell on top of him as he landed on the couch. His hands still held her ass. As she pushed against his chest, memories of TJ and his gentle touch and sweet caresses washed over her. Nothing like this. Bullet's erection pressed against her panties as he positioned her over him.

Was this wrong? She'd done it with TJ, so it couldn't be all bad. *But TJ's in love with you. This guy isn't. He's only looking for a quick hookup.*

God, what was she doing? This was crazy. *He can do a lot for your career.* TJ's words rang through her head. She was ready to screw some guy for his fame? Well, no she wasn't, but it's where this was headed if she didn't put a stop to it. Her head was too thick and mushy to think straight.

"No," she yelled as she managed to get her footing a few feet away from Bullet. "I don't want this kind of duet. If it's what you're looking for, I'm not interested."

Frowning, Bullet rubbed his erection, then rose to his feet. "Your loss, babe. But no hard feelings." He rubbed his cock again and smirked. "Well, there are *some* hard feelings, and I need to go find a fuck buddy to help. But as for singing together, I still want it, regardless of this"—Bullet waved his hand between the two of them—"You've got a great voice and song, and I have the fame to get us somewhere with it. Let me know."

He walked toward the door, then paused. "Last chance." He rubbed the front of his pants.

She shook her head.

"No prob. Later."

Once he walked out the door, she sank to the couch with her head in her hands. What the hell had just happened? She'd almost had sex with a famous rock star. Most of her friends would think it cool, but she was horrified. Damn, she was drunk. At least she hadn't gotten a tattoo. TJ would be proud of her.

Shit, no, he wouldn't. She'd let some guy paw all over her without a huge amount of resistance. She hadn't joined in, but she hadn't been fighting him off like she'd done with Dan. Boy, alcohol made you act stupid. She didn't need TJ to tell her.

Bullet wanted to sing with her, regardless of whether she slept with him or not. Well, he'd probably call it fucking. Doubtful, he was the type to snuggle next to a woman all night long. Like she'd done with TJ for an entire week. The most incredible week of her life. Her heart ached and cried out in agony. *Push him out of your mind. It will keep him and the pain of missing him as far away as possible.*

It didn't work.

Maybe it was the drink. Maybe it was having Bullet's hands all over in places TJ had touched. Had touched with sensitivity and care and yes…love. TJ loved her. And if she was reading her heart correctly, she loved him, too. It's why she couldn't do anything more with Bullet. The feelings weren't there. And they were for TJ. She loved him and had for a while. Earlier, she couldn't admit it because then she'd have to choose between love and career. Love would always win.

This summer, Erik had said, 'don't take what you have for granted.' At the time, she'd thought he meant her voice. Maybe he was talking about TJ. But she had taken him and his love for granted.

Finally, she'd found a man who loved her for being Sara Storm. And she loved him back. He'd been strong enough to share his faults and failings with her. Shared his emotions and most importantly his heart. And what had she done? Taken his heart and ripped it out of his chest, then stomped on it. And left him to deal with the mess. His newest song was evidence enough.

"His songs." Sara reached for the song sheets she'd originally brought in here to look at when she'd called TJ. It was still unclear why he made the deal for her to get them. His voice had been so cold and distant, she wondered if he was trying to make her feel guilty. Or maybe it *was* simply payment for her virginity.

Unfolding the papers, she scanned the first song. Her eyes began to water as she read the lyrics. This song was more upbeat, certainly more so than the one she'd heard earlier where he'd poured out his broken heart and tortured soul. This one spoke of being proud and holding your head up and being the best you could be. It talked about overcoming all odds and reaching your fullest potential. It also said to make sure to remain true to who you are.

Tears filled her eyes, and she blinked them away. Vivienne would think she was nuts crying over lyrics like this. But now she knew why he'd written these. It was his own little way of helping her in her career path, of supporting the life she'd chosen, even if it didn't include him.

But thinking back to their short conversation earlier, any feeling he had for her was most likely gone. Bullet's sexually laced comments had gone through the phone loud and clear, and now TJ thought the worst of her.

Collapsing on the couch, she cried.

What a mess. Her contract was being renewed, and she'd gotten some great songs. Why wasn't she on top of the world? The crowds were great, and she loved singing for them and hearing their applause and appreciation for her voice. But traveling from place to place wasn't nearly as glamorous as she thought it might be. Practice was for long periods during the day, then they performed at night. Going to the after-concert parties was pretty much expected, and she hated it. It was only in the early morning hours, she finally got to sleep. All to get up and do it again. And she missed her family. She spoke with her mom and dad a few times a week and kept up with her brothers who constantly asked if she was all right. But, God, she missed TJ. Not until she'd heard his voice had she realized how much.

She hadn't even said goodbye. Yet he still showed he cared by sending her songs to make her successful. A success he never wanted for her. She couldn't doubt his love. Even when he couldn't have her, he still wanted her to be happy.

Getting up, she locked the door to the room. The couch was comfortable and was less likely to be occupied during the night. Most people would head to the bedrooms. She'd grab the blanket on the back and sleep here. How much sleep she'd get was anyone's guess. There was a lot to think about. It might take her the whole night.

Chapter Twenty-Eight

"TJ? You got a minute?"

Looking up from unpacking a box of cups, TJ glanced at Mary, who stood in the backroom doorway. A strange expression crossed her face.

"Everything okay?"

"There's someone looking for a job. I thought you might want to talk to them."

"We don't need help right now." They'd hired a dozen temps for the Christmas rush, but they wouldn't need them in a few weeks. Something was up. He could see it in her eyes.

"I think you'll want to speak to this person."

He was about to argue again when Mary walked out, giving him the just-do-as-I-ask mother look. Setting the stack of cups back in the box, he followed her.

Mary had slipped behind the serving counter, but Darcy leaned on the bookstore checkout looking at him with major interest. What were these two up to?

Then he saw her. The blonde head was bent over Freckles, the woman scratching the dog behind the ears. He froze. His heart stopped, and his breath caught in his throat. Sara Sunshine.

Sara glanced up, then stood facing him, her face pale and tired. It had already started. They were draining the life from her. It wasn't something he needed to see. Why had she come back?

"Sara." *Keep the voice neutral. Don't let her see how much you want to grab her, hold her, and kiss those beautiful lips*. The ones she was biting because she was nervous. Had someone else been kissing those lips? Or doing more? The phone conversation they'd had a few weeks ago drifted through his mind. The masculine voice who'd called her 'babe' continued to play on a loop over and over. Bile rose in his throat at the thought of anyone else touching where he'd touched.

"Hi, TJ."

As she stood there, she twisted the bottom of her over-sized sweater. What was she so nervous about? She was the one who'd left him. His feelings obviously hadn't mattered.

"Is the tour over?"

"Yeah, it finished up a few days ago. I flew into Logan this morning."

Her appearance was different from his summer Sunshine. More casual in slim jeans tucked into high boots. And more make-up. Not a ton, but it was artfully done to emphasize her best attributes. Her hair was curled and pinned to one side. A much more sophisticated look.

"Did you want something? Or just slumming for the day?"

She flinched at his acerbic words, but he didn't care. Well, he did, but he shouldn't. The past four months, he'd struggled simply to stay above water.

She took a deep breath. "I wanted to thank you. For the songs. I didn't expect it of you."

Wasn't something he'd expected either, but it had

seemed right at the time. If he couldn't have her, at least he could make sure she had a chance in the music business. Right now, with her standing in front of him, reminding him exactly what he'd lost, he wasn't feeling so charitable.

"I got paid." He shrugged. "It's all that matters."

Her face fell, causing a knife to rip through his gut. Why was he being cruel? *Get away from her.* Standing here, making small talk, was killing him. Her thank yous had been said, so she could be on her way.

"Was there anything else? I'm kind of busy." Liar. There were only two people in the coffee shop sipping drinks. "I'm sure you have singing stuff to do. I'll let you go do it."

When he turned to walk away, she pulled in her lips and blinked as tears sprang to her eyes. G*et away. Move and don't look back. It's what she did.*

"Take care." Damn, he looked back. Why couldn't he simply walk away?

Practically running up the stairs, he ignored Darcy urging Sara to go after him. Would she? Did he want her to? He dashed into his office and leaned over the desk, breathing hard. Dammit. Why did she have to come back and torment him?

Footsteps sounded behind him, then the creak of the door closing, and the lock clicking. Was it Sara, or had Darcy followed him to ream him out?

"TJ?" Sara's voice held tears. *Steel yourself. Don't let her get to you again.*

"Why are you here, Sara? To pour salt in the wounds? Or did you want to show me all your new experience?"

When he finally turned, tears slid down her cheeks,

and he clenched his fists to keep from wiping them away.

“I’m not continuing the tour.”

His lungs stopped working. Had he heard her correctly? And what exactly did it mean?

“You’re not? You were doing so well. Why aren’t you going back?” God, he wanted one answer so badly he could taste it.

Her eyes narrowed. “How do you know I was doing well?”

Should he admit he’d kept tabs on her? “My manager and Vivienne have been in contact. She says the audience loves you.”

“Do you know Vivienne?”

Heat rose to his face. “I haven’t seen her in years, but she’s a friend of Celia’s. She’s a great manager.”

She tilted her head but didn’t seem upset. “Did you have anything to do with her becoming my manager?”

His gaze bounced around the room, then focused on Sara. “I told Celia she might suggest to Rawlins how good a fit Vivienne would be for you. She’s a sweet lady, and one of the only ones who used to treat Sonni and me like real people. You don’t need some douche bag who’d rip you off or not do any work.”

Sara took a step closer. His heart was about to jump out of his chest.

“Thanks for looking out for me. Viv is a great fit. I love her, and she’s been marvelous with my goals. She doesn’t know you’re James True. She hoped to figure out your real identity.”

“No one knows except my parents, Jim, and Mary. And you. How does Vivienne feel about you not finishing the tour? Or has she arranged something better?" The slim hope he had spread its wings and geared to take off.

"She's not thrilled, but we had a long talk, and she understands."

The lump in his throat made it hard to swallow. "What does she understand?"

"I missed my family. I missed you."

When she looked at him, the hope started to settle. But he couldn't let it get inside if it was only going to leave again. If Sara was going to leave again. No way he'd survive this time.

"You were right. I was miserable. It wasn't what I thought it would be."

Shoving his hands in his pockets kept him from reaching for her. Seeing her upset was hard, but he needed to hear what the bottom line was.

"I loved performing and hearing the people cheering for me. But all the times in between, I was lonely."

"Bullet didn't keep you company?" The words stuck in his throat. "He sounded plenty friendly when you called. Like you both had some things to do. Together." The images of what might have happened tortured him.

She shook her head, her eyes sad. "Everybody was nice enough, but I didn't fit in. You were right about the parties. Even in a crowded room, I felt alone."

"What'll you do now?"

Glancing at her feet, she twisted her hands in her sweater again. "I hoped you might have a job for me here."

"Really? Why would you think that?"

****

"I'm sorry." The tears she'd been fighting wouldn't stop, and she turned away. "Maybe I shouldn't have come. You probably hate me for what I did." The chill in his voice did little to dispel the thought.

But was it because she left him, or because he thought she'd slept with Bullet? Had she killed the love TJ had for her with her actions? When she peeked over her shoulder, his icy gaze sent a chill through her. Why did she think he'd jump at the chance to have her back? The black hole in her chest expanded, and she couldn't breathe. *Get out of here while you can still walk.* The lack of emotion in TJ's eyes cut through her.

She stumbled toward the door, but TJ grabbed her arm, spinning her around.

"I need to know why you came back. What you expect."

Taking a deep breath, she relished his touch, even through her thick sweater. "I came back because I missed you. Because this summer was the best time I ever had. Because being with you is better than anything else I've ever done."

She reached up, but he dropped his hand and stepped back. "You thought you'd come back here and slum for a while. What happened? Bullet find a new plaything? Or did he want someone with more experience, and you thought I'd help you again?"

Tears trailed down her cheeks faster than she could wipe them away. God, he really hated her. Should she just leave or try and make him understand? He'd sent those songs. They encouraged her to be strong and fight for what she wanted. Why had it taken so long to know she wanted TJ.

"I never slept with Bullet or anyone else."

His eyebrow rose. In disbelief?

“I’m not saying no one tried, but they didn’t do much beyond kissing. All I could think of was you, and how good *your* hands felt, and how sweet *your* lips were. I know it took me a while, but I finally figured it all out. I couldn’t…sleep with them for the same reason I could with you.”

His eyes bore into her, and she hoped what she was about to say would make a difference.

“I love you. I didn’t want to admit it before because then I couldn’t leave. But when I left, it all became clear. I love you, TJ.”

Something flared in his eyes, but he still didn’t move any closer.

“I’m sorry I didn’t realize it earlier. I had no idea what it felt like. It was only after being without you for a while I knew it had to be love. Nothing else has ever been this strong. I couldn’t stop thinking about you. Every minute of every day.”

He stared beyond her, and his jaw clenched. Was she too late?

“I know I hurt you, and I’m sorry. I never meant to. And maybe you don’t love me any more after what I did, but I don’t want you to hate me.” Her damn voice was going haywire. “I couldn’t live with myself if you did.”

She turned away from TJ’s cold glare, her steps slow to the door. As she reached for the lock, she closed her eyes and sighed.

“I don’t hate you, Sara.” His strangled voice sounded behind her. When she turned toward him, his eyes finally held warmth but also pain.

Her bottom lip trembled, and she bit down to stop

it. Lifting his hand, he ran his finger over her mouth. The gentle caress caused more tears to fall.

"You really love me?"

She nodded, blinking the moisture from her eyes.

"You're not going back on tour? You want to be with me?"

"Yes."

His lids lowered as he sucked in a huge breath. When he opened his eyes, tears glistened there, too. "I won't survive if you leave again."

"I won't, promise."

As she stepped closer, he scooped her into his arms and kissed her. Her arms tightened to hold him close so he couldn't escape. He tasted like cinnamon and apples. Like home.

"I love you so much, Sunshine. I've been miserable without you."

"Is it why you just treated me like crap?"

"I'm sorry." He stared into her eyes. "Your leaving killed me. I didn't want to go through that again."

She touched his face. "You won't."

"Are you sure you want to be here? Give up your music career?"

Easing back, she gauged his reaction. "Actually, I don't want to give it up. Don't be mad." Her words rushed out quickly. "I want to be with you, and I won't go on tour again. I didn't like it."

"You and Viv figured something out, didn't you?" He grinned like he knew her secret.

"I'm not finishing the tour, but Judd Ryker asked me to do a duet with him."

His body stiffened at the name.

Kissing him gently, she stroked his face. "That's

the important thing we needed to do when you heard him on the phone."

TJ's expression was dubious. "That's all he wanted?"

She rolled her eyes. "He would have liked more, but I told him singing together was all I'd do." No reason to tell him anything else.

"He wanted to perform the song at some of the concerts, then record it for a solo album. Viv and I figured I could go to a few of the New England concerts and perform the duet. They're all within driving distance, and I wouldn't need to stay away so long. Or be expected to go to the after parties as much."

"You've got it all figured out, haven't you?"

"Are you mad? Did you want me to completely stop singing?"

He held her face and looked deeply in her eyes. "Would you if I asked?"

Sara stared at the face of the man she loved. The man who would make her happy no matter what she did. He loved her, and she loved him. There was nothing more important in this world. She nodded.

"God, you're perfect, Sunshine." He crushed her to him. "I don't want you to give up music. I never completely left that world. I know when you have music in you, it's always in you."

"You're okay with my doing a few of the local concerts?"

"If you're real nice"—he smirked—"you might persuade me to go with you. To make sure you don't go all rock and roll princess on me."

"I won't, promise. I'd love you with me. How nice do I have to be? 'Cause I draw the line at cleaning the pool."

TJ laughed. "The pool's closed for the winter. Lucky for you. But I was thinking more along the lines of what we did in the Jacuzzi."

Heat spread through her, pooling between her legs. "Mmm, I could be persuaded to repeat it. I had a great teacher."

"You were a great student." He kissed her again, then trailed his lips down her neck. "I'm wondering if Earl could be convinced to let you be the opening act at the New England concerts, and split it with another group for the other leg of the tour."

She lifted her head, but TJ kept nibbling. "You'd be okay with that?"

"I never wanted to keep you from performing. I just didn't want you touring the whole damn country, living the wild life of a rock and roller. This way you still get to come home to me every night."

"Would I come home to you?"

"I couldn't think of anything nicer, but it depends on what you want. How would your family react? Do they realize how long you stayed with me this summer?"

Heat rushed into her face. "No, and you're right, my parents would be upset. I won't lie to them and say I had my own place. But would my boss pay me enough to have my own apartment?"

Lifting her hand to his mouth, he pressed kisses along her wrist. "What if they had something to look forward to? Like a wedding? Would that pacify them about your living with me?"

Her breath rushed out. "Wedding? You want to get married?"

"You don't."

"Well, of course, I just wasn't sure…I mean…"

"I want the whole thing, Sunshine. The Happily Ever After. The white picket fence and mini-van and a ton of kids in the yard. It doesn't have to be all right now, but eventually."

"My parents might be okay if they had something to look forward to. I think my mom felt a little cheated with Erik and Tessa's wedding. We might have to do something a bit bigger."

"Whatever you want, whatever she wants. No expense spared. Luckily, you're marrying a fairly wealthy man."

"I wouldn't care if you were the poorest man on earth. I'd still love you because you make me happy. Even when skies are gray."

TJ kissed her hand again, and she noticed a scar running along his thumb and into his palm. It was healed, but it hadn't been there before.

"What happened? You get into a bar brawl when I wasn't around to keep you under control?"

His glance hit the floor. "Actually, kind of. I cut it on the bottle of Chivas Regal I had in the kitchen."

What? Darcy said Jim had been worried about TJ. "Why did you have it down?"

TJ closed his eyes and sighed. When he opened them again, he couldn't look at her. Had he started drinking again, because of her?

"After you left, I was in a pretty bad place. It kept calling to me, promising it would make everything all right." One shoulder lifted. "I knew it would."

"Oh, TJ." Why hadn't she figured out her feelings before she'd left. Damn, stupid. This was her fault.

"I took the bottle down, poured myself a glass…then smashed the whole thing against the wall. Glass and all. I got this when I cleaned it up."

She released the breath she didn't know she was holding. "See, you are strong. You've got this beat."

"I admit I'm not as worried anymore about giving in to the need."

Wrapping her arms around his neck, she pulled him close. "Now I'll be here if you ever feel the need again."

Damn, his hands slipping under her sweater and caressing her back were wonderful.

"The need I'm feeling right now, Sunshine, is a very different one."

"What need would that be?"

"Why don't I show you?"

Within seconds he had her stripped and spread on his desk. His shirt lay on the floor.

"So I'm just another item added to your agenda, huh? Along with the invoices."

He picked up the papers near her and tossed them on the table behind him. "You're the only item on my agenda right now. *My* top priority."

Sara pushed at his chest, bare and tempting her to run her fingers through the swirls of hair. In no time, she'd undone his belt, had his khakis unsnapped and unzipped. When she slipped her hand inside, he was hard and ready.

"You got something to put on this guy?"

Stepping back, he muttered, "Oh, damn. I wasn't expecting you to show up today, and I don't normally have sex in my office."

A light came into his eyes, and he walked to a side

cabinet. "I almost forgot." After pulling something out of the drawer, he returned dropping two foil packets next to her. "I had to fire both Hunter and Cam about a week after you left. I caught them having sex in here. They forgot these. Lucky for us, huh?"

Sara pulled him closer and wrapped her legs around his waist. "I'm feeling very lucky right now."

His mouth crashed onto hers and their hands flew, caressing and exploring. Kissing his way down her torso, he lingered between her legs. Her cries erupted and she was helpless to stop them.

Finally, he rose and covered himself with the protection as Sara waited impatiently. She pulled at his hips and moaned when he slid inside her. Looking up, she saw love shining from his eyes. And something else.

"I have a confession to make."

"Now?" *What the hell*? "Isn't it my job to make confessions? Your job is to get moving."

Leaning over, he kissed each nipple causing her muscles to clench around him.

TJ groaned. "You're not playing fair. I wanted you to know, the last night we made love, and we almost forgot protection…when you first got on me, I remembered. I didn't say anything. For a second, I thought if you got pregnant, you wouldn't be able to go on tour."

Sara wiggled her hips, knowing she should be mad. But it only made her realize how far he was willing to go because he wanted her with him.

Pushing her heels into TJ's back, she growled, "If I forgive you, will you get moving?"

Chuckling, he skimmed his hands down her body

and thrust forward. A quiet knock on the door had them both groaning.

"Boss, you guys okay in there?" Darcy sounded unsure. "I'm just checking to make sure you haven't murdered each other or something."

"If you don't go away, Darcy," TJ threatened between clenched teeth, "I might have to murder *you*."

"Oh. Uh, Sara? You all right, too?"

His lips on her nipple ripped the laugh from her. "I'm perfect, Darcy. Everything is absolutely perfect!"

The footsteps wandered away, and as TJ started moving, whispering words of love, Sara knew it was.

Epilogue

The bottle was empty. Damn!

True Bannister stretched his arm out and placed the glass container on the night stand. Shifting in bed, he eased the eight-pound bundle closer to his side. She felt heavier. Maybe because his arm had fallen asleep as he fed her. Still seemed like she was hungry. He'd need to go search out more sustenance.

Swinging his legs out from the sheet, he planted them on the floor. As he stood, balancing his precious bundle, he realized he couldn't go traipsing around the house in only his shorts. Sara was in the music room giving an interview to Rolling Stone Magazine.

"Stay here, Little Mary Sunshine," he crooned as he placed the infant in her bassinet. "Daddy needs to put pants on."

Memories floated through his head of all the times without pants which had resulted in his tiny ray of sunshine. Every second had been enjoyable with his beautiful wife.

By the time he slid into old jeans and a T-shirt, Mary was fussing again. When he gently lifted her to his shoulder, she calmed instantly. Only a few weeks old and she already knew she was safe with her dad. His heart pounded with the love he never thought he'd feel again. It grew and expanded every day.

He padded across the house, then stopped outside

the music room. Sara sat on the piano bench, and the reporter, a middle-aged woman who looked like she belonged in Abe's entourage, sat in a chair nearby.

"You've got two songs in the top forty at the moment," the woman was saying. "Are you planning on releasing another album soon?"

Holding his breath, he waited for Sara's reply.

"It might take a while before the next album comes out. I'm thrilled at how well the first one did, but I have other priorities at the moment."

A secret smile transformed Sara's face when she saw him standing in the doorway. After mouthing 'I love you,' in her direction, he pressed a kiss to the sweet baby head resting on his shoulder.

"Going on tour would sell more of your music," the reporter said. "Why haven't you?"

"My manager's been pressing me to, but it's not really my scene. When I got my first big break, I was on tour for a few months. I missed my family."

"You make a bigger name for yourself when fans see you perform."

"I perform locally, and my husband and I travel to do a few of the smaller venues. I like having a more intimate audience."

Her thoughts came through clearly when she glanced at him. She liked having *him* more intimate, too.

"My husband and I are putting together a music video for a new song he wrote. He's got other songs he's working on to go in my next album. We're in no hurry. We've got more important things to do these days."

"What could be more important than your music

career?”

When he’d first met Sara, her answer would have been *nothing*. Now she was singing a different tune. At her smile this time, the reporter turned to see what she was looking at. Sara motioned for him to come in.

Walking over, he placed Mary in Sara’s arms. The reporter was speechless as she gaped at the baby.

“This is why you’ve been so private lately. Not like you’ve ever been very public about your life. It does make people wonder about you.”

“We don’t like being on display,” TJ finally spoke up. It hadn’t been his choice to have the interview so soon after the baby, but Vivienne reminded them Sara needed publicity so people wouldn’t forget her. Her career was growing, slowly. All he wanted was for her to be happy. And she was.

“True Bannister.” The reporter held out her hand. “Corrie Carlisle from Rolling Stone. Nice to finally meet the reclusive son of the rock world’s biggest couple. I’d think you’d be used to being on display.”

After shaking her hand, he rested his on Sara’s shoulders. “Not for the last twelve years.”

“How do Abe and Celia feel about being grandparents? Cramping their rock and roll style?”

Both his parents had been thrilled. They’d come for a visit a few days after Mary had been born and doted on their new granddaughter. Surprisingly, Celia had helped clean the house and care for the baby. No one had been more stunned than him. When he’d commented, she’d admitted she’d missed out on so much when he and Sonni had been little and regretted it.

Abe had cooed and waved at the infant and even

held her for much longer than TJ would have guessed. They'd arrived together, and it appeared they were actually trying to make their relationship work. And they'd come bearing gifts only the truly rich would bring. He wasn't sure how much of it Mary would ever use.

"Actually, they're loving it. They spent the first week here spoiling her."

"How old is she, and do we have an official name?"

Sara shifted the baby in her arms, showing her to Corrie. "She's two weeks old. Her name is Mary Sonata Bannister."

His lungs filled with air and his shoulders straightened. Mary Prentise had been thrilled when they'd named the baby after her. But if Mary hadn't given Sara the application and insisted TJ chat with her, none of this would've happened. He might still be living his lonely existence, unaware he was capable of such love.

"Can I take a picture of the happy family for the magazine? Abe and Celia's grandkid. People will eat this up."

He froze and glanced at Sara. The idea of exposing the baby to the notoriety at such a young age was one he hated. But he'd leave the decision to Sara. The two of them would be much more responsible parents than his own had been.

"I'd prefer you don't. Thank you for the offer." Always so gracious, his wife, making people lighter in so many ways. "You can take my picture in the recording studio TJ had built for me downstairs. If you're really persuasive you might convince him to be in one, too. But Mary isn't for public consumption."

"I understand. So tell me, has being married to Abe and Celia's son opened many doors for you?"

Her shoulders tensed. Sara hated people thinking she hadn't earned this on her own.

"Sara was noticed and offered a contract before we got together." Okay, maybe not physically together, but no one had known. The contract had been given on her own merit. "It was exclusively on her talent as a singer."

Corrie looked doubtful. "You didn't pull any strings with mom and dad? Whisper in someone's ear?"

"TJ tried to talk me out of signing a contract to go on tour."

"You didn't think she was good enough to make it in the business?"

"Sara has the most beautiful voice I've ever heard, but I was selfish and wanted her with me, not traveling all over the country. She's earned everything she's accomplished by herself."

"It doesn't hurt she's sleeping with award-winning composer, James True."

He grimaced. They'd let that little secret out of the bag once Sara's first album came out with all James True songs.

After kissing Sara's cheek, he stroked the baby's face. "She's my inspiration. Now I have even more inspiration."

"With the new baby, will you have to give up some of your career dreams?"

Sara gazed at Mary, then looked at him, love shining in her eyes. Love he would never take for granted. Love he would return until his dying breath.

"I'm happy with my career the way it is. And my true dreams…I'm living them right now."

A word about the author...

Kari Lemor has always been a voracious reader, one of those kids who had the book under the covers or under the desk at school. Even now she has been known to stay up until the wee hours finishing a good book. Romance has always been her favorite, stories of people fighting through conflict to reach their happily ever after.

Now that her kids are all grown and have moved out, she uses her spare time to create character-driven stories of love and hope.

https://www.karilemor.com/

Thank you for purchasing
this publication of The Wild Rose Press, Inc.

For questions or more information
contact us at
info@thewildrosepress.com.

The Wild Rose Press, Inc.
www.thewildrosepress.com